"What's the matter? Why are you crying?"

Misery choked her and Shea couldn't think how to answer him. She opened her mouth and willed excuses, or at least words of evasion up her throat, but nothing came.

"Oh, Shea," Cam murmured, tenderness rife in that soul-deep voice. He wrapped his arms around her.

Though she knew she had no right to accept what he was offering, Shea leaned into him. She nestled against the bulk of him, pressing her nose into the rough-woven poplin of his Saturday shirt. He smelled of fresh air and sunshine and hard work.

"You mustn't cry," he murmured. "You mustn't cry."

And when she couldn't seem to stop, he bent his head and kissed her.

It was a kiss that began with the gentlest graze of lips, a slide of warmth and texture. It became a consoling skim of his mouth on hers, a pure and gentle intimacy. It grew on a mingled breath and flourished with the brush of their tongues. Then all at once, that tender touch of solace transformed itself into something else.

It was as if one moment they were standing barefoot on a beach, the breakers foaming gently around them, and the next they were washed out to sea.

Also by Elizabeth Grayson

COLOR OF THE WIND

PAINTED
BY THE
SUN

Elizabeth Grayson

BANTAM BOOKS
New York Toronto London Sydney Auckland

PAINTED BY THE SUN

A Bantam Book / August 2000

ISBN 0-553-58013-2

Published simultaneously in the United States and Canada

Bantam Books are published by Bantam Books, a division of Random
House, Inc. Its trademark, consisting of the words "Bantam Books" and
the portrayal of a rooster, is Registered in U.S. Patent and Trademark
Office and in other countries. Marca Registrada. Bantam Books, 1540
Broadway, New York, New York 10036.

PRINTED IN THE UNITED STATES OF AMERICA

OPM   10 9 8 7 6 5 4 3 2 1

With love and appreciation to
Betty and Bob,
my adopted parents,
and
my birth mother, R.M.—
wherever you are.

The woman who makes photography profitable must have common sense, unlimited patience to carry her through endless failures, equally unlimited tact, good taste, a quick eye, and a talent for detail.

—FRANCES BENJAMIN JOHNSON
FEMALE PHOTOGRAPHER 1864–1952

Photography is a picture painted by the sun.

—AMBROSE BIERCE
WRITER AND JOURNALIST 1842–1914

ACKNOWLEDGMENTS

At the end of a book I am always filled with gratitude, not just for the fact that I have reached the final page, but also to the many people who have generously given of their time and expertise in helping me meld fiction with reality.

Perhaps the most daunting aspect in undertaking this particular story was learning about early photography. In my quest to track down early women photographers and their work, I wish to thank my good friend Joyce Schiller of the Reynolda House Museum in Winston-Salem for setting me on the trail of those lady pioneers.

I certainly would not have come as near to being able to reproduce the process of wet-plate photography without the assistance and expertise of Rob Gibson. Rob, who is practicing his Civil War-era art in Gettysburg, Pennsylvania, these days, not only shared with me pertinent facts, but gave me a sensory understanding of what it is like to work in this medium. He answered my thousand and one questions and was generous enough to review the section of the manuscript that dealt with sensitizing photographic plates and making photographs by this method.

In dealing with the law, trials, and lawyerly aspects of the novel, I turned to fellow novelist Kathleen Sage, and to my good friend John Villeneuve. John's patience in answering my highly speculative questions about jurisdiction and frontier law is something for which I am profoundly grateful. I will admit that I simplified some of the information he gave me in the interest of the story, so any derivations or distortions thereof are completely the fault of the author.

I would like to express my appreciation to the people working in the Western Collection of the Denver Public Library for their guidance, and especially to reference librarian Barbara Dey at the Stephen H. Hart Library in the Colorado Historical Society for answering pertinent questions I had about Denver in the period of the novel.

As always I owe enormous thanks to Eileen Dreyer, my critique partner, who has helped to shepherd one more book through to completion. Also I'd like to thank Meg Ruley, whose excellent questions helped me hone Shea's character. I also appreciate my companions at a particular dinner at the RWA conference in Anaheim who were willing to "talk plot." They helped me more than they will ever know.

And thanks to my husband Tom, of course, for putting up with the more-than-usual upheaval of his life this time.

I couldn't have done this without any of you.

PAINTED

BY THE

SUN

ONE

*C*ameron Gallimore hated hangings. He hated the gallows standing stark against the sky. He hated the way crowds gathered beneath it hours before. He hated the anticipation in their faces and the bottles of whiskey they passed from hand to hand. He especially hated hangings when he was the judge who'd condemned the man to die.

Drawing a dry, sharp breath of resignation, Cameron resettled the low-crowned Stetson on his head and stepped off the end of the boardwalk. The vacant lot near the edge of town where the gallows had been constructed was full of miners. As he waded in, the men closed ranks around him, clapping him on the back and offering congratulations.

Their approval rankled him. It wasn't as if he'd done anything to be proud of. It wasn't as if he'd earned the right to condemn a man by setting a fine example. He'd done his job. He'd done his job so well in the last four years, he'd sentenced eleven guilty men to the rope.

They'd hang the twelfth this afternoon.

Cam was pushing his way toward the base of the scaffold steps where he would stand to watch the sentence carried out when he caught sight of something he'd never seen at an execution before. Dead center and half a dozen yards back from the deck of the gallows a photographer had set up his camera.

The very idea that someone was going to immortalize Crazy Joe Calvert's execution stoked up a firestorm in Cam's chest. He came about in mid-stride and shouldered his way toward where the photographer stood all but hidden in the folds of the camera's focusing cloth.

Dear God! Cam thought with a shudder. What kind of a man took pictures of a hanging?

No kind of a man, as it turned out.

Cam stopped dead when he saw there was a green twill skirt flowing from beneath the drape of the camera's dark-cloth. Scuffed black leather boots with high heels and embroidered shanks peeked from below the skirt's fashionably banded hem. The hand adjusting the knob on the side of the lens was small, delicately boned, stained black at the fingertips—and distinctly feminine.

Feeling unaccountably more aggrieved, Cameron stepped closer and smacked his own big palm down on the top of the square oaken box. "What the hell do you think you're doing?" he demanded.

The figure beneath the heavy fabric jerked back, popping from beneath it like a gopher bolting out of its burrow.

The photographer was a woman, all right—a small, sweetly rounded woman; all startled and smudged and glaring mutinously. She'd hung her bonnet over one of the camera's tripod legs, and the friction with the dark-cloth had mussed her hair. It stood out in curly, gingery-brown wisps and straggled in corkscrews at her temples, cheeks, and nape. Her jaw angled gently above the high, banded collar of her jacket, and her mouth was bowed and soft as a baby's. It was a far more open and arresting face than Cameron had been expecting.

"And just who are you, sir," she demanded, narrowing eyes of cool, luminous green, "that you've a right to ask me what I'm doing here?" Though the words were clearly belligerent, they were sweetened with the hint of Irish brogue.

Around the two of them a few miners turned from the contemplation of their whiskey bottles to something that might, for the moment at least, prove more diverting.

"I'm the man responsible for all of this, and I can't say I recall giving a photographer permission—"

The woman straightened from her shoe soles, which brought her delicate, upturned nose almost level with the center of Cameron's chest. "I don't suppose I really need your permission to take this picture, now do I?" she asked. "This *is* a public street. This *is* a public event . . ."

Cam wasn't sure what was strictly legal, nor did he mean to debate with her, but the question was on his lips before he could help himself. "What purpose could you possibly have for taking photographs of a hanging?"

There was neither apology nor compromise in her demeanor. "Selling photographs is how I earn my livelihood."

"And someone will be willing to pay you for—for a picture of this?" he asked, incredulous.

"Newspapers back east," she confirmed. "If I send them the particulars, they'll write a story and make an engraving from my photograph. Sensationalism sells papers."

It was true enough. Newspapers these days would print anything.

All at once Cameron glimpsed the businesslike determination in the set of that jaw and the clear, hard practicality in those pale eyes. But then, it wasn't as if her reasons for wanting the photograph mattered to him. Even someone who'd stabbed his partner to death in front of witnesses deserved to die with a modicum of dignity.

"Well, I'm afraid you'll have to find something else sensational to send them," he said and reached for her camera.

"Here, now!" she cried, catching at his sleeve. "What do you think you're doing?"

A few more men turned to stare at them.

Though she clung like a terrier, Gallimore managed to shake her off and collapse the tripod. "I won't have you taking pictures of one of my hangings."

"One of your hangings?" she echoed, her voice rising. "Just how exactly is this *your* hanging? Is it your neck they'll be stretching?"

Some of the miners around them snickered.

Cam ignored the men and shifted the weight of the camera against his shoulder. He lifted the legs of the tripod off the ground. The contraption was a good deal heavier than it looked.

"I'm Judge Cameron Gallimore," he told her. "I presided over Mr. Calvert's trial, and I'm responsible for seeing his sentence carried out."

"Then go on and see to your job, Your Honor," she told him pointedly. "Just unhand my camera so I can see to mine."

"Go ahead and let her take her picture," one of the miners encouraged him. "What harm can it do?"

"Aw, don't t-t-t-take her c-c-c-camera, Your Honor," another pleaded. "M-m-m-making photographs s-s-s-sure doesn't seem like a c-c-c-crime to m-m-m-me!"

There was a slurry of laughter.

Heat blossomed along Cam's jaw. He wasn't about to let a few drunken miners interfere with him doing his duty.

"All the little lady wants, Judge, is a picture of Crazy Joe swinging," someone else called out.

Images from the last four years suddenly washed over Cam—memories of stockinged feet dancing their final dance, of inert forms spinning slowly. Of the crisp blue sky and the stench of death. They were visions that stalked him as he drifted to sleep, visions that prodded him awake at night. They were the memories that lurked at the edge of his consciousness every moment of every day.

He was right to take this woman's camera, to do what he could to prevent her from planting those barbarous impressions in anyone else's mind. "I'm confiscating your camera," he advised her grimly and turned in the direction of the sheriff's office.

"You can't do that!" she protested.

"I can do anything I damn well please on the day of a hanging."

The miners hooted as he stalked away. Above the sound of their derision Cam could hear her behind him, hurrying to catch up.

"Wait," she gasped, struggling to push her way through the thickening crowd. "Wait!"

He deliberately lengthened his strides.

She stumbled up beside him, breathless and panting. "Please let me have my camera back!"

"I'll see the sheriff takes good care of it."

"But I need to take that photograph!"

Cameron glanced down at her, recognizing something dark and desperate in her eyes. For an instant he hesitated. Then he imagined what he'd feel, being able to see the very moment of Joe Calvert's death frozen in time.

Chills chased down his back, and he hitched the camera higher on his shoulder. He caught the woman's elbow with his free hand.

She cheeped either in surprise or with the unintentionally hurtful strength of his grip. "What are you doing?"

"I'm taking you where you can keep an eye on the camera. You can have it back when the hanging's over."

"But that will be too late!" she snapped.

"Yes," he agreed and hurried her up the steps to the sheriff's office.

Shea Waterston wrapped her hands around the jail cell's stout iron bars and rattled the door. "Mary, Mother of God!" she fumed, glaring at where Judge Gallimore had disappeared into the front room of the sheriff's office. "I wasn't doing anything wrong!" She raised her voice. *"I wasn't doing anything wrong!"*

All she'd wanted was to take a photograph, a photograph that would have garnered money enough to ensure a warm place for her and her assistant to live and work this winter. Money enough so that if she was very, very careful they'd have a grubstake come spring. But now this damned principled prig was preventing her from taking it.

Oh, she knew he must have his reasons—proper, humane, and high-minded reasons. They were reasons she might have believed in herself if scruples didn't cost so much.

Shea rested her forehead against the bars. Sometimes she just got so tired of worrying and wondering, of scrambling to provide for the next day.

She'd known when she set out that finding her son was going to be difficult. She'd accepted that it would take time and persistence to locate a single child among the hundreds sent west on the orphan trains. She just hadn't imagined that after two years of searching out scores of children, of looking into their soft, expectant faces, that she'd be no closer to finding her boy than she was when she left New York.

She'd used every scrap of her energy to keep the photographic business afloat so she could finance her search, called on every bit of her ingenuity to keep turning up names and places where people had adopted city children. Taking a sensational photograph of this hanging and being able to negotiate her own price for it would have bought her time and breathing room. And a chance to rest.

But Judge Gallimore wasn't about to allow her that. He'd taken away her precious Anthony Camera and locked her up in this cell. And who knew how long he'd hold her? That thought set a whole new flock of worries swooping through her: Where her assistant might get off to. Why he'd refused to help her take this photograph. If he could be trusted to stay with the wagon in the midst of this crush.

Just then she heard Gallimore's voice from beyond the half-open door. It was deep and implacable as a death knell. "It's time to go."

Shea eased to her left, trying to peer through the

opening. One of the men in the outer office was facing something far worse than what she'd been worried about.

She'd caught a glimpse of the man they were going to hang as Judge Gallimore hustled her back to the cells. Somehow she'd expected a murderer to look older and more malicious, unrepentant and irredeemable. She'd imagined he'd be marked by what he'd done. Instead, Joe Calvert's face was young and guileless, with the narrow spade jaw of a youth still inching toward manhood and the mouth of a sulky child. Standing manacled between the sheriff and the parson, he'd managed to look both belligerent and scared to death.

In spite of knowing he was a killer, Shea couldn't help feeling a little sorry for him.

"Come along then, Calvert," the sheriff said. "You need anything before we go out there?"

Calvert must have shaken his head.

Shea shivered in the gust of wind and dust that boiled through the office as the men stepped outside. She heard the moment the crowd caught sight of them. The murmur of voices rose in a cheer that almost immediately disintegrated into a chorus of hoots and catcalls.

Shea glanced up at the narrow, barred window in the north wall of her cell. It faced the lot where the scaffold stood. The cell window was far too high for her to reach, a full two feet above her head. Even if she stood on the three-legged stool from the corner she wouldn't be able to see more than a bright square of sky. She listened instead, using the sounds to create her own gossamer images.

The lot must be more crowded than it had been earlier in the afternoon; the voices were louder. The men must be drunker; there was a harsh, raucous edge to their laughter. She wondered if the crowd was parting to allow Calvert a quick, smooth passage to the scaffold, or if the miners had pushed in close so that Sheriff Willoughby and Judge Gallimore were having to shove their way through and protect the man they'd come to hang.

Then, above the clamoring of the crowd, she heard the sound of footsteps ascending the stairs to the gallows. The brisk, heavy tread would be the sheriff's, impatient to get on with the business at hand. Calvert stumbled a bit as he climbed, as if fear were robbing him of his coordination. Lighter footsteps followed. They'd be the parson's, and Shea wondered whether he considered it a thankless chore to pray for a man who'd so willfully damned himself.

Judge Gallimore must be waiting off to one side. She could almost see him standing with his head high and his mouth pulled so taut it would be all but hidden beneath the drape of that luxuriant mustache. He'd be the very portrait of a man living up to his responsibilities.

The moment she'd flung back the camera's darkcloth she'd recognized him as someone of consequence. Beyond his intimidating height and the lean, leashed power of his body, there had been something in those sharp patrician features that bespoke intelligence, high standards, and influence, nobility—and outrage.

Then, she'd caught a flicker of the man behind that facade, shades of vulnerability in those night blue eyes. Before she could consider what she'd seen, he'd prodded her, asked why she was taking this photograph. She should have known better than to argue with a man like him, a man with such obvious authority. She should have held her peace—but getting this photograph meant too much.

From out where the gallows stood, Shea could hear the sheriff calling for order. She raised her eyes to the window and listened.

He began to read. "For being found guilty of murdering Ned Barstow in cold blood, the First District Court of the Territory of Colorado sentences Joe Calvert to death by hanging."

The crowd mumbled in agreement.

"Let us pray," the parson intoned. In a high, reedy voice he blessed the man Calvert had killed, asked repentance and redemption for Calvert himself, and finally prayed for everyone who came out to see justice done.

Shea bowed her head, and her own guilt lay heavy as God's broad hands on her shoulders. Repenting her own sins was taking everything she had, but she was trying.

People had begun to murmur and shift their feet by the time the preacher said "Amen."

"You have anything to say for yourself, Calvert?" the sheriff asked.

Silence fell and Shea could picture the crowd easing toward the gallows to listen.

Calvert must be standing in the very shadow of the noose looking out over that sea of avid faces. Did he realize these were the last words he'd ever speak? Small wonder they came so slowly.

"I'm so damn sorry I killed Ned Barstow," he said. "He was my best friend."

She could hear the regret in Calvert's admission. In spite of knowing what he'd done, her throat constricted.

"You should'a thought o' that b'fore you put yer knife in Barstow's belly," someone shouted.

"Just get on with it," another man urged.

"Hang the bleeding bastard!"

A haze of noisy agreement rolled out of the crowd like steam from a pot bubbling over the fire. It billowed, becoming a clamor; a babel, a roar. The rumble and churn reverberated off the walls of Shea's tiny cell. Out in the midst of the mob the volume must be deafening.

Then everything went still.

Though she had never seen a hanging, Shea realized what that silence meant. The sheriff was pulling a rough black hood over Calvert's head, tightening the rope around his neck, pulling it taut. It meant they were ready to—

There was the rattle of some mechanical device, the thud of wood rebounding against wood. In the vacant lot beyond her cell, the miners gasped.

Shea's knees wobbled and gave way. She reeled backward, collided with the three-legged stool in the corner of her cell, and sat down hard.

From beyond the wall a cheer broke out. The miners howled and hooted and might well be slapping each other on the back as if they'd accomplished something brave and wonderful.

Barbarous men, Shea thought, shuddering. How could they have watched that? How could they cheer?

Unbidden thoughts of Cameron Gallimore flitted through Shea's head. If he was out there among those drunken, yelling men, he'd be standing silent as a pillar of granite. No matter how deserving of condemnation Calvert had been, Shea sensed Judge Gallimore would have taken no satisfaction in his death.

Thinking of him, Shea suddenly realized how glad she was that she hadn't been at the foot of the gallows to take that photograph. She didn't want Calvert's death captured in silver on one of her glass plates. She didn't want to be able to make hundreds of copies of what she would have seen, or relive what happened every time she did. She didn't want to implant that image in anyone else's mind.

Any money she might have made from selling the photograph would have seemed like blood money. She was a photographer, a businesswoman, not a mercenary. She was proud of what she did, and she would never have been able to be proud of this.

As angry as she'd been and as much she could have used the proceeds from selling this photograph, she didn't regret that Judge Gallimore had intervened. She supposed she should thank the man for what he'd done—and knew she would not.

TWO

Shea had been pacing her cell for more than an hour when Sheriff Willoughby came to let her out.

"And Judge Gallimore said it was all right?" she asked with some asperity as he opened the door. "He's not going to charge me with public lewdness or disturbing the peace?"

The sheriff dipped his head a little to hide a smile. "Cam's a damn fine judge, ma'am," he allowed, leading her into the office proper. "He just didn't want you taking a picture of the hanging, is all."

"Well, he's had his way," she observed with a sniff. "Did he tell you to return my camera?"

He gestured to where the big box camera sat in the corner of the office. "We took good care of 'er."

"I should hope so."

Willoughby nodded toward the open door. "Can I tote that camera for you, ma'am?"

Shea thanked him and headed toward where her assistant, Owen Brandt, had parked their photography wagon across the street from the jail.

"All right?" Owen asked, as she approached. "You all right?"

Shea smiled up at the squat little man perched on the lip of the wagon seat. His shoulders were hunched, and anxiety had pinched harsh folds into his soft, apple-dumpling face.

"I'm fine, old dear, so don't you worry. *And* I got our camera back."

"Good," he said, the lines around his prim mouth easing. "Good."

Just as Shea turned to claim the camera from Sheriff Willoughby, two horsemen came galloping up the street whooping and hollering and firing their revolvers in the air. Shea and the sheriff pressed back against the side of the wagon as they swept by.

Drawn by the noise and excitement, miners spewed out the doors of the saloons on Main Street. They engulfed the horsemen, who fired a few more shots in the air, reholstered their pistols, and all but pitched out of their saddles.

Beside her the sheriff sighed and straightened. " 'Scuse me, Mrs. Waterston," he said with a tip of his hat. "I got me some drunken miners to toss in the hoosegow."

Several deputies came to help him make arrests and herd everyone still sober enough to stand back into the drinking establishments.

When things quieted, Shea glanced up toward the wagon seat and saw that Owen had disappeared. "Owen!" she cried as she leaned the camera against the wagon and scrambled up the side. "Owen?"

Shea found the old man crouched in the knee-well, shivering like someone in the throes of fever.

"Owen," she breathed in relief and reached for him. "Are you all right, old dear?"

His hat was gone, his bald pate shone with sweat, and his eyes glistened with incalculable terror.

"Owen, it's me," she murmured, reaching to lay her hand against his sleeve, stroking him like she always did when the demons chased him.

He stared at her and slowly recognition dawned across his features. An instant later hot shame flooded his cheeks, and he tried to push her hand away.

"You're all right, old dear," she crooned, still chafing his arm. "You're all right now."

It took a good long while to coax Owen out of the knee-well and onto the wagon seat, and then he sat gingerly, as if any minute he expected the thing to buck him off.

Seeing the worst was over, Shea shoved back a palmful of her unruly curls. "Will you be all right if I just go put the camera away?" she asked him.

Owen managed a jerky nod.

Shea climbed down to the street, reclaimed her camera, and proceeded around to the back of the photography wagon. Once she was out of sight her knees gave way. As often as she'd seen them, Owen's episodes of panic still unnerved her. Her husband Simon had been better at calming him than she was. But then, Simon and Owen had come through the war together.

Shaking her head, Shea furled the tarp that hung across the back of the Union ambulance Simon had converted to a rolling darkroom. It was the one he and Owen had taken to the army camps and battlefields, to places like Bull Run and Chancellorsville.

As she lowered the tailgate, she remembered how the tiny interior had been packed to the struts when they'd headed up to the mountains eight weeks ago. Now she could climb right in and put the tripod and camera away.

Owen was still clinging to the wagon seat when she got back.

Shea clambered up beside him and patted his knee. "You 'bout ready to leave this town?" she asked.

He looked over at her and chanced a wobbly smile. "Let's go, Sparrow."

Shea's heart pinched a little every time Owen called her by Simon's pet name. The endearment had been a joke between them, a reminder of how her husband had found her huddled in the snow outside his studio. Hearing the name on Owen's lips reminded her how hollow she'd felt since Simon died, how detached and rootless her life had suddenly seemed.

Well, finding her son was going to change all that, she told herself. Finding her son was going to change everything. Maybe once they reached Denver they'd be able to chase down word of him. Imagining their reunion, she picked up the reins and clucked to the horses.

Shea was repacking the wagon the morning of their third day out of Breckenridge, when a pair of roughly dressed men approached the camp. Without so much as a thought, Shea reached for the Winchester propped up beside her.

Caution was a reflex in such country as this. It was a wise—and not necessarily inhospitable—thing to be ready if trouble came at you.

"Morning, ma'am," the taller of the two men greeted her, pulling his horse up short at the edge of her camp.

"Good morning," she answered, then stood with the rifle nestled comfortably in the crook of her arm, waiting for him to state his business.

"We come down from Breckenridge day before yesterday," he continued, "headed toward Denver. You going that way?"

"We left Breckenridge ourselves two days ago," Shea volunteered.

The second man bobbed his head and gave a cackle of recognition. "You're that lady photographer, ain't ya? The one that wanted to take a picture of Joe Calvert's hanging."

Shea dipped her chin in acknowledgment.

"It's a damn shame how that judge treated you," the man went on. "Not letting you take that photograph, tossing you in the hoosegow because you argued with him. Wasn't I telling you about it, Lyle, just last night?"

"He said you was a feisty little thing to stand up to Judge Gallimore the way you did," Lyle agreed with a grin.

It was just as well these two men thought she was feisty, Shea reflected. They were rough, uneducated men, like hundreds she'd photographed over the last two years—drifters, working when and where they could. They'd take advantage of a woman if they thought she was weak, but Shea knew how to handle them. In this case, her reputation had preceded her. She lowered the Winchester.

If the first rule of the West was to be ready to defend yourself, the second was to offer what hospitality you could.

"Would you like a cup of coffee?" Shea inquired.

"Coffee'd be good, ma'am."

The two men dismounted and settled themselves. "My name's Lyle Smithers," the first man told her companionably. "And this here's Wally Barber."

Shea set the rifle well within reach and used a wad of rags to pull the coffeepot out of the coals.

As she poured a steamy brown stream into three tin cups, Owen came puffing up the rise. His sparse hair was slicked to his scalp and his face was pink from washing.

To Shea's eyes, he was a benign old man with more than his share of idiosyncracies. What she needed these strangers to think was that he was considerably more than that.

Shea raised her head and sliced Owen a glance that stopped him at the back of the wagon.

"I'm Mrs. Waterston," she offered as she handed over two of the cups. "And this is my traveling companion, Owen Brandt."

Lyle looked up at where Owen stood solid and square, braced against the wagon's tailgate. He'd hooked his thumbs in his belt on either side of the foot-long skinning knife he wore on his belt. These two drifters didn't need to know that all Owen ever used it for was cutting rubber tubing.

"Is Mr. Brandt going to be joining us for coffee?" Wally Barber wondered nervously.

"Mr. Brandt doesn't want any coffee," Shea answered for him. "Mr. Brandt is fine right where he is."

By then, both of the men were studying Owen, and it was clear something about his demeanor unsettled them.

Finally, Smithers returned his attention to Shea. "So—so you're a lady photographer, are you, ma'am?"

"For some years now," Shea said, sipping from her cup.

"And do you take pictures of things besides hangings?"

"I do every kind of photography."

"Could you take a picture of Wally and me?"

The request caught Shea off guard. "Now?" she asked him.

Her gaze drifted over them. Most people wanted to look their best when they had their portraits made. Men waxed their mustaches and slicked down their hair. Women decked themselves out in their Sunday best and put on fine lace collars. These two didn't look like they'd be ready to be photographed in less than a week of waxing and slicking and decking out.

"Sure. Now'd be good." Lyle grinned revealing gaps in both rows of yellowing teeth. "What should we do? Where should we stand?"

Shea looked up at the steep walls of the canyon, judging the light. "It—it would be difficult to do a sitting here," Shea hedged, hating to set everything up for the sake of a pair of tintypes. "It isn't bright enough down here in the trees, and we'd have to haul water to process the pictures."

Both men looked crestfallen.

"I'm sorry," Shea murmured. "Maybe I can arrange to take your photographs once we reach Denver."

"We're not going right into town," Lyle said on a sigh.

"I don't see why we couldn't take her with us to camp," Wally proposed. "Don't you figure the boys'd be tickled for a chance to get their pictures made?"

Lyle shook his head as if to warn Wally off. "I don't know that Wes would like it."

Shea wasn't sure it was wise to head off to some camp in the mountains with men she'd never seen before today.

"Oh, Wes won't mind," Wally enthused. "You know what a dandy Wes is. And the women . . . Well, don't you think having a photographer come to town will be a treat for them?"

Something about Wally's boyish glee convinced her. And if there were women and families in the camp, Shea figured they'd be safe enough.

Lyle looked unconvinced.

"What kind of a camp?" Shea asked. "A mining camp?"

"Um—well. Yeah, sure," Lyle fumbled. "A mining camp."

"And how many photographs do you think I might be taking?"

"Oh, twenty, at least," Wally volunteered. "Maybe more than that, if the men ain't been playing poker and cleaned each other out."

More than twenty photographs! If Shea could take twenty photographs she'd have the money to put them up in Denver long enough to decide where they were heading next.

She agreed quickly. "We'll be happy to visit your camp if you'll show us the way."

It was only a matter of minutes before Shea and Owen had the wagon packed and were following Lyle and Wally down the mountain.

A good-sized crowd had congregated in front of the mining camp's single commercial building by the time they pulled the photography wagon to a stop. Shea could see right off that these weren't the kind of folks she'd expected when Lyle and Wally had talked about the camp. What she'd hoped for were prospectors with full pokes who'd want pictures to send to their kin back east. What she got were a few bewhiskered miners; a goodly number of down-on-their-luck cowboys, four fading fancy women, and one lone boy who peeked at her around the women's skirts.

Still, Shea put on the best face she could and jumped down from the wagon to introduce herself. "Good afternoon. I'm Mrs. Waterston, a lady photographer lately of New York City. My assistant and I have come to your camp today to take the best photographic portraits you're ever likely to sit for." To prove her point she took out a tintype of a pretty saloon girl she'd photographed in Abilene and offered it for them to see.

A tall, blond man with a waxed mustache and pin-striped vest stepped forward and took the picture from her. He glanced down at the tintype in its cardboard sleeve, then raised his gaze and let it crawl over her.

Shea stood her ground in spite of the almost reptilian coldness in his heavy-lidded eyes.

"So you're a lady photographer?" he finally said.

Shea did her best to force a smile. "I make pictures of everything from church picnics to mountain scenery."

"But no pictures of hangings, huh?" Wally hooted from where he still sat his horse a few feet away.

Shea inclined her head. "I ran into a little unpleasantness in Breckenridge."

"She ended up in the calaboose!"

Lyle nudged Wally to silence, nearly knocking him out of the saddle.

The tall man's eyes slid over her a second time.

Shea's heart picked up speed. "It's not an experience I'm eager to repeat," she confessed.

Several men in the crowd snickered.

The man in the vest looked down at the photograph again.

"How much did you say you were charging for these?"

On the boardwalk back east, tintypes sold for a quarter. Out here where photographers were scarce, and especially considering the inconvenience of coming to their camp, Shea thought she could charge a good deal more.

"I figure a dollar," she told him. When no one complained, she pressed ahead. "So, which of you handsome gentlemen or fine ladies is going to be the first to be immortalized in a lovely photographic portrait?"

They all seemed to be hanging on what the tall man said. He looked down at the tintype, then up at Shea. "And you claim you can make us all look as fine as this?"

Shea shrugged. "A potter is only as good as his clay," she answered. "I make likenesses; I don't perform miracles."

One corner of the man's mouth twitched, though Shea wasn't sure if he was amused or offended.

"All right, then," he agreed and rubbed at his chin. "Will I have time to shave?"

Shea let out the breath she didn't realize she'd been holding. "Of course you will. A man wants to look his best when he has his portrait made."

"Good enough," he said with a nod. "I'm Wes Seaver. I expect you'll meet the others by and by."

"Indeed, I hope I will," she answered. Then she turned her attention from her customers to the narrow, sharp-sided valley. Bisected by a six-foot-wide ribbon of rippling stream, the camp consisted of cabins and mine tailings sprinkled along both banks.

"I'd like to set up my camera here on the rise where the light is good, if that's all right."

"It's fine with me," Seaver agreed. "I'll send my brother Jake out to the cabins so everyone knows you're here."

While Shea parked the wagon and tended the horses,

the crowd dispersed. By the time she climbed into the back, Owen was getting things unpacked.

"Don't like this," he grumbled under his breath. "Just don't like it."

Shea glanced across at him. "Well, it's not quite what I expected either, but we're here now and we're going to make the best of it. We'll be making mostly tintypes this afternoon, but have a few glass plates cleaned and ready, just in case."

Leaving Owen to organize the chemicals to his own exacting specifications, Shea picked up her camera and tripod and went back outside. The bench that sat in front of the general store and "dispensary" was a perfect place to pose her customers.

As she set up the camera, the boy she'd seen in the crowd earlier crept toward her. He was nine or ten, wiry, dark-haired, and grimy from head to toe.

"You really a photographer, ma'am?" he asked her, his eyes alight. He was all but dancing with excitement.

Shea couldn't help but grin. "Yes, I am."

"You really gonna charge a dollar for the photographs?"

Shea nodded, adjusting the tripod's legs.

"See, I ain't got but eighteen cents." He pulled a handful of pennies out of his pocket. "I earned most of it mucking out Old Digger McNee's cabin over yonder. I swear he had beans in his pot that went back to last spring!"

Shea laughed in spite of herself. "Maybe your folks can come up with the price of a photograph," she suggested as she ducked beneath the dark-cloth and twisted the knob on the lens to bring the bench into focus.

"That ain't likely," she heard the boy say. "My ma

died two years ago, and since then Pa spends most of our money on whiskey."

Shea was taken aback by the boy's forthrightness, and she couldn't think of a thing to say to him.

"Whatcha looking at under there, anyway?" he asked her a moment later.

Shea lifted one edge of the dark-cloth. "You want to see?"

"Sure!" His eyes fired up with excitement again. They were pretty eyes, set in a smudged and sunburned face, golden brown and flecked with green. Sharp eyes filled with eagerness and energy.

He ducked beneath the drape of fabric, and Shea positioned him in front of her. He had to stand up on his toes to see the image on the focusing glass, and instinctively she curled a hand around his shoulder to steady him. As she did she caught the sweaty, earthy smell of a boy who liked exploring these hills and digging in the dirt. She wrinkled her nose, but couldn't quite bring herself to back away from him.

"The store's upside down!" he exclaimed. "How come it's upside down? Will the picture come out upside down?"

Shea smiled to herself, remembering her own confusion the first time Simon had allowed her to look through the focusing glass. "There's a lens inside the camera that takes the light from things out front and flips it over. It's that light passing through the lens that makes an image on the photographic plate."

He looked back at her in the close confines of the tented dark-cloth. She could see him gnawing at the chapped curve of his lower lip. "What's a photograppic plate?"

Right then and there Shea made a decision. "All

right, boy, if you want to help me while I take the photographs, I'll show you how all this works."

"I'm good at helping," he hastily assured her.

Shea flipped back the dark-cloth. "I need to know what to call you if you're going to work for me."

"I'm Tyler Morran," he said and stuck out one dirt-encrusted hand. "But Pa calls me Ty."

"Ty it is, then." Shea took his hand gingerly in hers. "I'm Shea Waterston."

Shea took a moment to think what she wanted him to do. "Well, first," she began, "I want you to wash your face and hands all the way to the elbows. Handling plates and chemicals requires cleanliness. Then we can go inside the photography wagon, and I'll introduce you to my assistant."

"Am I your assistant, too?" the boy asked hopefully.

Shea hesitated, wondering if he'd expect her to pay him for his services. Then she acknowledged that even if he did, he needed the pittance she'd give him far more than she. "I guess you are," she answered.

The boy snuffed and spat. "Hot damn!" he said.

After giving Ty soap, Shea climbed inside the wagon, where Owen had things all laid out.

"Water reservoir?" he asked her, indicating the collapsed rubber bladder that would hang from one of the ribs in the wagon's top so they'd have running water during the processing.

"I'll have our new helper take care of it."

"Some kid," he guessed.

Shea just laughed.

"Better than the last?" he murmured.

"Well, yes, I know the last one tried to pocket two of our lenses," she admitted. "But I'm sure this one is far more—"

"Mrs. Waterston?" Ty called from just outside. "I'm all washed up."

Owen gave a snort of derision.

"Come on in, Ty," she shouted.

The boy climbed into the wagon. "I can't say as how I've ever seen so many of the men washed up and clean at once!" he declared, reporting back from the stream.

Shea bit her lip to suppress her smile. "Do you suppose you could bring us a bucket of clear water?" she asked him.

Ty nodded and took the bucket.

"Better than some," Owen allowed.

They were just filling the rubber bladder with water when someone rapped on the side of the wagon.

"We'll be ready for you in a few minutes," Shea called out. Tying the edges of the flap at the back of the wagon closed to keep out the daylight, Shea went to where Owen had everything mixed and ready. It was warm inside the wagon, and the only light came through the yellow calico window in the top, giving the tiny space a dim, orangy glow.

"Now we're going to flow the plates," Shea told Ty in her most instructive voice.

There were two kinds of plates, ones made of black coated iron and others of glass. She took one of the metal plates and dusted the japanned surface with a camel-hair brush. Carefully balancing the plate on the fingertips of her left hand, Shea took up a bottle with her right.

"This is the collodion," she said pouring a substance about the consistency of thin molasses into the center of the plate. She turned her wrist as she did, tipping the plate carefully in what she'd always considered a graceful sleight of hand. The liquid ran slowly toward her thumb, then, with another tip, toward her forefinger. She moved the plate side to side, coating it evenly.

A cloying drift of vapor rose from the liquid as she worked. "Collodion is made from ether, alcohol, and guncotton," she said, holding the bottle beneath the last corner of the plate and dribbling the excess into the neck. "Collodion can catch fire or make you dizzy because of the ether. It dries fast, so we work quickly. Once the plate is tacky, we'll dip it into a chemical that will react with the collodion and make the plate sensitive to light."

Ty looked up at her and nodded.

"While I am posing our subjects," she went on, "Owen will be sensitizing the plates and putting them in the plate holders. What we'll need you to do, Ty, is bring the plates to me out at the camera. Do you think you can do that?"

Once he'd assured her he could, Shea tested the edge of the plate with the tip of her index finger. "Perfect," she pronounced, and showed Ty how to set the plate into an inverted-T-shaped holder. "This is the dipper," she said as she lowered the coated plate into a canted, black envelope-like apparatus that was filled with clear liquid.

"This is silver nitrate," she explained. "It makes the plate sensitive to the light that comes through the lens of the camera." She supposed to a boy Ty's age all this must seem like sorcery.

"Now I'm going to pose the first of our customers. I'll need you to bring me the plate when I call for it."

Outside the wagon five miners were lined up to have their photographs made. Shea gestured the first one forward, settled him on the bench, and eased him into the stemmed, semicircular headrest Owen had set up for her behind the bench. The headrest functioned as a guide to help the sitters remain in position long enough for Shea to make her exposure.

After she'd collected her fee, Shea strode to the back of the camera, ducked beneath the dark-cloth, and looked through the lens. "Take off your hat," she instructed. "Hold it in your lap if you like. Otherwise it casts a shadow on your face, and we won't be able to see you."

Moving carefully so as not to dislodge the headrest positioned behind his ears, the man did as he was told.

"Ty," she shouted and checked the focus one last time. "I need that plate."

She was just replacing the lens cap when the boy eased out of the wagon. Moving with exaggerated care, Ty brought her the loaded plate holder.

"The plate sort of glowed when Owen took it out of that silver nite-tate stuff," he whispered.

Shea took the rectangular wooden frame. "I'm pleased you carried this plate holder just the way Owen showed you."

The plate holder had a latched wooden door on one side where Owen had inserted the sensitized plate, and a slide on the other. Taking care to keep it upright, Shea eased the plate holder into the slit on the side of the camera so it—and the sensitized plate—were positioned in front of the lens.

She turned to her subject. "I need you to sit absolutely still for this," she told him.

Once she had judged the strength of the sun streaming over her subject's face and calculated the exposure, Shea pulled the wooden slide with her left hand and removed the lens cap with her right. She allowed light to enter the camera for a count of six, then replaced the cap and pushed in the slide.

"You're done," she told her sitter.

"That all there is to it?" he asked her.

Shea removed the plate holder from the camera and sent Ty into the wagon. "Sitting for a tintype is easy, isn't it?"

"How long before I can pick up my picture?" he wanted to know.

"An hour," she told him. For all his eccentricities, Owen had been one of the most skilled and efficient photographic processors in New York City. "And I'm sure you'll be delighted with the picture when you see it."

The next man took his place on the bench, and Shea went through the posing again. They worked methodically all afternoon, and as the men saw how a sitting worked, they began to include things in their poses that gave hints to their personalities. One pretended to be playing his guitar. Someone else brought his shovel and pickax. Two of the women posed together, each wearing a lovely lace mantilla.

When one of the sitters seemed particularly colorful, Shea made a second exposure on a glass plate. Though she didn't explain what she was doing, these pictures were for her. After she and Owen were settled somewhere, she'd take the glass negatives and make copies to sell back east. The easterners fancied almost anything that captured the feel of the West, and these men were as much a part of it as the prairies and the mountains.

Midway through the afternoon Wes Seaver showed up and took his place on the little bench. He'd shaved, slicked back his luxuriant blond hair, and rewaxed his mustache. He'd donned a handsome broadcloth jacket, a jay blue vest, and a black string tie. Before seating himself, he eased a fancy pearl-handled revolver from the holster on his hip.

Shea noticed he wore his holster tied down like the

gunfighters she'd seen in Dodge City and in Abilene. He seemed unaccountably comfortable with that pistol. But then, many of the men who'd fought in the Civil War handled firearms with the same unnerving nonchalance.

Seaver struck a pose, and once Shea had exposed the plate for his tintype, she asked Ty to bring a second plate.

"What are you doing?" Seaver asked her.

A guilty shiver slid up her back. None of the other men whose pictures she'd taken for herself had questioned her.

"I think you moved during the first exposure," she lied, her heart thumping. "I'm making a second to be sure you're happy with the portrait I make of you."

"Oh, all right," Seaver answered. He settled back on the bench and carefully turned his gun so the beautifully etched barrel and the polished grip showed to best advantage.

Shea's last customer was preparing for his photograph when a rail-thin man wove down the inclined path from one of the nearby cabins.

"Ty?" he called out, as the boy climbed out of the wagon, balancing the plate holder in his two hands. "Ty, what are you doing there? You're not bothering that lady, are you?"

"Hullo, Pa," Ty called out to him. Giving the photographic plate to Shea, he ran up the rise to meet his father. "I'm glad you're awake, Pa. There's someone I want you to meet."

As the two of them came toward her, Shea could see that the man's hair was mussed and his eyes were bloodshot.

"This is my pa, Sam, Mrs. Waterston," Ty made the

introduction. "Mrs. Waterston's a photographer, and I been helping her."

Morran laid his hand on his son's curly hair. "And you are a good worker, aren't you, lad?"

Why wouldn't a man who touched his son so gently see that he was bathed and fed and wearing clean clothes? Shea wondered. How could any man sleep away the afternoon when his son was hard at work?

I'd take better care of Ty if he were mine, Shea found herself thinking.

"He's been a big help to me, Mr. Morran," Shea said, wanting to be sure Ty's father knew how much she appreciated his son. She'd even seen Owen give the boy a nod of approval. "I'm afraid we've kept Ty running most of the afternoon."

Ty beamed at her praise of him.

"Hey, what about me?" Shea's last customer shouted from the bench where he was posed and ready. "You gonna jaw all day or take my picture?"

While Ty gave his father an explanation of everything photographers did, Shea took the photograph. When she was done, Ty looked up at his father. "Can we have our picture made, Pa? It costs a dollar."

"Aw, no, Ty. I don't think we can afford—"

"I got eighteen cents," he went on hopefully and dug into his trouser pocket.

Shea couldn't bear to watch him offer up those hard-earned pennies, and spoke impulsively. "I'll take the photograph for free! I—I had intended to pay the boy for his help, but if Ty would rather have a tintype made . . ."

Tyler's eyes glowed. "You'd do that, Mrs. Waterston?"

Shea smiled. "For such a fine helper, indeed I would."

"Oh, son, I don't know," Ty's father began, smoothing down his boy's hair.

"But we don't have any pictures of Marna," the boy cajoled, "and sometimes I wish . . ."

The grief that flared in Morran's eyes was proof of the man's feelings for his dead wife.

That's why he doesn't take care of Ty. There isn't room in him for anything but his pain and loss. The flash of insight made Shea twitch inside her skin. It wasn't something she wanted to know about this boy, or about his father. She shifted on her feet, unsettled and angry, convinced that Ty deserved better than his father was giving him.

"Please, Mr. Morran," she found herself saying. "Let me take the picture for the boy's sake."

Morran must have read her judgment of him in her eyes, because he took a moment to compose himself, then looked down at his son. "All right," he agreed.

Shea positioned the two of them side by side on the bench. She straightened Morran's hair as best she could and noted it was no cleaner than his son's. She tugged at the frayed collar of his work shirt and draped his arm around his son's narrow shoulders.

Ty snuggled in, absorbing the contact with his father like rain seeping into dusty earth. He laid his own small hand on his father's thigh.

The hunger in that simple gesture made Shea's throat close up, and she couldn't help remembering her own da's spontaneous hugs. He'd always had a place on his knee for one of them, and stories to tell by the cottage fire.

She sensed that Tyler Morran's father never told his son stories, never held him close, never made him feel safe. With the realization, a knot of conviction tightened beneath Shea's breastbone.

When she found her son, she'd take *such* good care of him. She'd feed and care for him. She'd hold him in the evenings and play games with him and spin tales for him. She'd make sure he knew he was loved, knew he was safe. Every child deserved that, even if he wasn't hers.

Shea peered at Ty and his father through the focusing glass, determined to get the photograph taken before they lost the light. Owen was humming when she went in to retrieve the last plate they'd expose this afternoon.

When she returned, she adjusted the focus one last time, put in the plate holder, and pulled the slide.

"I'll give this tintype to Ty when we are done," she told Morran as he pushed to his feet the moment they were finished.

"You sure you don't mind having him underfoot?" he asked her, shifting uneasily and glancing to where the lights had come on in the dispensary.

"Heavens, no! Ty's been a wonderful help this afternoon."

"Good," Morran said. "Good." Then without another word he went inside.

It seemed that the dispensary was a gathering place for many of the men at the close of the day. As Shea put away the camera, she could hear them in there talking and laughing.

As the voices got louder and louder, Shea and Owen hurried to finish the last of the developing. They kept Ty busy drying and varnishing the tintypes, putting them into their folded-cardboard cases and delivering them to their customers.

"I know Wes said it was all right for you to be here," Ty offered after his second trip to the dispensary, "but sometimes the men get to drinking and acting crazy. I think you should leave as soon as you can."

When the last of the tintypes was processed and delivered, Ty helped them hitch up the horses, then climbed into the wagon. "I'll show you a way out that's quicker than the way they probably brought you here."

The boy was as good as his word. Settled between Owen and Shea on the wagon seat, Ty guided them across the stream and down a narrow, jolting trail that wound through the dark denseness of a pine forest, then out to what was clearly a more traveled route through the mountains. Looking back the way they had come, Shea wondered how anyone ever found their way into that little valley.

As they pulled onto the main road, Ty clambered over Shea's knees and jumped to the ground. In spite of his eagerness to get them out of the camp, he seemed reluctant to let them leave.

His hesitation tugged at Shea. "Well, good-bye, Tyler Morran," she finally said, then leaned over the side of the wagon to shake his hand. "I thank you for your help today."

"I thank you for the tintype of Pa and me." He patted the front of his shirt where Shea had seen him tuck the picture away, and she sensed she'd managed to give the boy something he'd treasure.

"You're welcome, Ty. You earned it," was all she said.

Owen clucked to the horses and rattled their reins. When she turned to look back as they made their first turn, Ty was still standing on the fringe of the road—a frail, small figure, as lost in his way as her own child.

THREE

It took Shea and Owen two more days to wend their way out of the mountains, and Shea chafed with every mile they traveled. She could barely wait to reach Denver, could barely wait to get the boxes of photographic plates they'd exposed this summer on a train to New York. She was even more eager for the bank draft that would arrive once Anthony and Company accepted her views into their collection of western stereography. Only when she had that money safely deposited in a Denver bank would she be able to breathe, to replenish their supplies, or to consider their winter accommodations.

Yet as impatient as she was to reach the city, Shea was not blind to the rugged grandeur of the land around her. Gilded stands of aspens spilled down the rocky mountain sides like living flame. Bristling pines stood velvety counterpoint to those slim, bright torches of gold. The mountain air crackled with the breath of fall, and when the morning mist laced thick along the bank of the stream they'd been following, Shea was awed anew by the pure, primal power of this wilderness. They paused often to record what they saw, adding to the store of negatives they'd send back east.

They were making their final descent through the rocky foothills in the hopes of making Denver by suppertime, when they rounded a bend in the road and came upon a scene right out of some western melodrama.

Three men on horseback were preparing to lynch a fourth.

Owen hauled back on the horse's reins.

Shea reached for the Winchester braced beside her on the wagon seat. As the wagon clattered to a stop, she sprang to her feet and leveled the rifle at all of them.

"Stand where you are," she shouted, "or I'll be looking to put a hole in you!"

Owen dove into the knee-well beside her, taking cover.

All of the men turned to stare at her, gone so still they might have been posing for one of her photographs. Three were miners, by the worn, shabby look of them. One of them had flung a rope over the limb of a tree at the edge of the road. A noose dangled menacingly at the end of it. The other two held pistols on the man they meant to hang.

The fourth, the man with his hands in the air, was bigger and better dressed. It took Shea a moment to recognize him—His Honor, Cameron Gallimore!

Astonishment sizzled all the way to her toes.

"You just go on your way, ma'am," one of the miners called to her. "This don't concern you."

"Oh, but I'm afraid it does," she shouted back. Her voice might have wavered a little, but the Winchester didn't. "Now if you'd be so kind as to throw down your weapons . . ."

Shea raised her rifle, prodding them.

The miners hesitated.

As they did, Judge Gallimore leapt from his horse toward the man with the rope. He grabbed him across the shoulders and bowled him out of the saddle. The two of them landed like a sack of shot down among the horses' hooves. The other miners' ponies whinnied and shied, danced frantically sideways.

From the floor of the wagon box, Owen tugged at the hem of Shea's skirt.

"Not now, old dear," Shea whispered. She didn't dare take her eyes off the men thrashing in the dirt. Didn't dare turn from where the other miners were fighting to rein in their mounts.

Shea could see that Judge Gallimore punched like a bare-knuckles champion. He'd reared back on his knees to slam his fist into the hangman's face, when one of the other horsemen wheeled.

He fought his pony for control, then pointed his pistol at the judge's back.

"Look out!" Shea yelled, but she knew Gallimore probably couldn't hear her.

She sighted down the barrel of her Winchester and pulled the trigger. The rifle jumped hard against her chest. The stink of powder seared up her nose. Her eardrums pulsed with the report of the rifle.

On the far side of the road the gunman reeled out of his saddle.

She'd shot a man.

A fierce, hot burn of remorse flared along Shea's nerves. She hesitated, shaken by what she'd done. Shaken by what she'd been forced to do.

The last horseman turned his pistol on her.

Shea heard Judge Gallimore shout. She saw him scramble away from the man he'd been fighting and

lunge toward the one on horseback. But Gallimore was
too far away.

She struggled to ratchet another round into the
chamber of her rifle so she could defend herself.

Before she could, the man fired.

Orange flared out the barrel of his gun. An instant
later the impact of the bullet knocked her sideways.
Numbness dropped through her. The rifle tumbled
from her hands. Her knees gave way.

She lost her coordination, lost her balance. She made
an instinctive grab for the side of the wagon, felt the
struts and canvas tear out of her grasp. She teetered at
the edge of the wagonbox and felt herself fall.

Pain blasted her world apart in a shower of sparks.

"She better not be dead, goddamn you!" Cameron
roared and charged the man with the pistol.

The gunman swung around in his saddle and tried
to aim. Cam was on him before he could. He battered
the pistol out of the gunman's hand. He hauled the
man off his horse and threw him to the ground. Strad-
dling him on his knees, Cam wrapped his hands
around the gunman's throat.

Pure, crimson rage burst through him. His lungs
burned. His scalp tightened. Fury howled in his ears
like a thousand banshees. His thumbs crushed down on
the gunman's windpipe.

The man thrashed beneath him. He fought for
breath.

Through a haze of red, Cam saw his hands squeezing
and squeezing. He watched the gunman's chest spasm
and his eyes roll and suddenly realized he was the cause
of it. He loosed his hold and sat back, panting. The
man gagged and gasped for breath beneath him.

"She just better not be dead," Cam whispered and hitched himself to his feet.

He recovered the miner's pistol a few yards away and wheeled in the direction of the photography wagon. As he broke into a trot, the man on the ground shifted, crab-crawling backward. Cam caught the movement from the corner of his eye. He turned, sighted on the gunman's thigh, and pulled the trigger.

The man yowled in pain.

"You stay where I put you, God damn it," he shouted. "I'm going to check on the lady you shot, and you better be here when I get back."

Cam turned toward where the woman lay at the edge of the trail like a bundle of wet wash.

What in the name of God was this photographer woman doing here? he wondered as he pelted up the rise. Why in hell hadn't she stayed out of this? He'd have found a way to handle it.

He came to his knees beside her, and only when he reached out to her did he see how his hand was shaking. He balled his fist, sucked down a ragged draught of air, and reached again. He eased her gently onto her back.

She lay limp in his arms, blood flowing freely along her temple and jaw from a deep gash at her hairline. A scuffed-looking graze marred one pale cheek.

Cam slid his hands over her, examining her with an impartial expertise he'd perfected during the war. *Never blink,* he found himself thinking. *Never let them see how bad it is.*

But in this case the wound was far from serious. The bullet had passed through the fleshy curve of the woman's arm a little more than midway up the sleeve of her dark, close-fitting jacket. With a doctor's care and a little binding, she'd be right as rain inside of a week.

Cam was just finishing his assessment of the woman's wound, when he became aware of a soft, low-pitched whimper from the wagon. Worried that someone else was hurt, he used his coat to pillow the woman's head and got to his feet.

When he peered over the side, he found a small, bald-headed man wedged beneath the wagon seat. He was chalk white, shivering, and moaning softly.

Recognition dropped through Cameron like a sinker into a pond. He knew what it was.

"Mister," he said softly, almost crooning. "Mister?"

The little man blinked, as if he was fighting his way back from someplace far away. He looked up at Cam.

"She—she hurt?" he whispered.

"She's going to be fine," Cam murmured. "The wound's not serious. She's going to be all right. Are you wounded, too?"

The man swallowed and shook his head.

"Then do you think you can find me something to use for bandages?"

"Bandages?" the little man breathed. He wiggled out from beneath the seat. "Bandages," he repeated and disappeared into the back of the wagon.

Cameron knelt again beside the lady photographer. What was her name? Waterman? Waterhouse?

Damn it all, what was she doing here? And why had she tried to help him?

Cam heard the wagon springs creak, and a moment later, the bald-headed fellow appeared out the back. He approached Cam cautiously, holding out a roll of gauzy cloth and a canteen.

"Bandages?" he offered, holding them out stiff-armed, as if he didn't want to get too close.

Cameron nodded and tore off a length of cloth. He moistened it with water from the canteen, and began to dab at the gash on the woman's head.

"Will you tell me your name?" Cam asked as he worked.

"Owen," the fellow whispered. "Owen Brandt."

"And her name?"

"Shea Waterston."

"I'm Cameron Gallimore," he offered. "I think your friend is coming around, Mr. Brandt."

Shea Waterston shifted and moaned. Her lashes lifted over ice green eyes that were unfocused and filled with confusion. Instinctively Cameron laid his palm against her brow, meaning to soothe her.

She blinked at him and shifted away. "You're not going to take my camera, are you?"

Cam smiled in spite of himself. At least her wits hadn't been addled by the bump on her head. "Your camera's safe from me," he assured her. "Do you remember what happened?"

She blinked again and put her hand to her brow. "There were men trying to—to hang you. Is that right? And I shot someone . . ."

"That you did, Mrs. Waterston. And took a bullet in the arm for your trouble. The wound doesn't look too serious, so I'm just going to bind it up to stop the bleeding." He unfurled another length of gauze and talked as he worked. "I've got a farmstead not ten miles ahead. We'll take you there and have the doctor come have a look at you. Is that all right?"

Once he'd tied up her arm and fastened a bandage in place around her head, he eased her into a sitting position. "Do you think you can stand, Mrs. Waterston?"

"I—I don't know. I'm feeling a little light-headed . . ."

With a murmur of sympathy, Cam slid one arm around her back and worked the other beneath her knees. He lifted her gently, taking care not to jostle her wounded arm. "You're going to be just fine, Mrs. Waterston," he assured her.

Cradled against his chest, she nodded.

"Owen," he said, turning toward where Owen had retreated at the back of the wagon, "is there someplace Mrs. Waterston can lie down in there?"

Owen climbed up into the back and hastily spread their bedrolls atop a collection of wooden boxes. Cameron followed him inside and eased Mrs. Waterston down on the makeshift bed.

"You're going to be fine," he said again, though he didn't like how lax and waxen she suddenly seemed. "It'll just take me a minute to collect my horse and what's left of the men who jumped me, then we'll head for the farm."

The woman nodded again and closed her eyes.

He turned and found Owen Brandt standing at his elbow. "Be all right?" the little man pressed him.

Never let them see how bad it is, the echo of other times rang through his head. A shiver prickled the length of Cam's back.

"She'll be just fine, Mr. Brandt," he said with an assurance he didn't quite feel. "You count on that."

Cam couldn't ever remember being so glad to get back to the farm. As he eased the team and photography wagon up the drive, he recognized Emmet Farley's buggy pulled up at the gate—and let out his breath.

For once, when they had need of a doctor, they had one close at hand.

He pulled the wagon to a stop and glanced toward where Shea Waterston lay in the back. She'd been drifting in and out of consciousness most of the way, but the last few miles she'd fallen silent. Cam set the brake, jumped down from where he'd been sitting with Owen on the wagon seat, and went around back.

When he'd finished tending Mrs. Waterston up in the hills, he'd found his would-be hangman had taken away the body of the man Shea had shot. Only the miner he'd threatened and wounded himself had remained, and the fellow sat trussed up and bandaged on the floor beside Shea Waterston's makeshift bed.

"She don't look so good to me," his prisoner offered as Cam let down the tailgate and climbed inside.

Cam didn't think Mrs. Waterston "looked so good," either. Yet neither the bandage on her head nor the one around her arm showed signs of additional bleeding. He felt for the pulse at the side of her throat. It was weak and tripping erratically; her skin seemed chill beneath his fingertips.

An answering chill wormed its way to the pit of Cam's belly as he eased one arm beneath her shoulders and the other under her knees. The moment he lifted her clear of the bed he knew what was wrong. Blood pooled in the hollow beneath her. It darkened the blankets and had seeped into the feather tick. It shimmered damp down the side of the wooden boxes and on the floor.

"Jesus God!" Cam whispered. The Waterston woman was bleeding to death, and he hadn't realized it.

Clutching her against him, he scrambled out the back of the wagon. "Emmet!" he bellowed. "God damn it, Emmet, get out here!"

Cam caught a glimpse of his sister Lily's profile as she peered out the kitchen door to see who'd come into the yard, just before Emmet Farley brushed past her. Sandy-haired, long-legged, and tall, he crossed the porch in two long strides.

By the time Farley reached him, Cam had kicked his way through the picket gate.

"What's wrong?" the doctor demanded.

"This woman's been shot and is bleeding to death!"

Emmet held open the door, and Cam carried Shea into the kitchen. Lily had already swept the plates and teapot they'd been using into the sink and was wiping down the scrubbed pine table with a cloth that smelled of vinegar.

Emmet bent over the woman the moment Cameron put her down. "How did this happen?"

"I ran into some trouble coming out of the mountains," Cam answered, suddenly mindful that his sister was listening and shading his words accordingly. "Mrs. Waterston rode in at the wrong moment and got shot when she tried to help me."

Lily clasped his arm, her soft, gray eyes widening with concern. "And are *you* all right, Cammie?"

Cameron realized how he must look, battered and scuffed and bloodstained. "I'm fine," he assured his sister. "This wasn't anything I couldn't have handled by myself."

"Well, we'll have to take very good care of this lady after all she did to keep you safe," Lily murmured.

Cam turned back to where Emmet had grabbed up Lily's paring knife and was slicing open the Waterston woman's dark, tight-fitting jacket. As the fabric gave way Cam saw that the muslin bodice beneath it was soaked with blood.

"Oh, Shea! Oh n-o-o-o!"

At the sound of the keening, Cam turned and saw that Owen Brandt had followed them into the house. He stood wavering just inside the kitchen door, his mouth hanging lax and his face as white as the winter moon.

Cursing under his breath, Cameron hustled Brandt out onto the porch. He thrust the little man down on the weathered bench and handed him a bucket.

"Blood!" Brandt moaned, then shivered and gasped and lost his breakfast.

Cam laid one hand on Owen's shoulder and felt how he was quivering. "The sight of blood upsets lots of folks," he soothed, squeezing gently.

"Only since the war," the little man all but sobbed. He shuddered, panted, and was sick again.

The war had scarred everyone who fought in it. That's how war was. Cam stared down at Brandt's sweat-damp shirt and heaving shoulders. He understood; *he knew how this went.*

"Just breathe deep, old man," Cam advised him.

He heard the hitch and rasp of Brandt's indrawn breath, the reedy gust of his sigh as he fought his way back from wherever it was he'd been. "Shea?" he somehow managed to croak.

"She couldn't be in better hands."

Cam spent a good long while on the porch with Owen Brandt, standing there, watching over him, steadying him when he needed it. By the time he returned to the kitchen, Cam felt a good deal steadier himself.

While he was gone Emmet and Lily had undressed their patient and tucked her beneath a sheet. She lay as if she were made of melting wax, the skin of her neck and shoulders all but translucent.

Fear gripped Cam when he looked at her. "What
didn't I see?" he asked in a whisper.

Emmet looked up from the basin of carbolic acid
where he was washing his hands. "You bandaged her
arm competently enough, but the bullet passed right
through it and lodged in her side."

Going to where Shea Waterston lay, Emmet peeled
back the sheet.

At first all Cam could seem to see was an expanse of
that fragile, blue-white flesh. The cup and rise of her
collar and breastbone, the mounds of her breasts
crowned by nipples the pale pink of cherry blossoms.
With an effort, Cameron tore his eyes away from all
that lush femininity and adjusted his focus to where
a seeping, rough-edged hole defiled the soft, faintly
pleated arc of her ribs.

"Trussed up the way she was, that wound was almost
impossible to find." Emmet shot Cam a meaningful
glance. "*Anyone could have missed it.*"

Still, Cam blamed himself. He should have looked
for other wounds; he should have been more careful.
"Are you going to be able to get the bullet out?"

Emmet's expression tightened as he lowered the
sheet and turned away. "That slug was probably de-
flected by a rib and could have gone almost anywhere.
With as much blood as she's lost already, I'm not going
to be able to do much probing."

Cameron stared down at the woman on the table.
She'd been wounded because of him, because he'd been
in trouble and she'd tried to help. Responsibility con-
gealed in his chest like bubbling tar, the heat of it all
but choking him.

"What can I do?" he managed to ask.

Emmet immediately put him to work. He helped
turn Shea Waterston onto her side and agreed to

administer chloroform if she began to come around. He'd done it a time or two during the war when there hadn't been anyone else to help the surgeons.

But mostly Cam held her arm up and out of the way as Emmet worked. As he did, her hand lay cupped and lax in his. It was a small hand with an oddly crooked little finger, a hand that hardly seemed strong enough to heft a gun, much less fire it.

Shifting his gaze from the patient, Cam saw that Lily had taken up duties as Emmet's nurse. She was handing him instruments, vials of carbolic acid and powdered opium, pads of lint and rolls of bandages.

Emmet worked with wordless concentration. His long, skilled fingers moved gracefully on the scalpel and probes. At last he removed a misshapen piece of lead and dropped it with an ominous clang into the basin Lily held out to him. As he cleaned the wound, Shea Waterston's blood stained the sheets beneath her, pooled at the edge of the table, and dripped onto the floor.

Cam wondered how anyone could lose so much blood and live.

Out on the porch he could hear Owen Brandt's boot soles scuffling over the planks, could sense the little man's fear hovering like a miasma just over their heads. What was going to happen to this odd little man if Shea Waterston died?

After Emmet had bandaged his patient's side and arm, and stitched the gash at her hairline, he stepped back and swiped the sweat from his brow with the back of his wrist.

"Will she live?" Cameron asked him.

Emmet shrugged, the gesture eloquent, chilling. "We'll keep her quiet and make sure she doesn't open those wounds again. But even if no infection develops, it doesn't look good for her."

"We'll pull her through," Lily said with quiet determination as she went about gathering up the blood-soaked bandages and Emmet's instruments.

The doctor's gaunt face softened and his eyes warmed as he turned to her. "I don't want you getting your heart set on that, Lily. Too much could go wrong."

"Well, we'll just have to see that it doesn't."

Cam glanced at his sister, seeing something in the set of that softly rounded chin that reminded him of the girl she'd been years before.

"If Lily says she'll pull Shea through, she will," he told Emmet, wanting to reassure his sister.

Wanting to reassure himself.

As if his words had settled everything, Lily gestured toward the front of the house. "I thought we'd put Mrs. Waterston in your room, Cammie. The sheets on the bed are clean, and with me sleeping right next door, I'll hear her if she needs something in the night." She glanced at her brother for approval.

"I'll bunk in the attic with Rand," he offered.

"I just hope all this optimism is justified," Emmet observed with a doctor's practiced scowl.

Bending, Cameron carefully lifted Shea Waterston and followed his sister through the well-appointed dining room and parlor. He waited while she turned back the covers on his bed, then settled Shea on sheets that smelled of lye soap and sunshine. The woman seemed even paler against the soft, sun-bleached linen, more fragile than the tatted lace Lily had sewn in rows along the hems of the pillowcases.

Lily must have sensed his thoughts, and she laid her fingers on his arm. "Mrs. Waterston will be all right," she whispered. "We'll pull her through this—the two of us together. If she came to your aid, we owe her that."

Cameron nodded, and with a reassuring squeeze, Lily brushed past him toward the kitchen.

He stood looking down at the small woman who seemed all but lost in his big bed. He could barely believe she'd been the one who'd tried to photograph Joe Calvert's hanging, the one he'd tossed in jail for defying him. She looked like bisque china now, yet she'd brandished her rifle at those miners this afternoon like a warrior queen. She'd even shot one of them to protect him. What kind of a woman did that? What manner of woman was Shea Waterston?

He bent and smoothed back the strands of her gingery hair. The curls that had been lush and tousled the other afternoon lay slack as seaweed across the placid surface of fresh-pressed bedding. He brushed her black-stained fingertips with his, and all but shivered at the chill. He tucked her hand beneath the covers and just stood staring.

He needed to know where she'd come from and what she'd been doing in the mountains. He needed to know why she'd saved his life and what he owed her for the service.

Cameron Gallimore paid his debts and honored his commitments. He might not like what some things cost, but he lived up to his responsibilities. He'd make this up to Shea Waterston, he told himself—if she lived.

Turning from the woman on the bed, he saw that Lily had laid Shea Waterston's clothes across the chair. He picked up the skirt and rubbed the fabric between his fingertips. It was good, heavy twill. The serviceable petticoats she'd worn beneath it were stained with red,

and her stockings, collapsed into loose rosettes of knitted cloth, were thin and often mended.

He reached for the bloodstained remnants of her
close-fitting jacket. A tag sewn into the seam proclaimed the name of a clothier in New York. He'd surmised she was from somewhere back east. The lilt in
her voice and her unconventional occupation bespoke
someplace a good deal more cosmopolitan than Colorado.

Then, amid the untidy tumble of books and papers
on his desk, he noticed three pieces of jewelry that
must belong to Mrs. Waterston, too. There was a narrow wedding band, a pair of filigree earbobs, and a
good-sized silver locket. He opened the piece expecting
to see a likeness of Mr. Waterston. Instead a yellowing
square of newsprint fell into his hand.

It was dog-eared and creased in a dozen places. Cam
unfolded it carefully and tipped it toward the light.
"CHILDREN TO GOOD HOMES," the headline
read. The story beneath gave the particulars of the arrival of an orphan train and enumerated the qualifica-
tions for prospective parents.

A trickle of recognition ran through him.

He looked toward the bed, wondering why, of all
things, Shea Waterston should have this article tucked
away. Why would this newspaper story mean so much
to her? Had she adopted a child from one of the orphan trains, or did she want to? And if she'd taken one
of those children, where was that child?

He turned to where she lay inert, unnaturally still.
She hardly seemed to be breathing.

"Who are you?" Cameron whispered. "And why did
you risk your life to help me?"

FOUR

$\mathcal{S}$ometimes Cameron forgot what had happened to Lily during the war. Sometimes when he was away from the house for days at a time, he was able to divorce himself from what the fighting back in Missouri had done to her. But it always came back—came back to surprise him, to catch him unaware. To remind him of a part of his life he could never live down.

As he approached the doorway into the kitchen from the front of the house, Lily stood lighting the lamp that hung suspended over the table. With the globe raised and the kerosene flame flaring bright, the shiny skin and pale striations that puckered the right side of her face and neck were sharply illuminated. They crimped the corner of her eye and tugged at her mouth; they ran down her jaw and throat like melting wax. They turned her from a lovely woman into an outcast, someone who would be stared at and pitied—*if she ever left the farm.*

Cam paused in the shadowy dining room just out of her sight waiting for the shock of being reminded to dim and the hot flush of self-loathing to seep away.

"Are you going to stay to supper, Emmet?" he heard Lily ask as she turned to where the doctor was putting instruments into his satchel.

"I can't tonight. I need to get back to the office. I've got two patients whose babies are due any day, and I have to be where their husbands can find me."

"Oh, who?" Lily asked. "Who's having a baby?"

Emmet glanced toward her and then away, as if he heard the wistfulness in her voice as clearly as Cameron did. "Mrs. Phillips, the wife of the man who runs the feed store."

"How many children do they have now?" Lily asked, crossing her arms against her waist.

Cameron realized Lily spoke of the Phillipses as if they were people she nodded at in church or passed on the street. Of course she did quiz Emmet and him about the families in and around Denver. She heard from Rand about the boys who attended his school, and she read the newspapers every day. Cam knew Lily kept track of the births and deaths and marriages because she often asked him to deliver notes of congratulation or condolences, flowers from the garden, or a crock of soup to someone who'd fallen ill. He'd just never really considered the degree to which these phantom neighbors, this phantom community had become real to her. Nor had he noticed the resonance in her tone when she spoke of them.

He stood listening as Emmet answered. "This will be the Phillips's eighth child. And the Halversons, out east of town, are having their first." The doctor gave a rueful smile. "Matt Halverson was chewing nails and spitting rust the last time his wife came into the office. I'm more concerned about him making it through the delivery than I am her."

Cameron recognized the sadness in his sister's smile. "They *will* be all right, Emmet, won't they?"

Farley reached across to squeeze her hand. "I'll take good care of them."

Lily's expression softened. "Of course you will. With two new babies coming, I suppose I'll have to get busy knitting booties."

Cameron cleared his throat to announce his arrival and crossed the threshold into the kitchen. "Shouldn't Rand be home?" he asked. "It's getting on toward dark."

"Rand has begun taking violin lessons on Wednesdays after school," his sister reminded him. "He should be along any time now."

"Right," Cam acknowledged. Then he noticed that Owen Brandt was still hovering outside the kitchen door. "I guess I need to have a word with Mrs. Waterston's companion," he went on, "then see to their wagon and the horses."

"I'll head out with you," Emmet offered, hefting his bag. "I thank you, Lily, for the cake and tea. If Mrs. Waterston takes a turn, you send for me. Otherwise I'll be along tomorrow to look in on her."

The moment Cam stepped outside, Owen Brandt sprang at him. He seemed smaller than he had earlier this afternoon, wizened and brittle, as if the waiting had scorched the life from him.

"S-S-Shea?" he whispered fearfully.

Cam laid his hand on Owen Brandt's shoulder. "The doctor's done his best for her."

It wasn't much reassurance and both of them knew it.

Emmet Farley paused to add a few words of encouragement. "You listen here, Mr. Brandt. Lily Gallimore's a damn fine nurse, and she's determined that your Mrs.

Waterston will recover. I'd pin my hopes on Lily's nursing if I were you."

Brandt bobbed his head, his eyes welling. "Th-thank you."

Emmet patted his arm, then turned toward his buggy. Cameron and Owen followed him out to the drive where they'd abandoned the photography wagon this afternoon. The horses, still in their traces, glanced up from where they'd been nibbling the thick, sweet grass that grew along the edges of the lane.

Cam went around back to see about the prisoner he'd taken this afternoon and found the man was gone. He shook his head in exasperation and figured it served him right. He'd left the man unattended for hours, forgotten about him completely until just now. Well, at least he'd had sense enough not to steal Cam's horse.

Just then Cam's son turned up the lane, his violin case tied to the back of his saddle.

"Pa!" Rand cried when he saw his father and dismounted on the fly. He flung his arms around Cam's middle and held on tight. "I'm so glad you're back. What's going on? Whose rig is this? Is that blood on you?"

No matter how good it was to get back to the house, Cam never truly felt at home until he saw his son. It seemed as if the boy had grown these last few weeks. He looked taller and seemed more sure of himself. The changes unsettled Cam a little, so he took a moment to rumple his son's thick, reddish hair, to trail his palm along the curve of that broad-jawed face. He hugged the lanky ten-year-old again before he explained.

"The rig is Mr. Brandt's," Cam said and hastily made introductions. "Mr. Brandt's companion, Mrs. Waterston, got hurt this afternoon. They're going to be staying with us while she's convalescing."

Rand's eyes went wide. No one but Emmet ever came to the farm. "What happened?" he wanted to know.

Though he didn't want Rand worrying about him when he was away, Cameron explained as much as he could. "Emmet's done his best," he finished, "and now your aunt Lily's looking after her.

"Mr. Brandt and I were just about to take the horses down to the barn," Cam went on as he turned to catch the near-side harness. "Are you willing to help us get them settled?"

"Sure, Pa!" the boy answered eagerly.

Once Emmet took his leave, Cameron, Rand, and Owen Brandt led the horses to the big log barn that sat a hundred yards down the lane and off to the left of the house. They parked the photography wagon beside it and unhitched the team.

Feeding and tending both Shea Waterston's horses and his own animals took Cam some time. If it hadn't been for Brandt, Cam would have lost himself in the work. He liked the rich, fecund smell of the stable. Pitching hay and milking the cow and the goats helped clear his head, especially after the demands of holding court. But tonight Owen Brandt was here, and the puzzle that was Shea Waterston preyed on Cam's mind.

In truth, he wasn't sure how much he could learn from Brandt. He'd seen men like him before, men whose minds were shattered by what they'd seen or done during the struggle with the South. But then, the war had marked everyone who fought in it. It ruined people's lives—people who were innocent, people whose lives had no cause to be ruined. It's how war was.

Sensing the little man's agitation at being away from Shea, Cam spoke as quietly, as soothingly as he could.

"So what are you and Mrs. Waterston doing out here in the West?"

Brandt looked up as if he was startled to be addressed directly. "Taking pictures," he finally answered.

"You were up in the mountains taking pictures?" Cam looked up from where he was pouring oats into the horses's troughs just in time to see Owen nod. "How long were you up there?"

"Since June."

"It's beautiful country," he observed.

Brandt inclined his head.

"But a damned rugged place," Cam continued. "How did you and Mrs. Waterston manage?"

"Had a guide."

Some of the old trappers did that, took hunting parties or mapping expeditions up into the Rockies. Cam should have been surprised that Shea Waterston was so intrepid, but after what he'd seen this afternoon, not much she did would surprise him.

"Photography seems to be an unusual profession for a woman," he observed. "How did Mrs. Waterston start taking pictures?"

Owen slid him a sidelong glance. "Husband taught her."

Shea Waterston was married, of course. She wore a wedding band and used her husband's name. But there was also something unfettered about her, something that spoke of self-determination and self-reliance. It made him wonder what her husband was like.

"And Mr. Waterston, where is he?"

"Dead." Owen bit the word off short, as if it scared him. As if he wanted to say it, then run away.

Cam refused to let him do that. "What happened?"

"Consumption."

The little man seemed unaccountably rattled by the

exchange, and Cameron paused to rub his horse's muzzle so Brandt had a chance to settle again. It gave Cam time to think through what he'd learned already.

Shea Waterston wouldn't have been traveling with a man who'd been dying by inches. She couldn't have cared for him in a photography wagon, couldn't have kept him clean and warm and dry. So when had Mr. Waterston died? How long had she been wandering, stopping to sell her wares, then moving on?

In Cam's experience, women wanted security, a home, a settled life. "What's she doing out here?" Cam wondered, half to himself.

Owen Brandt must have heard him. "Looking," he muttered.

Cam turned and stared at him. "Looking for what?"

Owen's mouth went tight, as if he thought he'd said too much, as if he were trying to swallow his secrets. Shea Waterston's secrets.

"Owen? What is it she's looking for?"

Brandt didn't seem capable of lies or evasions. Instead he simply let his attention drift. Without a word, Owen turned and wandered toward the small, dim tack room and the cot Cam and Rand had made up for Brandt to use. He closed the door behind him, shutting himself off, going to ground like a fox seeking the safety of its den.

With a grunt of frustration, Cam went about finishing up his chores. When he was done, he looked around for his son and found him at the far corral feeding windfall apples to his neat roan gelding. Watching Rand and Jasper together, Cam was struck again by how good Rand was with horses, how gentle and patient, how eagerly they did what he asked. Not once in all his years of riding and tending stock had Cam seen anything quite like the way Rand handled animals.

Just then Lily rang the big iron bell mounted on the porch, calling them to supper. At the sound Rand looked up, wiped the horse slobber from his hands onto the seat of his trousers, and came running toward the barn. The two of them knocked on the door to the tack room.

"Supper's ready," Cam told him when Owen Brandt peered out at them. "Come up to the house and have some dinner."

"Dinner?" Brandt asked.

"It smelled like pot roast to me," Cam encouraged him.

"You'd best come with Pa and me, or Aunt Lily'll be down to get you herself," Rand warned him and laughed.

When it looked like Brandt was going to refuse in spite of the warning, Cam sweetened the pot. "You can look in on Mrs. Waterston after we eat."

"Shea?" Brandt asked hopefully.

"She'll probably still be sleeping, but you can sit with her if you like."

Owen Brandt stepped out of the tack room and closed the door behind him, securing his nest.

"Come along then, Mr. Brandt," Cam encouraged him. Slinging his arm around Rand's bony shoulders, they turned toward the house. "Supper's waiting."

Cameron Gallimore's farm nestled up to the Platte River the way a wife snuggles up to her husband at night, the swell of her sandy bottomland tucking into the protective arc of his sinuous length. Cam hadn't even been sure they were going to stay in Colorado when they'd come to look at this place, but the moment they'd turned the carriage up the drive, it had felt like home.

It still felt like home eight years later. Cam reined in his horse halfway up the shady lane and let the warmth and welcome of the place envelop him. Years before, someone had raised a ramshackle cabin out by the road, but Cam had built his home on the rise above the river. In the harsh fall sunlight, it gleamed white as a moonstone, with each shutter and each window box, each turning of the porch posts etched in sharp detail.

The place had begun as a cozy four-room structure. Four years ago he'd added a good-sized kitchen wing out the back, with narrow porches tucked beneath the overhanging all around it. Last year he'd built a veranda across the front, where Lily assured him they'd sit on summer evenings and sip lemonade with company. Of course, no one but Emmet ever came.

As he eased his horse past the house on his way to the barn, Cam glanced at the front bedroom window and wondered how Shea Waterston was. She'd lain all but insensible for these last three days while Lily plastered poultices on the woman's wound, wiped her down with basins of cool water, and, when she roused, fed her beef broth from an invalid's cup. Emmet had come nightly to examine Shea and shake his head, but Lily refused to be daunted.

Once inside the barn, Cameron unsaddled his horse, then took his time feeding and currying him. The routine of brushing, the smell of the barn, and the twitter of birds in the rafters soothed him. Some days he imagined he'd be perfectly content to work the land, give himself over to a kind of endeavor where he had no life-and-death decisions to make, no questions of fairness and justice, no moral ambiguities. The original parcel of land had not been big enough to amount to much, but he'd been slowly buying up the acreage to the north and east just in case. And maybe someday . . .

Cam sighed, gave Barney, his big gray gelding, a final pat, and turned toward the house. He'd promised Lily he'd keep an eye on Shea Waterston this afternoon while his sister finished canning tomatoes.

But as he passed the photography wagon that was parked just to the left of the barn, he couldn't help but stop and peer inside. This dim, cramped wagon was Shea Waterston's domain, the whole of her world while they were traveling.

Prodded by a curiosity he couldn't in any way justify, Cam let down the tailgate and climbed inside. A dry sink with deep drawers beneath it nestled behind the driver's seat. The astringent smell of photographic chemicals assaulted him when he opened the top drawer. It was filled with an array of big, glass-stoppered bottles labeled with the names of the liquids. A second drawer held working paraphernalia: rubber trays and wooden tongs, measuring beakers, glass stirrers, and a spirit lamp. Another was filled with what he assumed were plate holders and printing trays and padded boxes of lens caps.

Cam stepped back and slid the lid from one of nearly a dozen wooden crates sitting side by side on the floor. Inside, fitted into grooves to keep them from clattering together, were a score of glass plate negatives. These must be the photographs Shea Waterston and Owen Brandt had taken while they were up in the mountains.

He looked through their foodstuff and camping supplies and bedrolls, finally finding what he was looking for—a scuffed leather valise. Though he knew he had no business pawing through Mrs. Waterston's things, he wanted to learn everything there was to know about the stranger he'd brought into his home. He needed to discover what he could about the woman who'd appeared out of nowhere and had probably saved his life.

In truth, there wasn't much inside Mrs. Waterston's bag, just a brush and comb, a few sturdy, dark-colored skirts and bodices, two pair of stockings, some serviceable underthings, and an extra pair of boots. At the bottom he found a neatly kept ledger, a Bible and a rosary, a bound cardboard folio of children's photographs, and a big tin box fitted out as a sewing kit.

Shea Waterston clearly was not a woman who indulged herself. There were no lengths of ribbon or lacy collars, nothing frivolous or pretty. It was as if this woman had pared her life down to the essentials, narrowed her focus to the thing that mattered most to her: her photography.

Cameron stared at her belongings arrayed before him and knew there were no insights into her character here. There was nothing at all to tell him—Cam frowned in exasperation—*to tell him whatever it was he needed to know about her.*

With an oath of irritation, Cam stuffed the clothes back in the valise and headed for the house. The steamy smell of stewing tomatoes greeted him halfway across the yard.

"How is she?" he asked as he pushed open the kitchen door.

Lily stood at the stove, doing her best to allay any anxiety she might have about Shea Waterston's recovery with tomatoes, salt, and canning crocks. She broke off the hymn she had been singing and glanced at him.

"Her wound's not nearly so inflamed as it was yesterday," she answered, trying to sound encouraging. "But she hasn't stirred. Owen's with her." The narrowing of Lily's mouth gave evidence as to what she thought of Owen Brandt's bedside manner.

Cam himself understood it. "I'll just go look in on them," he suggested, and strode toward the front of the house.

In Cam's bedroom Owen sat hunched beside Shea's bed. His hands were clenched between his knees as he rocked back and forth, back and forth.

Cam cleared his throat to warn Owen he was standing in the doorway. The moment he turned, Cam was swamped by the wave of Owen's agitation and panic. He did his best to fight through it, fight free of it, then rode the swells of his own answering emotions like a skiff in choppy seas.

When he felt steady again, Cam laid his hand on Owen's shoulder. "How is she?"

"No better," the little man reported.

"Well, healing takes time," he reassured him. "Lily says Shea's wound is looking better."

"Has to get well," Owen mumbled, glancing up at Cam with red-rimmed eyes.

Cameron couldn't imagine what Owen Brandt would do if this woman died. Shea Waterston seemed to be all he had in the world, his only friend, his only tether.

"Lily and Emmet are doing their very best for her," Cam said quietly. "Would you like me to sit with her for a little while so you can get a breath of air?"

So you can escape to somewhere safe.

Owen nodded, all but quivering with relief. He pushed hastily to his feet, then still seemed reluctant to leave. "Call me if she . . ."

Cam patted him again. "Of course I will."

Once Owen was gone, Cam settled into the chair beside the bed and took Shea's hand. It lay small and limp and cold in his. He covered it with his opposite palm and chafed it gently. He'd been preoccupied with this woman ever since he'd confronted her at the hanging in Breckenridge, and plagued by her presence every moment since she'd risked herself to protect him. Her bravery and determination confused him; that he'd needed her help disturbed him in ways he preferred not to contemplate. That he owed her upset the balance he was always fighting to maintain within himself.

He figured he'd feel less beholden if he could talk to her, if he knew who she was and why she'd tried to help him. But she couldn't say, and those questions would poke him like a stone inside his boot until he got his answers. *If he ever got the answers.*

He scowled down at where Shea Waterston lay so silent and still. Her eyes were closed; her face was as blank as a sheet of fresh parchment.

"So are you going to get well, Mrs. Waterston?" Cam asked, as if she could hear. "Or will you leave us here to puzzle after you?"

The sea lifted in a swell of liquid jade, poised in sharp anticipation, then rushed in leaping, frothing waves toward the jagged shore. It shattered on the beach, shimmering like spilled gems that winked amber and scarlet in the fading light. The voice of the sea roared back from the craggy headlands that cradled this narrow crescent of sand. And as the sea howled around her, Shea Waterston spun and danced on the ocean's threshold amidst the fizzing, ice-cold foam.

She laughed with joy at being here again, just down the path from the cottage where her da had brought her mam the night they were wed, from the cottage where she had been born and lived as a girl. She laughed again and fought for breath as the wild wind tore at her hair and flapped the hem of her wet skirts against her legs. It hummed around her, its melody fierce and familiar, as old as time. As comforting, in its way, as a lullaby.

Then above the wail of the wind came a shout, a voice she did not recognize. Shea turned from the crashing waves and saw a boy at the crest of the path that led up to the windswept headland. She ignored the bawl of the tumbling sea and fought to hear what he was saying.

"Mam!" the boy was shouting. "Mam!"

The cry reached her, and warm, sweet recognition wrapped around her heart. "Liam!" she cried and reached out to him.

Her son waved in reply as she ran toward him across the cold, packed sand of that crescent beach. She scrambled up the rocky path as fast as her shaking legs and sodden skirts allowed her. With her heart hammering and the breath puffing dry in her throat, Shea crested the rise.

"Mam," he cried again.

Liam was running toward the rocks at the very edge of the earth, toward where the headland merged with the sky, toward where the streaks of amber and orange had stained the surface of the shifting sea.

"Liam," she cried and scampered over stones turned coppery in the dying light. She darted over deep fissures nibbled into the promontory by raging storms and restless tides, between patches of lichen that carpeted the rocks.

At the edge of the cliff the boy turned to her. The setting sun was at his back, limning the outline of his head and shoulders, casting his face in shadow. She reached for him again, wanting to hold him against her heart, to embrace him for the first time since he was a babe. But before she could claim him and take him home, that silhouette winked like the guttering of a candle flame and disappeared.

Shea stood sobbing for breath, staring at the last slice of blazing sun as it bled into the darkening sea. The light faded, leaving her helpless, hopeless, blind and lost, her mind echoing with an afterimage of what might have been.

Then light flared again, brighter than before. She blinked against the glare as it resolved itself into the flame of a kerosene lamp set on a table beside the bed where she was lying.

Her boy was sitting just beyond the arc of lamplight. She could see his smooth, soft face; his wide pale eyes. His hair was the color of years' old rust and fell crisp against his collar.

"Liam," she whispered and pushed up in the bed, reaching again, determined to clasp him to her this time.

Pain ripped through her, swelling in a fierce, inexorable tide. It filled her chest, roared in her ears, and rose before her eyes like a veil of fire. She gasped in agony and fell back. Beyond the pain the image of the boy faded, engulfed in a blackness so dark and deep it might well have been the depths of eternity claiming her.

"Awake again, are you, my dear?" someone asked her.

Shea shifted sluggishly in the center of the big bed and blinked to clear her vision. A tall woman in a plain black gown was standing over her. She was slender and dark-haired, and would have been pretty except that one side of her face seemed puckered somehow. Shea did her best to squint those puckers away, then realized the woman was scarred, burned perhaps some years before.

Frowning a little, the woman bent nearer and

pressed the back of one rough-skinned hand against Shea's cheek. Something about the gesture and the faint lavender scent that lingered afterward made Shea think of her mother.

"I think your fever's down," the woman said, in a warm, throaty voice, "but I'll warrant you feel as if you've been wrung out and hung up to dry."

Shea wasn't sure how she felt. She was beginning to realize she was occupying a sunny room where sheer muslin curtains fluttered at the windows and ivy-printed paper ran up the walls. Surely Owen hadn't been so foolish as to squander the last of their money putting her up in some fancy hotel, had he?

"What is this place?" she asked, then was surprised at how raw and strained her own voice sounded.

"This is my home. My brother's home," the woman corrected herself. "I'm Lily Gallimore."

Gallimore. Shea recognized the name, but for the life of her, she couldn't place it.

"My brother brought you here," Miss Gallimore went on.

Gallimore. How did she know that name? Her thoughts stirred lazily like weeds beneath the surface of a pond.

"My brother's a judge," Lily offered helpfully.

Judge Gallimore.

"Oh, damn," Shea whispered. The memory of Judge Gallimore tossing her into jail the day of the hanging sharpened as if she'd turned the focusing knob on her camera. "Him? The judge brought me here?"

"Yes." Cameron Gallimore's sister seemed to be biting her lip to hide a smile. "He'll be glad to know you remember him so fondly. From what he tells me, you came to his rescue when he—How did he put it?—ran into some trouble coming out of the mountains."

Shea had a hazy impression of three men trying to lynch a fourth. "Is he all right, your brother?"

"Right as rain—for which I'm profoundly grateful to you."

"I don't know that I did anything much," Shea responded, trying to remember. The effort made her almost unbearably weary, but she fought the urge to sleep long enough to ask one last question. "Is Owen all right? Did the judge bring him here, too?"

"Owen's fine. We've put him up in the tack room out in the barn," Lily Gallimore told her as Shea closed her eyes. "I'll see that he's here when you awaken."

The woman was as good as her word. Owen was settled in a chair beside her bed when Shea next came to herself.

"Owen!" she breathed in relief.

Tears welled in the old man's eyes, and he reached to take her hand. "Here, Sparrow," he whispered. "You better?"

"You dear old thing," Shea murmured, touched by his concern. "I'm sorry if I worried you."

It seemed odd to have Owen hovering over her. She was used to looking after him.

"Doctor was worried, too," he informed her.

Shea nodded and tried to take stock of herself. Her head ached, and there seemed to be some sort of stiffness along her hairline. Beneath what must be a borrowed nightgown, a bulky bandage encircled one arm, and her chest was bound tight enough to make breathing a misery.

"What happened? I can't seem to remember."

"Saved Cam's life."

"Cam?" she asked.

"The judge."

With Owen's help Shea managed to put together the

bits and pieces of that day on the road. She remembered the miners and their intention to hang the judge. She'd forgotten she'd shot a man in his defense, and her stomach dipped queasily when Owen reminded her about it.

"Did I kill him?" she asked, not sure she wanted to hear the answer.

Owen shrugged in that way he had when he wanted to avoid something upsetting.

She tried again. "How long ago did all that happen?"

"A week."

"I've been lying here for a week?" In spite of her weakness and the pain that tore along her side, Shea pushed up on her elbows. "What have you done about the plates we exposed up in the mountains?"

Owen bobbed his head. "Safe."

"Where are they safe?"

"In the wagon."

"You didn't send them to New York?" she demanded.

"Now, Sparrow," he cajoled.

"We need to get those plates off to New York," she insisted.

"Ask Cam," Owen suggested as if Judge Gallimore were the final authority on everything that went on here.

In spite of her concerns about the photographic plates and the money they needed to live on, it was only a few more minutes before Shea's eyes drifted closed.

The woman—Lily—awakened her a good while later and fed her soup. The doctor came, a slow, soft-spoken southerner from the sound of him. He rebandaged a wound in her arm and another along her ribs. He told her she was doing better than any of them had a right to expect. When he was done, he dosed her with laudanum to make her sleep.

Night had darkened the windowpanes when Shea next opened her eyes. The room was dim, illuminated only by a lamp turned low on the desk in front of the window. A dark-haired man sat hunched beneath it, poring over the papers and books piled high on the desk's cluttered top.

His back was to her, but she recognized the impressive breadth of his shoulders and the shape of his head from that afternoon in Breckenridge. This was Judge Cameron Gallimore, the man who'd confiscated her camera and thrown her in jail. The very thought of that confrontation turned her breathless.

Still, Judge Gallimore had been kind enough to bring her here when she was hurt, and he'd seen that she was cared for. Surely he couldn't be as single-minded and dictatorial as she remembered.

Unsettled by the very sight of him, Shea let her gaze drift around the room. Beyond the foot of the bed, a simple chest of drawers stood beside the desk. Tumbled piles of socks and handkerchiefs were scrambled across the top. Sleeve garters, belts, and elastic braces sprang out the half-open drawers. Neckties in several colors and designs hung haphazardly from the mirror above the chest and looped through the pressed-iron drawer-pulls.

A washstand with a cream-colored china bowl and graceful ewer stood in the corner near the room's side window. On pegs opposite it slumped pants and shirts and a dark woolen jacket. On a hook by itself was a well-worn gun belt with a pearl-handled pistol peeking out the top of the holster.

This was his room, then—His Honor, Judge

Cameron Gallimore's room—as tumbled and unkempt as a child's. Uncomfortable with the idea that she was intruding here, Shea shifted a little on the bed.

Judge Gallimore must have heard the springs creak beneath her, because he turned in his chair and looked at her. Eyes of dark, rich blue shone bright from beneath shadowing brows.

"I'm glad to see you're awake, Mrs. Waterston," he said. "Is there anything I can get for you?"

Shea shrank back against the pillows, not sure what she should say to him.

With a single lithe movement, he rose and came toward her. "Would you like a drink? Lily brought fresh water in from the pump a little while ago."

Shea dared to nod.

He poured water from a delicate gold-rimmed pitcher and sat beside her on the bed. He slid an arm beneath her shoulders and lifted her gently. He'd done this more than once, she realized, and wondered who it was he'd tended so carefully.

She wished she had strength to sit up by herself, yet it was pleasant enough to nestle against him feeling his warmth and strength soak through the soft, well-washed fabric of her nightgown. She raised her hand, intending to guide the glass of water to her mouth, but her arm fell lax on the coverlet.

"Oh, damn," she whispered, shaken by her own frailty.

"You've been very ill, Mrs. Waterston," Gallimore offered, putting the glass to her lips. "The doctor says you're over the worst of it, but give yourself time. Soon you'll be feeling stronger."

Shea nodded and drank, the water cool and fresh in her mouth. It eased the dryness down her throat.

Up this close, Judge Gallimore's face was all planes

and angles. His brow was broad, his cheekbones high and sharply cut. His chin was just square enough to hint at both obstinacy and strength. Something about the bow of his mouth just visible beneath the thick drape of his mustache gave the impression that there were fine, gentle things inside him.

Something about his concern made her feel unexpectedly protected, utterly safe. It was such a profound and completely unfamiliar feeling, that it took a full minute for her to realize what it was.

She was still grappling with that sense of safety when the door to the bedroom opened. "Pa," came the sound of a child's voice, "Aunt Lily said to come in and say good night to you."

Judge Gallimore turned, and beyond the bulk of his shoulder, Shea could see the boy who'd been beside her when she'd first awakened.

Liam. The name shot unbidden through her head, but now that she was more herself, she could see this wasn't the boy she'd been dreaming about.

"Come in, boy," Gallimore said. "I was just helping Mrs. Waterston to a drink. Mrs. Waterston, let me introduce you to my son Randall."

Shea did her best to nod, but she was too busy staring.

Cameron Gallimore's son was a handsome boy, tall and spare, with red-brown hair and eyes the color of weathered copper. His face had that same width at the cheekbones and breadth at the jaw his father's had, and she could see the boy would be every bit as imposing when he got older.

"I'm very pleased to meet you, Mrs. Waterston," Randall said. "Aunt Lily tells me you're feeling ever so much better."

He spoke as if he'd swallowed an etiquette book, and

to Shea's eyes looked far more neat and proper than any child should. Even now at the end of the day his shirttail was still tucked into his trousers, and there wasn't so much as a spot of his dinner down the front.

"I'm pleased to meet you, too," Shea murmured, trying to summon up her company manners. "Were you with me when I first woke up?"

"Yes, ma'am," the boy agreed. "You called me by some name I'd never heard before."

"Liam," she said.

"Yes, that's it."

"It's the Irish form of William. You—you reminded me of—of someone."

"Who?" the boy wanted to know. "Someone in Ireland?"

"Rand," his father said shortly, warning him about his manners. Then he eased Shea back against the pillows and turned to his son. "Did you finally finish those arithmetic problems you were puzzling over?"

"Aunt Lily helped me," Rand answered. "But as soon as we solved the last of them, she said I had to go to bed."

From the way he lifted his eyebrows Shea could see he was angling for a reprieve.

"I'm afraid she's right," the judge agreed. "And I'm afraid I'm not going to have time to read with you tonight, either."

"Aunt Lily said you have a meeting in the morning."

"I'm afraid I do. Do you think *The Three Musketeers* will keep for one more day?"

"It'll be awfully hard to wait to find out what's going to happen," Rand offered hopefully.

Gallimore reached across and hugged his boy. "We'll read two chapters tomorrow. I promise."

Something about the unabashed affection in that

simple gesture, and the way Rand wrapped his arms around his father's waist, made Shea's throat close up. For whatever else she might think of Cameron Gallimore, he clearly loved his son.

With a final pat Judge Gallimore sent Rand off to bed.

"He seems like a fine boy," Shea said when he was gone.

"He is," Gallimore confirmed, still staring after him. "Lily's done a wonderful job raising him."

All at once Shea had half a dozen questions she wanted to ask him: where Randall's mother was, and how Lily Gallimore had ended up taking care of her brother's child. But most of all Shea wanted to know how she'd gotten here, and what had possessed him to take her in. Before Shea could muster the courage to ask, the judge refilled Shea's water glass and set it beside the bed.

"Is there anything else you need?" he wanted to know. "Will it disturb you if I continue working?"

In truth, even this much conversation had tired Shea almost beyond her endurance. She shook her head. "I'll be fine," she said. "I'm going to sleep."

"Sleep will help you regain your strength faster than anything," he confirmed. He went toward his desk and the papers strewn across the top. "I'm glad you're feeling better, Mrs. Waterston," he added as he settled into his chair again.

"So am I," Shea agreed quietly.

He readjusted the books and papers, then dipped his pen. But as much as Shea thought she'd sleep, she lay watching him through her lashes until he blew out the lamp a good while later.

FIVE

$\mathcal{B}$y the end of the third day, Shea had had her fill of being ill. She'd sipped enough fever tea to float a ship, memorized the twists and turns of every sprig of ivy on those papered walls, and was thoroughly bored with her own company.

As the light beyond the window turned rosy, Shea strained to hear the voices of the people gathered in the kitchen. Lily had been singing all day and sounded pleased to have company for supper. Dr. Farley's slow drawl gave counterpoint to Lily's faintly breathy tones and Owen's reedy ones. Cam spoke with a quiet resonance, and when Rand told them about something that happened at school, everyone laughed.

Shea slumped low on her pillows and scowled. She hated being sick! She should be getting her photographic plates off to New York and finding winter accommodations, not lying here in bed. She'd navigated as far as a chair in the parlor this morning—with Lily's help—then slept for hours afterward.

In spite of her discontent, Shea must have dozed,

because supper was well over when Lily came to look in on her.

"It's such a lovely evening," she began, rubbing her hands together as much with nervous energy as with happy anticipation, "we decided to have cake and coffee on the veranda. Are you feeling well enough to join us?"

"Oh, yes!" Shea answered eagerly, not caring about anything but being out of bed.

At Lily's summons, Cam came and carried Shea out to the front porch. Though her head was reeling by the time they got her tucked up in blankets and nestled on the wide porch swing, it was well worth the effort. From where she lay she could see a swath of mauve and crimson sky draped behind a ridge of jagged mountains off to the west. She could hear the rustling of the cottonwoods that sheltered the house and smell the soft musk of fall in the languid breeze.

Once everyone had finished their lemon cake, Lily turned to Rand. "Why don't you go get out your violin and play us that piece you've been practicing?"

The boy flushed and did his best to disappear behind the pot of geraniums at the head of the steps.

"I think your father would like to hear what you've been learning," she prodded him.

"Oh, Aunt Lily!"

Cam spoke up right on cue. "I certainly would like to hear you."

"My da used to play his fiddle in front of the fire in the evening when I was growing up," Shea offered, smiling at the boy.

"Your da?" he asked.

"That's what we call fathers in Ireland," Shea clarified. "He was really quite an accomplished fiddler. He'd play with some of the other men at parties or in the pub." The melodies drifted through her head, rousing reels, melancholy laments, and songs with words that fomented rebellion.

The judge inched forward in his chair. "Where in Ireland are you from, Mrs. Waterston?"

"From the west country," she answered. "My father was gamekeeper at an estate near Clifden."

"And what brought you to America?"

Though the question was innocuous enough, Shea sensed the lawyer in him and saw the way those bright, appraising eyes bore into her.

He made her want to pull the blankets up around her ears and refuse to answer. Or perhaps the reason she was reluctant to speak was that she had no intention at all of telling him the truth. What business was it of his that her father had lost his position because he'd agreed with men opposed to British rule? Nor was she about to explain the strife that had torn her country and her family apart. Some memories just didn't bear thinking about, and they most certainly weren't meant to be shared with the likes of Cameron Gallimore.

She lifted her chin. "I came to America for the opportunities, to be sure."

Then, to avoid more of the judge's scrutiny, she turned to Rand. "You will play for us, won't you, child? I do so miss the sound of fiddle music."

The boy scowled and grimaced and pushed to his feet.

"I'll accompany him on the piano," Lily offered, following Randall indoors.

With the windows open to catch the breeze, the strains of "My Old Kentucky Home" floated out to them. Rand played haltingly, yet Lily managed to fit her accompaniment around his squeaky passages and uneven rhythms.

As she listened, Shea couldn't help wondering if *her* son had inherited his grandfather's gift for music, or his uncle Sean's way with horses, or old Auntie Maura's second sight. She wondered if Liam looked like his da or her, and she couldn't help wishing that she'd be able to see a bit of the people she'd loved and lost in Liam's face when she finally found him.

Shea and the three men applauded as the duet wound to a close.

"Cammie," Lily called out, her voice gently teasing, "shall I bring you your guitar?"

Cameron scowled and grimaced, duplicating his son's expressions of reluctance. "Oh, I suppose," he conceded.

After he'd tuned the fine instrument to his satisfaction, Cam glided gracefully into "Barbara Allen," a tune Shea immediately recognized.

He played well, and his voice, warm and rich as peat smoke, wrapped around Shea, enveloping her in the story of lost love. Midway through the second verse, Emmet Farley shifted forward in his chair and slid a slim, silver mouth organ from the inside pocket of his jacket. The reedy tones and trills he breathed from that simple instrument added a melancholy counterpoint to the simple tune.

Swept up in the ballad, Shea drew breath and began to sing. Though her voice wobbled a little at the start, it gradually bloomed and gained momentum. As it twined in delicate harmony around the judge's lush baritone and merged with the plaintive whine of Emmet Farley's harmonica, Shea seemed to share some unexpected connection to these two men, to everyone here. It felt so good to be part of a family again, no matter how fleetingly.

Once they finished the last stanza where the rose and

the briar "twined themselves into a lovers' knot," Lily applauded with delight. "That was wonderful!" she exclaimed.

Shea laughed breathlessly, feeling warmed and welcomed, more safe and contented than she had in a very long while.

"Why, Mrs. Waterston," Cameron offered, leaning toward her across the waist of his guitar. "I had no idea you sang so well."

Shea basked in the warmth of his teasing smile. "I dance a fair jig, too, though I'm afraid I must plead my infirmity this evening."

"You'll demonstrate it for us another time, perhaps?" he suggested, those night blue eyes alight.

"Perhaps, Mr. Gallimore, I'll do exactly that."

"Could you teach me to dance a jig?" Rand piped up, drawing her attention from his father. "Men dance jigs, too, don't they?"

"And hornpipes and reels," Shea assured him, resisting the urge to reach over and muss his hair.

"Maybe she'll show you when she's feeling better," Cameron suggested.

"I will indeed," Shea promised.

Emmet returned the harmonica to his pocket, then pushed to his feet. "I'm afraid I'm needed back in town. Thank you, Lily, for another delicious dinner," he said and sketched a bow. "And thanks to everyone else for such fine entertainment."

Before he left he turned his professional regard on Shea. "Now, even if you're feeling better, missy," he told her sternly, "I don't want you doing too much."

"She won't," Lily answered for Shea, standing over her.

Shea bristled a little. She was used to seeing to herself, used to looking after others as well. Yet how lovely it was to have someone show her such charity and concern. How beguiling it was to be taken care of, to feel so safe.

And the Gallimores did make her feel safe: Lily with her bustle and concern, Rand with his open-handed friendship. And Cam, who stood like a bulwark for the rest, a calm, quiet man with depths that drew her in spite of herself.

Still, Shea knew better than to rely on strangers' kindnesses. Simon might have taken her in, might have been willing to marry her, but she'd paid a price. She didn't regret the years she'd given him. She'd loved Simon, and he'd taught her so much. But those years had also convinced her that the only person she could truly rely on was herself. To think otherwise was dangerous—and could break her heart.

So Shea looked up at where Dr. Farley was standing over her and gave him her own answer. "I promise to behave myself."

Cameron set his guitar aside. "Since you're bent on leaving, Emmet, why don't you let me give you a hand with your horse?"

Owen rose from the far end of the porch to follow.

"I'm coming, too," Rand chimed in.

"Oh, but I'm afraid you're not. You have school tomorrow," Lily reminded him, "and it's time for bed."

"Aw, Aunt Lily!"

"Maybe we can read another chapter of *The Three Musketeers* tonight," Cameron suggested.

"I've been reading it to Mrs. Waterston in the afternoons," the boy put in. "We're two chapters ahead of where you left off."

"I'll catch up," Cameron assured him, following Owen and Dr. Farley down the path.

Shea liked reading with Rand, liked listening to him, liked sharing his excitement at the musketeers' adventures. She liked watching his face and imagining the kind of man he would become. The kind of man she'd always hoped her own lost boy would be, she thought, and couldn't help wishing Rand was hers.

Once Rand had dragged reluctantly into the house, Lily began loading their cups and plates onto a tray.

Shea turned to her, smiling. "This has been such a pleasant evening. I had no idea you were all so accomplished."

"Mama taught piano to Cam and me when we were little," Lily answered almost wistfully. "He learned to play the guitar during the war."

"Rand's doing well with his violin," Shea observed. "He's such a good boy, Lily. You and the judge must be so proud of him."

"We are," Lily confirmed, gathering up the tray.

Shea inclined her head. "And what happened to Mrs. Gallimore?"

"My mother?" Lily asked in surprise.

"Cameron's wife."

Lily turned so abruptly the cups and plates on the tray clattered together. "His wife?"

Shea hadn't meant to pry and felt a flush creep into her cheeks. "I only thought that if Cameron had a child, he must have been—"

"No! Oh, heavens, no! Cammie has never been married!" Lily proclaimed, then fled into the house.

By the time he got back to the porch, Cam could see that Shea Waterston was wilting like pansies in high summer. Her head drooped against the back of the swing, as if she were too weary to hold it up, and there were lines of exhaustion around her mouth.

"If you're ready," he suggested, "I can take you back to bed."

"But it's been such a pleasant evening," she murmured, sounding like a child who'd been allowed to sit with the grown-ups.

"There's always tomorrow," he said gently. Without waiting for her assent, he bent and slid his arms beneath her shoulders and knees, and lifted her against him.

For more than a week he'd been trying to reconcile this dab of a woman with the avenging angel who'd bolted upright in that wagon box bent on saving his life. Feeling how small and frail Shea was, and remembering what she'd done back there in the foothills, made Cam go hot and tight inside.

He wasn't sure he deserved the sacrifice she'd been willing to make, wasn't entirely sure he'd wanted her to risk herself for him. Now he owed her, and he couldn't think how he'd ever even the score with a woman who'd come so close to dying to keep him safe.

Scowling at the thought, he shouldered through the screen door, crossed the parlor, and bore Shea into his bedroom. The place had been transformed since she'd come here. Though he'd managed to maintain a toehold by refusing to relinquish so much as one square inch of space on his overflowing desk, the rest of the room had been commandeered and feminized.

Several fresh, neatly folded nightdresses were piled on the corner of his dresser. Combs and brushes and ribbons had overrun his socks and handkerchiefs and were scattered across the top. The skirt and bodice Shea had been wearing when he brought her home had been mended and laundered and pressed. They hung

on the pegs by the window, all but veiling the dangerous, masculine shape of his mother-of-pearl-handled
pistol and holster. The bar of lavender soap on the
washstand seemed to scent the whole damn place with
spring.

With her caught up close in his arms, he realized
Shea smelled of lavender, too. It was the fragrance his
sister usually wore, but the scent seemed sweeter on
Shea's skin, more earthy and provocative. It made him
want to press his cheek into the tumble of her caramel-
colored curls and nuzzle her temple.

A hot dart of conscience shot through him. This
woman was ill. He'd offered her his protection, and
here he was, thinking about nuzzling her skin. *What the
devil was wrong with him?*

Tamping down the notion, Cam bent and lowered
Shea down between the bed's opened sheets. As she
settled back, the hand that had lain lax along his neck
trailed down his chest. At that simple touch, he became
vividly aware of its weight and warmth against him. It
made his breath snag in his throat and set off an unwelcome tingling that rippled all the way to his groin.

Cam scowled again and pulled the covers all the way
up to her chin, intent on cloaking her from his view.

Shea must have noticed his gruffness. "I'm sorry to
be such a bother," she murmured fretfully. "I hope you
won't have to cart me about like this for very much
longer."

He deliberately gentled his voice and, ignoring every
gram of his common sense, reached out to stroke back
a few straggling strands of her hair. "I really don't
mind. Besides, now that your fever's gone, you'll be
getting stronger every day."

"It *was* pleasant though, wasn't it, sitting on the
porch this evening?"

He heard the wistfulness in her voice. How often did she have a chance to have her evening coffee on a veranda? Moving around the way they did, she and Owen had to live a solitary life. And Brandt, for all his loyalty, could hardly be mistaken as an affable companion.

Cameron had already begun to take back his hand when Shea reached out and caught it in her own. "I'd like another word with you if you have the time."

Cam looked at her, aware of how weary she seemed, aware that he'd promised to read with his son. Still, something in Shea Waterston's eyes, something in the taut line creasing her brow convinced him to give her a few more minutes.

He settled on the edge of the mattress. "What is it?" he asked her.

She raised those pale green eyes to his; they were wide and filled with doubt. It made him want to gather her up and hold her until whatever was paining her melted away.

The muscles in her delicate throat worked before she spoke. "Owen says I shot a man up in the mountains . . ."

Cam waited for her to go on, his chest filling with dread and anticipation.

". . . I want to know if that is true."

"Those were Joe Calvert's friends," he said remembering how the miners had come tearing down out of the rocks before he had a chance to defend himself. "They were men who didn't agree with the sentence I passed on him."

"I need to know." She paused and swallowed hard. "I need to know if I killed him."

He could see what this forthrightness was costing

her, saw how she pressed her lips together to stop their trembling. Still, he couldn't bring himself to lie to her.

"If it's any comfort, your shooting him saved my life." It was the first time he'd admitted that, even to himself, and the knowledge dragged on him. "You traded my life for his," he went on. "What you need to decide is whether you think it was worth it."

"Of course it was worth it," she answered without reserve, sounding more sure of his value than he was himself. "I suppose what I need to know is—is how you live with yourself afterward."

The question set off tremors in his hands and he balled them into fists to still their shaking.

"What makes you think I'd know?" he asked her.

She pressed those soft full lips together as if to firm her resolve. "Lily said you fought in the war, so I thought—I thought you'd be able to tell me."

The war again. The war, always and forever—staining him, marking him the same way it had marked a whole generation of men who'd marched off to fight for causes that had gotten obliterated in the heat of battle.

He looked past her, out the window to where the memories lingered in the dark. Memories of firing his gun more times than he could count, of looking over the field after the battle and wondering how many of the men lying dead were ones he'd killed.

"You tell yourself what you did was justified," he finally answered, his voice gone raw. "You tell yourself you had no choice. But you never forget what you did, and the remembering tempers everything you do from that day on."

He hunched at the edge of the bed, knowing he should have lied to her. The truth was too harsh, to hard to tell, too ugly for her to live with for the rest of her days. He should have refused to answer. He should have—

Shea slid her hand across the coverlet and curled her fingers around his wrist. His pulse beat hard beneath her cool soft flesh, and when he dared to raise his gaze to hers, what he saw in her eyes was understanding and compassion. No one had ever offered those things to him; no one had ever understood how badly he needed them. The moment of contact burned fierce and hot between them, then abruptly Cam pushed to his feet.

He needed to put distance between this woman and himself, to break off the strange communion. His head was reeling a little as he stood over her. "I can't imagine that a conversation as grim as this is going to lead you into pleasant dreams," he apologized as he bent to dim the lamp.

"Ah, no." Her voice came soft in the dark. "But I think that it was necessary. I thank you for telling me the truth."

The truth, Cam thought as he closed the bedroom door behind him, was one more thing in life that was vastly overrated. Lies, evasions, and denial were so much easier, so much safer. But then, Shea Waterston didn't seemed to be afraid of the truth. He was beginning to wonder if she was afraid of anything.

His sister was wiping dishes when Cam passed through the kitchen on his way to check the animals for the night.

"I think Shea enjoyed being out on the porch, don't you?" Lily said stopping him halfway to the door. "And goodness, what a lovely voice she has."

"The singing tired her out," Cam observed. He felt churlish and itchy inside his own skin; he needed to be by himself for a while.

"Is she all right?"

He couldn't set Lily to worrying because he was out of sorts. "She'll be fine once she's slept."

"Cammie?"

He'd put one hand on the knob when he recognized the low, precarious note in his sister's voice. He turned and looked at her. Her head was bowed, and she was worrying the delicate garnet band she'd worn on a ribbon around her neck ever since the night their mother died.

"What's the matter?"

"Shea asked me about Rand's mother."

He froze. "And what did you tell her?"

She raised her head. He could see the V nipped into the delicate skin between her eyes. "I spoke before I thought. I told her you'd never been married."

He went to her, closed his hands around her arms, and drew her against him. "It's all right, Lil. She's only curious."

"But, Cammie, no one here knows where Rand came from."

He could hear the apprehension in her voice, and looked down into her ravaged face, into those wide, worried eyes. He stroked her withered cheek and loathed himself for not being able to protect her.

"No one will ever know about Rand unless we tell them," he soothed her. "There's no reason to worry. I promise you."

He gathered her nearer and felt her turn her face into the curve of his throat. Cam shifted his weight, rocking her gently. No matter how he'd failed her in the past, he was here now. He'd always be here to protect and care for her and his son. He'd made his promise.

"It *will* be all right," he whispered.

"You're sure of that?"

"As sure as I am that we'll have snow this winter." He smiled to himself and rested his cheek against her hair. "As sure as I am that you'll be hanging washing on the line come Monday morning."

"As sure as I am that the last piece of lemon cake will be gone before you go to bed," Lily said, and he could hear the smile come back to her voice.

It was a game they'd played since childhood, after their father had died and left their mother with the two of them to raise. Cameron couldn't remember how the game had begun, but somehow the assurances still worked for them.

"Maybe it was *you,* not Rand, Shea was wondering about," Lily suggested slyly.

She might as well have gigged him with spurs. "What do you mean?"

She stepped back and looked him up and down. "Perhaps Shea was asking because she finds you—"

"For the love of God, Lil!" Cameron's own unsettling awareness of Shea Waterston sent a heat creeping up his jaw. "I don't want some woman finding me anything!"

"Don't you?" she asked, genuinely surprised. "Don't you ever want—"

Her voice trailed off, but Cam knew what she wanted: a husband, children of her own, to be part of the world around her in spite of her scars. He would have sold his soul to give those things to her, but he was powerless to change the past. Powerless to alter the course her life had taken. Or his own.

He touched her sleeve to let her know he meant what he said. "I'm content the way things are, Lil. Truly I am."

She smiled at him. "You're a good man, Cammie. Any woman would be proud to—"

With a snort of irritation, he turned away. "I'm going out to the barn."

This time he managed to make it out onto the porch, but one glance toward the barn reminded him that Owen Brandt was there. What Cam wanted was solitude. He headed for the back of the house and half-stepped down the rise toward the river. He ambled through the rustling thigh-high grass that grew all the way down to the riverbank and stood watching the Platte ripple past on its thousand-mile journey to the sea. On nights like tonight he liked to lose himself in something just that vast and mute and powerful.

Shea Waterston was disrupting all their lives. Rand was dancing attendance and bringing Shea flowers. Lily was worried she'd unearth their secrets.

And as for him—the woman shook the very bedrock of who he was. The more he saw of her, the more he wanted to seek her out. The more he learned of her, the more questions he seemed to have. The more he tried to turn away, the more compelling she seemed. Even here by the river, he could not still the mumbling in his blood or quench his errant thoughts of her.

SIX

*W*hat the devil's going on at the photography wagon? Cam wondered as he rode into the barnyard several days later. The tailgate was down, and two big boxes of what he knew were photographic plates sat at the lip of the opening. Once he'd unsaddled his pony and shooed it into the corral, he stepped around to the back of the wagon to see what Owen was up to.

Shea was crouched on the floor of the wagon instead.

"Just what the hell do you think you're doing out here?" he boomed at her.

Shea started, shot to her feet, then lost every hint of color in her face.

Cursing, Cam vaulted into the wagon and caught her as her knees gave way. "Are you going to faint?"

"My ears are buzzing," she slurred, toppling against him.

"I don't for a minute doubt it."

There wasn't enough room to lay her down on the floor, so he eased her back across the jumble of boxes. It couldn't be very comfortable, but Cam wasn't sure that mattered. With a clatter that sounded like tin cups and silverware, he upended another box and propped her feet on top of it.

Shea lifted her head. "Don't you dare break any of my photographic plates!" she admonished him, then fell back moaning.

"Take deep breaths," he instructed her. Cam figured that was the single most useful bit of medical advice he'd ever heard. He knelt beside her and fanned her with his hat.

"What the hell are you doing out here all by yourself?" he muttered. What could Owen and Lily have been thinking to let her come to the wagon alone? Shea hadn't even had on proper clothes until yesterday.

"The goats got out," she answered. Her voice faded a little between the words, and she didn't have so much as a dab of color in her cheeks. "Lily and Owen went off chasing them."

"And you just strolled on down here." He fanned harder, irritated with everyone involved.

"I had to stop twice to rest."

Twice in a little more than a hundred yards, but she'd kept coming. Damn stubborn woman, anyway.

"What was so blasted important?"

"I wanted my things." Her voice had steadied some, and she didn't look quite so much like bone china.

"Someone would have brought them to you."

She nodded and closed her eyes. "I suppose."

He could see she didn't like being less than whole, didn't like being beholden. He could understand her wanting her things. Women seemed to set great store in having their own belongings around them.

Then he realized what Shea had been doing when he came around the corner. "You weren't exactly gathering

up your handkerchiefs when I got here," he accused
her. "You were going through those photographic
plates."

"I didn't come down here to do it," she admitted on
a weary sigh, "but someone has to. Owen and I won't
have a penny to bless us come winter if we don't get
those plates off to New York."

Shea's worry was perfectly justified; Owen Brandt
wasn't going to take care of this. Owen Brandt had all
he could do taking care of Owen Brandt.

Still, Cam was overwhelmingly peeved at her. "Well,
damn it, it serves you right."

"What serves me right? Being penniless?"

"Fainting."

"I didn't faint," she insisted, with a little more vigor.
"I got muzzy is all, and I wouldn't have done that if
you hadn't popped around the corner and scared me
half to death."

Cameron scowled, irritated with himself this time.
Why hadn't he realized shouting like that would startle
her? He let out his breath in exasperation. "Well, I'm
sorry."

She turned her head and looked at him. "You're
sorry?" She sounded as if the declaration amazed her.
"Why, I didn't think judges *ever* apologized!"

"What on earth gave you the idea—" Cameron began gruffly, then caught himself. Shea Waterston was
teasing him! No one but Lily ever teased Judge
Cameron Gallimore. No one dared.

Cam fumbled for a few glib words, something sharp
and clever to fob her off. He couldn't seem to come up
with anything but the truth. "I'm afraid this judge has
a great deal to apologize for. Scaring you and tossing
you in jail is the very least of it."

Her eyes narrowed as if she knew exactly how much

he'd just admitted. Yet when she answered him her tone was light. "I've been meaning to thank you for doing that."

Cameron sat back on his heels. "Thank me for locking you up that day in Breckenridge?"

"Well, not that precisely," Shea clarified. "But in the end I was glad you kept me from taking that photograph."

"Why?"

She drew a long, deep breath. "I'd never been to a hanging. I didn't know what went on. All I was thinking about was how much money I could make selling that photograph. But I'm glad I never had the chance to take it."

"You are?"

Her clear gaze locked with his, and he could see her eyes darken with conviction. "In the end I was glad I didn't see the hanging. Just hearing it—" He saw a shiver run through her. "Just hearing it was enough to convince me I don't ever want to attend one. I don't want to photograph one. And I most certainly don't want to be responsible for making the last desperate moments of a man's life available for everyone to see."

Shea Waterston understood. Something shifted inside him. Without him having to explain, Shea had seen how wrong it would have been to immortalize something as barbarous as Joe Calvert's death.

When he'd accepted the appointment as territorial judge, Cameron had understood the kind of decisions he'd have to make, the hangings he'd be duty-bound to order. He'd taken the job because he believed in the law, because he thought he could administer justice fairly. He'd done just that, but each of the murder trials he'd presided over and each execution he'd witnessed was engraved in his mind as if it were etched in steel.

"How do you do it?" she asked softly, tugging him back from the dark places those memories had taken him. "How do you bear it?"

Cameron shifted uneasily, startled by her perceptiveness. He wasn't sure he wanted to admit to anyone how much each of those hangings had affected him.

"How do I watch those men die?" He felt the words burn in his throat and was appalled by how close to the surface his feelings were. "I don't do it very well, I'm afraid. Even though I've made certain each of those men deserved the sentence I've passed on him, I hate the hangings. I hate the noise and the people who come to watch. I hate knowing I'm responsible."

He started as Shea's small hand closed around his larger one. Her fingers were cold, but her grip was solid and reassuring.

He looked down at their linked fingers, remembering how he'd held that same hand as Emmet worked over her. He'd held her fingers in his and willed her his strength. Now she seemed to be repaying him in kind.

When he finally found the courage to raise his gaze to hers, her eyes were calm, filled with a compassion that was nearly as unnerving as it was seductive.

But with his responsibilities to Lily and Rand, Cam didn't dare allow himself to be seduced. He wrenched his hand away and shot to his feet. He needed to put some distance between them and snatched at the first thing he could think of to divert her.

"So which of these boxes need to be sent to New York?"

Shea hesitated just long enough to let him know she saw through his evasion before she gave her answer. "The two boxes down by the tailgate are ready to go. The three at this end of the wagon stay with me. I've been trying to sort through the rest and divide up the negatives."

Shea pushed up on her elbows, then eased cautiously into a sitting position. She wavered a bit, and Cameron steadied her.

"If I get everything ready," she said on a sigh, "perhaps I can convince Owen to venture into Denver—"

"Venture into Denver? Denver's barely a half hour drive. Rand and I ride into town every day," he told her. "I'll put the boxes on a train myself."

"You'd do that?" Her expression softened and her words were tinged with amazement and gratitude.

How long had it been since anyone had done things for her? Cam found himself wondering. How long since she'd allowed anyone in close enough to help?

"I wouldn't offer unless I meant it," he assured her. "Besides, if I'm ever going to get you and Owen out from underfoot"—he let a smile dawn across his face— "I have to see you have the wherewithal to find other quarters."

Shea stared at him askance for a moment, then realized *he* was teasing *her*. She laughed with surprise and reached across to brush his hand again.

Even that fleeting touch sent a tingle of sensation rippling across his flesh. Her warmth seeped through the pores of his skin and sank deep. He resisted the urge to rub the spot.

"Do you want to go through the rest of these now," he asked her, "or would you like to do them when you're feeling stronger?"

"I'd like to do them now, if we can," she answered.

They reviewed the plates one by one. Most of the negatives were views Shea had taken with a stereoptic camera. Its double lens produced two small, dense images side by side. When the negative was printed on cards and used in a stereoptic viewer, the scene would jump to life giving the illusion of reality.

As they held the negatives up to the light, Cam could see how well she'd captured the grandeur of the mountains and recognized several of the landscapes. She'd crept close enough to photograph elk grazing in a meadow ringed by mountains, and caught the pristine details of the alpine wildflowers.

Even looking at the negatives with darks and lights reversed, Cameron was captivated by Shea's skill. Working in what must have been nearly impossible conditions, she had made magic with the contrasts, the shapes, the poetry of the high country.

What courage and determination it must have taken to record the places few women had ever seen! Cam was inexpressibly proud of her.

Shea seemed pleased with the negatives, as well. But by the time they'd gone through all the plates, she was drooping with weariness.

"If I promise to come back after supper and seal these boxes," he proposed, "will you let me escort you back to the house?"

"Are you sure it won't be too much trouble for you to send these off for us?" she asked, still fretting about accepting the favor.

Cam scowled at her. "Now just how much trouble do you think I'll have taking these five boxes to the railroad station?"

Finally convinced, Shea allowed him to lift her down from the wagon. He steadied her on her feet, then slid an arm around her and drew her against his side. The fluff of those gingery curls barely reached his shoulder, and he was surprised at how small she really was. Somehow the practicality and determination in her made her seem so much more hardy.

As he matched his footsteps to hers, her warm not-quite-lavender scent rose in his nostrils. Her hand came to rest in the furrow of his spine, and for all that it wasn't a particularly intimate touch, Cam found it strangely unsettling.

"Shea," he said as they ambled down the lane, "you know if you need help, all you need to do is ask for it, don't you?"

Her gaze rose to his, and he could see that some of the wariness he'd sensed in her earlier had ebbed away. "I know it now," she answered softly, and together they walked back to the house.

"King me!" Rand whooped as he snapped a black checker down on the game board directly in front of where Shea was sitting.

She scowled at him across the kitchen table. It was Sunday afternoon. Lily was singing hymns and finishing up the dinner dishes, while Shea was losing her third—or maybe it was her fourth—game of checkers to Rand. She could hear Owen's boot soles scuffling, keeping the battered rocker out on the porch in motion. Cam had gone off to deliver a crock of Lily's chicken broth to someone who'd fallen ill.

"Aren't you going to king me, Shea?" Rand prodded her.

"Oh, all right." With an exaggerated sigh she stacked a second checker on Randall's king.

"Are you *sure* you've played this game before?" he asked with a sly smile.

"Of course I've played it," she sniffed. She carefully considered her next move and eased one of the checkers forward. The instant she lifted her finger she knew she'd made a mistake.

Rand cackled with delight and jumped Shea's last three men. "I won," he announced unnecessarily.

"I can see that." Shea did her best to scowl at him, but he was such an engaging child with that breezy grin and affable manner. "If you want me to keep playing with you," she muttered peevishly, "don't you think you should let me win just once?"

"He's just like his father," Lily put in, working the last of the spoons through the folds of her towel. "He likes to win. I think half the reason Cammie went back east to study law was so he could prevail in any argument."

"Oh, your brother's not so bad as that," Shea offered, thinking how Cam had apologized for locking her up the day of the hanging.

"Well, Cammie was different before he went off to fight," Lily conceded. "He was brash, full of himself, far more stubborn and argumentative. The war—" Shea glanced up just in time to see Lily rub her withered cheek. "The war changed him."

Shea fastened her curious gaze on Lily.

"How did it change him?" Was the war what put the wariness in those night blue eyes? Was the war what created that shadowy second self that no one but her seemed able to see? Was the war why he was more committed to his sister than a husband to a wife?

But Lily seemed disinclined to discuss how her brother had changed. Instead she hefted the brimming dishpan and headed toward the door. Shea hurried ahead to open it, then trailed Lily into the yard.

Walking gingerly, Lily carried the sloshing basin toward the double row of rosebushes blooming along the foundation of the house. "Cammie says there's snow in the mountain passes," she said, as she rationed out the soapy water. "I suppose that means I should be cutting my roses back, but I just can't bear to lose the flowers yet."

Shea knew she should be preparing for winter, too. As soon as they got a bank draft from New York, she'd be able to look for winter accommodations and restock their supplies. Since she'd sold Simon's studio in New York, she and Owen had wintered wherever they were at the season's end. They'd set up a studio in Nebraska City last year and been money ahead come spring. With the month or more they'd lost while Shea was ill, they'd probably be holing up in Denver this winter.

Once we're settled, I can start writing letters again, Shea found herself thinking. Through the dozens of letters she'd written last year, she'd been able to discover which of the orphan trains had taken Liam west. This year she hoped to learn exactly where that train had stopped and when her son had been adopted. Perhaps, if she was lucky, she might even discover the name of the people who'd taken her child.

"Shea?" Lily asked, reaching out to touch her arm. "Shea, have you heard a word I've said?"

"You said you need to cut the roses back?" she guessed hopefully.

"I said that a good long while ago," Lily said with a laugh and tucked a deep pink blossom from one of the bushes behind Shea's ear. "That color suits you," she said, seeming pleased with the effort.

Shea reached up to brush the petals with her fingertips. "I've always liked pink roses," she replied. "Thank you."

Just then Rand burst out the kitchen door. The bang it made bouncing back on its hinges all but launched Owen out of the rocker.

"And where do you think you're going, young man?" Lily asked, stopping Rand in his tracks.

"Down to the corral."

"Did you put the checkers away?" she asked him.

"Yes, ma'am, I did."

"Have you appropriated more of my perfectly good carrots to feed that animal of yours?"

Rand paused at the gate. "It's Sunday, so I figured Jasper deserved a treat."

Lily sighed helplessly. "Oh, I suppose he does."

Rand grinned at her and raced off down the lane, letting the gate slap closed behind him.

"He loves that horse," Shea murmured watching him.

"He loves *all* horses," Lily corrected her. "And he'd feed them a whole field of carrots if I let him. Since Cam's not here, I suppose I ought to keep an eye on him. Do you feel up to walking as far as the corral?"

Shea had been staying up longer and walking farther every day. She linked her arm through Lily's. "I think I can, but it would be nice to have someone to lean on."

Together they started off. Though the sun was shining and the sky was china blue, the wind carried the breath of that distant snow. It tugged at their hair, nipped color into their cheeks, and slapped their skirts against their legs. Lily shivered and Shea found herself wishing she'd grabbed their shawls from the peg inside the kitchen door.

When they got to the corral, Rand was riding bareback on a compact little roan, guiding him with the press of his hands and the shift of his weight. Rand and the horse seemed attuned somehow, moving in perfect accord.

He rides the way Sean did, Shea found herself thinking. Her brother had always had a way with horses, a gentleness and ease that was as much a part of him as breathing. Rand had that, too.

"He's a fine horseman," Shea observed, glancing across at where Lily had climbed up onto the first rail of the fence beside her.

"He is, isn't he?" Lily agreed with more than a bit of pride. As she watched Rand and Jasper lope around the corral, the wind teased several long sable strands from Lily's chignon. They caught on her lips and her eyelashes, and without giving the impulse a second thought, Shea reached across and tucked them back.

At the brush of Shea's fingertips against her cheek, Lily stiffened. "What are you doing?" she gasped and jerked away. "I never let anyone touch my face!"

When she'd smoothed back Lily's hair, Shea hadn't even noticed the scars. It was just how Lily was—imperfect in a way folks could see instead of ways they couldn't.

But before Shea could think what to say, Lily had pushed back from the fence and bolted toward the house.

Shea was ready to go after her when Rand nudged Jasper up close to the fence. "What happened to Aunt Lily?"

Shea turned and confronted the child's far-too-curious eyes. "She left something on the stove." She lied instinctively, protecting Lily.

Rand smiled ruefully, taken in. "She let some eggs boil dry one time when she was practicing piano. And, boy, did they stink!"

Shea couldn't help being relieved when Rand went on. "Want to see the trick Jasper and I have been working on?"

She could almost hear her brother Sean shouting,

"Watch me! Watch me, Shea!" before he made his father's gelding high-step across the paddock or jump some impossibly high fence.

Smiling at the memory, she nodded to Rand. "Of course I want to see."

Easing Jasper to a lope, the boy raised one foot, then the other, and slowly pushed himself into a standing position. Balanced upright in the center of the roan's broad back, he made one circuit of the corral and then another.

As Shea applauded, Emmet Farley bellied up to the fence beside her. "Don't you fall off that pony, boy," he warned. "I'm planning to have tea with your aunt this afternoon, and I don't want it disrupted to bandage that head of yours!"

Rand laughed and waved and kept right on circling.

Shea looked up at the doctor. His long, angled jaw wore a bristly coat of sandy-colored whiskers, and his clothes seemed creased into the joints of his gaunt, long-boned frame.

"I didn't expect you to come by this afternoon," she said.

"I just delivered a fat baby boy down the road at Mayhew's," he said around a yawn, "so I thought I'd stop and see you since I was out this way."

Shea slid him a sidelong glance. "*I* think you came to see if there's any of Lily's apple cobbler left over from dinner the other night."

"I do have a certain fondness for Lily's cobbler," he allowed, then turned to look down at her. "So how are you, Shea?"

"Stronger than I was yesterday, but not as strong as I'll be tomorrow."

He nodded, pleased with her answer. "I'd still like to

check your bandages. Would you mind if we headed back?"

Shea waved at Rand then threaded her hand through Emmet's elbow. As they walked, Shea tried to scrape up courage enough to ask the question that had been plaguing her for weeks, the question that had come to a head this afternoon. "What happened to Lily Gallimore's face?" she finally asked.

Emmet stopped dead in his tracks. "Is that why Lily seemed so upset when I drove in?"

A hot flush flooded up Shea's neck as she explained what had happened.

When she was done, the doctor shook his head. "I keep hoping she'll find a way to make peace with those scars. I keep trying to find something that will get her off this farm. I'm not sure she's been farther than the end of the lane since Cam brought her out here."

"Is she afraid that people will stare at her?"

"Or worse yet, offer pity."

Shea nodded thoughtfully. "Yet she's curious about Denver. She reads the newspapers and asks you and Cam all sorts of things about town. And she sends notes and gifts—"

"—to people she's never seen and doesn't know. It doesn't make sense, does it?"

Shea shook her head. "Maybe one day she'll just get curious enough to pick up and go into town."

"Maybe pigs'll sprout wings and fly," Emmet all but growled at her.

"Can you tell me what happened?"

Emmet slid a thin, dark cheroot from the pocket of his jacket. "I'm not sure I know the whole of it," he said, striking a match and exhaling a long plume of smoke. "She and Cam don't say much. Just that Anderson's Confederate guerrillas raided the town where Lily

and her mother were living during the war. And that
after the raiders ransacked the house, they set it ablaze.
Apparently Lily's clothes caught fire while they were
escaping."

Shea shivered at the thought and raised her hand to
her own smooth cheek. What would it be like to feel
those withered striations where smooth, soft flesh had
been?

"Lily couldn't have been more than a girl," Shea
breathed.

"She was just sixteen." Emmet's voice caught and
she could hear sadness in him, regret that ran deep, and
compassion that ate at him for Lily's sake. "Just sixteen."

Instinctively Shea reached for the doctor's hand.
"And Cam wasn't there to protect them?"

"He must have come home not long after. I think
he's always blamed himself for not being home when
they needed him. His mother died the following spring
and he's devoted himself to Lily and Rand ever since."

Emmet threw down his half-smoked cheroot and
ground it to powder beneath his boot. "I hate that Lily
has sacrificed so much of her life to those damned scars.
I keep thinking that when they put her in the ground
all she'll ever have been is Cameron's sister and Randall's aunt, when there's so much more she could have
had and been."

"But would it be so terrible—if she was happy?"

The stiffness went out of Emmet's back. "No, it
wouldn't be terrible if she was happy." He drew a suddenly shaky breath. "But the loss would be a goddamn
shame for the rest of us."

The sound of the dinner bell clanging startled them
both. Lily was standing on the back porch waving at
them. In the last half hour she seemed to have regained

her composure. "I've put the tea on to steep," she called out. "Won't you come in and have a cup?"

As he turned to her, Emmet Farley's face softened and warmth supplanted the regret in his eyes. "We'll be right there, my dear," he shouted back.

SEVEN

$\mathcal{S}$hea stood on the kitchen porch ringing the bell to call the men in to breakfast. It was the season's first truly wintry day, and as she watched Cameron, Rand, and Owen tramp down the frozen lane puffing clouds of breath, she realized she couldn't expect Owen to sleep in the unheated tack room for very much longer. It was time she accepted her responsibilities and got the two of them settled somewhere for the winter.

Not that they hadn't liked being here at the farm. Owen had settled in better than Shea had ever dreamed he would. She and Lily had become fast friends. Rand was bright-eyed and inquisitive, headstrong and rambunctious, funny and dear—everything she hoped her own lost boy would be like when she finally found him.

Then there was Cameron, whose deep, rough voice she liked far too much. Who smelled too good. Who lit a strange, unexpected warmth inside her. She admired his intelligence, his wit, and his rare rich laughter. She liked that he took her ambitions seriously.

As Cam ushered Rand and Owen through the gate

and up toward the house, Shea felt his protectiveness
enfold her, too. Cam made her feel so safe. They all
made her feel safe. It had been a very long time since
she'd been safe. But if she meant for Owen and her to
earn their keep, if she meant to find her son, Shea
couldn't be seduced by that semblance of safety.

As the men stomped up onto the porch to wash,
Shea went back into the kitchen to help Lily finish
dishing up breakfast.

It was Saturday morning. The early chores were
done, and all of them had gathered in the kitchen to
enjoy the rarity of a leisurely breakfast. Banners of sunlight draped across the scarred pine table. The glassware
and utensils twinkled in the light. Gold-edged steam
rose in swirls from the heaping platters of eggs and
bacon and biscuits.

They clasped hands once everyone was seated, and
Lily offered a blessing. With Owen's cold fingers
tucked tightly in her left hand and Lily's work-
roughened palm clasped in her right, Shea felt so connected to these people, so grateful for their friendship.

A sharp burr of emotion caught in her throat. She
wanted to save this moment, tuck it away forever. She'd
done that with the evenings her father had played his
fiddle by the fire, the rainy afternoons in the big house
in New York when the women servants had gathered to
do their mending, and the days when Simon had been
well enough to walk with her in the park. They were
the memories she took out and fingered when she was
lonely and afraid. Yet sometimes, when finding Liam
seemed hopeless, Shea wondered if this small store of
memories were all she'd ever have.

Shea had just poured second cups of coffee all
around when Cam turned to her. "Shea," he said,

fishing in the pocket of his corduroy vest. "I have something here I want to give you."

"Something for me?" Shea couldn't fight the swell of anticipation that crept up her chest, or the quick pinch of eagerness. No one had given her anything since Simon died.

Cameron caught her hand in his and gently pressed a key into her palm. Shea closed her fingers around it, feeling the irregular shape of the metal against her skin and the warmth of Cameron's body.

"Why are you giving me this?" she managed to ask him.

Across the table Rand was squirming in his chair. Lily favored Shea with her one-sided smile, and Cam's eyes sparkled with mischief.

Shea's heart gave a sharp little kick of excitement.

"It's the key to the cabin down by the road," he told her.

"Down by the road?"

"The hired man's cottage," he went on. "It's small, and no one's lived there for more than a year. It needs some repairs and a good cleaning to make it habitable, but we thought you and Owen might like to use it for the winter."

Gratitude poured through her like sunshine. These people had done so much for Owen and her already that she could never repay them, and now they were offering them even more.

Then, on the heels of that flush of appreciation came an inexplicable wariness, the drag of unexpected reluctance. It was confusing, unsettling when just a few minutes before she'd been thinking how much she was going to miss the Gallimores.

"I can't think what to say," Shea murmured, fumbling for time to sort things through.

"Why don't we all walk down to the cabin so you can see exactly what it is we're offering you," Cameron suggested.

Owen hustled out the door, ten paces ahead of everyone else.

The rustic log house at the end of the lane had been the first building on the property. A trapper had raised it years before, and Cam and Lily had made do living there while the house on the rise was being built. The cabin had been improved several times since then and occupied by a series of hired hands. It consisted of one main room with a loft above and a lean-to grafted onto the back to serve as a bedroom.

"The roof's sound enough," Cameron observed, standing in the center of the main room with his hands on his hips staring up at the ceiling. "Though God knows the place does need cleaning and sprucing up."

Shea could imagine that with the cobwebs swept away and a fire glowing on the hearth, the cabin would be every bit as snug as the cottage where she'd grown up.

"I've a length of blue calico put by," Lily enthused, her face alight. "We could turn it into some perfectly lovely curtains . . ."

"I'll bring in wood every day," Rand promised. "And if you're here all winter, maybe I can teach you to win at checkers."

Shea laced her arms across her chest and surveyed the place a second time. "There isn't light enough to do photography here," she commented dubiously. "And surely no one would come all this way to have their portrait made."

"You could rent a studio in town and live out here," Cam suggested. Both he and Rand rode into Denver every day for work and school.

The Gallimores' open-handed generosity beguiled her. Lily's smile, Rand's excitement, and the warmth in Cam's eyes beguiled her. So why, Shea wondered, was she resisting?

"Before we decide, I think I'd like to go into Denver and see if there's studio space available," Shea hedged.

"Does that mean you don't want to stay with us?" Rand asked, clearly disappointed.

"It means she's a businesswoman who must consider her options," Cameron explained, though she could see the pleasure in his face had dimmed, as well.

Shea couldn't bear to look at Lily.

"Perhaps we should give Shea and Owen a chance to look over the cabin on their own," Cam went on, and he ushered his sister and Rand toward the door.

Once they were gone, Owen turned to her. "We staying?"

Shea could see unexpected hopefulness in Owen's face. "Is that what you want?"

He shifted from foot to foot.

Not once since Simon's passing had Owen questioned her decisions or expressed an opinion about where they went or what they did. What made taking this cabin so important? she wondered, and asked him outright.

"Like it here," Owen admitted, ducking his head.

Shea had always prided herself on being attuned to Owen's feelings, but she hadn't realized how he felt. Still, if she'd been so taken by the Gallimores, why wouldn't Owen feel the same?

She pressed him anyway. "What is it you like?"

He cringed like a turtle drawing back into his shell.

"What is it you like?" she persisted.

"He knows," Owen finally whispered.

"Who knows?"

"Judge."

She hadn't realized that Owen had formed such an attachment to His Honor. "What does the judge know?"

Owen hung his head. It was a full minute before he answered her. "About the war."

What exactly did Cameron Gallimore know about the war? Lily had said Cam fought for the Union, but Shea hadn't heard him moaning in his sleep caught in the throes of terrible dreams. He didn't appear to be terrified of gunfire. Cam didn't wall himself off the way Owen did.

But then, she didn't doubt Owen's word. If Owen said Cameron understood about the war, she believed him.

Owen rubbed his hands together. "Stay here, Sparrow. Please?"

Shea was stunned by the sudden lucidity in the old man's eyes. How could she have known him for all this time, traveled all these miles in his company, and never once caught a glimpse of this clarity, this other Owen?

No matter how wrong it felt to accept the cabin from the Gallimores, no matter how remaining on the farm seemed to threaten her own interests, Shea couldn't bring herself to refuse him.

"All right, we'll stay," she promised.

"Good." He nodded twice before his eyes clouded over again. "Good."

Shea left Owen in the cabin to contemplate their new home and headed for the photography wagon. The promise she'd made him lay like a rock in her belly, and she hoped that an hour or two of sweeping, scrubbing, and reorganizing the wagon would aid her digestion.

In truth, she was feeling better when Rand peeked around the back a good while later. "Shea?"

She looked up from the list of supplies she was making and smiled at him. "Come on in."

Rand accepted the invitation and climbed aboard. He settled on one of the wooden boxes across from her. "So, what *is* all this?" he asked her.

Shea suspected he'd been in the wagon before. What boy worth his salt wouldn't have come in and poked around? Now that she was here, he wanted to know what he'd seen.

She handed him a piece of the japanned steel. "This is the metal we use to make tintypes," she began in her most instructive voice. "These"—she pulled open the drawers beneath the dry sink—"are bottles of the chemicals that make that metal sensitive to the light."

She went on to elaborate, remembering how she'd gone through all this with the boy they'd met up in the mountains. Tyler Morran had been about Rand's age, and his eyes had shone with this same curiosity.

"Are you going to take a photograph of Pa, Aunt Lily, and me?" Randall asked when she was done.

Mindful of what Lily might think of having her likeness made, Shea answered carefully. "I'll discuss it with your father, and then we'll see."

Rand's shoulders slumped. "I was hoping you'd make our photograph and let me watch."

"I'll show you how this works when we get a studio in town," she promised him.

Rand seemed momentarily satisfied, though judging from the way he perched on the edge of the box, there was something more on his mind.

"Shea," he began, though he couldn't quite bring

himself to look at her. "If—if someone overhears two people talking about a secret, should he let them know what he overheard?"

Shea put down her pencil and gave the boy her full attention. "I suppose it depends on the secret and the people involved," she answered carefully.

Rand frowned, a crease deepening across his brow. He raised his gaze to hers. "I wasn't snooping. Honest, I wasn't."

Though her belly began to tighten, Shea did her best to draw him out. "I know you wouldn't pry into things that don't concern you."

He shifted again and looked down at his hands. "Well, this does concern me. It concerns Pa and Aunt Lily and me. They were in the kitchen talking when I came up on the porch."

Family secrets were dear things, especially to close-knit folks like the Gallimores, and Shea knew neither Lily nor Cam would welcome her interference.

Still, Rand wouldn't have come to her unless he needed someone to talk to—someone who wasn't part of whatever was bothering him. Perhaps he'd come to trust her in the weeks she'd been here. The notion sent a soft, sweet warmth sliding through her.

She shifted closer. "They didn't mean for you to hear what they were saying?"

"I don't think so."

Shea pursed her lips. Should she hear Rand out, then tell Lily and Cam what was bothering him? Should she suggest Rand go directly to his father? That's what Cam would want her to do, but she wasn't sure she could convince—

"They were talking about how Pa adopted me."

Rand's words sizzled down Shea's backbone with all

the heat of a lightning bolt. She straightened abruptly. "He adopted you?"

Worried sage green eyes looked up at her. "If he adopted me, it means Pa isn't my real father, doesn't it?"

At the uncertainty in his voice, tenderness closed like a fist around her heart. Shea shifted across the aisle to the box where Rand was sitting and wrapped her arm around his shoulders.

She shouldn't be the one explaining what adoption was; it wasn't her place. Still, Rand had brought his questions to her, trusted her with his uncertainties. In the instant she had to frame an answer, Shea did her best to think what Cam would want her to say to his son.

"It's true that being adopted means you and your father aren't related by blood. But being a parent is—" The dark specter of her own secrets and regrets rose before her. "Being a parent is more than blood. It means taking care of a child every single day. It means seeing that he's healthy and happy. It means guiding him as he grows."

She hauled in a ragged breath, thinking of Liam.

"Being a parent means loving a child with all your heart," she continued with fierce conviction. "You know how much your father and your aunt Lily love you, don't you?"

Rand nodded.

"I can see how much they love you, too," she confirmed, just to be sure he knew. "You must never doubt for a moment that you're your father's son in every way that matters. You're your father and your aunt Lily's child because they've loved you and cared for you." Shea spoke the words unequivocally, determined that he would believe her.

"Even if they got me from an orphan train?"

If his first revelation had stunned her, these last two words seared into Shea as if they'd been dipped in acid. "An orphan train?"

"That's what they said."

The faint waver in his voice tore at her, and she tightened her arm around him. She longed to tell him all she'd learned about orphan trains—how city children like Rand and her Liam were herded on. How they were marched out onto the platforms of stations thousands miles from anyplace they knew and paraded in front of prospective parents. Her child must have been picked just that way, like a puppy from a litter. And so had Rand.

Shea bit down hard on the bitter words. Rand had just told her his most terrifying and closely guarded secret. What he needed was to be reassured and comforted.

She wrapped both arms around him and felt him nestle against her. He was more solid than she'd expected him to be, broader across the back and shoulders, outgrowing his childhood by leaps and bounds. Yet he was still just ten years old, and he needed the right answers.

"Do you know what orphan trains are?" she asked him.

"Sort of."

If she were wise, Shea thought, she'd climb right out of this wagon and take Rand to his father. If she were wise, she'd let Cameron explain this to him.

Instead she stroked Rand's hair. "Orphan trains brought children from crowded cities back east out to the West, where life wouldn't be so hard for them," she began. "People who wanted to open their homes and their hearts to the children met the trains and picked the boys and girls they wanted."

"And Pa and Aunt Lily picked me?"

She could still hear Rand's uncertainty and groped for words that would make him feel as if he was wanted, privileged, unique.

"They must have been able to see right off what a good boy you were," Shea said, squeezing his shoulder gently. "They realized even then what a fine, upstanding man you were going to grow up to be. They chose you, Rand, because they could tell you were special."

"They picked me because they thought I was special?" His voice wavered a little, and she hugged him closer.

"Very special," Shea rested her cheek against his hair. "You're the kind of child any parent would be proud to claim."

Cam and Lily were exactly the kind of parents every mother dreamed would take the child she'd given up.

"What I think," Shea went on, "is that it's time for you to tell your father what you've just told me. I think you need to hear what he and your aunt Lily have to say about how they came to adopt you."

Rand sat back and looked at her. "You don't think he'll be angry I found out?"

"Your father loves you," she encouraged him. "I think the questions you have left are ones only he can answer. Why don't you and I go find him?"

"Now?" His eyes widened. "You want to go find him *now*?"

"I'll go with you," she offered and rose to stand over him. "I'll help you explain how you found out you were adopted."

Rand didn't budge. "I don't want to talk to him. I don't want him to know I was listening."

She ached for him, for all that contrition and confusion and uncertainty. She held out her hand. "Your father loves you. He'll want to explain this to you in his own way."

"I don't want to talk to him about it!" Rand insisted, and sprang to his feet. "That's why I came to you."

"Rand, please! This is what's best!"

"No, it isn't!" he cried and pushed past her. He leaped out of the back of the wagon and was halfway to the corral by the time she'd clambered to the ground.

As Rand scrambled over the fence, Jasper lifted his head and trotted toward him. The boy threw his arms around his pony's neck, and the neat little roan turned his head to nuzzle his boy.

Shea stood watching them for a moment more, then let out her breath. Rand had owned up to a lot today. He needed time to think this through, time to gather the courage he'd need to face his father. There was nothing to be gained by pushing him.

She sagged back against a wagon wheel, weary now that Rand was gone. Her hands were shaking and her heart was chugging like a freight on an uphill run. She couldn't help wondering if she'd said the right things to Rand, the things that would convince him to talk to his father. To the father who loved him.

She gave a long, bone-deep shudder as she realized what it was she'd just done. In telling Rand about the orphan trains, she'd put herself in the place of someone who'd adopted a child—not someone who'd given one up. She'd cried a lifetime's worth of secret tears because she'd given up her boy. She'd wrapped her hopes and dreams around finding him. Yet in the space of a few short sentences she'd disavowed all that heartache.

What if it was people like Lily and Cam who had taken Liam? What would she do if Liam had come to love his adopted parents the way Rand loved the Gallimores? What right did she have to arrive unannounced and disrupt the only life her son could remember? And why, in God's name, was she trekking all over the West looking for a boy who might not want his mother back?

Shea swiped at her eyes with the back of her hand. "My boy does want me," she insisted under her breath. "He is waiting for me to come for him. Once I have him, once he's mine, I'll make a wonderful life for both of us."

Shea straightened slowly, feeling years older than she had half an hour before. She raked her fingers through her hair. She drew a breath and let it go.

No matter what her own concerns, she needed to let Cam know what Rand had discovered. At first she didn't have any idea how she was going to do that, then she realized that back in the wagon she had just the thing to open their conversation.

Shea had been dreading this moment all day. The rock that had lain in her belly since early this morning had migrated north, lodging at the base of her throat, making breathing all but impossible.

"Please help me find the right things to say to Cam," she whispered, then hastily crossed herself. She hadn't had all that much to say to the Lord since she'd given Liam up, but she could use a little help tonight. A little wisdom and insight.

Her hands shook as she reached for the pressboard portfolio she'd taken from the bottom of her valise. She clutched it against her chest like a shield and headed resolutely toward the kitchen.

Once she'd begun to recover from her wounds, Cameron had taken to working at the kitchen table in the evenings. That's where Shea found him now, his books and papers spread beneath the golden glow of the kerosene lamp.

With his head bent in concentration, lamplight threaded his crow black hair with veins of amber and highlighted the steadfast lines of his brow and jaw. He had such strong features, such an uncompromising face, that for a moment Shea lost her courage.

If she had come here for her own sake, she might have quailed. But knowing she was doing this for Rand, so he'd have no doubts about where he belonged, held her steadfast. She curled her clammy fingers around the edge of the portfolio, and stepped across the threshold.

"Shea," Cameron greeted her, one of his rare, slow smiles dawning through the drape of his mustache. "What are you doing up so late?"

Shea had deliberately waited to talk to him until Lily and Rand were abed. She didn't want either of them overhearing. "I've brought something I'd like to show you," she said, "if you've a moment to spare."

"I was just finishing up," he said and closed his books. "What is it you've got?"

Shea perched on the chair beside him and opened the portfolio. "These are some photographs I took while we were traveling," she explained, hoping the images would speak more clearly than she could herself.

The top picture showed a girl and slightly older boy seated on the steps of a neat, brick farmhouse. The girl's face was wreathed in smiles, and the boy's arm lay protectively across her shoulders. It could almost have been a photograph of Cameron and Lily in their younger days.

"Paul and Susan are children I met near Nebraska City," Shea told him. "Their family was one of the first to homestead in the area."

"I can see the farm is very prosperous." He indicated the rows of fruit trees visible at the side of the house. "But I thought itinerant photographers usually made pictures of the entire family."

"And sometimes even the family cow," Shea confessed with a smile. "I did do that kind of photograph for these folks, too," she went on, her belly quivering, "but I also wanted a picture with just the children. All of these are pictures of children."

She felt his regard slide over her, astute, curious. Her stomach rolled. She wasn't willing to own up to her reasons for taking these pictures if she could help it, but Cameron didn't question her.

She turned to the next photograph, one of a boy of eight or nine clinging to the bridle of a spotted pony. "This is John," she said. "He's apprenticed to a blacksmith."

She'd taken to John immediately, liking his brashness and his curiosity, seeing a bit of herself in his bright grin and curly hair. Until she'd talked to his parents, she'd all but convinced herself she'd found her son. But John had been placed out only the year before—far too late to be her Liam.

Cam slid her another sidelong glance. "The boy looks like he enjoys his work."

Shea had showed him half a dozen other photographs when he covered her hand with his. A shiver of his energy danced up her arm.

"Shea," he began, "is there a particular reason you're showing me these photographs?"

Her pulse rate surged. This was the question she'd been wanting him to ask, the very reason she'd showed him the children she'd photographed while she was searching for Liam. Still, the words came hard. "All these children were sent west on orphan trains."

Shea felt his fingers flex on hers, quick, involuntarily.

"Orphan trains?" he asked. Wariness darkened the blue of his eyes, as if he knew what she'd come to tell him and wanted to forestall her. "Is there some reason you thought I'd be interested in photographs of children from orphan trains?"

She swallowed around the constriction in her throat. "Rand came to talk to me today."

"What was it he wanted?"

She turned her hand beneath his and clasped his fingers in her own. "Rand knows how he came to be your child," she said gently. "He knows you chose him from an orphan train."

She saw a succession of emotions flicker across Cam's face: dread and resignation, confusion and concern. "Is Rand all right?" he asked her.

Shea curled her opposite hand over his. "He's confused. He needs to have his questions answered."

Cam's shoulders bunched defensively. "How did he find out?"

"He overheard you and Lily talking."

She could see the blame settle over him like fine dust, gathering in the creases at the corners of his eyes.

"I've been wanting to tell him how he came to us for months," he said on a weary sigh, "but Lily keeps insisting he's too young."

"She needs to hang on to him as long as she can."

Shea knew now why Lily stood on the porch in the morning and watched Rand ride down the lane. She'd seen how carefully she smoothed her boy's clothes before putting them away, and knew that there were always molasses cookies in the cookie jar because they were Rand's favorites. Lily had wrapped her life around this child. Small wonder the idea of telling Rand he'd had another mother, another life threatened her.

"But why would Rand go to you instead of coming to Lily or me?" Cameron asked her.

She squeezed his hand, wishing she could dispel the raw note of disillusionment in his voice. "He came because I'm a stranger here, because I've got no part in this."

He came because he trusted me.

Shea treasured that trust, even if she'd risked losing it by telling all this to his father.

She looked into Cameron's face. "Rand's whole world changed when he heard you and Lily talking. He isn't who he thought he was, and you aren't who he thought you were, either."

But didn't she mean to change Liam's world just this way? Didn't she mean to reveal that he was someone else entirely when she finally found him? The insight appalled her, and she hastily shoved it away.

She had to make sure Cam talked to his boy and got things settled. Shea leaned in close at Cameron's shoulder. "Rand discovered the truth without having anyone to tell him what it meant," she explained, "without having anyone to reassure him. He wants to talk to you, Cam, but he just doesn't know how."

He dropped his head into his hands. His voice came ruffled on a sigh. "God knows, it seems like Rand's been ours forever."

Though she knew she had no right to ask, the question was on her lips before she thought to hold it back. "How is it you came to adopt him?"

Cam steepled his forefingers against his lips. "Do you know how Lily came to be scarred?" he asked.

"Emmet told me."

Desolation skimmed the surface of his eyes like scudding clouds reflected in a night blue lake. That resolute mouth lost its resolution, the strength in that strong jaw eroded. As ghastly as Lily's burns were, as devastating as losing her beauty must have been for her, this was worse. Whatever Cam was remembering ate at the very core of who he was.

Yet when he finally spoke his voice was low and cool. "Our mother died not quite a year after the guerrillas came through Centralia, and it was then I realized what Lily had become. Though she'd physically recovered from her burns—" Cam pressed his lips together as if just speaking of this took unimaginable courage. "—She was barely alive. She wandered the house like a wraith. She rarely spoke. She never saw anyone. I moved my law practice into a room downstairs because I didn't want her to be alone there."

Shea could imagine how Lily must have felt—disconnected from a world she'd once been part of, walled off, separate, terrified of how people would respond to her.

"Once I was there every day, I began to notice she kept her own kind of schedule. I'd find her peering around the edges of the curtains every morning and every afternoon. She was watching the children going back and forth to school. She watched them with such intensity, with such longing, that I got it into my head that what Lily needed was a child."

Shea nodded, encouraging him.

"It was a good while later that I found an article in the newspaper announcing that orphan trains were coming to Missouri." His tone warmed, and Shea

thought the memories of that time must not be quite so
bleak. "I made inquiries and when the next train was
due, I bought Lily a bonnet and mourning veil and
loaded her into the carriage. She cried for two whole
days, all the way to St. Joe. I wasn't even sure she'd go
and see the children once we arrived, but I didn't know
what else to do for her."

Shea's throat went dry. "You—you adopted Rand
from a train that stopped in St. Joseph, Missouri?"

Cam nodded. "There was a little frame church not
too far from the St. Joe station. They'd already begun
letting people select the orphans when Lily and I arrived. The children were lined up in chairs on a platform across the front of the sanctuary. They were a
ragtag lot. Most of them looked scared to death; some
of the younger ones were crying."

Shea's stomach twisted. This was just what she had
imagined—children put on display to be poked and
prodded and haggled over. Liam must have gone
through exactly what Cameron was describing.

"The older children seemed to have been chosen
first by folks who were looking for hands to work their
farms, and a few of them managed to convince their
new parents to foster their brothers and sisters, as well.
But inevitably some of the younger children were left
behind. Though the Children's Aid Society agents were
busy making out the indenture papers of the foster parents to sign, they did their best to keep track of the
families so the brothers and sisters could at least write
to each other. But still, it was a sad thing to watch
those boys and girls going to different families."

Shea knew how it tore your heart to lose every tie
you had, to see people you loved manacled and hauled
away, to hold your mother's or your sister's hand as

they lay dying, to wake from dreams of home with the smell of peat in your nostrils.

Cam took up his story again. "Finally only a handful of children were left. There were three boys and two girls about six or seven, and four or five toddlers not much over two years old.

"One of the agents told us it was unusual for the Society to place out children so young, but because there were so many older girls on this particular train, they'd sent the little ones west to find new homes."

"But, Cam, how did you choose?" she whispered. "How could you look into all those little faces and pick just one?"

Shea had never been sure which would have been worse—to sit on that platform waiting to be chosen or to have to choose a single child.

"In the end," he said, "it was Rand who chose Lily and me."

"How?" she asked him. "How did he choose you?"

Cameron smiled with the memory. "As the crowd thinned, we went and sat at the edge of the platform. At first Lily refused to uncover her face, but I said whichever child we took had a right to see who we were and decide if he wanted to go with us."

Shea could imagine how difficult saying that must have been for Cam, how horrifying it must have been for Lily to lift her veil and reveal her scars to strangers. "What happened?"

"Two of the children cried and ran away. But one boy—he wasn't much more than a toddler, really—came toward us. He looked us up and down"—Cam's voice deepened—"and then he reached right out and pressed his fingers against Lily's withered cheek.

"When that baby touched her, Lily came alive for the first time since she'd been burned. She reached out and pulled him into her arms. 'I think this one picked me to be his mother,' was all she said. And that's how Rand came home with us."

Shea swallowed around the knot in her throat. "It's a wonderful story," she told him, imagining the joy in Lily's eyes, a joy that echoed in them today. "It's exactly what Rand needs to hear from you. He needs to know that from the first you belonged to him. That he belonged to you. That he's the one that made you a family. You need to tell him as soon as you can."

Now that she'd come to know the Gallimores and seen how they loved their boy, how could she think about interfering with another family to reclaim her son? Yet how could she turn away after searching all this time?

Shea shook her head and pushed away those unanswerable questions. She couldn't consider them here or now. She couldn't consider them when every day brought proof of how happy their adopted child had made Lily and Cam. And what wonderful parents they'd been to him.

Hastily she pushed to her feet and began gathering her pictures—pictures of the more than three dozen orphans she'd managed to find. They were pictures of children whose lives she'd have disrupted in an instant if she'd thought they were Liam.

Cam rose and stood over her. "I know this can't have been easy for you to tell me. I can see how affected you are by the orphan train stories. But I want to tell you how much I appreciate your letting me know what's on Rand's mind."

Shea's fingers fumbled on the photographs and all at once she realized that in exchange for the truth about Rand's concerns, Cam had given her a few more bits of information to add to the store she'd been collecting.

Then it struck her that if she asked exactly the right questions, perhaps he could tell her even more.

"Do you remember the name of the church where they'd taken the orphans?" she asked carefully, averting her eyes lest he see more in them than she wanted him to see. If he could tell her that, maybe she could write the pastor. Maybe he would remember one particular child and know what had become of him.

"It was a Baptist church." Cam narrowed his eyes as if that would bring the past into clearer focus. "First Baptist Church, perhaps?"

"And just when was it you got Rand in St. Joe?"

"It was the year before we came here. 1866."

Shea straightened abruptly, but she dared not look at him. "What month exactly?"

"November."

Around her the world took on a particular brittle clarity. She became unaccountably aware of the coals hissing in the stove, and the screen door creaking in the rising wind. She became unbearably aware how the blacks and whites in her photographs shaded to gray.

This couldn't be happening.

"November of 1866." Her words came on a shuddering breath.

Because so few rail lines had gone west nine years ago, many of the orphan trains had passed through St. Joe. Only the winter before had Shea finally learned when Liam had been placed out. It was when he was almost two years old, in November of 1866.

In the space of a heartbeat, a dozen coincidences converged: that Rand's hair had the same reddish sheen as hers, that he cocked his head in a way that reminded her so much of her mother, that he handled horses with her brother Sean's innate skill. And his father's gentleness.

It wasn't possible.

After these years of searching, of tracing dozens of children, of writing letters and ferreting out the tiniest shreds of information on Liam's placement, how could she have found her son by purest chance?

Fate couldn't be so cruel.

Certainly it wouldn't have led her here, to these people and this boy. To this family she'd come to care for so deeply. Rand wasn't the son she'd searched so long to find—was he?

Her mind raced. Even if Rand was her son, how could she think of taking him away? How could she destroy the Gallimores? How could she deny Lily the single thing that kept her alive? And Mary, Mother of God! How could she make a better home for Liam than this fine place, or be a better parent than Cam or Lily?

But if she refused to acknowledge this boy was her son, she'd be giving up the only dream she'd ever allowed herself.

Shea closed her hands around the photographs, pictures of children who weren't her boy, and struggled with her need to claim the child who was. She clutched the papers tighter, as the future she'd imagined for herself disintegrated around her.

A tear plopped unexpectedly into the center of the photograph she'd made of Paul and Susan. Another rolled down the edge of the portfolio. A third spattered onto the back of her hand. Shea stared at the drops, hardly realizing what they were.

Cam must have seen the tears, because he tucked a finger beneath her chin and raised her face to his. "Shea, what is it? What's the matter? Why are you crying?"

Misery closed her throat, and Shea couldn't think of a way to answer him.

"Oh, Shea," Cam murmured, tenderness rife in that soul-deep voice. He wrapped his arms around her.

Though she knew she had no right to accept what he was offering, Shea leaned into him. She nestled against the bulk of him, pressing her nose into the rough-woven poplin of his Saturday shirt. He smelled of fresh air and sunshine and hard work.

She wanted desperately to absorb the comfort he was offering. But how could she accept succor from this man when only moments before she'd realized that his son was her own lost boy? When she could, only hours and days from now, be telling him she wanted her son back?

Unaware of how she could destroy his world, Cam bent over her, smoothing his palms from her shoulders to her waist, conforming her body to his.

He felt so good against her, so sure, so safe. So comfortable and welcoming. A sob worked its way up her throat.

"Oh, Shea," he whispered and tipped her face up to his. There was such tenderness in his fingertips as he swiped the tears from her cheeks. There was such sweetness in his eyes.

"You mustn't cry," he murmured. "You mustn't cry."

And when she couldn't seem to stop, he bent his head and kissed her.

It was a kiss that began with the most gentle graze of lips, a slide of warmth and texture. It became a consoling skim of his mouth on hers, a pure and gentle intimacy. It grew on a mingled breath and flourished with the brush of their tongues. Then all at once, that tender touch of solace transformed itself into something else.

It was as if one moment they were standing barefoot

on a beach, the breakers foaming gently around them, and the next they were swept out to sea.

They floundered amidst a swirl of sensations neither of them had anticipated or was ready for. Just that quickly the world of consolation and consequences liquefied. Their breath raged rough and ragged in their throats. Their hands clutched, hers charting the bow of his back and the breadth of his shoulders. His palms slid down to the soft, full curve of her derriere, and he drew her against him.

Shea shivered as all that was female in her melted into him, going fluid and soft and welcoming. He raised his hand to her breast, cupped his palm to the shape of her.

"My God! Shea," he whispered and her soul caught fire.

"Pa."

Before either of them had time to consciously recognize the voice, they jerked apart. Shea stepped back dazed, her senses humming, her mind grappling to understand why she was standing here alone, while Cam stood three feet away devouring her with his eyes.

"Pa?"

The sentient cloud of physical allure that had rolled up so unexpectedly between Cam and her blew away like a squall before a freshening wind.

Rand was poised on the threshold into the kitchen, tousled, barefoot, blinking in the light.

This boy.

Her son.

The realization swamped her, set her head to spinning with wonder and incredulity. Her son was here before her now, solid and real after so many years of living only in her imagination. Joy burgeoned in her chest, filling her, making laughter bubble in her throat and fresh tears sting her eyes.

She needed to reach for him, hold the weight of her child against her chest the way she had when he was hours old. She wanted to feel the rise and fall of his breathing beneath her palms. She wanted to savor his scent, stroke the hair at the nape of his neck with her fingertips.

She wanted to tell Rand who she was—*and who he was.*

Instead Shea stood crushing the orphan train photographs against her chest, as ten years of guilt and loneliness and self-denial clamored that she speak.

"Pa?" Rand said again, beginning to sound uncertain as the silence in the kitchen lengthened.

"What—what are you doing downstairs?" Cam's own voice seemed a little frayed.

And then Shea realized all at once what they'd been doing in front of this child. In front of *her* child. A flush scorched to her hairline.

She could see the boy was flustered, too. "I—um—came—um—down for a glass of water."

"The bucket and dipper are there on the sink," Cam directed unnecessarily, following after the boy, dipping a cup of water for him as if he were a far younger child. He stood with his hand cupped to her boy's back with a gentleness that tore at Shea's heart.

How could she tell this boy who she was, if it meant destroying something so precious as this father's love? How could she hurt these people who had been so good to Owen and her, so wonderful to her boy?

Shea turned away, fumbled the photographs into her portfolio, and jerked at the strings.

"I—I was just going off to bed myself," she said.

Her voice was trembling, but she didn't even try to control it. "So I bid you good night."

"Good night," the boy and his father echoed.

Once she'd been swallowed up in the shadows of the dining room, Shea looked back at her son. In the lift of Rand's arced eyebrows and the quirk of his mouth, she rediscovered the man who had been his father. She caught the play of a dimple that reminded her suddenly of her sister Mary Margaret. And though she was seeing Rand Gallimore with new eyes, she realized this boy was everything she dreamed he would be.

Then as she watched, Cam bent close to the boy, speaking to him with concern etching the contours of his lean face. With love in his eyes, he spoke to the boy in a way that excluded everyone else. Including her.

And in that moment Shea knew she couldn't stay on at the farm. She couldn't stand by and watch how Cam was with her son, or see proof every day that her boy was the light in Lily's world. She couldn't stay here and make the decision she had to make, the decision that could change everything and disrupt every one of their lives.

She needed time. She needed space. No matter what she'd promised Owen this morning, they had to leave.

Cameron stared after Shea, his body still thrumming with the unexpected longing her kiss had fired up in him, his mind churning with all she'd said about his son. He turned back to where the boy was drinking water as if his life depended on finishing every drop.

How much of what had gone on between Shea and him had the boy seen? Too much, Cam suspected.

But that wasn't what he needed to talk to his son about tonight. He had to speak with Rand about his adoption, tell him how he'd come to be with Lily and him. Rand needed to hear how much they loved him. Every child deserved to be secure within his family and if Rand had doubts, a father's job was to reassure him.

Cam shifted on his feet and cleared his throat. "Shea and I were talking about you just before you came down to get a drink," he began, then did his best to ignore the glance Rand slid across the rim of the cup at him. It was a glance that said he knew exactly what his father and Shea had been doing when he'd interrupted them—and it hadn't been talking.

Embarrassment scorched up Cam's jaw, but he didn't let his own discomfort deter him. "Shea seemed to think," he went on, "that you had some questions I needed to answer."

Rand set his cup on the edge of the sink. "She told you I found out about the orphan train, didn't she?"

Cam inclined his head. "She thought it would make it easier for you if she told me."

Rand looked down at his bare toes. "I—I didn't know how to tell you what I heard. I thought you'd be mad at me for listening."

Cam reached across and clasped Rand's shoulder. "It's been weeks since your aunt and I had that conversation, and you've been stewing over this ever since, haven't you?"

"I couldn't figure out why you hadn't told me about being adopted."

Cam squeezed his son's shoulder gently. "Where did you think you came from?"

"I thought you had been married and my mother ran away," the boy confessed in a rush. "I thought that's why you never talked about her. I—I thought because of that you were . . ."

Cameron squeezed again. "Were what?"

Tears rose in Rand's eyes and Cam could see how hard he was trying not to cry. "I thought you were ashamed of me."

Cam pulled his son close, cradling him against his chest as he had cradled Shea not so long before.

"Oh, Randy," he murmured. "I could never be ashamed of you. You're the finest son any man could have." A shiver of feeling crept into his own voice as he went on. "No one's ever been prouder of a boy than I am of you. I'm proud of how hard you try at school, proud of how much you help around the farm, proud that you're honest and thoughtful and kind to people. And your Aunt Lily thinks the sun comes up in the morning because you're here with us."

He felt the boy shudder in his arms. "Does—does Aunt Lily really think that?"

Cam hugged his son tighter. It was closer to the truth than the boy would ever know. "Why do you think she goes around singing in the morning the way she does?"

"I like it when she sings."

"So do I," Cam admitted. There was a time in his life when he thought Lily's song had been silenced forever. Adopting Rand had taught her a whole new melody; he'd saved her life.

Cam held onto his son in silence, feeling the warmth and life in him, a promise to the future every man wanted to believe in. And he most of all.

"Did Shea tell you anything about orphan trains?" he asked, when Rand's tears had abated to sighs and sniffling.

He felt Rand nod against his chest. "She said children were sent from the city on the orphan trains so they could have a better life. She said people out here took children because they wanted to make them part of their families."

Cameron blessed Shea for giving the boy such a comforting view of a controversial enterprise. "Well, Shea would know," he observed, his suspicions about Shea's interest in the orphan trains sharpening.

"She said you picked me off the orphan train because I was special."

Cam leaned back far enough to look into his son's face. It was tear-streaked, and his eyes were red. Cameron gently smoothed down his sleep-tumbled hair.

"You have no idea how special you were to your aunt and me," he confirmed, thinking back. "Do you remember anything that happened before we came here to Colorado?"

"I remember the old house in Missouri. There was a swing in a tree out back, and Aunt Lily used to swing me. You had a horse named Ned, and there were children next door I played with."

Rand paused to think. "And I remember being in church. I remember sitting in the front of it, not like we sit sometimes in the rows of benches. And Aunt Lily was on the edge of this little stage."

Cam stared at him. "You really remember that?" Rand couldn't have been more than two years old when they'd gone and gotten him in St. Joe. "Well, that's a very good thing for you to remember. It was the day we got you. The day you picked us."

Rand sniffed in surprise. "I picked you?"

Cameron could see that day now just as clearly as when he'd described it to Shea earlier. He remembered the terror in Lily's eyes and how afraid he'd been that he was making a mistake by forcing her into this.

"When some of the children saw your Aunt Lily's face, they ran away."

"Because of her burns, you mean?"

Cam nodded. "But you came up to her and put your hand right on her cheek. And we knew the moment you did that you were meant to be our boy."

He hugged Rand close again, and his own throat went tight as Rand hugged him back. "Don't doubt for a moment how much we love you," he whispered hoarsely. "No two people could be more pleased and proud of any boy than we are of you. No parents could love their son more. If you ever have any doubts about that, I want you to come to me. To me or your Aunt Lily."

"All right," Rand promised.

They clung together for a moment more before Cam stepped away. "Are there any more questions you want to ask me?"

Rand thought for a moment, then beamed up at him. "No, Pa."

Cam let out his breath, feeling weak-kneed and battered, yet strangely content.

"I'm going to tell your Aunt Lily that you and I had this talk," Cam warned him. "And I wouldn't be surprised if there are things she'll want to say to you, too. But I don't want you worrying about that. She loves you every bit as much as I do. She's every bit as proud of you as I am. You understand me?"

"Yes, Pa," the boy answered.

"Good," he said on a nod. "Then let's head on up to bed. Dawn seems to come earlier than I ever expect it to."

"But in the morning Aunt Lily will be singing, won't she?"

Cam reached to douse the light. "You bet she will."

He heard his son's voice in the dimness. "Pa?"

"Yes."

"You shouldn't be embarrassed that I caught you kissing Shea. I think she's really pretty."

Cam burst out laughing. "So do I," he agreed and slung his arm around Rand's shoulders.

EIGHT

"*I* think I've got just what you're looking for, Mrs. Waterston," Agnes Franklin, the buxom proprietress of the millinery shop on Sixteenth Street, assured Shea as they climbed the flight of exterior stairs that led to the rooms above her shop.

Shea certainly hoped Mrs. Franklin was right. It was Monday afternoon, and she and Owen had been traipsing around Denver since early this morning making inquiries and looking at rooms to let. So far, they hadn't found anything even remotely appropriate for a studio. Each disappointment left Shea feeling a little more frantic about leaving the farm.

Mrs. Franklin jingled her ring of keys and stopped on the landing. "Mr. Allen kept a photographic studio here for well over a year, then just picked up and moved back to the States. *And* he left owing me a full month's rent!"

While Mrs. Franklin unlocked the door, Shea did her best to evaluate the studio's location. The place was half a block off Denver's busy Larimer Street, tucked

into an alley between two respectable shops. The building was brick, neatly kept and with freshly painted
trim. The steps themselves were in good repair and
hemmed by a stylish wrought iron banister.

"Now don't you mind the mess," Mrs. Franklin
went on. "The rooms have been vacant for months,
and with so many women wanting new hats this fall, I
haven't had a moment to get up here and clean things
properly."

The older woman's words proved all too true. Shea
lifted her skirts so they wouldn't drag in the dust as she
stepped into the first of several spacious rooms. Mrs.
Franklin had clearly been using the place for storage;
boxes of feathers and fabrics and trims overflowed
across the floor. An army of spiders had strung their
intricate lace across the corners, and there were signs of
mice. Though the place was far from habitable, Shea
could see potential here.

With the addition of a rug, some chairs, and a gallery of photographs, this entry hall would make a perfectly adequate reception area. To the right was a small
second room with windows overlooking the street
that was big enough for a bed and a few personal belongings.

But it was the studio through a wide double doorway beyond the entry hall that settled things. A large
skylight facing north provided ideal illumination for
taking photographs. They had access to the roof so they
could lay out their negatives to print in the sun, and a
small side room—a closet, really—had obviously been
used as a darkroom by the previous tenant.

Shea haggled over price, then gave Mrs. Franklin
nearly every cent she had toward their first month's
rent. If they meant to eat, she'd have to get the studio
up and running almost immediately.

With a final bit of advice about which merchants in the neighborhood to patronize and which to avoid, Mrs. Franklin handed Shea the keys and went back to her customers.

Shea took another turn around the rooms before she came to where Owen was hovering just inside the door. He was standing wringing his hat in his hands, seeming so unsettled it was all Shea could do to keep from throwing her arms around him as if he were a six-year-old.

"Well, then, old dear," she began. "I've rented this studio for the winter and decided to live here in town."

Owen furrowed his brow and looked around the rooms again. "Cabin?" he reminded her.

"I know Cameron has offered us a perfectly good place to spend the winter," she began, "but I don't think it would be very convenient to have a studio here and stay out at the farm."

"Not far."

In truth it wasn't all that far, a little more than half an hour's ride. Cameron and Rand made the trip twice every day, but Shea's determination to break her bond with the Gallimores didn't leave room for negotiation.

"It would seem like a very long way if the weather was bad," she pointed out. "And there have been several holdups out that way."

"Like it there," Owen insisted.

Owen almost never argued. That he was arguing now gave an indication of how very strongly he felt about staying with Cam.

"I know you like being at the farm," she conceded. "Cam understands things, doesn't he?"

Owen hung his head.

"I know you haven't had anyone who understands about the war since Simon died," she offered consolingly, thinking of her husband and the secrets she'd never realized he had.

Owen nodded, then nudged against her arm like a cat that wanted petting. She curled her fingers around his sleeve, massaging with her thumb.

"Would you—" She took a breath, surprised at how it tugged at her that Owen might value his and Cam's common past above the years of her companionship. Still, if he felt safe with Cameron Gallimore, Shea couldn't begrudge Owen that security. "Would you like me to talk to the judge and see if he'll let you stay on at the farm?"

Owen glanced up at her and then away.

"I really wouldn't mind being here in Denver by myself," she went on, encouraging him. "After you've ridden back to the farm for the night, I could retouch and mount the prints we need to deliver the following day."

A spark of what seemed to be genuine insight fired up in Owen's eyes, almost as if he could see past her explanations to the conflicts she was harboring. Still, Owen had no way of knowing Rand had come west on an orphan train, and he certainly wasn't privy to her belief that the boy was her son.

Owen's mouth puckered as if he were tasting bitter fruit. "Stay, Sparrow," he murmured and covered her hand with his. "Stay with you."

Shea thanked him, feeling as if she had forced him to make some sort of impossible choice. "We'll do well here," she whispered. "I promise."

It was almost dark when they got back to the farm, and by the time they'd seen to the horses, Lily was putting dinner on the table.

"Did you have a productive day?" Cameron asked once they were settled and had spoken the blessing.

Shea forked pot roast, carrots, and potatoes onto her plate. "Indeed we did. I've taken a very nice studio on Sixteenth Street. It's knee-deep in dirt and needs to be scrubbed from bottom to top. But once I've spruced it up and found some secondhand furniture, it'll be perfectly adequate."

"We've got some old furniture out in the barn," Rand volunteered, "don't we, Pa? Maybe we can let Shea have some of that."

Rand's offer warmed her and she smiled at him across the table. It was proof of her boy's generous heart.

"Most of the pieces out in the barn are pretty rickety," Cam put in, "but we'll have a look."

Rand grinned at her. "And I can come by after school and help. Except on Wednesdays; Wednesdays I have violin lessons."

She knew she should refuse him outright, but the prospect of having time with Rand drew her irresistibly. Now that she knew he was her son, she had so much to learn about him, so much she wanted to share and show him and teach him. She didn't delude herself. She knew each moment with her son was stolen time, time Cam and Lily would never allow her if she told them the truth, time she'd have to fight to claim if she meant to get him back.

"Well, we surely wouldn't want you to miss your violin lesson, but I'd welcome the help of a big, strapping lad like you any other day," she found herself saying. "Goodness knows, I need to get the studio open if we mean to eat."

"I'll come by and lend a hand, as well," Cam volunteered.

Shea looked up at him, torn by gratitude and dismay. She'd decided to take a place in town so she could escape this constant contact with the Gallimores. She was just opening her mouth to refuse when Lily mumbled something under her breath.

"I beg your pardon?" Shea asked, sure she'd misunderstood.

"I—I said," Lily murmured, her voice quivering ever so slightly, "that I'd like to help, too."

Everyone at the table turned to where Lily was closely examining the pile of carrots on her plate.

"You mean you'd be willing to come into town and help me put the studio in order?" Shea croaked incredulously.

Lily's mouth crimped and the color receded from her cheeks. "Y-y-yes."

"But Aunt Lily," Rand burst out. "You never go to town!"

Shea looked across the table at Cam, who was chewing at the corner of his mustache and looked every bit as baffled by Lily's offer as she was.

No matter how incomprehensible that offer was, Shea knew she couldn't refuse it. No matter how much distance she'd hoped to put between herself and the Gallimores, that Lily had volunteered to leave the farm was a miracle happening before their eyes. It didn't matter why Lily had made this choice. What mattered was that she had.

"Well, then," Shea said, doing her best to sound matter of fact. "I'd certainly welcome your help. There's lots of work to do, and you're so good at making things pretty."

As if she'd suddenly realized what she'd done, Lily raised one hand to her withered cheek. Lily was already worrying about going into town, wondering how people would respond to her.

Shea didn't give her a chance to change her mind.

"Now haven't I seen a veiled bonnet around here some-where?" she puzzled.

"It's on the hat rack in the parlor, isn't it, Lil?" Cam answered.

Lily turned on her brother, her eyes wide with re-proach. She'd clearly expected Cam to rescue her from this momentary madness and was stunned by his de-fection.

"I really do need you, Lily," Shea went on, clasping Lily's hand and feeling how cold her fingers were.

"I—I suppose I could come just once and help you clear away the worst of the mess," Lily conceded.

"Thank you for agreeing to help," Shea said. "I'll expect you first thing in the morning."

"Tomorrow?" Lily squeaked.

"I'd planned to take the carriage into town tomor-row, anyway," Cam put in.

"Oh, well, yes," she conceded, already fluttering with nervousness. "I suppose I can ride in with Cammie in the morning."

Shea wanted to take this pale, slim woman in her arms and tell her it was going to be all right, that once she'd mustered her courage to do this, it would get easier. She wanted to tell her that neither she nor Cameron would let anyone hurt her. But even if she did, Lily would never believe her.

"Good," Shea answered instead. "I'll expect you at the studio about eight o'clock."

Rand carried most of the dinner conversation after that with tales from school.

Once Shea had helped Lily wash up the dinner dishes, she grabbed a shawl and headed outside. The move into town wasn't going at all the way she'd envi-sioned, and she needed a breath of air to reflect on this change of plans. But when she stepped out onto the porch, she found Cameron leaning against one of the posts smoking one of the slim, dark cheroots he indulged in now and then.

She didn't say so much as a word to him, just drew the tails of her shawl more closely around her and stared out toward the faint sawtoothed ridge just barely visible in the distance.

"I want to thank you for whatever it was you said that made Lily offer to go into town," he finally murmured, breaking the silence between them.

"I didn't say anything much. You heard her; she made the offer of her own accord."

He shook his head. "Emmet and I have been trying to coax her into Denver for years, but she just wouldn't go."

"Well, maybe the time's just right," Shea offered, looking up at him. "Maybe having complete strangers foisted upon her has worn down her reserve."

One corner of Cam's mustache twitched in wry amusement. "Well, whatever it is, I'm grateful."

Shea acknowledged the comment with a nod of her head.

He looked back toward where the mountains lay dark and passive off to the west. He drew on his cheroot then tossed it away in a smooth, glowing arc. "I take it this means you and Owen have decided not to stay at the cabin."

Shea felt the heat creep into her cheeks. "As generous as your offer was, I believe Owen and I will do better with our photography if we live in town."

Cam hesitated, frowned, and then turned back to her. "It isn't what happened between us the other night that made you—"

"No!" Shea denied, her cheeks burning hotter. It wasn't the kiss. It wasn't the rich, dark roux of emotions that kiss had set bubbling between them that made her want to leave.

Realizing Rand was her son was what prevented her from accepting Cam's offer. Her indecision and her impotence when it came to declaring herself made it impossible for her to stay on the farm. She'd spent ten years yearning for this child. Now if she meant to claim him, she'd have to destroy this home, this family. Destroy everyone involved, including Rand, and she couldn't bear being reminded.

Cam shifted uncomfortably beside her. "What I mean to say," he went on, "is that I didn't intend for that kiss to happen. What I mean to say is that I can— control—myself where you're concerned."

Shea glanced up at him, pleased to have something to divert her from her own irresolute thoughts. "Now, isn't that just the kind of compliment every woman yearns to hear from a man who's kissed her?"

She hadn't realized how stiffly he'd been holding himself until she heard him chuckle and saw the line of his shoulders soften.

He rubbed at his chin and something that might have been a smile curled one corner of his mouth. "It isn't that I didn't enjoy it," he amended.

"I suppose I should be grateful to hear that."

He hitched an eyebrow in her direction. "Does that mean that you enjoyed it, too?"

Oh, God help her, yes! Her mouth tingled just remembering how his lips had moved on hers, how his tongue had explored her. Her body ached to feel the imprint of his again, with the need to feel his arms around her, drawing her close. He'd stirred to life things she had never experienced. He'd given her her first, lush taste of unruly passion.

Liam's father had been as shy and as unseasoned as

she was the night they'd come together. Simon had been kind, but years older than she and ill most of their married life.

For all the semblance of a staid, almost monastic existence, Cameron knew what a woman wanted. He knew how to give her pleasure. Shea understood that instinctively with just one kiss. But she couldn't let this unwelcome attraction influence the decisions she had to make.

She drew her shawl closer still. "I thought the kiss was lovely," she answered.

He leaned closer, bending over her. "I was hoping for a more enthusiastic adjective."

His breath feathered over her face. She could feel his warmth through her clothes. She longed to raise her mouth to his, taste the flavor of him again, and chance whatever came. But Shea Waterston was a practical woman, a woman who recognized danger when she saw it. So instead she stepped away.

He drew back as well and looked off toward the mountains again. "No," he agreed. "That wouldn't have been wise. Not for either one of us."

She was glad he understood that her responsibilities came first—just as his did—and yet the hot tremble of unrequited anticipation was slow to die in her. She stood there not wanting to turn and go back into the house, yet not knowing what to say to him, either.

"So when do you think you will be ready to open the studio?" he asked her.

She let out her breath, grateful he'd bridged the gap between them, glad they had something to talk about that didn't involve either Rand or that soul-deep kiss.

"Longer than I'd like," she admitted. "If I could open the studio by mid-November, I'd be able to take advantage of people who want portraits done for Christmas."

"Do you need money for supplies and groceries until then?" he inquired.

"Oh, Cam!" she breathed and turned to where that strong, half-illuminated profile stood out sharply against the deeper dark beyond the porch. She couldn't remember more than a time or two in her life when anyone had been so thoughtful, or so generous. "If our money arrives from New York anytime soon, we'll be all right. I think the shopkeepers will extend credit to me until I establish myself."

"Good," he told her and straightened as if he meant to go into the house. "Good. I just want you to know you can come to me if you need—well—if you need anything at all."

"I will," she promised. "Cam?"

He paused, looking down at her.

It was her turn to avert her eyes. "You've been really good with Owen these last weeks. He says you understand what happened in the war."

Though he didn't move, she sensed a sudden and peculiar tension coil through him. It was a moment before he spoke, and when he did his voice was low.

"The war scarred everyone who fought in it," he answered carefully. "It scarred folks who had no reason to be hurt."

He was most decidedly speaking of his sister, but Shea sensed his empathy ran deeper than that. To Owen, and maybe Dr. Farley as well, who'd fought for the South. Hearing Cam speak of it made Shea wonder what the war had done to him and how he managed to hide his scars so well.

"I just wanted to thank you," was all she said.

"That makes us even, then." He made it all the way

to the door this time. "Come on into the house. Lily
will have my head if I let you freeze to death."

I hope this isn't a mistake! Cameron thought as he drove
the carriage up Sixteenth Street and pulled to a stop at
the stairs to the left of the millinery shop.

He glanced across to where his sister sat beside him,
veiled from head to toe in black. She hadn't said so
much as a word the whole way into town. He figured
she was scared to death—and he couldn't blame her.

Lily hadn't left the farm since they'd moved into the
house not quite eight years ago. She never went anywhere to shop. She didn't attend church. She'd never so
much as set eyes on their neighbors. Coming into Denver today, Lily was like a chick breaking out of its shell,
leaving somewhere safe for worlds unknown.

Watching her, he felt like he had when he'd taken
Rand to school for the first time. Eager and apprehensive, and determined not to let his feelings show.

He just hoped everything would go all right. He
hoped he wouldn't be sorry he'd encouraged her. God
knows, he had so much to regret where Lily was concerned already.

Still, for all her evident trepidation, Lily didn't seem
cowed by being here. She carried herself like the lady
their mother had raised her to be, sitting beside him on
the buggy seat with her chin up and her back straight.

Setting the carriage's brake, Cam jumped down. As
he came around to help her to the ground, the chilly
October wind ruffled the dark scrim of her chest-length
mourning veil.

She batted the fabric back in place, took a breath
that was deep enough to visibly lift the wall of her
chest, then accepted his outstretched hand to negotiate

the steps to the ground. It was early and the streets in downtown Denver were empty, except that the proprietor of the shop next door was sweeping the walk.

He looked from his work, and dipped his head in greeting. "Morning, Judge. Miss Gallimore."

Lily's fingers bit into the muscles of Cam's arm.

Cam tipped his hat. "Morning, Mr. Nicholson."

They were halfway up the stairs to Shea's studio when Lily squeezed his arm again. "How does he know who I am?" she whispered.

Cam decided this wasn't the time to tell her she wasn't as anonymous as she thought. He patted Lily's hand reassuringly. "Mr. Nicholson was only guessing it was you on my arm."

Shea must have heard them coming up the steps, because she was waiting when they reached the landing. "Good morning!" she greeted them, and with a laugh and flourish swept them into the studio.

"Now I want you to imagine this with the cobwebs knocked down, the boxes gone, and the floors polished," she instructed breathlessly. "Imagine a nice rug out here in the reception hall, and a curtain between it and the studio. What do you think?"

"Goodness!" Lily answered with a little laugh. "Give me a moment to catch my breath!"

Shea chattered eagerly as she showed them around, extolling the virtues of northern light for making photographs, opening the door to what would be their darkroom, showing them the alcove behind it where Owen would sleep.

Since the photography wagon had been gone when he went to the barn for early chores, Cam surmised Shea had been here cleaning since before sunup. God knows she looked it. Her hands and the apron around her waist were smudged with black, and her hair frizzed around her head like a halo of down. But beneath the sheen of perspiration on her brow and the bit of fuzz stuck to one cheek she was glowing with excitement.

She loved this. He could feel her enthusiasm as if she were giving off sparks. He could feel them crackle along his skin, and saw that Lily was energized by her, too.

Before he knew it, Lily had whisked off her bonnet and was taking a folding rule from her reticule. She measured the width of the doorway between the reception room and the studio.

"Green curtains, I think," Lily was saying, half to herself. "Velvet would be lovely, but I think we could make do with something not quite so grand."

"I just knew you'd know how to make this place presentable," Shea agreed.

"And wallpaper," Lily went on. "The reception room needs just the right wallpaper to set if off. And brass sconces . . ."

With a frown of practicality Shea gently reined in Lily's enthusiasm. "I can't afford wallpaper, or sconces, either. We'll only be here until the roads are passable in the spring, so I daren't spend much on decorating."

"Well, then, we use paint. A nice soft color, something that will flatter the ladies' complexions. Cammie will paint the reception room for you."

"I will?" Cam spoke up. But then, he would have agreed to anything short of highway robbery to see his sister so bright and animated. "Maybe I can get Emmet to help."

"Emmet!" Lily laughed and wrinkled her nose. "He may be unsurpassed when it comes to using a scalpel, but he doesn't know one end of a paintbrush from the other. Do you remember the time, Cammie, when you asked him to help you paint the fence?"

Cameron shot an explanatory look in Shea's

direction. "He ended up spattered from head to toe, and with picket stripes all down his trousers."

Shea bit her lip to hold back a smile. "Owen paints; so do I. And it sounds as if we're a good deal more accomplished than our friend the doctor."

Cameron laughed and the tension seeped out of him. Lily was doing fine here. In a few more minutes she would be tying an apron around her waist and taking up a broom. She was safe here, and he knew he could count on Shea to keep her safe.

He was preparing to head for his office when someone thumped insistently on the door to the studio. Lily started in surprise and lost her smile.

Shea turned toward the reception room, her features sharp with curiosity. "I'll just go see who that is."

Cameron followed her and arrived just as she opened the door. A ragtag boy about Rand's age stood outside.

"Why, Tyler Morran!" Shea greeted him as if she knew him well. "Whatever are you doing in Denver?"

"Pa and me come to town for the winter," the boy said. "Pa's been coughing something fierce since the weather got cold, so I figured town'd be the place for him this winter."

"How on earth did you find me?" she asked him.

"I sweep up over at the Golden Spur on Blake Street," he told her, "and heard a lady photographer was opening up a studio. Then I saw your photography wagon parked in Mr. Johanson's livery stable and figured I'd stop by."

Cameron moved up a little closer behind Shea, taking note of the boy's rumpled hair and dirty face, his ragged shirt and inexpertly mended trousers.

He could tell by the way Shea's mouth narrowed that she was every bit as appalled by the boy's appearance, but when she spoke it was clear she was more concerned about other things. "It's Tuesday, Ty. Why aren't you in school?"

He studied the toes of his battered boots. "Me and school don't get on too good," he explained to her.

Cam saw concern for the boy gentle her features. "Are you here looking for work, Ty?"

"Well, yes, ma'am, I am," the boy answered. "Like I said, I been sweeping up some, and I work at the livery when Mr. Johanson needs me. I figured maybe you'd be needing some help—like up in the mountains."

Shea reached out to the boy and curled her hand around his narrow shoulder. "And a fine helper you are, too."

The boy's face lit up like the Fourth of July.

"Well, let me see," Shea went on. "I suppose I'll be needing someone to sweep up here, and maybe run some errands."

"I could do that," Ty assured her. He scuffed his boot soles and stepped into the studio. "And it looks like you got the makings of a fine place here, too."

The boy looked up at Cam and nodded, as if he had been raised to be polite. Then his gaze moved beyond Cam to where Lily stood in the studio doorway.

Before anyone could stop him, Tyler Morran stepped in close and looked up at her. "What happened to your face?" he wanted to know.

Cam turned, ready to grab this ragamuffin by the collar and haul him out the door. But when he saw Lily was nearly as absorbed in the boy as he was in her, he decided to wait.

"I got burned in a fire," she answered, tipping her chin just a little so he could see the scars more clearly.

The Morran boy looked at them intently. "I bet that hurt."

"It did," Lily confirmed.

"It hurt anymore?"

"Not at all."

"Good," he said, and just that quickly, the boy moved on to the things that were more interesting and important. "So are you a lady photographer, too?"

Cam saw the twinkle of appreciation come into Lily's eyes. "No, I'm not a lady photographer," she answered. "I came to help Shea get ready to open the studio."

"Me, too," Ty agreed and turned to where Shea stood watching them. "So, Mrs. Waterston," he asked, "what is it you want us to do to help you?"

Shea made hasty introductions, then offered Lily an apron and broom, and dispatched Ty to the store.

As they scurried off in all directions, Cam slumped back against the wall and let out his breath in a whoosh. He'd known that, no matter how careful they were, Lily was bound to confront a stranger eventually. That this boy—this child—had faced her, looked at her scars, and then dismissed them, was something for which Cam was profoundly grateful.

He didn't stay long after that. He kissed Lily's cheek and squeezed Shea's arm by way of thanks. He went off to the law offices feeling more lighthearted than he had in months.

Fresh paint always smelled like new beginnings. Hopes and aspirations. Dreams dreamed and promises made.

Shea snipped off the thread she'd been using to hem what was going to be a pair of green twill drapes and looked with some amazement around her studio. When she'd rented these three dusty rooms she hadn't meant for this to be a new beginning. She'd imagined it as a way station, a place to spend the winter, a way to break her ties to the Gallimores. But the Gallimores didn't seem ready to let her go.

As Shea rose from the table beneath the skylight, Lily Gallimore looked up from where she was industriously stitching on her half of the drapes. "These are going to look wonderful," she enthused.

Shea paused to stroke the dark green twill. *Everything* was going to look wonderful when they were done. Mrs. Franklin had come up from the millinery shop this morning to have a look and had oohed and aahed over the improvements. Though Lily had turned the scarred half of her face away, she had allowed herself to be introduced. Lily was opening to the world one petal at a time, and Shea was continuously amazed by her courage.

"I'm just headed out to see how the painting's going," Shea told her and turned toward the entry hall.

Of course her gaze immediately fell on Rand, with his paint-speckled face and air of concentration. Her heart turned over every time she saw her child. She wanted to go to him, dab at him with a cloth dipped in turpentine, touch him, and make sure he was real. But doing that would have been unseemly, too intimate an act for a mere friend. It would have revealed far more than she was ready for anyone to know about her relationship to the boy, so Shea held back.

"So what do you think?" Cam asked, drawing her attention from his son to where he was balanced on the second-to-last step on the ladder. She turned and for a moment was content to just watch him paint. There was something soothing and hypnotic about his long, smooth brush strokes, something in the grace of his movements that pleased her.

"You missed a spot," she pointed out.

He arched an eloquent eyebrow in her direction.

"You planning to climb on up here and do your own painting, missy?"

"Rand and I painted yesterday," she reminded him. "But I do think it's fortunate you have the law to fall back on so you don't have to earn your keep painting walls."

"I don't know," Cam countered, tapping his brush against the rim of the paint bucket. "It seems to me Michelangelo got his start just like this."

"No," Shea corrected him. "What Michelangelo painted was *ceilings*."

"Who's Michelangelo?" Rand piped up.

Shea smiled down at where the boy was dabbing at the baseboard. "He's a man who painted and sculpted in Italy several hundred years ago."

"He painted ceilings in churches," Cam added.

"He's one of the world's most gifted artists," Lily said, coming up behind them. She flashed Shea a smile. "This may not be art, but I do like the color *very* well."

They'd picked a warm beige tone, softened with the slightest hint of rose. Shea had managed to find a scrap of figured rug at the mercantile in shades of rose and green, probably a remnant from the carpeting in one of the new brick mansions going up at the end of Fourteenth Street.

Shea nodded. "I like the color, too."

"Yes," Owen agreed, looking up from where he was cutting in around the doorjamb.

Just then, Shea heard running footsteps on the stairs and Ty Morran burst in the door.

"I came as soon as I could," he puffed. "Sweeping up at the Golden Spur on Saturday morning's a 'normous job! But I'm here now. You got painting you want me to help you with?"

He'd bathed since the last time Shea had seen him,

and though the clothes he wore were faded and patched, at least they were clean. She ruffled his curly hair and ushered him toward the others. "I think you know everyone, except maybe the judge's son, Rand."

Ty sized Rand up, then extended his hand. "Glad t' know you."

Rand put down his paintbrush, scrubbed his palm against his pants, and took Ty's hand. "I'm pleased to meet you, too."

As they shook, Shea couldn't help noticing the differences between the two boys. Rand was tall and, even spattered with paint, had an undeniable poise and presence. Ty, thin and wiry, was excitable as a bantam rooster. Even now that his hair was clean, curls whipped up in all directions. His clothes seemed a size too big and were more than a little askew.

"What I need, Ty," Shea began, "is for you to run to the mercantile." She crossed the studio and took several things from the table. "I need thread just this shade—" She gave him a length of green from the wooden spool. "—and thirty curtain rings like this one. You can tell Mr. Sands to put everything on my account."

"Sure enough," he assured her and pocketed the things she'd given him.

"May I go, too, Pa?" Rand asked as Ty turned for the door. "You gave me my allowance this morning—"

"And it's burning a hole in your pocket," Cam observed.

"I put *half* of it by for Christmas," the boy wheedled.

"Oh, let him go," Lily said with a shake of her head. "He won't be happy until he's bought another of those tin soldiers he's been collecting."

"Since your aunt says it's all right," Cam agreed,

picking up his brush again, "you can go. But do your best to stay out of trouble."

Not half an hour later, Rand came pounding up the stairs and burst inside. "Pa!" he shouted. "You've got to come help! It's Ty!"

"What is it?" Shea demanded, rushing toward Rand, who stood hovering in the doorway. "Is he hurt? Is it his father?"

"The sheriff's got him!" Rand reported, his eyes gone wide.

Shea stumbled back a step, colliding with the breadth of Cameron's chest. He curled his hands around her arms to steady her, and for a moment she let herself lean against him. She'd forgotten how good it felt to have someone there when you needed them.

"What does the sheriff want with him?" Cam asked.

"He says he's going to haul Ty off to jail!"

Cam shifted one hand to the small of Shea's back and urged her forward. "Well, let's just go see what's happened here," he offered quietly, "before we jump to any conclusions."

They didn't have far to go. Just as they started down the stairs to the street, the sheriff came around the corner of the building, dragging Ty by the scruff of his neck.

"Ty!" Shea cried and flew down the steps to the boy wriggling in the sheriff's grip.

"He yours, ma'am?" the sheriff asked her.

"No, he's not," she answered laying her hand on Ty's shoulder, claiming him in spite of the denial. "But he was on an errand for me just now, so you'd better tell me what's happened."

"I'm afraid I'm going to have to arrest the boy for thievery."

"Thievery!" she echoed. Shea looked down at Ty's

bowed head. He wasn't even denying the accusation. She squatted down beside him so she could look into his face. "Did you take something from the mercantile?" she asked him.

Ty shook his head.

"Did you pick someone's pocket?"

"No."

"What exactly did he do, Sheriff Cook?" Cam asked, reaching the bottom of the steps with Rand close at his heels.

"He stole those clothes off Mrs. Gordon's wash line," the sheriff reported.

Shea saw bright red shame creeping up Ty's jaw.

He'd taken those sad, ill-fitting clothes, Shea realized. Those patched and mended trousers. That faded shirt. If Ty was going to go to the trouble of stealing something to wear, why on earth didn't he steal something in better condition?

"Ty?" She curled her palm around his arm and drew him closer. "Did you take the clothes, Ty?"

The boy's flush deepened.

"Did you take them?"

He raised his eyes to hers. She could see that he was trying not to cry, but those pretty brown eyes were suspiciously shiny.

"I took a suit of clothes for both Pa and me," he admitted, his gaze never leaving hers. "I picked the oldest and the holiest ones I could find 'cuz I figured nobody'd miss 'em."

Shea patted the boy, pleased that he'd told her the truth, though she was faintly appalled by his reasoning. He'd taken these clothes because they were someone else's castoffs, because he didn't think he deserved anything better. That filled her with outrage that had nothing to do with his dishonesty.

She looked up at the two tall men towering over them. "Well, what are we going to do about this?"

"I can't do much but put the boy in the hoosegow, if Mrs. Gordon presses charges," Sheriff Cook informed her.

Shea wasn't about to let Ty go to jail. She wondered briefly if she should ask where Ty's father was, so Sam Morran could assume responsibility for his son. The instant the thought crossed her mind, she rejected it. From what she'd seen and heard, Sam Morran wasn't capable of taking responsibility for himself, much less for Ty.

"Would it be possible for me to pay this Mrs. Gordon to replace the clothes?" she asked him.

The big man scowled. "I don't rightly know that'd do much good. Not like keeping the boy in a cell for a night or two. Gotta catch a thief young and teach him stealing's wrong. There wouldn't be so damn much crime in this part of Colorado if folks would just beat a boy black and blue when he strays from the straight and narrow."

There had been several spectacular robberies around Denver in the last few months. Just last week, the stage had been stopped by five armed men and the strongbox opened. Still, Shea was appalled that the sheriff would advocate beating and sending a boy of Ty's tender years to jail.

"Well, then, Sheriff," Shea went on, "if what you want him to learn is responsibility, I'll give Mrs. Gordon a reasonable price for the clothes and see that Ty pays me back. He's working for me, anyway, so it won't be difficult to hold back a portion of his wages."

Before the sheriff could answer, Ty turned to her. "You'd do that for me, Shea? You'd pay good money to keep me out of the calaboose?"

"I'd do it once, Ty," she told him, holding his gaze with her own, "and you'll have to pay back every cent. But if you steal again—if you take so much as a stick of licorice candy—I won't lift a finger to help you."

"I won't steal anymore. Honest, I won't." There was conviction in his voice when he made the promise.

Cameron nodded his approval. "So what do you say, Dan? Will you let Mrs. Waterston handle this?"

"Aw, Cam!" The rangy sheriff snuffed and spat. "You know I don't hold with mollycoddling law-breakers."

"He's just a kid, Dan," Cameron nudged him. "And Mrs. Waterston's willing to vouch for him."

Sheriff Cook blew out his breath. "All I can do is talk to Mrs. Gordon."

Cam patted the sheriff's shoulder. "Thanks, Dan. We'll be upstairs painting until the end of the day."

Only when things were settled did the sheriff turn his attention to other matters. "So, Mrs. Waterston, you're opening a photographic studio up in Mr. Allen's old quarters, are you?"

Shea came to her feet, resting her hands lightly on Tyler's narrow shoulders. "I expect to open in the middle of the week. Would you be thinking of having a portrait made?"

The sheriff gave her a sheepish smile. "I might just. I got me a daughter in Omaha who's been asking me for a picture."

"I'd be happy to do one for you, then," she invited him.

"You having a grand opening and all, Mrs. Waterston?" he wanted to know.

"I thought I might." It had been on Shea's mind all morning. Once the rug was down, the curtains hung, and the furniture in place, the studio was going to look marvelously elegant. "We invited a few people in when we opened in Nebraska City last winter. It was a good way to drum up business."

And Shea would need all the business she could get, since she'd just agreed to pay Ty's debt as well as her own.

"I should think that would be a wonderful way to showcase your photographs and let people see what you can do," Cam offered, thinking aloud. "I'll warrant you could sign people up for portrait appointments while they're here."

"I bet Aunt Lily would help with food and stuff," Rand put in.

"I've been thinking about putting a notice in the newspaper . . ." Shea murmured.

"And between us," Cam added, "Emmet and I know pretty much everyone worth knowing in Denver. We could start issuing invitations."

The idea of having an opening seemed to have taken on a life of its own. Shea felt a little stunned by how quickly it was taking shape. "Well, I suppose we could have everything ready by next Saturday night."

And how much she had to do between now and then!

"You will stop by later to let us know what Mrs. Gordon has to say about the clothes, won't you, Dan?" Cam suggested as the sheriff turned to go.

"I sure will." Sheriff Cook paused as he was turning to go. "And Cam?"

"Yes?"

The sheriff grinned. "I just wanted you to know, I think that pink stripe you're wearing looks damn fine down the middle of your mustache."

NINE

Was everything ready? Shea pressed her hand against her midriff to calm the nervous flutters, and tried to think what more she had to do to get ready for the opening. The punch was made, the food laid out, and the rooms—

She looked around with a swell of pride. The rooms had been positively transformed. Here in the reception area, the rug and the fresh paint complemented each other perfectly. Three wooden armchairs sat shoulder to shoulder along the wall opposite the door. Samples of her portrait work hung in a double row above them. On the shawl-draped table that served as Shea's appointment desk lay a stereopticon and a selection of cards made from the photographs they'd taken during their travels.

With the green twill curtains tied back, Shea could see into the studio proper, where a green velvet chair, a chest-high Grecian column, and several potted ferns stood beneath the skylight ready for posing. Just as the studio in New York had been Simon's domain, this was hers. That felt good, empowering, and even after all this time, oddly liberating.

As she waited for their guests to begin to arrive, Owen wandered out of the alcove behind the darkroom wearing a freshly laundered shirt, a string tie, and his best vest. Though his eyes were bright, he was worrying the buttons down the front as if they were a rosary.

"Pretty, Sparrow," he said quietly when he looked up from the pewter studs.

"Thank you, old dear," she murmured and caught a glimpse of herself in the faintly spotted looking glass they'd found in Emmet's attic. Lily had recut one of her mother's old gowns for Shea, and the turquoise faille hugged the high, full curves of Shea's breasts, nipped tight at her waist, then draped gracefully into a bustle at the back of the skirt.

Shea fingered the locket that lay framed in the gown's gently V'ed neckline—the locket where she kept the frayed, yellowing newspaper clipping about the orphan trains—and considered the boy she'd found here in Denver. She smiled, thinking of how Rand burst into the studio every day after school, thinking about how bright and eager he was and how much she treasured the hours she spent with him. Thinking what a miracle it was she'd found her son after all this time.

Clutching the locket tightly in her palm, Shea ached with the decision she knew she'd have to make. She ached with the knowledge that when she did she would destroy either the Gallimores' world or every dream she'd ever had.

But then, as her thoughts drifted toward things that could only make her sad, Emmet and Ty arrived in a flurry of masculine energy to divert her.

"Boy, do you look nice!" Ty exclaimed as he burst in the door.

"So do you," she answered, smoothing down his curls.

The doctor looked her up and down, then gave a decisive nod of agreement. "Everything seems to be ready," he said. "Cam and Rand not back yet?"

Shea shook her head. "They came by earlier to take Lily back to the farm."

"It's a shame we couldn't convince her to stay," Emmet mused.

Shea patted his sleeve. "I did try to convince her."

Emmet inclined his head. "I know; so did I. I guess now that she's begun to emerge from her cocoon, I'm hoping for too much from her."

"She'll come around," Shea offered in encouragement, but before she could say more the first of their guests arrived, and Emmet began making introductions.

In the next half hour, he must have introduced her to half the town. There was Mr. Ruther, the telegraph operator; Mrs. Wyman, the cook at the Windsor Hotel; Mr. and Mrs. Sands from the dry goods store. Mrs. Fenwick brought her lovely twin daughters, Virginia and Violet, and immediately made an appointment to have the girls' portraits made.

Several ranchers in town on business asked for Shea's cards to pass on to their wives. Reverend Maplethorp wanted her to photograph the First Baptist Church's choir on the church steps before their Christmas concert. Mr. Ryerson asked her to take a picture of his house, one of the recently completed villas on Fourteenth Street, and Mr. Hense set up a time to have a family portrait made to send to his sister in Pittsburgh.

A goodly number of cowboys wandered in off the street, drawn by the sound of the fiddle music. Denver's three most eligible bachelors, the Sutherland brothers, stopped by on the way to a private party. The mayor, three city councilmen, and four of the county commissioners arrived to welcome Shea into the business community and shake their constituents' hands. Reporters from all three of Denver's newspapers came by, and the one from the *Rocky Mountain News* assured Shea that the opening would be mentioned in Monday's early edition.

The crush in those three rooms became so thick that it was nearly impossible to pass from one to the other or hear above the babble of conversation. Only Cam and Rand were missing.

Where were they? Shea wondered, watching the door and fidgeting, shaking hands and fidgeting, writing appointments in her appointment book and fidgeting.

In the midst of all that, Ty managed to weave his way through the crowd to bring Shea a glass of punch. "Mrs. Franklin thought you needed this," he told her.

Shea caught her landlady's eye and raised her cup in salute, thanking her both for the drink and for maintaining the refreshment table. Agnes Franklin lifted her own cup in reply, knowing full well that traffic to and from the studio was bound to enhance business at the millinery shop.

Shea took one sip of the punch Mrs. Franklin had sent and laughed. The punch was liberally laced with brandy.

"What's so funny?" Ty asked her.

"Just happy is all. Just pleased that the party is going so well." She took another sip of punch and slid an arm around his shoulders. "You're looking particularly handsome this evening."

Ty looked down at himself. "You should like the way I look. You bought this shirt for me."

"I just thought it might not be wise," she offered in a confidential tone, "to wear your 'borrowed' things to the party."

"Yeah, well, the shirt's real nice," he allowed and rubbed at the sleeve. "I like all these blue stripy things."

Shea smiled with a certain proprietary pride. "And what do you think of the party?"

He looked around. "I didn't suppose folks got so noisy as this when they ain't been drinking whiskey."

Shea laughed and listened to the din of a hundred voices, the clink of glasses, and people clapping to the fiddle music. If there'd been room, they would have been dancing. It reminded her of Ireland.

She smiled down at Ty. "People are pretty much the same all over. They like a good time."

"I bet with all the swells you got here, there won't be any fistfights."

Shea burst out laughing. "Are you disappointed?"

"Sort of," Ty admitted with a shrug, then leaned in close enough that she could smell the pomade Owen had used to help Ty slick down his hair. "Shea," he began, "I wanted to know how you ended up with that picture of—"

"Ty?" She squeezed his arm, interrupting him. "Isn't that your father coming in?"

Ty wheeled around. "What's *he* doing here?"

"Maybe he's come by to see you," she offered hopefully.

"He could'a seen me at home," Ty muttered and started toward where his father had come in with several rough-looking companions.

Even from across the room Shea couldn't help noticing how dissipated Sam Morran looked. His clothes

rippled loose against his ribs and flanks, and the skin of
his face lay flaccid against the bones.

No wonder Ty's been so worried about him, Shea
found herself thinking. As she drew closer, she could
see Morran had clamped a hand around the boy's
shoulder and was wavering on his feet.

"Good evening, Mr. Morran," Shea greeted him. He
gave off whiskey fumes like heat from a candle flame.
"How nice of you to stop by. I've been hoping to get a
chance to tell you what a wonderful help Ty's been here
at the studio."

"Regular little gentleman," Morran sneered.

"Well, yes he is," Shea answered for Ty's sake, confused by Morran's attitude. When she'd met him up in
the mountains he'd seemed an ineffectual father. Now
he was drunk and angry with his son, almost resentful.
But of what?

Another moment gave Shea her answer.

"Bet you're the one who's been filling his head with
all that 'Yes, ma'am' and 'No, sir' stuff he's been spout-
ing," Sam Morran accused. "Bet you're the one who
convinced him he needs to clean his teeth and take a
bath every week."

"Pa!" Ty hissed.

"I admit I *have* encouraged Ty to take care of himself," she answered evenly. "And if I've influenced him
to mind his manners, so much the better."

"You think he's too good a boy to have a pa
like me!"

"Oh, Pa!" Ty moaned.

Shea heard the misery in the boy's voice, the embarrassment, the regret—as if his father's behavior was *his*
fault.

Shea felt the heat come up in her face. "Please, Mr.
Morran," she started, holding onto her temper for Ty's

sake. "If you're determined to discuss this, let's step into the other room where we can do it privately."

"I know he comes by here every day, trying to cotton up to you," he declared, ignoring her request. "Tonight he's wearing this fancy new shirt you bought him and look how he's slicked down his hair!"

Morran's voice had taken on an even more strident note, rising above the hum of conversation. She sensed that people were faltering to silence around them, turning to watch the three of them. After a moment the music faded, too.

Shea had a mouthful of things she was aching to say to Sam Morran, but she knew this wasn't the time or place to say them.

"Shea ain't done nothing wrong," Ty spoke up, defending her. "She *pays* me to sweep up here, and she's my *friend*. All of them are my friends—Rand and Lily and the judge—"

Morran stiffened and his grip on Ty's shoulder tightened. The boy did his best to flinch away.

"I don't want my son coming here," Morran shouted, color suffusing his sallow cheeks. "I don't want you talking to him. I won't have you buying his affection with new clothes and such. He's my boy and I won't let you or anyone interfere with how I'm raising him!"

Cursing, he gave Ty a shove in the direction of the studio doorway. "Now git on home, boy," he shouted, "before I lose my temper."

Whether Morran had meant to push his son as hard as he had, or miscalculated his own strength, Ty all but flew across the room and out the open door that led to the stairs.

"Ty!" Shea cried and bolted after him in alarm.

But before she could make a grab at Ty, the boy

slammed into the waist-high baluster at the far side of the landing. He staggered with the momentum, then rebounded headlong down the steps.

"It sounds like a good party," Cam said to Rand as they pulled up their horses in front of the millinery shop. From where the studio door stood open in invitation, he could hear the rumble of conversation and the high, sweet notes of a violin. The fiddler Shea had hired for the evening was playing "Lorena."

As he was tethering his horse, Rand glanced up toward the studio. "You think Ty's there, yet?"

Cam paused and looked at his son. "You and Ty get on together, don't you, boy?"

Rand grinned at him. "Sure we do. He runs really fast and is a dead aim with a slingshot. He can juggle three chestnuts at a time, and he knows things."

Cam looped his horse's reins around the post. "What things?"

"Well, he knows how to cheat at poker, for one."

"Cheat at poker?" Cam couldn't help being taken aback. "Is—is knowing that important?"

"If you're going to gamble, I guess it is."

"Is that what Ty means to do with himself? Be a gambler?"

"Oh, no!" Rand vehemently shook his head. "Ty says playing cards is a big waste of money. While he was sweeping up over at the Golden Spur he saw some man lose a hundred dollars on a single hand of cards! But Ty says it's important to know how to cheat, in case you get into a game with someone who's doing it."

Cam couldn't fault either the Morran boy's reasoning or his good sense, though he wished Ty wasn't being exposed to life in a saloon quite so young.

"Well, I'm glad you like each other," Cam said, draping an arm around Rand's shoulders. "I think Ty needs friends like you and Shea right now."

"Him being new in Denver and all?"

That wasn't quite what he'd meant, but Cam nodded anyway. He nudged Rand toward where Shea's freshly painted sign pointed the way to the studio. "So are we going to go to this party or aren't we?"

They were halfway up the stairs when Cam heard someone in the rooms at the top start shouting. A tingle of alarm shot the length of his back.

"Go wait for me at the bottom of the steps," he instructed, his heartbeat quickening. Rand must have recognized the urgency in his tone because he obeyed without question.

Cam cupped his palm to the reassuring shape of his holstered pistol as he climbed the stairs. Up above a man was shouting, his voice loud and slurred. He heard Shea answer, quiet, insistent, and—unless he'd misjudged her—furiously angry.

He had almost reached the top of the steps when Ty came careening out the studio door. He slammed into the railing at the far side of the landing, all but toppling over it. He stumbled half a step then came rebounding directly at Cam.

The boy slammed into Cam's chest like a sack of corn, with force enough to knock both of them down the steps. Clutching Ty against him, Cam teetered and reeled, somehow managing to keep his balance on the narrow stairs.

After several frantic moments of struggle, both Cam and Ty managed to find their footing.

"You all right, son?" Cam asked, steadying the boy. Ty nodded and sniffed.

"You sure?"

Cam glanced at the people crowding out onto the landing. He immediately spotted Shea and saw she was restraining a rail-thin man who stood wavering at the edge of the top step. Cam figured this drunkard must be Ty's father.

"I'm fine," Ty insisted.

But Cam heard the faint waver in the boy's voice, felt the tremors wrack his narrow shoulders. A low, familiar hum tuned up deep inside Cam's skull.

He eased the youngster past him down the stairs. "Rand's waiting there at the bottom," he instructed. "You go stay with him while I find out what's happened here."

Ty did as he was bid, and Cam turned his full attention to Morran, who was calling curses down on his boy's head.

No matter what he'd told Ty, he really didn't need explanations. It was clear enough what was happening; this man was abusing his son.

Fighting to hang onto his composure, Cameron climbed the rest of the steps. The humming inside him tuned to a higher pitch. "I'd like to have a word with you in private, Mr. Morran," he said.

"And just who the hell are you?" Morran demanded with bleary belligerence.

"I'm Judge Cameron Gallimore, sir," he answered, his voice taut, but scrupulously polite. "Please come with me now so we won't have anything to regret about this later."

"You say what you got to say to me right here."

The drone in Cam's head gained intensity. He breathed deep and caught the faint metallic sting of blood and gunpowder in his nostrils.

"I'd like to speak to you down in the alley," Cam clarified.

"I don't want to speak to you anywhere," Morran sneered. "I mean to stay and enjoy the party."

"I will have a word with you, sir," Cam told him, stepping closer. "One way or another. Now if you'll just come with me . . ."

Something about the low, raw timbre of Cam's voice, or the way each syllable rang like a blacksmith's hammer, must have made Morran reconsider. He looked Cam up and down, straightened his shoulders, and wove past him down the stairs.

"I'll give you a word," he blurred, "but nothing more."

Cam stepped back to let him pass, taking care not to touch Morran. He took care not to think too much about how good it would feel to jam his palms against Morran's bony shoulders and shove him down the stairs. How good it would feel to mash Morran's face with his fists and consider the consequences afterward.

People spilled down the steps as they made their descent. Cam could feel them trailing in his wake, their eyes burning into his back, avid with excitement and speculation.

He heard Shea call his name, but he couldn't break his concentration long enough to answer her.

At the bottom of the steps, he brushed past Rand and Ty and herded Morran across the alley. Looming over the man, using his height and the breadth of his shoulders, Cam forced him back against the wall.

He braced his hands on either side of Morran's head and leaned in close enough to smell the whiskey on the man's breath and the stench of his unwashed body. Contempt flared up in him.

"I don't want you laying a finger on that boy of yours," he instructed, quiet as a knife thrust. "If I hear there's so much as one bruise on him anywhere—"

Cam paused and dropped his gaze to the center of
Morran's chest. "—I'll find you, Morran, and I'll cut
out your heart."

In half-light Cam saw Morran pale.

"Do you understand me?" he whispered.

Morran's head bobbed as if it were barely attached to
his body.

"Good," Cam whispered. "Good." He sucked in a
breath and stepped away.

The instant he did, Morran lit out up the street. He
stumbled, righted himself, and set off running again.
Somehow Cam wasn't surprised when Ty went after him.

Once Morran was gone, Cam's world shifted, frag-
menting, tilting beneath his feet.

People poured down the stairs to engulf him. Rand
rushed over, and before Cam could stop him, threw his
arms around his waist.

The vicious, mindless need to strike out roared
through him. Heat surged up his spine and detonated
behind his eyes. His palms burned. His scalp shifted.
He knotted his fists, fighting the white wash of fury
that leaped along his nerves—the old, acrid residue of
too much wrath and too much misery.

Cam fought the madness, taking one breath and
then another, closing his eyes, squeezing down the
clamor. Finally, he opened his eyes and looked down at
his son. His face came into focus; his words came clear.

". . . really scared Mr. Morran! I never thought a
grown-up could run so fast!"

Cam pressed his hands flat against his son's shoulders, steadying himself on the bulwark of that innocence, the sweet pure feel of that uncorrupted life.

At the periphery of his vision he saw Emmet pushing determinedly nearer. Owen trailed half a step

behind him, clear-eyed and resolute in a way Cam couldn't remember seeing him before. They did the best they could to insinuate themselves between him and the press of the crowd.

Still, men encroached, saying things Cam could not bear to hear. They praised him, complimented him. He all but came apart when someone smacked his shoulder with the flat of his hand.

Through it all he clung to Rand like a handhold in the face of a cliff and managed to weather the intrusion. He nodded when people spoke to him and tried to remember to breathe. He did his best to stay on his feet while sweat ran down his back and the shakes rumbled through him.

He caught sight of Shea at the periphery of the throng and stared at her, drinking in her sweet, unconventional beauty. He let her remind him that the world could be caring and fine and good.

As the crowd around him began to thin and Rand ran off to look for Ty, Shea inched nearer. Cam watched her approach, wanting to clutch her against him, wanting to ward her off.

Emmet stepped between them, fierce and protective. "You all right, Cam?" he asked.

Cam saw Shea's gaze sharpen. She looked from Emmet to Owen and from Owen to him. Recognition dawned across her face. She knew what this was, goddamn her.

She'd probably seen the old man like this, sweating and shaking and glassy-eyed. Cam supposed that should make him feel better. Instead he felt weak, angry with himself for being like this, for letting her see. Angry with her for being so perceptive.

Thick, black despair filled up his chest. He hated what he'd done tonight, hated that he'd had to do it.

He hated that these three people knew how much that simple act of decency had cost him.

"Cam?" Emmet's tone was sharp, reproving. "Cam!"

Shea's lush mouth bowed with distress.

Cameron swallowed hard and dragged himself back toward composure by his fingernails. He slumped back against the wall and wiped the sweat from his face with his forearm. "I'm all right."

Shea didn't look like she believed him. She reached right past Emmet as if to take his hand—then hesitated.

Cam stared at her in surprise. She really did understand how it was with him, yet he could see neither judgment nor fear in her eyes. There was nothing but empathy, nothing but solace and compassion and warmth. *And dear God, how he needed her warmth.*

He inclined his head granting her permission.

Shea grasped his hand, and with that touch something vital passed from her to him. Something warm and pure and life-affirming. He clung to her fingers as hard as he could, drawing on her vigor and letting it feed him.

"Mrs. Franklin has some brandy upstairs," she said, urging him upright. "I think you've earned a shot of it."

"I'll go see if I can round up the boys," Emmet offered and disappeared up the street.

Shea was as good as her word. She brought a punch cup and a bottle of good French brandy to the studio's little front room. As the party wound down outside, Cam slumped at the edge of the bed, watching as Shea filled and handed the cup to him. He drank down two long swallows, liking the way the brandy lit up the hollow in his chest. He closed his eyes and willed the bitter silt of the past to settle again.

"I'm sorry that happened," he told her when he had drunk enough brandy to voice the words. "I'm sorry I caused a scene and spoiled your—"

"Now what could you possibly be sorry for?" she interrupted, and startled him by stepping in close. She cupped his jaw in the curl of her palm, her touch gentle, unbearably compelling. "You kept Ty from going headlong down those stairs. You confronted his father. Maybe you even managed to put the fear of God in Sam Morran for a little while. You've no reason in this world to be apologizing."

She took the empty cup from him and filled it to the rim again. This time before she gave it back, she took a long, deep swallow of the brandy herself.

Cam fancied he could detect the taste of her, her subtle warmth along the rim of the glass when he put it to his mouth. The sensation sent a strange tingle of pleasure creeping through him.

That tingle intensified as Shea eased close again and rested her palms against his shoulders. "I think confronting Morran cost you dearly," she murmured. "Are you truly all right?"

Cam looked away. Emmet and Owen understood this. They'd gone where he'd been tonight. They knew what it was like to all but drown in the scum of fury and despair the war left in each of them. But how could Shea know? How could she understand what this was and still be here with him?

He took a long breath and nodded for both their sakes. "I'm all right."

"Then I want to thank you for what you did for Ty."

Cam glanced up at her. "I didn't do much. Not nearly as much as you've been doing."

"I'm only giving him work," she said. "You let him know he deserves something better than what he has."

"And he went off after his father anyway."

She squeezed his shoulder as if to say that didn't matter, that what Cam had done was right. He found such simple ease in that reassurance, such satisfaction in her gentleness.

"I think it's only the money Ty earns that's been keeping them afloat since they came down from the mountains," she mused.

"Was Ty's father any different then?" Cam asked.

"I only saw them together for a few minutes and didn't realize how much Morran depended on Ty," she answered. "I think his father began to drink out of loneliness and grief when Ty's mother died, and I'm sorry for him. But damn it, Cam, that boy needs someone to look after him, too. He needs a home and security. He needs to be in school."

"If they're settled here in town," he offered, "I could have the truant officer look in on them."

Shea thought that over, then shook her head. "If you did, I'm afraid they'd disappear into the mountains again."

"Then I think you're doing all you can. You're befriending Ty, giving him work—"

Shea shook her head, dismissing her own efforts. "It's not fair that there are people desperate to be parents who don't have a child," she said bitterly, "and parents who refuse to look after the children they have."

Cam saw her eyes sheen bright with tears and saw her touch the locket that lay at the base of her throat. For a moment he thought she was going to explain about the children in the photographs, the children from the orphan trains. But just then Owen appeared at the half-open doorway.

"Boys are back," he reported.

"Thank goodness," Shea breathed and stepped away.

Cam couldn't be sure if it was the boys' return or avoiding the conversation they'd been about to have that pleased her more. He pushed to his feet and followed her into the reception area.

Shea skimmed a hand along Rand's shoulders in gratitude on her way to where Ty was standing just inside the door. She smoothed his hair, his tear-smudged cheek, then hugged him against her.

"Are you truly all right?" she asked softly.

Cam draped his arm around his son. "Where was he?"

"Down at the river throwing rocks."

After the scene Ty's father had made tonight, it seemed a remarkably reasonable thing for a boy to do. "I'm glad you and Emmet brought him back. Shea's been worried."

Rand slid his father a knowing glance. "I figured she would be."

Cam pulled Rand closer. Across the entry hall he gave Emmet a grateful nod. Emmet had proved his friendship twice tonight.

It was as Ty was trying to apologize for his father that Owen exclaimed that one of the portraits was missing from the display in the entry hall.

"Now whatever could have happened to that photograph?" Shea wondered aloud, going to inspect the gap in the double row of pictures. "We put those up just this afternoon!"

Cam noticed Ty's eyes widen as he stared at the empty space. "Well, *I* didn't take it!" he declared hotly.

She turned to him. "My heavens, Ty! No one said you did! Besides, what would you want with a portrait of a perfect stranger? What would anyone want with it?"

Cam saw something in the set of Ty's shoulders and the sudden dip of his head that made him wonder if Ty knew more about the missing picture than he was letting on.

"You don't have any idea about who might have taken that print, do you, Ty?"

Ty looked up, desperation crimping deep, tight lines into that childish face. "No!" he answered. "I don't know a thing about that photograph!"

Cam took care to nod as if he believed him.

TEN

When Shea unlocked the door to the studio the Monday morning after the opening, three people were waiting on the stairs to see her photographs. Notes began to arrive at midmorning, requesting appointments. Two buxom, well-dressed sisters stomped up the stairs just after lunch and demanded that she make their portraits *immediately*.

As Shea posed the first one in the velvet armchair beneath the skylight, she couldn't help asking, "And how did you find out about my studio?"

"Oh, my dear!" she answered, beaming up at Shea. "When we saw the article in the newspaper and read how you and Judge Gallimore had befriended that young boy, sister and I said to each other, 'Now there's someone we ought to patronize,' and here we are."

"There was an article in the newspaper?"

"You mean you haven't seen it?" The second sister produced a copy of the *Rocky Mountain News* from her voluminous canvas shopping bag. "It makes you quite the heroine."

Shea scanned the column on the second page. It was more or less a factual account of what had gone on Saturday night, except that it portrayed Cam and her as if standing up for Ty were more than common decency.

Maybe this newspaper story was why Ty hadn't come by the studio this morning, Shea thought as she removed the lens cap on the camera and counted to ten. Maybe Sam Morran had seen it and wouldn't let Ty come.

Though the reporter had given neither the child's nor his father's name, Morran would surely recognize himself, and there was no telling how he'd react. When she'd met Morran up in the mountains she thought he was a negligent father, but one who truly cared for his boy. After Saturday night, she wasn't sure what kind of father he was, and she worried about Ty's safety.

As she posed and photographed the second of the two sisters, Shea's nerves began to hum. Once the women left, she grabbed up her jacket and set off to find Ty.

But Ty wasn't working for Mr. Johanson at the livery stable this afternoon. He wasn't sweeping up at the mercantile, and when she peeked through the doors at the Golden Spur, she couldn't see any sign of him there, either. The only other place Shea could think of to look for him was the shack the Morrans had rented down by Cherry Creek.

Though she tried to convince herself she wasn't afraid to face Sam Morran, Shea found herself standing in front of the building where Cam kept his office a few minutes later. Without taking time to consider the co-incidence, Shea climbed the stairs, passed through the well-appointed outer office, and knocked on the door to the private one beyond it.

When Cam shouted for her to come in, she passed

from the impersonal neatness of that outer room into the warm, tempest-tossed chaos of the sunny corner office. The overflowing shelves and filing cabinets, the tipsy towers of books and sheaves of papers, the yards of unruly clutter all belied the calm, well-ordered mind of the man who sat at his crowded desk with his back to the bank of bowed corner windows.

Shea scuffled her way through the crumpled foolscap pooled on the floor around the wastebasket and confronted him. "Have you seen the newspaper?" she asked by way of greeting.

Cam looked up from what he was writing. "Ridiculous pap," he snorted. "All we did was stand up for the boy."

Shea nodded in agreement. "Indeed it is. Still, I'm worried that Mr. Morran has seen the paper and taken it out on Ty. He was supposed to be at the studio first thing this morning, and I haven't seen hide nor hair of him."

"Do you think Morran would hurt the boy?" Cam asked with real concern.

Shea shook her head. "I don't believe he meant to put Ty in jeopardy Saturday night, but I don't trust him. Who knows what he might do if he's seen this story? I've been looking all over town for Ty and no one's seen him. I want to go over to where they live, but I—I—"

"Would you like me to go with you?"

"Oh, yes!" Shea exclaimed, and was halfway down the stairs by the time Cameron had grabbed up his coat.

The weather-beaten shack where Ty and his father lived was tucked into the alley behind one of Denver's most notorious saloons. While Cam rapped on the battered door, Shea danced a little from cold and nervousness.

If she could just see Ty was safe, perhaps the snarl of concern in her belly would ease; if she could just make sure he'd be at the studio tomorrow, she'd be able to breathe. She didn't need to lay hands on him, she told herself. But if he wasn't here, she wouldn't rest until she knew what had become of him.

"Pa?"

Shea heard the hopefulness in Ty's voice as he pulled open the door; she saw how his face fell when he realized who it was. She recognized that she wasn't the only one worried about someone today.

"Hello, Ty," Cam greeted him.

Ty looked them up and down. "What are you doing here?"

"When you didn't come by the studio this morning like you promised, I thought I'd come and find out where you were," Shea said, trying not to sound anxious and proprietary—and failing miserably.

Cam looked down at the boy. "Your pa's not at home?"

"No, sir," Ty answered.

"Do you know where he is?"

The boy shrugged, trying to pretend it didn't matter. "Some men from up in the mountains came by Saturday afternoon. It's them that took Pa drinking and got him all riled up. It's their fault he was the way he was at the party."

Shea supposed that was about as much explanation for Sam Morran's behavior as they were likely to get. Now that Ty mentioned it, she had recognized a couple of the men from the mining camp in the crush at the studio.

Cam laid his hand on Ty's shoulder. "And your pa?"

Ty hung his head. "I left him at the Golden Spur Saturday night. I ain't seen him since."

As dismayed as she was to find that Ty had been alone here all this time, Shea couldn't help drooping a little with relief. If Sam Morran was still carousing—or sleeping off a drunk—he probably wouldn't see the article in the newspaper.

"Then why don't you come back to the studio with me?" she suggested. "We've got cookies and cake left over—"

"No, thanks." Ty cut her off, then stood staring down at the toes of his boots. "I— I'm not sure I can keep sweeping up for you, either."

Shea's belly flip-flopped. If Ty wasn't coming by the studio, she'd have no way to keep an eye on him. "Did you decide that," she asked him, "because your father doesn't want you seeing me?"

Ty's gaze came up to her, those pretty brown eyes dark with worry. "I'll cause trouble if I come," he said. "Bad things will happen."

"Oh, Ty," she said, reaching out to him. "I won't let any bad things happen."

Yet here she was standing on his doorstep because she'd been afraid for him. She hadn't been able to prevent his father from belittling Ty in a roomful of strangers, or from manhandling him, either. How much trouble would *she* cause *him,* if she persisted?

She looked to Cam, willing him to come up with some way they could help.

He hunkered down and spoke to Ty in that quiet, earnest way of his. "Has your father been treating you all right, son? He doesn't hit you, does he?"

Ty's chin came up. "Oh, no! Pa never hits me."

"Because if he hurts you there are things judges can

do to make him stop," Cam said softly. "There are places you can stay where you'll be safe."

"He'd never hurt me on purpose," Ty denied. "Please, I want to stay with him. He's my pa."

Cam looked up at Shea as if he were seeking her sanction, then turned back to the boy. "Of course you can stay with your father. But I want you to know I'm going to keep an eye on things. Is that all right?"

Shea saw Ty nod before Cam continued. "You know you can come to Shea or me if you need us, don't you, Ty?"

The boy fidgeted and stared at his boots.

"You know we'd help you no matter what."

Ty glanced up, quick and disbelieving. "No matter what?"

The boy's incredulity tore at Shea. How long had it been since Ty had had someone he could turn to or depend on?

Cam's voice deepened. "We're friends, Ty. You and Shea and Rand and me. Friends help friends—always. No matter what."

Shea could tell by the shine in Ty's eyes when he looked at Cam that he believed him.

"You'll remember that, won't you, Ty?" Cameron insisted.

"I'll remember," the boy promised. Then, as if he'd accepted all he could from them, he ducked back into the cabin and shut the door.

"Do you think he'll really come to us if he's in trouble?" Shea asked as they made their way up the garbage-strewn alley toward the street.

"I think we've done all we can right now."

Tears simmered at the back of Shea's eyes. "If he were mine," she promised fiercely, thinking of Rand, "I'd take such good care of him."

"I know you would."

"I'd see he got enough to eat and had a clean bed to sleep in." Her voice quavered. "I'd make sure he went to school, and I'd keep him safe. I'm not sure that little boy back there has ever had anyone who made him feel safe!"

Her throat ached with the conviction. Shea herself had only begun to rediscover what safety was and to mark the distinction firsthand.

"You've done everything you can for him, Shea," Cameron assured her gently. "He trusts you; he likes what you can teach him. He'll come back to the studio when he feels he can."

Shea let her breath out on a sigh. "Somehow that doesn't seem like much."

As they turned up Larimer Street, Cam slid her a smile from beneath the curve of his mustache. "You know, Shea, you should have a child of your own someday."

His soft, half-teasing words ignited a fierce, raw heat beneath Shea's ribs. They ignited a firestorm of guilt, a sear of terrible confusion, a flare of hope and wonder and regret.

I do have a child, she wanted to shout at him.

Some miraculous twist of fate had brought her face to face with the boy she thought she'd lost. After years of wishing and yearning and seeking, she had finally found her son. Through circumstances too extraordinary to question, she was able to see him every day, share a portion of his life.

Now that that child had become a real and essential part of her life, she ached to acknowledge him. Though Cam was the very last person on earth with whom she should share this secret, Shea wanted to tell him about her boy—not who he was, or that she'd found him—but that she'd had a child to love, once long ago.

The secret she'd kept so long—and so well—pressed up her throat. She came so close to speaking the words that she could taste the sweetness on her tongue. She could sense the relief she'd feel by admitting the truth.

"I do have a child," she whispered.

She thought she'd spoken softly enough that Cam might not have heard, but he stopped right there in the middle of the street. He caught her hand and turned her to face him. "You do?"

Hot color flared into her face as the full scope of what she'd revealed caught up to her. In telling Cam about her son, not only had she acknowledged her boy, but she'd opened the door to scores of questions. If he asked, she'd have to own up to being a woman of easy virtue, to the shame of bearing a child who had no father. Why hadn't she remembered the contempt she'd seen in people's eyes when they realized she'd borne her child unwed and alone, when they realized her son was a bastard? Could she bear to see that in Cam Gallimore's eyes when he learned the truth? Could she face either his questions or his scrutiny?

"But, Shea, where is your child?" Cam asked her, still clasping her hand.

To say more would mean owning up to what she'd done, to becoming an outcast all over again. It would mean courting the censure of a man she liked and respected. A man who could keep her from Rand if he found her an unworthy companion.

Old, enduring guilt and bright, new fear pierced her vitals. She jerked her hand out of his grasp and fumbled for words to fob him off. "It's a very long story, I'm afraid," she said and started off up the street.

Cam caught her in three long strides. He caught her

hand again and drew it through the crook of his arm. "I'm a lawyer, Shea," he said, falling into step beside her. "I like long stories. You can spend the rest of the afternoon telling me this one."

Shea stood in the tall, bowed window of Cam's office staring up Larimer Street. Though the sun beat warm through the glass, it could not penetrate the stone-cold dread that lay at the very heart of her.

What had she done?

She linked her arms across her waist as if she could hold tight enough to keep from coming apart. Behind her she could hear Cam making tea, setting the kettle on the wood stove, unearthing a teapot and canisters from the tumult of that cluttered office.

As he boiled and brewed, as the windows steamed and a faintly herbal scent filled the air, Shea tried to fathom what had possessed her to talk about her child. She supposed that seeing Rand every day had made him real to her in a way he'd never been before. Smelling the chalk and cold on him when he came in from school, wrapping her arms around him and guiding his hands as he focused her big box camera, shaping his observations of a world he was just beginning to discover had put a face on the phantom she'd been chasing. It had made it impossible for her to deny her son a moment longer.

Shea just wished she'd found someone else to confide in.

"Tea?" she heard Cam ask.

With a shiver of dread, she turned from the window and saw that he was offering her a delicate porcelain cup and saucer. While the tea had been steeping, he'd cleared the clutter from the two leather wing chairs that sat before his desk and was waiting for her to join him.

Reluctantly she skirted his broad desk and closed the distance between them. Taking the teacup into her trembling hands, she lowered herself into one of the chairs.

Cameron settled in the opposite one and sipped his tea. "So tell me about your boy," he invited.

"My boy?" she echoed. His assumption surprised her. "How can you be sure my child is a boy?"

Cam appraised her over the rim of his cup. "I've seen the affinity you have for Rand and Ty, so I thought you might have a son—maybe one about their age."

A chill trickled down her back. Cam was far too bright, far too perceptive. He knew things without being told, knew them with a sharp and almost uncanny intuition.

"*He is* about their age," she admitted almost reluctantly.

"And where is your son that he isn't with you?"

She stared down into her cup breathless and terrified, knowing exactly where her answer would lead. "I'm not entirely certain where my son is."

"Oh?"

Shea heard a thousand inflections in that single word, and she didn't know how to respond to any of them. How could she reveal to this fine, upstanding man the things she'd done and watch disillusionment steal across his features? How could she deliberately tell him things that would taint his opinion of her forever? How could she risk his friendship when it meant so much to her?

How could she tell him even part of the truth without Cam guessing the whole of it?

"I've always thought," he observed in that deep, beguiling voice, "that the wisest place to start anything is at the beginning."

Shea gave the slightest of nods. Back in the days when Cam had been a lawyer instead of a judge, surely these walls had heard secrets far more damning than the one she had to tell.

She straightened in her chair before she spoke. "Then I suppose I should start when my sister and I left Ireland." Cam inclined his head, and Shea's voice became stronger as she remembered. "I was just sixteen when my sister Mary Margaret and I signed papers with an agency that guaranteed girls from good families passage to America and jobs when we arrived in New York."

She could almost see the day they sailed, how the mists hung low over those green, green hills, how the wind had whisked the bay to whitecaps as they spoke their good-byes. There were only the three of them left of a family of eight: Jamie standing with his new wife, determined to make his way in Ireland; proud, practical Mary Margaret, clutching her valise and impatient to be off; and Shea, not knowing where she belonged or what she wanted. It wasn't a teary good-bye. They'd wept too much over other tragedies to squander tears on a simple parting.

Shea glanced across at where Cam sat watching her, his head tipped a little to one side as if he were listening to more than her words.

"But poor Mary Margaret," she went on, "for all her excitement at coming to America, fell ill our third day at sea and died the morning after. I arrived in New York alone to take up what had been my sister's adventure.

"The agency placed me as a housemaid with a family

that lived near Washington Square. It wasn't a bad life, really. I didn't mind the work, and Mrs. O'Halloran, the housekeeper, saw we got enough to eat. But I missed my sister; I missed my family."

It was the first time she'd understood what loneliness was.

"I was having a good, loud weep about it out back of the carriage house not long after I arrived, when the coachman came to say I was scaring his horses. Michael was his name, and he gave me his handkerchief."

That handkerchief had smelled of sweat and hay and horses, honest smells she'd come to associate with her father and her brothers and home. It had made her cry all the harder, and Michael had moved in on her like she was one of his high-strung strutters. He'd put his arms around her and let her cry herself out against his chest.

"So you fell instantly in love with this coachman," Cameron prodded her.

Michael had been a lovely man. Wiry and quick and dark-haired, with wonderful eyes—rich, warm brown that crinkled at the corners.

"No," she answered after a moment. "I didn't fall in love with him; we became the best of friends. We'd walk out together in the evenings or sit on the back steps. He'd tell me about all the fine places the mistress went for tea, or about the countryside up north of the city where the master had holdings. It was a pleasant life. But then the war came—and the war changed everything."

With the mention of the war she saw the darkness creep into Cam's eyes, and when he spoke she could tell it was from that raw, cold place inside him. "War changes everything."

She leaned across and gently touched his wrist,

speaking as if she were waking him from a dream. "Cam," she said gently. "I know the war changed the world for you, but you've come a very long way since then."

He nodded after a moment, his gaze lingering on her as if he were grounding himself. He nodded slowly. "Go on," he murmured. "Tell me the rest."

Needing to put some small distance between them, she set her cup on the pile of books between their chairs and pushed to her feet. She crossed to the desk and turned to him. "Early in the war, everything seemed exciting and glorious. Parades went past the house. Several of the footmen enlisted. Then the reality of it all set in. Casualty lists went on and on. There were calls for more and more men. Riots swept the city when they began the draft."

"And Michael?" he asked as if he were anticipating her story or had heard its like before.

"He finally had to go." She twined her arms across her midriff, trying to gather her courage for what she had to admit to him. "The night before he was to leave, we sat together on the steps one last time. It was a lovely spring evening. The air was warm and I could smell the lilacs blooming at the back of the garden. Michael tried to be brave, but I could see how afraid he was. I wanted to hold and reassure him, but that wouldn't have been seemly there on the steps. So we went to his room above the stables."

Shea tightened her fingers around her arms and bowed her shoulders, curling in upon herself. Now that she'd begun, she needed to say the words before she lost her nerve. "We sat together on his little cot. I held onto him as hard as I could. He kissed me and I kissed him back. In the end—well—in the end we made a child.

By the time I realized what we'd done, Michael was dead, killed at Cold Harbor."

"And they fired you from your job when they found out about the baby." Cam didn't even phrase it as a question.

"Mrs. O'Halloran said she was sorry, but she couldn't condone what I'd done. I didn't know a soul in New York when they cast me out, but I'd saved enough of my wages to get a room. I did piecework until my little Liam was born, but afterward I fell ill . . ."

She retreated to the far side of the desk. She could feel the sun beating through the window at her back, but it did nothing to warm her. No heat could penetrate the cold, hollow places in her heart. No tears could wash away the shame of what she'd done or the longing she felt for her child.

"It was winter," she whispered, "I had no money for food or heat. My landlord turned us into the streets. Finally, I couldn't feed my child anymore."

She looked down at her hands, the hands that had held and bathed and soothed her precious boy. The hands that had laid her little Liam on the steps of a foundling home nearly eleven years before.

As if he'd heard the sob worming its way up her throat, Cam rose and went to her. He grasped her shoulders as if he could will her the strength she needed to concede the rest of it.

"If I'd kept him—" she whispered, "—he would have died."

Cam gathered her up in his arms.

"I didn't want to leave him at the foundling home."

"I know."

She panted for breath. "I loved him so much."

"I know."

She'd stood within sight of the foundling home and looked into her son's face for the very last time. She'd caressed his feathery brows and lashes, his petal-smooth cheeks, the bow of that sweet baby mouth. She'd nuzzled him one last time, breathed his scent and brushed his forehead with her lips. Then she had taken him where she knew he'd be safe.

The sobs rose in her throat, choking her. Cam spread his big warm palms against her back and sought to pull her against him.

She didn't deserve the comfort he was offering, didn't deserve to have his arms enfold her, didn't deserve the bulwark of his strength to lean on. Shea tried to twist away as the sick, raw anguish ran through her. But as hard as she pushed against him, he bound her effortlessly against the length and breadth of his body.

She struggled for a space, crushing her face into his shirtfront, giving vent to her grief and guilt that was as fierce and raw as it had been the day she'd given her son away.

Cam held her without saying a word, swaying on his feet, rocking her as if she were a child. He stroked her hair, her shoulders, the length of her back. Gradually she melted against him, resting her head against his shoulder, accepting his comfort.

When she had quieted, he bent close against her ear. "It must have taken such courage to give up your child."

For an instant Shea couldn't think, couldn't even draw breath. How could he say such a thing to her? Didn't he realize she'd given her baby away?

She raised her head, seeking censure in that strong, dark face, in those fathomless blue eyes. Instead there was understanding and tenderness.

His deep, liquid voice poured over her. "Don't

doubt for a moment that what you did was right. You gave your child life a second time."

Those few softly spoken words all but brought her to her knees. Her heart twisted inside her. Fresh sobs tore up her throat. She wrapped her hands in the folds of Cam's clothes and clung to him.

No one had ever understood how much giving up that baby had cost her—not even Simon. No one knew that the first thing she thought about when she opened her eyes was that child, or that she ended each day with a mumbled prayer for his welfare. No one knew that every year she marked the day he'd been born—and the day she'd given him away.

Tears she'd been saving since that night outside the foundling home spilled down her cheeks. They were tears that threatened every time she saw mothers and children together, tears she'd swallowed as she photographed each of the orphan train children. She could let them loose after all this time because Cam knew, because he was still here with her in spite of the desperate deeds she'd confessed to him.

What she'd expected from him was condemnation, and what she'd found was absolution. She'd expected denunciation and found benediction. She wasn't sure she deserved what Cam had given her, but she was more grateful than she'd ever be able to tell him for what he'd offered her this afternoon.

Still, there was the rest of the story to tell, and Shea's last and most closely guarded secret to protect. She stirred against him, pushed away. This time he let her go.

"After I'd given little Liam up," she said, pacing the breadth of the window alcove, "I didn't care what happened to me. I wandered the streets, and one night I took refuge from a storm in the doorway of a photography studio.

"Simon found me there the next morning. I was half frozen to death and terribly ill, but he refused to let me die." Shea pressed her hands together at her waist, remembering Simon's gaunt form bending over her, remembering his determination that she would live. "When I was better, he gave me a job at the studio. Over the next months we came to love each other, and gradually I told him everything. Once we were wed, I went back to reclaim little Liam."

Shea shuddered as she recalled the cold, barren office where she'd waited at the foundling home, and the spare, dour woman who'd come to speak with her.

"What happened?" Cam murmured.

She shifted on her feet, her muscles burning with tension, her throat closing again. "He wasn't there," she choked out. "They wouldn't tell me where he was. They said I had no proof I was his mother."

His deep, soothing voice rolled over her. "But you've kept searching."

"Every day," she whispered, conceding the vow she'd made years before. "Since then I've visited every orphanage in New York, talked to dozens of matrons, and held hundreds of children in my arms."

"How long was it before someone told you they'd sent your Liam west on an orphan train?" he asked softly.

Her gaze rose and clashed with his.

He knew. And if he knew about the orphan trains, what else might he be astute enough to discover?

"How did you . . ."

"I saw the newspaper clipping in your locket when you were ill." Shea's hand flew to her throat. "You showed me the photographs you'd taken of all those children, children from the orphan trains. What else was I to think?"

He'd seen things in her she hadn't expected anyone to see, concluded things she hadn't thought anyone would figure out. Could he possibly have deduced the last and most devastating part of her secret—the part that touched him and his son?

The pulse throbbed in her throat as she stood staring at him. Her hands curled into fists. Would he ask about the rest? Would he ask her about his son? And if he did, could she tell him the truth, or would she lie?

But Cam didn't ask. He came toward her instead, curled his hand around her shoulder, seeming intent on questions of his own. "If you find your boy," he asked instead, "what is it you mean to do about him?"

That question had become as much a part of her in these last days as the child himself, but she was no closer to having an answer now than she had been that night in the kitchen.

"It would be easier to cut out my own heart than to give Rand up," Cam declared softly, but with a fierceness in his face that hinted at the kind of soldier he must once have been. "I can't imagine that it would be much easier for anyone else who'd taken in one of those children."

Shea had known that claiming Rand would have been like depriving Lily of sustenance, depriving her of breath. She could see now that taking her boy from Cam would tear a hole in his heart that would never mend.

What was she going to do when she found her child?

Shea did her best to frame her answer so it lay at the threshold of truth. "What I set out to do was find my son and make a life with him. But after seeing you with

Rand and how Rand is with you and Lily, I realize it will never be that simple."

She shrugged out of Cam's grasp and went to where her teacup sat forgotten on the pile of books. She put the cup to her lips. The tea was cold and bitter on her tongue, but no more bitter than the truth had been.

She was separated from the Gallimores, the people who had come to mean so much to her, by the very thing that bound her to them. Her son.

She set her cup aside. "So there's my tale. It's a long and maudlin story, I'm sorry to say. But you did ask to hear it."

Cam came to stand over her as she pulled on her jacket and prepared to go. "You did the right thing, Shea. I hope one day you'll find your boy."

She stood for a moment, her throat knotted tight, trying to think what she should say to him. He'd given her so much this afternoon, understanding and tenderness—and even the absolution she'd been seeking so desperately. What he hadn't been able to offer—what there might not be anywhere in the world—was resolution.

She raised her gaze to his, looked into his eyes. "Thank you," she whispered. They were the only words she was able to speak as she turned to leave. But even if she said them a thousand times, she knew they'd never be adequate for what he'd done for her today.

French silk rustled and the heavy scent of gardenia perfume wafted through the studio as Shea ushered the subject of her last sitting of the day toward the door.

"I think you'll be very pleased with the portrait, Mrs. Greene," she offered, easing one of Denver's most prominent matrons into her fur-trimmed pelisse.

"You come very highly recommended, my dear," the woman answered, adjusting her hat, "so I doubt I'll be disappointed."

"I expect the picture will be ready at the first of the week. Shall I have someone bring it by your house?"

"Send that boy I read about in the newspaper, if you will. I'm surprised he isn't here with you this afternoon."

"I expect he's just getting out of school," Shea said, though in truth Ty wasn't attending school, and Shea hadn't spoken more than a dozen words in a row to him in a fortnight.

He'd been staying away from the studio, staying away from her since the day she and Cam had gone looking for him. Except for seeking him out at the bottom of the steps while he was waiting for Rand, she wouldn't have known whether Ty and his father were still in Denver.

The boys had been going off together every afternoon, running Ty's errands or hanging around the livery stable helping Mr. Johanson. Rand usually returned to the studio rosy-cheeked and windblown just in time to meet his father for the ride back to the farm. He sometimes came back dirty, and once his trousers had been ripped at the knee, but neither she nor Cam had questioned him about it. Rand was giving Ty the friendship he seemed so hungry for, and Ty was teaching Rand a kind of self-sufficiency he never would have learned in his life at the farm. Shea suspected their afternoons together were as good for one of the boys as it was for the other. If Cam was concerned about how they spent their time, he never let on.

After Shea had seen Mrs. Greene to the door, she crossed to the desk and leafed through her appointment book. Every sitting was taken from now until

Christmas, a phenomenon Shea was sure she owed it to the article that had appeared in the newspaper following the opening. She and Cam had become heroes of sorts for what they'd done, though she would have given up the notoriety, and the appointments as well, if she'd been able to have Ty where she could keep a better eye on him.

Sighing, she pushed back a handful of curls and headed for the darkroom. Taking care to knock before opening the door, she stuck her head inside.

"How are you coming?" she asked.

Owen turned to her, looking frazzled. No matter what he was like outside it, Owen was almost never frazzled in the darkroom. This small, smelly room lit only by a single spirit lamp was his domain, his empire.

He broke off his tuneless humming to answer her. "Too much work!" he complained.

Shea couldn't help laughing. "There's no such thing as too much work."

"There is," he argued, then pointed to a two-inch-high stack of finished prints. "They need colorin'."

Painting colors onto that many prints was a daunting prospect, even for Shea. "I'll work on them all evening," she promised, glad for something to keep her occupied.

Owen had nearly surprised the life out of her a few days after the studio's opening by informing her he intended to move into Emmet Farley's spare room. When she had been able to catch her breath to ask him why, he'd explained.

"It's not proper."

"You don't think it's proper for us to be living here together?" she'd asked incredulously. "But, old dear, we've traveled thousands of miles, just the two of us."

"Save your reputation."

"I'm not worried about my reputation. How can *you* be, after all this time?"

"It's different here," he insisted.

"In town, you mean?"

He'd nodded his head, leaving Shea stunned and a little hurt by his defection.

"And you'll be comfortable living with Emmet?"

Owen had lowered his head just the way he had in the cabin that day at the farm. "He understands," Owen murmured.

Something had changed for Owen when he and Emmet had swooped down to offer Cam a very particular kind of shelter after he'd confronted Sam Morran. In offering up that part of himself, Owen had taken a step away from who he'd been. He'd taken a step away from her. Going to live with Emmet was taking another step.

Once Owen had gathered up his belongings, Shea discovered she didn't like being by herself. She missed the rumble of someone moving about, the security of having another soul to turn to if she was lonely. The hours dragged. She slept fitfully, but didn't let on. The change in Owen, the calmness in him, the new steadiness of his hands, was worth her small discomforts.

Shea glanced across the darkroom at Owen, then picked up the stack of prints to be hand-tinted. "I'll just go and get started on these," she told him and took them to the desk in the entry hall.

She had finished seven of the prints from the stack and was beginning the eighth when Cam came by for Rand almost an hour later.

"You're hard at work," he observed, pulling a chair up to the far side of the desk. He always managed to spend a bit of time with her when he came for Rand at the end of the day, and Shea had taken to straightening her skirts and repinning her hair in anticipation of his arrival.

Things had changed between them since that day in his office. Their friendship had ripened, deepened in ways Shea wasn't sure she could explain. They'd revealed not just secrets, but parts of themselves they'd never shared with anyone else. It had made them each more aware of the other, more attuned somehow.

"I *am* hard at work," Shea answered him, gesturing to the prints stacked up beside her. "I've enough work here to keep me busy until dawn. I'm not complaining, mind you, but I really don't know how we're going to keep up with the printing and the coloring and the framing, with the number of sittings we have scheduled before Christmas."

"Is there anything Lily could do to help?"

"Lily?" she asked, looking up from the gilt buttons she'd been painting onto one of the prints. "Is Lily lacking for things to keep her occupied out at the farm?"

Cam shrugged. "She's been doing her Christmas baking, but it looks to me like she's already made enough fruitcakes to provision every man, woman, and child in Denver." A conspiratorial smile curled beneath the silky droop of his mustache. "Though she'll never admit it, I think she misses coming to town."

Shea warmed with pleasure, both at the news and at the way Cam's gaze lingered on her. The way a twinkle sparked up in those deep blue eyes. The way he seemed to be looking directly at her mouth.

Shea licked her lips, then realized what she'd done and flushed to the hairline.

Cam seemed highly amused by her maidenly blushes.

"Does—does Lily really miss coming here?" she

asked, sitting back in her chair. "Would she come in and help if I asked her?"

"She volunteered the last time," Cam pointed out.

"Then I'll write her a note."

"Good," Cam said with a nod of satisfaction. "Good."

Shea was just signing her name to the request for help, when Rand came thundering up the stairs and burst into the studio.

Shea's heart swelled at the flushed, rumpled sight of her son, and it was all she could do to keep from going to him, admonishing him to button up his coat against the cold, and smoothing down his windblown hair.

"Look at this!" he exclaimed as he charged toward them. He held up a flat copper disk. "Ty showed me how to put pennies on the train tracks so they'd get squashed flat!"

"You weren't playing on the tracks, were you?" both Cam and Shea gasped simultaneously. They glanced at each other and burst out laughing.

"You sound like my mother!" Rand complained, turning to Shea as if she had no right to correct him.

But the boy's half-teasing words ripped into Shea like talons.

The truth leaped into her throat. *I am your mother!* she longed to shout.

Shea swallowed the truth, though the words burned all the way down. "You think I sound like your mother?" Shea managed to murmur. "Imagine that!"

Cam had turned his attention to Rand. "Now, what's this I hear about you playing on the railroad tracks?"

"We were careful," Rand cajoled.

Shea knew no child was ever careful enough.

"I know you like spending time with Ty," Cameron

went on, his voice low and deliberate, "but Ty isn't always as careful as he could be. That's why I need to be able to count on you to be the responsible one when you're with him."

Even as rattled as she was by what had gone on moments before, Shea noticed the way Cam talked to the boy, the way he spoke of his confidence in Rand's good judgment instead of admonishing him for his mistakes. Would she have been able to speak to him as patiently as Cam did if she knew Rand had put himself in danger?

This was Cameron at his best, as a man and as a father. This was the calm, reasonable soul everyone turned to and counted on—even her. She saw how his eyes warmed as he talked to the boy, saw how he curled his fingers around Rand's shoulder, drawing him closer to show him how precious he was, even as Cam was correcting him.

Her chest constricted as she realized how precious Cam himself had become to her. How she'd begun to listen for his tread on the stairs, how he could warm her with a look or a word. How much time she spent when she was alone remembering what it had been like to kiss him.

She found herself watching him as he spoke, watching his mouth form the words and knowing the tart, fresh taste of him. Seeing the breadth of those shoulders and that chest, and knowing what it was like to lean into him. Remembering the surge of desire that had rushed between them.

She hastily lowered her eyes to her work. It was ridiculous for her to be thinking about such things, especially when there had been nothing between them since that night in the kitchen but a little harmless flirtation.

". . . so I expect you to look out for Ty as well as

yourself," Cam was saying. "Do you understand me, Rand?"

"Yes, sir," the boy answered, then held up the flattened penny again. "But isn't this amazing, even if I'm not supposed to make one again?"

Cam shook his head. "I suppose it is. But maybe we'd better not mention the penny and playing in the train yard to your aunt Lily. You know how she is."

"Won't Aunt Lily have supper ready soon?" the boy asked, his thoughts jumping to more practical matters. "I'm so hungry I could eat a horse!"

"I'll have to warn Jasper," Cam answered drolly, adjusting his hat.

Shea handed the note across to him. "Encourage Lily to come," she admonished him.

"Oh, I will," he promised. "I'll do my best to get her here in the morning."

Shea was whisking the night's dusting of snow off the steps the following morning when Cameron and Lily pulled up in the carriage.

"Lovely day, Mrs. Waterston," Cam called out, flashing a smile at her again as he rounded the carriage to help his sister alight.

Shea couldn't seem to help the warm rush of exhilaration that tumbled through her as she smiled back. "And good morning to you, Judge Gallimore."

Cam looked especially fine today in his tan, leather-collared duster and flat-crowned hat, more like a cowboy than a judge, more rough-hewn and compelling than usual. He flustered her a little and made her glad she'd taken special care with her hair and dress this morning. Once he'd helped Lily down, he waved and climbed back into the carriage. Somehow Shea couldn't help watching him down the street.

Lily was just starting up the stairs when someone called out to her.

"Miss Gallimore?" Mr. Nicholson, who owned the hardware store next door, came rushing up the alley. "Is that you, Miss Gallimore?"

Lily paused, easing ever so slightly back toward the wall of the building as Nicholson approached. "Yes?" she answered. Shea started protectively down the steps.

"It's me, Miss Gallimore," the man said, stopping at the bottom and tugging off his hat. "It's Abe Nicholson. I don't want to trouble you, ma'am. I just wanted to say how much the flowers and the note you sent when we lost our Amy meant to the wife and me. Yellow roses were always Amy's favorites."

Lily stared at Nicholson, and at first Shea thought she wasn't going to reply. Then she bent and hesitantly pressed her slim, gloved fingers to where his hand lay against the banister. "I'd just read in the newspaper about Amy winning that prize at school, so I could barely believe it when Dr. Farley told me about you losing her."

"Yes, ma'am. Amy was the light of our lives all right." Nicholson's voice wavered a little as he spoke. "Anyway, I just wanted to thank you for your thoughtfulness."

"I—I'm glad the roses were a comfort."

With that, Nicholson turned back to his work, and Lily hastened up the stairs to the landing. Shea saw how unsettled she was as she brushed past, and followed her inside.

"Did Mr. Nicholson upset you, Lily?" she asked.

"No!" Lily denied hotly, hurriedly unpinning and tugging off her hat. She stood for a moment stroking the thick black veil. "I—I guess I didn't think anyone would know me in this."

Shea stepped closer and slid an arm around the taller woman's waist. "That veil hides your face, Lily," she offered gently. "It doesn't make you invisible. Besides, you knew who Mr. Nicholson was."

"I had read about Amy in the newspapers, and when Emmet told me she'd died, I . . ." A flush came up in Lily's cheeks. "Sending a note and a few of my roses seemed the least I could do."

"You keep up with lots of people here in Denver through newspapers, don't you?" Shea asked softly.

"And through Emmet and Cam."

Shea nodded thoughtfully. "And are those folks real to you, Lily, even though you've never set eyes on them?"

"Of course they're real."

"And you send those real folks notes and flowers and crocks of soup," Shea went on drawing Lily closer. "You knit their children booties and remember the old people at Christmas. Isn't that right?"

"Yes, Shea, I do. What is it you're getting at?"

"I think you need to realize that with sending those notes and gifts you've made yourself real to them, too. They're grateful for what you've done—and they're curious."

"You mean they all know who I am?" Shea heard the distress in Lily's voice, and the dawning of wonder.

"You've been as good a neighbor to these people here as anyone could, and I think all they want is to be neighborly back."

Shea could see that the idea had shaken Lily's perception of herself, see it in the way she dipped her head and pursed her lips. Shea pressed her cheek to Lily's unblemished one and gave her an affectionate little squeeze. Then she deliberately went on about her work, giving Lily time to think things through.

A few minutes later, when Shea looked from the print she was coloring, she saw that Lily had joined her.

"I can't imagine what I can do," Lily said. "I don't know the first thing about photography."

"You learned watercolor painting when you were in school, didn't you?" When Lily said she had, Shea continued. "Then you can do this. Just let me show you what I need."

In preparation for Lily's arrival, Shea had set up a table in the bedroom and laid out her retouching pencils and brushes and paints. In a few minutes of instruction, she showed Lily how to selectively and delicately add color to the photographs. She stood over her as Lily tried her hand at her first print. It was nearly done when people began to arrive in the entry.

"That must be Mrs. Fenwick and her girls come for their sitting," Shea told her and turned toward the door. "Just keep working. I've made notations on the back of the prints if there are certain colors you should use."

"You'll come and see that I'm doing this right, won't you?" Lily asked, still sounding uncertain.

"You'll be fine," Shea assured her and bustled out to greet the Fenwicks.

It was almost noon when Shea got back to the front room, and by then Lily had tinted an entire bed full of photographs.

"It wasn't all that difficult once I got the hang of it," she confided.

Lily had a good eye. The results of her hand-coloring were subtle and flattering to the sitters. "You're doing nearly as well as photographers who've been hand-retouching prints for years," Shea told her, then settled on the corner of the bed and began to fit the finished photographs into their pressboard frames. "Owen will have another stack of prints ready this afternoon, if you're willing to tackle them."

"Oh, I imagine I can give it a try," Lily said.

As Shea worked, Lily turned to her. "Shea . . ."

Something in the tone of Lily's voice made Shea look up.

"You've done such a wonderful job photographing everyone, especially the women . . ." Lily hesitated. ". . . that—that I was wondering how you managed to make even the matrons look so lovely."

"Well," Shea began, "some of it is the light. Part of it is posing a person properly to show her at her best, and putting her at ease in front of the camera."

"I see," Lily murmured, staring down at her watercolor-speckled fingers.

Shea reached across to her. "Lily? Is there something you wanted?"

Lily raised her head; her eyes were brimming with uncertainty. "I—I wondered if you could take my photograph. I wondered if you could show me at my best."

Shea shifted closer and let her practiced gaze run over Lily's face. "We can pose you so the scars are away from the camera," she answered. "But they'd still show here at your brow." She feathered the tips of her fingers over Lily's withered flesh, pleased when she didn't pull away. "And here at the corner of your mouth."

"You can't make me look the way I did when I was sixteen?" Shea could hear the heartbreak in Lily's voice, the yearning to turn back time.

Shea closed her hands around Lily's fingers, holding them firmly in her own. "Photography may bend the truth, but it can't lie," she offered very softly. "I can use my skills to show you in the most flattering way, but no photographer can change what's there."

"I'd just—hoped," Lily said on a soul-deep sigh.

"I can make an exposure this afternoon," Shea suggested, "and then we'll see—"

"No," Lily said, withdrawing her hands from Shea's. "No, it was just a thought. Nothing for you to be concerned about."

But Shea was concerned. Lily was on Shea's mind when she climbed into bed hours later. She couldn't help but think Lily's questions about taking a photograph were a good thing, just as her coming into town had been, just as her interest in the other residents of Denver obviously was. She was reaching, exploring, trying to find a new place for herself.

What else could Shea do to encourage Lily, to open the world to her a little at a time? she wondered as she nestled into her pillows. Perhaps she could ask Lily to accompany her to the freight office to pick up her supplies. Perhaps she could encourage Lily to attend the Christmas program at Rand's school. She closed her eyes. Emmet would be so pleased when he heard about this.

Shea didn't know how long she'd been asleep. She didn't know what it was that awakened her. All she knew was that she came to consciousness with her heart thudding in her ears and an undefinable menace pressing down on her.

She lay utterly still, straining to catch the slightest sound, her ears ringing with the effort. The embers glowing in the stove gave off just enough light to assure her that she was alone in the room. But just beyond the half-open door, the entry hall lay black as the bottom of a pit. Prickles danced across her skin.

If only Owen were here, Shea found herself thinking, knowing Owen would be no help at all.

As the wind gusted up the alley, the door at the top of the stairs seemed to rattle. She hadn't ever noticed it did that. She hadn't noticed that the sign beneath her window creaked, or that she could hear train whistles from over near the river.

The door to the studio rattled again, louder this time. Almost as if someone was trying it. Shea froze, the air trapped in her lungs and her heart thundering. Then, with a muffled curse, she rustled her way out of bed. Her bare toes curled when her feet hit the icy floor, and she scampered toward the corner where she'd kept her rifle.

Her fingers closed around the stock. She ratcheted a round into the chamber. Feeling better with the gun in her hands, she crept out into the entry hall. Her gaze swept the room and the studio beyond it. The brightness of the winter sky shone through the skylight. Snow was dusting down in huge feathery flakes.

The door rattled again. She thought she heard the handle turn. A wave of malevolence broke over her.

She wheeled toward the sound, pointing her rifle, ready to fire. Her nerves sang with tension. Her heart battered around inside her chest. She stood there waiting, waiting. Waiting.

She stood there for a very long time, her eyes trained on the stout wooden panel. She heard the wind moaning up the alley and faraway laughter from up the street. Her muscles quivered with tension.

At last she lowered the rifle and went to press her ear to the door. She couldn't hear anything. The sense of malevolence had faded a little. She should open the door to make sure there was no one outside, but she couldn't bring herself to do that.

Shea crept back into the bedroom and set the rifle where she could reach it. She crawled into bed and pulled the covers up around her ears. It was then the shivers took her, shivers of cold and reaction and relief. She'd only imagined that someone was there, she told herself. She was foolish to get so wrought up over nothing. Still, it was almost dawn when she finally drifted off to sleep.

She awoke not much more than an hour later, tired and out of sorts, carrying the weight of her sleeplessness around with her. She got up and stoked the fires. She washed and dressed. She put the kettle on to boil.

Just before seven o'clock she went out to sweep the steps and found footprints on the landing. They were big and deep, stamped into the freshly fallen snow. A chill of fear slid down Shea's back.

ELEVEN

Could anyone have a happy Christmas in such a place? Shea wondered as she rapped on the battered, gap-toothed door of Ty and his father's little cabin. For as much as Ty had been avoiding the studio, avoiding her, Shea hadn't been able to let the holiday pass without seeing him. She wanted to be sure Ty had a gift to mark the day, and she couldn't convince herself that Sam Morran would even remember it was Christmas. So here she stood shivering on their doorstep, hoping Ty was alone inside the cabin.

After a moment the boy cracked open the door and stood staring out at her. In his arms he held the biggest, scruffiest, meanest-looking calico cat Shea had ever encountered in her life.

"When did you get a cat!" she exclaimed.

Ty shrugged. "Me and Rand found him down by the river a couple weeks back."

Which meant the boys had been exploring another one of the places Cam had specifically told them not to go.

"Does—does your kitty have a name?" Shea asked, fighting the urge to admonish him about playing too near the water.

Ty ruffled the fur beneath the cat's chin. "I call him Rufus."

"Well, hello there, Rufus," Shea said, reaching to give the animal a scratch.

Rufus took exception to being fondled by someone he didn't know. He reared back in Ty's arms and hissed at her.

Shea gave a startled laugh and withdrew her hand, taking the moment to look Ty over. He seemed to have grown taller in the weeks since the opening, and the pants he was wearing were two inches too short. Dark circles lay beneath his eyes like smudges of lampblack. He seemed thinner, too. It made her want to bundle him up, take him back to the studio, and feed him until he was too full to swallow.

"I—I just stopped by to wish you Merry Christmas," Shea told him instead. "Would you mind if I came in?"

Ty glanced over his shoulder, then shook his head. "Pa's still sleeping."

Sleeping off a drunk, Shea thought. But then, at least Ty wasn't alone today.

As if Ty realized she wasn't likely to go away, he stepped outside and set Rufus on the ground. She could tell by the way he shifted from foot to foot how uneasy Ty was at having her here. Rufus seemed to sense that, too, and hissed at Shea for good measure.

"All I wanted," she went on, determined not to make him any more uncomfortable, "was to give you this, and wish you a merry Christmas." She held out the striped paper cornucopia she'd made and filled for him.

The boy stuffed both his hands in his pockets instead of reaching for the bright paper cone. "I don't have anything to give you."

"Christmas is a day for giving *children* gifts," she insisted, holding out the cone again. "Please, Ty, won't you take this?"

"I don't know as how I should," he allowed, "after the way Pa took on when you gave me that shirt."

"This is nothing but an orange, some nuts, and a few pieces of candy. Surely he can't object to that." She hesitated before she went on, and was a little ashamed of herself for resorting to blackmail. "You know, I'm not going to be able to enjoy Christmas unless you take this."

Ty ducked his head, but made no move toward the cornucopia. "So, are you going out to the Gallimores' farm?"

Shea couldn't think when she'd heard such longing in anyone's voice. What had it been like for him before his mother died and his father had given himself over to grief and alcohol? Had Ty ever had a proper home, with proper meals at proper hours, and a proper bed to sleep in? Or for that matter, a proper Christmas Day?

"Why don't you come out to the Gallimores' with me this afternoon?" she offered impulsively, thinking how wonderful it was going to be having Christmas with her son. "Rand would be so pleased to have you, and Lily always cooks enough food for an army."

Shea regretted the invitation the moment the words were out of her mouth. Ty's eyes went stark with a wistfulness she knew all too well. She'd been alone often enough in her life to know how much a body yearned to be part of something.

But then Ty slid a glance back toward the cabin and shook his head. "I need to be with Pa today."

Shea stiffened, even angrier with Sam Morran than she was with herself for making Ty choose. Would Sam Morran even know it was Christmas? Would he appreciate the sacrifice his son had made to be with him? How could this man inspire such loyalty, such love in this boy?

How could anyone stand helplessly by and watch this man strip away the years of Ty's childhood, one day at a time?

She swallowed down the shards of anger and held out the cornucopia of candies. "I'd really like you to have this."

Ty looked at the cornucopia, from the frill of paper lace around the top to the crimps of trailing ribbon. His brown eyes darkened the instant before he gave in to temptation and reached for the cone of candy. "Thanks," he said.

Before he could escape, Shea bent and pecked a kiss on one windburned cheek. "Merry Christmas, Ty," she said and turned away.

Halfway up the alley she paused to look back. Ty was still standing in the cold staring after her, the cornucopia of candy in one hand and the calico cat curled up against his feet.

Christmas at the Gallimore farm was like something Shea had read about in books. After a drive through fields lightly dusted with snow, Cam had welcomed Emmet and Owen and her into a house that smelled of evergreens and wassail spices, of roasting meat and fresh-baked pies. She'd turned from a red-bowed wreath that hung on the front door into a parlor where a spruce tree stood glittering with decorations. A kissing ball dangled innocently in the archway into the dining room, where the table had been dressed with ribbons and holly and Lily's best china.

They'd barely arrived when Rand came racing out of the kitchen to greet them, his face flushed and his green eyes bright with excitement. Shea wanted to catch him up in her arms and give him a Christmas kiss like she had Ty, but she would have felt presumptuous doing that in front of Cam and Lily.

Not long after they arrived, the six of them settled down at a table groaning with holiday bounty: roast pork and duchess potatoes, brown-sugared squash and green beans, applesauce and yeast rolls. As she watched Rand dig into his heaping plate, Shea couldn't help wondering if Ty was getting anything to eat today at all.

They were only just finishing their pie when Rand glanced wistfully toward the decorated tree in the corner. "Is it time to open the presents yet?" he asked hopefully.

Instead there was food to put away and dishes to wash. Once they'd finished Lily herded everyone in toward the piano. "I thought we'd sing a few carols," she suggested, "before we see what's in all of those lovely packages."

"Oh, Aunt Lily!" Rand complained. "How come we always have to sing before we get our presents?"

"You know how much your aunt Lily likes Christmas carols," Cam reminded his son with a wink. "Besides, anticipation makes the sugar sweeter."

"My an-tissy-pation's sweet enough!" Rand huffed and plopped down beside Lily on the piano bench. She gave him a conciliatory squeeze, planted a kiss on the top of his head, then struck up the first chords of "O Come, All Ye Faithful."

Watching Cameron stand over Lily and Rand as they

sang, Shea realized that this was how the Gallimores always spent Christmas: with a special meal, caroling around a piano, and gifts beneath a tree hung with popcorn chains and delicate blown-glass ornaments.

Hot jealousy pierced her heart when she thought about all the Christmases these people had had with her son and the traditions they shared. Even her happiest holidays with Simon had been tainted with regrets, marred by wondering about the child she'd given up.

It wasn't fair, she thought, watching the three of them together, that while she'd been pining for her son, Rand had been happy in a world of his own. While she'd been traveling thousands of miles in search of him, her boy had been going to picnics and hayrides and skating parties, had been doing chores, playing games, and attending school. He'd been having Christmases with the Gallimores, just like this one.

Seeing the three of them clustered together at the piano this afternoon, seeing the love and history that bound them together, tore at Shea. It made her realize just how much of Rand's life she'd already missed.

She hadn't been there to nurse him through bumps and mumps and chicken pox. She hadn't been around to applaud him when he rode a horse for his very first time. She hadn't been the one to teach him his letters, or how to harness a wagon, or the trick to spitting watermelon seeds farther than anyone else. It made her angry that she'd forfeited so much, angry that in her disgrace and poverty she'd had no choice.

Now that she'd finally found him, Shea yearned to tear this child out of Cam and Lily's arms. But what right did she have to destroy the only home her son had ever known? What did she have to offer him, compared to all of this? And how could she hope to prove that he was hers?

Yet after years of struggling and searching and yearning for her son, how could she turn away from him? What purpose would she have in life if she gave him up?

Shea did her best to swallow down the bitter draught of melancholy. She had a great deal to be thankful for. She'd loved Simon and had learned so much from him. She had Owen's loyalty and companionship. She had her work and her independence and the kind of adventures most women would never experience. Yet she didn't have what she wanted most, because nothing could give her back the years she'd lost, or stitch her into the tight, sleek weave of the Gallimores' lives.

Shaken by the effort of acknowledging that, Shea linked her arm through Owen's and swayed with him in time to the music. He patted her hand and smiled up at her from beneath his brows, and just that moment of his simple kindness made her chest constrict.

Then, as the last notes of the carols echoed away, Lily rose from the piano. She slid her arm around Shea's waist, and drew her to sit beside her on the settee. Cam lit the candles on the tree and began to pass out packages wrapped in butcher's paper and remnants of cloth, parcels bound with bits of ribbon and string, adorned with holly, a candy cane, or a pinecone.

Rand exclaimed over a tin wind-up train his father had ordered from Philadelphia. Owen beamed at Shea and threaded his new string tie beneath his collar. Lily fondled the elegant embroidered gloves Emmet had brought for her.

"For your trips into town," he told her, his eyes alight.

The three Gallimores presented Shea with a length of sturdy wine-colored twill. "Because you'll spend every penny you have on photographic supplies and nothing on yourself," Lily told her, laughing.

Shea fidgeted as Rand took up the gift she'd brought for him, watching those broad, impatient hands tear through the wrappings. Shea hadn't known what to get, but she'd never given her son a gift and wanted so much for him to like it. Her stomach twisted as she waited for his reaction.

"Oh, Shea!" He turned to her, his eyes alight. "Some of the older boys in school have lead pencils, but no one's is as nice as this. Look how it slides together!"

"It telescopes." Cam gave him the correct word.

"Telescopes," Rand mumbled, looking around for something to write on.

Shea let out her breath. Her son liked what she had given him. Her face warmed with pleasure.

"That pencil's something special. Take good care of it," Lily admonished gently.

"I'll treat it like it was made of gold!" Rand beamed at Shea. "It isn't, is it?"

"No, not gold," she assured him, laughing.

Lily and Cam opened their gift from Shea last, and both of them oohed and aahed over the portrait Shea had made of Rand. She was pleased with the picture, too, thinking she'd managed to catch an excellent likeness of her son, not just that open face, but the goodness and wonder inside him. A blending of what she'd passed on to her boy and the things the Gallimores had given him.

While she was at it, she'd made a copy of the photograph for herself—then had immediately hidden it away in the bottom of her valise. She supposed she'd done that because having the photograph and being able to study the child she'd borne almost exactly eleven years ago still seemed an illicit pleasure. Just as being with her son on Christmas did.

After Lily had hugged Shea to thank her for the photograph and arranged Rand's portrait amid a cluster of greens on top of the piano, she bustled into the kitchen to pour coffee.

She was just returning with a tray of cups when Emmet waylaid her beneath the kissing ball. "I've caught you now," he said, grinning down at her.

"My hands are full," Lily protested, doing her best to step around him. "I can't properly defend myself."

Emmet shrugged, indifferent to her plight. "I caught her fair and square, didn't I, Cam?"

Lily's face went pink.

Cam laughed at his sister's obvious discomfort and shook his head. "I'm not getting involved with this!"

"I think I deserve a Christmas kiss," Emmet persisted.

Knowing there was no sense arguing, Lily wrinkled her nose distastefully. "Oh, all right, you damn fool," she said with more than a little consternation. "Kiss me quick and get it over with."

Smiling with anticipation, Emmet stepped in as close as the tray of cups would allow and, with consummate tenderness, curled his hand along the arc of Lily's withered cheek. He lowered his head and tipped her mouth to his, taking her gently.

Why, Emmet is in love with Lily! Shea realized as she watched them. What she had dismissed as southern gallantry and profound respect was love. It was a pure and abiding love Emmet would probably never bring himself to act on, for fear of offending Lily's sensibilities—but it was love, nonetheless.

Emmet kissed Lily chastely, but thoroughly. Then,

grasping an elbow to steady her, he broke the kiss and stepped away.

Lily blinked at him, flushing darker this time—and all the way to her hairline.

Cam and Rand hooted, taking great delight in Lily's embarrassment, completely oblivious to what was happening right before their eyes. Then, caught up in their foolishness, Rand scrambled to his feet and went to buss Lily on the cheek. A moment later Cam did the same.

"Now if you boys have had your fun," Lily sniffed, "do you suppose we can drink this coffee before it gets cold?"

They had barely settled down with their cups when someone galloped up the lane and came bounding up onto the porch.

"Is Dr. Farley here?" the gaunt, bearded man demanded of Cam when he answered the knock.

"What is it, Mr. Young?" Emmet asked, stepping to the door.

"It's my boy Fred. He started running a fever last night and has been talking out of his head since noontime. I hate to disturb your Christmas, Dr. Farley, but my wife and me would sure feel better if you could come have a look at him."

Emmet asked a few questions, then nodded. "My bag's in the buggy, Mr. Young. Just give me a minute to grab my coat and hitch up my horse."

As Lily scurried around gathering up Emmet's things, Cam pulled on his own coat, ready to help Emmet hitch up. "Stay with the Youngs as long as you need to," he assured Emmet. "I'll see Shea and Owen get back to town."

Emmet sought Lily on his way out. "You're the best

cook in three counties, Lily. It's been a wonderful day, and I thank you for everything."

For an instant Shea thought he might kiss Lily again, but then he turned and went outside. Shea and Lily watched from the window as the menfolk hitched up Emmet's buggy. Then, with a wave, he whipped his horse down the lane and turned in the direction of Denver.

Lily stood at the window a good long while, her eyes lingering on the point where Emmet Farley had disappeared and her hand pressed gently against her mouth.

Cam couldn't have asked for a better night to drive Shea and Owen back into town. He liked the way the moon hung heavy and milk-white against a heaven stippled with stars, and how the icing of fresh snow turned the fields on the sides of the road to shimmering yards of pale blue satin. As he drove nearer, he could almost feel the warm yellow glow of Denver's gaslit streets envelop them.

He and Shea bid Owen good night in front of Emmet's house on Arapaho Street, then proceeded up the block.

"It was a lovely Christmas," Shea murmured, glancing across at him. "It was good of you and Lily to invite us to share the day with you."

Cam inclined his head and turned the buggy into Sixteenth Street. "I'm glad you and Owen enjoyed it."

"I just wish Ty could have been there," he heard Shea murmur on the drift of a sigh. "I went by their cabin this morning to wish him a happy Christmas, and I invited him to come out to the farm."

"And what did he say?"

Cameron saw the wedge of worry settle between her

graceful brows. "He said he needed to be with his father."

He reached across and gave her hand a consoling squeeze. "Then, Shea, he made his choice."

She shifted uneasily beside him. "I just can't stop worrying about him! I think it's only what Ty earns that keeps the two of them going. And now that he's not working for me . . ."

Cam eased back on the reins, slowing the carriage at the cross street. "Well, then, I suppose it's a good thing I mentioned Ty to Mal Ruther down at the telegraph office."

"You got Ty a job delivering telegrams?"

Cam could hear the delight in her voice and couldn't help being pleased with himself. "I think Ty and his father are doing all right for the time being. And Rand's keeping an eye on things for me."

He saw the rigidity melt out of her shoulders, and she looped her hand through the crook of his arm. "Thank you, Cam."

He smiled at her thinking he had never in his life met a woman who was so concerned for children that weren't her own. But then, he supposed that made a particular kind of sense. He could see the shadows in her eyes, see what he thought was longing for the child she'd given up. He'd seen it today at the house when she looked at Rand. He'd have bet half his next year's wages that while they were standing around the piano she was thinking about her own lost boy and wondering how he was passing Christmas.

Giving that baby up had marked her, tempered her, given her an abiding concern for children. Or maybe an abiding concern for all lost souls. He saw how she was with Owen. The way she'd brought Lily along had

been little short of miraculous. And the night he confronted Morran . . .

He shivered a little.

Without so much as a thought, Shea pressed her
fingertips to his forearm, as if she meant to soothe him.
Shea understood his uncertainty and his turmoil, his
longing and his guilt. She was so perceptive sometimes
it scared him to death. Still he liked the awareness between them, that strange connection.

Cam pulled the carriage up in front of Shea's studio
and was just as glad for the diversion from his thoughts.

As he handed her out, Shea turned to him. "So what
did you make of Emmet catching Lily beneath the kissing ball?"

Emmet's actions had surprised Cam a little, but he
hadn't "made" anything of them. "That's what kissing
balls are for, isn't it?" he said with a shrug.

"Oh, indeed," she agreed with him.

Still, he heard something he couldn't quite identify
in her tone. "Why else would he kiss her?"

Shea raised one eyebrow in answer as if to say he'd
missed something important. He fumbled for a moment, wondering what that was. "Did you want me to
catch you under the kissing ball?" he guessed.

Shea gave a gust of delighted laughter. "Oh, Cam!"
she chuckled, shaking her head.

"Well, it might not have been so bad cornering you
for a Christmas kiss," he defended himself, realizing it
was true. It had been a long time since that night in the
kitchen, and he hardly had to be reminded how much
he'd liked kissing her. He'd held her more than once
since then—and teased her and comforted her. But he
hadn't kissed her. He hadn't so much as tasted those
plush rosy lips or plumbed the depths of that soft,
sweet mouth. He hadn't had the opportunity.

But now it was dark between the buildings. The streets were deserted. And it *was* still Christmas.

They'd climbed barely half a dozen stairs when Cam paused. Shea paused on the step above him. As she did, he curled his hand around her wrist and drew her toward him. When she realized what he intended her eyes widened but she came to him quite willingly.

Her lips themselves were cold, but the soft inner margins were warm and lush and so damnedably inviting he couldn't help but sample deeper. He had meant this to be a simple kiss, something delicate and fleeting, a Christmas greeting passed from mouth to mouth. Instead, the kiss welled with a delicious, soul-enhancing magic.

The communion between them that night in the kitchen had been a surprise. Because they'd become confidantes, champions, friends, this kiss was a revelation. Each of those connections amplified the wonder and intensity between them. The wonder and intensity of the needs this kiss stirred up in him.

Cam pressed Shea back against the wall, suddenly hungry for her, for the feel of her hips and belly and breasts against him. He longed to run his hands along the curve of her back and draw her against—

"Cam!" Shea gasped with laughter and wriggled against him. "You can't just ravish me here on the stairs!"

Despite her protest, her breathing was fast and nearly as unsteady as his and he saw the soft sensuality in her face. She hadn't wanted him to ravish her on the stairs, but she hadn't prohibited ravishing someplace else. Her bedroom came to mind, that small, simple bedroom, that iron bed made up with sheets that smelled of lavender. He grabbed her hand and started up the steps again.

Halfway to the top he jerked to a stop. Alarm shot deep into his belly. Footsteps had been tramped into the newly fallen snow. A faint drift of smoke and kerosene tweaked his nostrils.

"What is it?" Shea murmured.

He squeezed her hand, then flicked back his duster and pulled his pistol. He climbed the stairs noiselessly and paused when he was level with the landing. The door to the studio stood open not quite halfway.

A familiar humming tuned up inside of him.

Shea crowded up close behind him. "I locked that door before I left. I swear I did."

Cam shoved her none too gently against the wall. "Stay here," he mouthed, then stole up the last few steps.

He rushed the door, kicking it hard enough to send it banging back on its hinges. The noise was thunderous. He waited, hanging at the lip of the landing, but nothing shifted, nothing stirred.

He burst inside and pressed flat against the wall of the reception room. His hands were slick as he clung to the sleek, polished grip of his pistol and probed the thick, black caverns of these familiar rooms. He strained his senses for any hint of movement, but all he could hear was the ragged roar of his own breathing and a faint crunch of something beneath his boots.

There was no one here, but above the smell of spilled lamp oil came the stench of some lingering malevolence. His skin tightened and crept with gooseflesh.

"What is it?" Shea hissed, looming up in the doorway.

Cam swung on her, his heart resounding like a spiker's hammer. He jerked his pistol skyward, when he realized who it was.

"Light a lamp," he ordered, and holstered his gun.

Shea crossed to the reception desk and struck a match. As she raised the lamp, illumination flared across the ceiling and down the walls. Shea whimpered with distress at what she saw.

The place had been ransacked, willfully demolished. Here in the reception area the chairs were overturned and the portraits had been ripped from the walls. Shards of glass from the frames sparkled like a carpet of stardust. That carpet led directly into the studio.

Shea rushed ahead, raising her lamp and gasping at the carnage. Beneath the skylight her camera lay on its side, the box crushed and the legs of the tripod lying broken on the square of rug. The velvet posing chair had been slashed and was leaking drifts of stuffing onto the floor. The plaster column lay strewn across the rug like something from a Grecian ruin.

Cam was still taking in the wreckage when he heard Shea cry out, "Mary, Mother of God! They dumped my boxes of negatives!"

Her glass plates spilled across the floor in a hundred shattered images, an acre of glittering mosaic. A host of broken memories.

Shea rushed directly to one particular box and righted it. "The children!" she cried and staggered to her knees amidst the shimmering glass. "Oh, God! I've lost the children!"

She wept as she picked through the shards around her, clasping fragments of the children she'd found and photographed and treasured. The orphan train children. *Shea's lost children.*

Cam went and bent beside her, stroking her hair, the bow of her back. "Take care, love," he murmured. "You'll cut yourself."

He gathered her up as gently as he could, stood her on her feet, and shook the crumbs of glass from her skirts. He righted the posing chair and steered her into it.

She looked at him, her eyes wide and wet with a grief that went well beyond the destruction here. "The children are gone," she whispered. "All my children. Every one."

He heard the heartbreak in her words echoing down a decade of regret. He put his arms around her.

"I'm sorry, Shea," he murmured, holding her, rocking her as if she were broken, too. "I know how precious those children were to you." He knelt beside her for a very long time, stroking her, letting her cry, giving her the simple comfort of his closeness. Knowing it was all he could offer when she'd lost so much.

After a good long time she quieted and he sopped up her tears with the pads of his thumbs. "I need to check the other rooms," he murmured and rose to stand over her. "Will you be all right while I go do that?"

Shea sniffed and nodded.

Finding another unbroken lamp, Cam set off. The bedroom was tumbled as if it had been searched, but nothing seemed missing or broken beyond repair. But the moment he stepped inside the darkroom, a haze of smoke and the chill of that strange malevolence enveloped him.

Gooseflesh chased along his skin as he scuffled through the charred debris to the pile of ashes crumpled in the corner. When he braced his palm against the wall and bent to examine them more closely his hand came away dark and gritty with soot.

For a moment he stared at his blackened fingertips. Remembering another fire, another loss. An old and painful tragedy.

The room dipped and swirled around him, and he was there again—riding.

Riding hard. Riding fast.

Smoke.

Oh, God, smoke.

Smoke rising from my town. Fire at the end of my street. Flames roaring through my mother's house.

My mother's house.

Let them be safe.

Orange flames licking up the walls.

Let them be safe.

The house enfolded in flame, screeching, crumbling. Vaporizing.

Please let them be safe.

Women huddled in the yard. Singed hair and smoking clothes. Two of them. Two.

Thank you. Thank you.

Dismounting. Running toward them.

Are they all right? Please let them be all right.

Catching Mother in my arms. Holding close, holding fast. Lily lying in the grass. Hurt.

Please not hurt.

Bending over her, reaching out.

Her face. Oh God, my sister's face.

Cam crumpled to his knees there in Shea's darkroom, gasping for breath. His throat ached raw with smoke. Sweat soaked his clothes, crawled down his chest, slid down his neck and ribs and back. He couldn't stop shivering.

He curled in upon himself and did his best to breathe in and out. He'd had this before. He knew what this was. He knew it would pass.

He didn't think it would ever pass.

He squeezed his eyes closed and fought to steady himself. He was sane outside of this. *Somewhere.*

That sanity returned by slow degrees. Cam became aware of the small, smoky room around him, of the studio beyond it, of Shea waiting. Dear God, how long had she been waiting?

He pushed to his feet and stood there quivering. He was hollow inside, wasted, spent—and this wasn't even his tragedy. It was Shea's, and he needed to go and see to her.

When he finally picked his way out of the darkroom, Shea was crouched on the floor again sorting through the shattered photographic plates. She'd gathered some of the largest pieces on one of the rubber developing trays and was looking for more she could salvage.

He knelt beside her and stilled her hands. "Shea," he said as gently as he could, "whoever did this set a fire in the darkroom, too."

"A fire?" she echoed, as if she wasn't quite able to believe that someone would set a fire deliberately. "But we store ether in there. Ether's terribly flammable." A new fear flickered across her face. "There could have been an explosion."

"Yes," he said and tightened his grip on those slim, vulnerable wrists. What would have happened if she'd been at the studio when the vandals arrived? Would she have been hurt? Might she have been killed?

He drew her closer, becoming unaccountably aware of her pulse beating beneath his fingertips, the warmth of her flesh, the flow of her breathing. He drew her nearer still. "I think they wanted to destroy the place, to put you out of business."

She let out a ragged sigh. "Well, they've succeeded, then. My portrait camera is broken beyond repair. Most of my lenses are gone . . ."

"Can you get the things you need to start again?"

"Start again?" she asked, looking lost. "It would cost the sun and moon to start again."

For the first time since he'd known her, Shea

Waterston seemed lost, utterly defeated. Somehow Cam couldn't allow that.

"We'll get you what you need," he promised. "We'll find a way for you to keep the studio going."

He drew her closer, needing to hold her, needing to protect her. Needed to know she was safe. He needed it the same way he needed to be sure about Rand, sure about Lily—almost as if Shea belonged to him.

He wanted to go on holding her, but Shea eased away. She climbed to her feet and rose to stand over him. "I'm going to get the broom."

"Shea," he began, halting her, "have you had any kind of trouble here at the studio."

"Trouble?"

"Has anyone threatened you? It's possible drunken cowboys did all this, but I don't think that's who it was."

"You don't?"

Cam rose and went to her. "Has anyone who's come to the studio made you uncomfortable?"

"Beyond Sam Morran?"

"He hasn't been back to bother you, has he?"

Shea shook her head. "But someone *did* steal a photograph at the opening," she reminded him. "And I woke up one night a week or two ago, thinking someone had tried the door."

Cam's new protectiveness warred with irritation. "And you didn't tell anyone about it?"

"And just who would I have told, Cam?"

"You could have gone to the sheriff," he suggested. "Or come to me."

"And what would I have said? That I got spooked being here by myself?" She compressed her lips, and he could see she was disgusted with herself for being skittish.

Cam knew Shea Waterston was no shivering miss who pulled the covers over her head. "So what did you do?"

"That night?" She smiled a little ruefully. "I made sure my rifle was loaded and looked around. The door rattled a time or two, but it might have been the wind. There *were* footprints in the snow the next morning, but anyone could have made them."

He couldn't argue with her, yet the missing picture, her midnight visitor, and now this destruction worried him far more than he cared to admit.

"You need to report this to the sheriff," he insisted. "It wasn't the bogeyman who came tonight."

"No," she acknowledged, staring with deep sadness across the floor carpeted with shattered glass. "I suppose not."

"I've been picking through these broken plates hoping I could salvage something, but it's hopeless." Then she sighed, squared her shoulders, and turned. "This time I really am going to go get the broom and dustpan."

While Shea was gone, Cam looked at the pieces she'd set aside. She'd been gathering up bits of the children from the orphan trains, and he found himself scanning the floor for more of them.

But instead it was a large fragment of a portrait that drew his attention. He was intrigued by the subject's narrow, long-fingered hands and the competence with which they were holding his pistol. It was the gun the man was holding that sent cold swooping into the pit of his stomach. For a moment he simply stared at it, trying to rearrange the image somehow, convince himself he wasn't seeing what he thought he was.

"Shea," he called out, hoping she wouldn't hear the tremor in his voice. "What plates are these you'd kept?"

She came back into the studio with her broom. "I sent almost all the landscapes to New York. I'd been keeping the children's negatives here with me, and the rest were portraits I made this summer and fall."

"Pictures you took here in Denver or up in the mountains?"

"Both," she answered. "Why?"

Now that he looked more closely at the fragment of negative, Cam could see the picture hadn't been taken in the studio. The subject was seated on some sort of rustic bench. But again, it was the gun that drew him. He would have recognized it anywhere.

It was a double-action Navy Colt pistol, with gold fittings and silver chasing along the barrel. The grip was of mother-of-pearl, polished to a moonstone sheen. The gun was half of a commemorative set his troops had given him when he'd made major back in the spring of 1863. He'd sworn he'd treasure the pair of them always, but always hadn't lasted as long as he thought.

Cam took one last look at those long elegant hands, at the gun that they were fondling—the twin to the one he was wearing on his hip. Without even being able to see his face or the color of his hair, Cam knew who this man was. His name was Wes Seaver, and if Seaver was here in Denver, Cam's past was catching up to him.

TWELVE

*S*hea opened the studio door one morning several weeks after Christmas and found a big wooden box on the landing. When she stepped out to examine it, she found the crate unmarked, unlabeled. Clearly it wasn't the photographic equipment she'd been expecting from New York.

She glanced down to where Mr. Nicholson was sweeping the walk in front of his store. "G'morning, Abe," she called to him. "Did you see who left this box for me?"

Nicholson paused and shook his head. "Haven't seen anyone 'cept Mrs. Franklin going into her shop. Must be the weather."

Shea glanced at the gray, fleecy sky. They'd have snow before nightfall. She could feel the cold, damp bite of it in the rising wind.

Frowning, she looked down at the pine box, then nudged it with her toe. Something rustled inside—something alive.

Shea stepped hastily backward. It had been nearly

three weeks since someone ransacked her studio, and neither Cam nor the sheriff had been able to discover who it was. Had the same person left this box for her? Was this another threat?

The faint rustling came again. Were there snakes inside the box? Or rats?

Her skin crawled with the possibilities. For an instant she considered going for the sheriff, then she straightened with an exasperated sniff. "Don't you be a fool, girl," she admonished herself. "Just open the damn box, and have done with it."

She went inside to get her hammer—and her Winchester. Then, bracing one knee to hold the top in place, she pried out the nails around the edges. The whine from the nails set Shea's teeth on edge, and the movements of whatever was inside the box became more agitated. Once she'd pulled them all, Shea took up her rifle and flipped open the top.

A huge calico cat leaped gracefully onto the floor of the landing.

Shea stumbled back against the door frame. "Rufus!" she squeaked.

Rufus looked her up and down—and hissed.

Shea laughed, feeling both foolish and relieved. It was just Ty's cat!

Setting her rifle aside, she hunkered down and extended a hand. Rufus hissed and swiped at her.

Giving up on making friends with Rufus, Shea examined the box more closely. Inside was a tattered piece of blanket, a chipped pottery bowl, and a hastily folded paper.

She opened the note and read the scrawled, uneven letters:

DEER SHA
PLEZE FEED MY CAT.
TYLER MORRAN

They must be gone, Shea thought on a sharp wave of concern. Though she'd spoken to Ty directly only half a dozen times since Christmas, she kept up with him through her son. As long as Ty and his father were in Denver, as long as Rand and Ty were friends, she was able to keep an eye on him. If there had been trouble, she was near enough to help. If he'd needed money or food or medicine, she'd have found a way to provide it.

Now that tough, brave, self-sufficient, and vulnerable boy was out of her reach. He was at the mercy of a father who was so wrapped up in his own misery that he could barely acknowledge the world at large, much less his son.

Shea couldn't even be certain where the two of them were. They'd gone back to the mountains, she supposed, back to the mining camp. But why would they go in the dead of winter? Had they run out of money? Were they one step ahead of the law?

Shea wanted to grab up her shawl and run over to the cabin to see what she could learn, but first she needed to get Rufus inside. She was still down on her knees trying to coax the wily calico close when Owen came puffing up the steps.

"What's all this?" he asked her.

"Ty and his father seem to have left town. He asked me to take care of his cat," Shea explained. "Ty calls him Rufus."

As if drawn by the sound of his name, Rufus tiptoed around the far side of the box and blinked at Owen. Owen blinked back, then extended his hand.

"He isn't very friendly," Shea warned him.

Just to make a fool of her, Rufus nuzzled up against Owen's fingers and began to purr.

"Such a nice kitty," Owen crooned and scratched behind the cat's ears. "Nice Rufus."

Rufus immediately rolled over and exposed his tummy, inviting more extensive scratching.

"Must just be *me* he doesn't like," Shea murmured, pushing to her feet. She carted the box inside and set it in one corner of the studio, wondering what she was supposed to feed this troublesome creature.

Owen scooped up Rufus and followed her in. "We finish painting today?" he asked her.

They'd been working on the studio since the day after Christmas. They'd swept up the glass, repaired the furniture, and repainted the walls. Once the new camera and supplies arrived, Shea could begin to reschedule her portrait sittings and see if she could pick up where she'd left off. But the incident had shaken her confidence.

She could see that the vandalism had disturbed Cam, too. He'd become more protective since that night, more attentive. More apprehensive somehow. She could sense a brittleness in him that was strangely incompatible with the man she'd come to know. It was almost as if he was waiting . . .

But waiting for what?

Shea gave a snort of impatience and dispatched Owen down the block to see if he could find something Rufus might like for breakfast.

Cam was still on her mind when he burst through the door a few minutes later. "Are they here?" he demanded. "Have you seen them?"

"Seen who?" she asked. Cam was rumpled and unshaven. She heard a ragged edge of panic in his voice. Alarm spiraled through her.

"Rand and Ty."

"Rand?" she echoed, her throat pinching tight.

"This was the only other place I could think of to look for them," he told her, trying to catch his breath.

"I found Ty's cat outside my door this morning. I think he and his father have left Denver. Did Rand go with them?" she asked incredulously.

Cam pulled a crumpled paper from the pocket of his coat. "I found this when I went to wake Rand this morning."

The note was written in Rand's careful copperplate script.

> *Dear Pa and Aunt Lily,*
> *Ty's father went off yesterday. Ty says he thinks he knows where he is, so we are headed out to find him. We should be back in a couple of days. Please don't worry.*
>
>> *Love,*
>> *Randall Cameron Gallimore*

> *P.S. I took Jasper and some food with me.*

Shea looked up at Cam, at the taut, pinched lines between his brows, and the narrow set of his mouth. New shadows haunted the blue of his eyes. She reached for him, catching his hand, feeling his warmth and sinewy strength beneath her fingertips.

"Surely they'll be all right."

Cam shook off her hold and paced from one end of the studio to the other. "Do you have any idea where they went?"

"Well, there's a mining camp up in the mountains—"

"Where is it?" he demanded. "How far?"

"A full day's ride when the weather's good."

"When the weather's good," he echoed, the lines in his face settling deeper. "But it's going to snow . . ."

Hot threads of apprehension darted through her. It might very well be snowing up in the mountains already.

"Oh, Cam! They're such little boys to be up there all alone." *Her* little boys—Rand, her precious son, and Ty, the child she'd been mothering in Rand's stead.

Cam clasped her hand in his, giving back the assurance she'd given him. "They'll be all right. Now can you tell me how to find that camp so I can go and bring them home?"

She shook her head. "I'm going with you."

"Oh, Shea," he protested. "I don't think—"

"The turnoff to the camp could be hard to spot, especially if it's snowing," she argued, thinking how easy it would be for the boys to get lost up there. Besides, she wasn't going to sit in Denver when her son was missing.

"It's damned rough country," he warned her.

"I know what kind of country it is."

"The temperature's dropping, and if it's started to snow—"

"Then, don't we need to dress warmly and get on our way?"

Something about her pragmatism won him over. "I'll be back in half an hour with supplies and horses." He paused halfway to the door and glanced back at her. "You're a damn stubborn woman, Shea Waterston."

Coming from him, the words sounded like a compliment.

• • •

They'd trekked a good long way up into the mountains before it started to snow. At first Cam tried to convince himself that what he saw ahead was fog creeping down from the high country, but soon enough the whorls of white resolved themselves into tight, dry flakes. As the snow thickened around them, Cam glanced back and saw that Shea was staying close on his heels in spite of the pace he'd set for them.

She was bundled up against the cold in a heavy woolen skirt, a sheepskin jacket she'd borrowed from Owen, and two pairs of gloves. A long knitted scarf tied down her hat.

Had Rand thought to dress as warmly? Cam wondered. Had he brought matches, food, and blankets in case he and Ty got stranded? Did Ty know the way to this camp well enough that they wouldn't get lost? Speaking those worries aloud would have made them far too real, yet they wore at him with every step.

"They'll be all right," Shea said, nudging her horse up close beside his on the narrow trail, speaking the reassurance as if she'd read his mind. "Ty's as resourceful as they come, and Rand won't let him take any foolish chances."

Still, beneath the broad brim of her hat, Cam could see Shea's face was every bit as set and grim as his own.

They pressed ahead. Here along the edge of the ice-skimmed stream they were sheltered from the wind, but ahead, where the trail wound higher, all Cam could see was roiling clouds of white. The snow fell faster the further they went. It blew in their faces and piled up in the folds of their clothes.

They lost the light as the clouds settled low and the velvety pines closed in around them. The trail turned slick and treacherous underfoot. The horses labored, chuffing with the altitude and the effort it took to keep plowing ahead. Only when Shea's horse stumbled in a belly-deep drift did Cam ask about stopping for the night.

"I'm afraid I'll miss the turnoff to the mining camp if it gets too dark," she admitted, shivering.

The world around them had gone silent, opaque. The swirling snow had a milk blue shimmer that obscured everything but this one dim notch between the trees.

"There's an old trapper's cabin not far ahead," Cam conceded. "We'll stop there and wait for daylight."

With every step they took Cam prayed he'd find the boys holed up in that battered shack, but when they reached it, the snow blown against the door lay undisturbed. Fighting down desolation, Cam sent Shea into the cabin while he saw to the horses.

By the time he brought in their saddles, Shea had a fire going. She'd unfurled their bedrolls across the floor and had melted snow enough to make tea. He hunkered down on the bedding closest to the flames to warm himself. With the heat of the fire and the flickering orange glow dancing over the walls, the shack might have seemed snug, almost cozy if he hadn't been so worried about the boys.

"Surely they've found someplace to shelter for the night," she said hopefully, though he could sense the tautness in her, too.

"If the boys left Denver at dawn," Shea went on, offering him a steaming mug of tea, "they may have made it to the mining camp before the weather got bad."

Cam gave a low, noncommittal grunt and unbuckled his gun belt before he accepted the tea.

Shea sipped from her own cup, then set it aside. "Do

you mind if I have a look at your pistol?" Shea asked him.

Cam ignored the sharp twist of uneasiness in his gut. "Of course not."

She slid the pistol from his holster, handling the weapon carefully, but without a woman's squeamishness. She settled her palm around the mother-of-pearl grip and, taking care to turn the barrel away, she examined the inlay and the chasing.

"Where have I seen this gun before?" she asked him.

Apprehension jolted along Cam's nerves. "It was hanging in my room while you were recovering."

"You've taken to wearing it more often lately," she observed.

Cam nodded, nursing his tea. "For the same reason I've been having Rand ride back and forth to town with me. Because there are more miscreants in Colorado this year than last."

She frowned running her fingers along the gun's delicate silver traceries. "I don't think that's why I remember it."

The broken photographic plate flashed before Cam's eyes. She'd seen a gun just like this one when she'd taken that photograph of Wes Seaver. He just prayed she wouldn't remember.

"The pistol is one of a pair my men gave me after the Rapidan," he volunteered, hoping to divert her.

She glanced at him. "Why?"

He swallowed down more of his tea. It tasted gritty and sulfurous as cannon smoke. "Well, I'd made major, for one thing, and I'd managed to keep more than half my troopers alive through three years of battle."

It didn't sound like much, but considering what those years had been like, it was little short of a miracle.

"What happened to this gun's mate?" she asked instead.

"I lost it," he said shortly.

"How?"

Trust Shea to ask. He hesitated trying to decide how much of the truth to tell her. More rather than less, he thought.

"Toward the closing days of the war I was assigned to a roughshod detachment of soldiers and was fool enough to take that fancy rig with me. Right off one of the officers offered to buy the guns. When I wouldn't sell, he tried to win them at poker. That didn't work, so he had his orderly try to steal them. Finally he took my horse from the picket line and deliberately mistreated him." Cam shrugged. "I couldn't tolerate that, so I picked a fight."

"And you lost?"

Cam stared down into his tea. "Yeah."

It hadn't been a fair fight. Riding with outlaws, he shouldn't have expected it to be. Still, losing to Seaver had rankled him. He'd been sprawled on his face breathing dust when Seaver propped a foot in the small of his back and pulled the pistol from the holster at Cam's hip.

"I'm leaving the other of these fine guns for you," Seaver had drawled. "So that every time you draw it, you'll remember I'm the better man."

"And the officer kept the gun?" Shea asked him.

Her question jarred Cam, chased the memory away. "He took it as his due."

Shea admired the Colt a moment longer, polished the fingerprints from the barrel with the hem of her skirt, and slid the pistol into its holster.

The wash of relief came so strong Cam felt almost drunk on it. If she didn't remember now where she'd seen this gun's mate, she'd never connect him to Wes Seaver.

Shea went to rummaging through the saddlebags, pulling out bread and cheese and apples for their dinner. Cam's stomach rumbled as she set the food before him, and he couldn't help worrying about what Rand and Ty were having for supper.

"And you're sure this mining camp is where Morran would go?" he asked her.

Shea looked up from slicing the bread. "Didn't the barkeep over where he and Ty were living tell you some of Morran's cronies came and got him?"

"Which for miners is odd," Cam reflected. "Winter isn't a miner's most productive time. So why would Morran hightail it back to this camp? And what would prevent him from taking Ty?"

"Could they have made some kind of a strike?"

"That's possible," he allowed, but knew it wasn't likely. "I just wish the boys hadn't been as brash and reckless."

Shea's mouth tipped up at the corner, and she slid him a sidelong glance. "I'll warrant you were every bit as brash and reckless when you were younger."

"Oh, I don't know," he said with another shrug. "Has Lily been telling tales on me?"

"She *did* say you won medals in the war. That sounds brash and reckless to me."

The mention of the war caught him like it always did, quick and hard. Drenching him in memories.

"It's war that makes men brash and reckless," he said with more than a modicum of bitterness. "It makes them do things against their beliefs, against their conscience. War forces men to deny their humanity, and when what they've done has turned them into beasts, the government gives them medals for doing it."

Shea might have seen how it was with him the night of the opening and understood some of it. But not all—and he wasn't about to enlighten her.

He took a slice of bread and a piece of cheese and shifted back onto his elbows, putting some distance between them. "So tell me about growing up in Ireland," he suggested. "I'll wager you weren't the most staid and docile of children, either."

She laughed as if she were pleased that he'd given her leave to speak of happier things. As they ate, she told him about her life in the cottage by the sea. She spoke of her da and mam, of her brothers and sisters, of boating and fishing and riding over miles of rolling countryside at her father's heels.

She was so lovely sitting there in the firelight, her eyes alive with memories, the lilt in her voice deepening, her words flowing with a special kind of music. The glow of the fire set the copper lights to shimmering in her coppery curls and deepened the ruddy flush the wind had scoured into her cheeks.

It seemed all at once like a very long time since he'd touched her softness or tasted her warmth. He yearned for that tonight, for comfort and surcease. He longed for the vitality of her flesh beneath his hands and the sweetness of her mouth. He wanted to lie down with her, wrap her in his arms, and forget how cold and weary and worried he was about the boys.

But he couldn't bring himself to compromise Shea any more than he had already compromised her by bringing her here. He couldn't take advantage of either her womanliness or her warm heart. Still, he needed some harmless bit of contact.

From where he was propped up beside her, listening to her tales of her home, he could reach the thick, brushy bloom of curls at the bottom of her tightly wrapped braid. He raised his hand to stroke those gingery strands, to rub the silky corkscrew tendrils between his fingertips. Her hair was as soft and vital as Shea was herself. And as mesmerizingly lovely.

At his touch, she paused, an unfinished sentence still poised on her lips. She closed her eyes, and for a score of heartbeats went utterly still. When she turned to him, he could see the same lonely desperation in her face, the same yearning for tenderness and succor he was feeling.

His chest filled with warmth, filled with wonder.

"Shea," he whispered, wanting to offer her what she needed. "Oh, Shea."

Tightening his hold on her braid, he drew her toward him.

Shea hesitated; her eyes darkened and her mouth bowed. For an instant he thought she might pull away, but then she sighed and came to him.

He kissed her gently at first, his lips barely grazing hers. Her mouth was succulent and even softer than he remembered— plush, pillowy pink and fresh with the taste of apples. His lips settled over hers, lingering and then withdrawing, sipping and pressing.

Her mouth moved sinuously beneath his, caressing, retreating and giving back. She grazed his upper lip with the tip of her tongue, rasping along the bristly edge of his mustache, then returned to slick his lower lip.

As they kissed, he pulled the ribbon from her braid and began to untwine her soft, thick hair. He spread the loosened strands against her shoulders and back in a mass of tumbled coppery-gold curls. He filled his palms with that softness as he eased her down across their bedrolls.

Lying beside her length to length, he was reminded

how small she was, how delicate, how deliciously
feminine. He pulled her close and raised his hand to
cup her cheek. He tipped her mouth to his and lavished
those full, sweet lips with the swipe of his tongue.

This was what they needed, Cam decided hazily.
Closeness and comfort, the balm of touching, the companionship of these few shared intimacies. They needed
shelter from the cold and from the fear that had dogged
them every mile they rode today. Surely no harm could
come of giving and receiving something so simple,
something so basic.

They kissed for a very long time, slow, lazy, languorous kisses. Kisses that rode the rhythm of their breathing. Kisses that shuttered the world and their worries
away. Kisses that teased and probed and promised.

Her hands slid over him as they kissed, going around
his ribs and up his back. Cam drew her closer, telling
himself comfort and succor were all he meant to give—
and all he wanted for himself.

He should have known better.

Tangled there before the fire, their kisses ripened.
Deepened. Darkened. They skimmed the ragged edge
of passion.

As innocent as Cam had meant those kisses to be,
they kindled a thick, rich heat between them. Cam's
senses sang with his awareness of Shea's earthy lavender
scent, with the oddly provocative way she moved beneath him, with the soft, appreciative sighs she gave as
he raised his mouth from hers.

How much he longed to ease her out of her clothes
and lie with her skin to skin, to tangle his legs with
hers, and skim his hands the length of her back. He
wanted to savor that closeness, savor that heat. *He
wanted to make love with her*.

The admission sobered him, and before he could act,

Cam rolled away from her. He sat up at the edge of the blanket, dizzy and disoriented.

"I need to—to go check on the horses," he managed to mumble.

But as he reached for his holster and his pistol, Shea caught his hand. "The horses will be fine," she assured him, her thumb caressing the curve of his wrist where the blood ran hot and close to the surface. "I want you to stay with me."

He shook his head and swallowed. "If I stay," he whispered, "I'm going to end up making love to you."

Her dusky green gaze rose to his. Her eyes were soft and bottomless with yearning. "I know," she answered.

His breath caught in his throat and he stared at her. "That is isn't why I brought you here."

Shea nodded and came to kneel beside him. Slowly she lifted his hand and curled his fingers around the top button in the row that ran down the front of her bodice.

"Shea?" he managed to whisper.

She inclined her head.

Desire condensed inside him like breath on glass.

Cam slipped one whorled pewter button from its buttonhole. With fingers that trembled, he undid a second and a third. Shea's bodice began to part, revealing a long, ivory white V of skin, and the wash-softened folds of her underthings.

He reached to skim that soft freshly exposed throat, the creamy billow of her breasts above the neckline of her chemise. He pulled the satin bow at the neckline of the quilted jaconet she'd worn for warmth, and loosened the hooks along the front.

Then he pulled her against him and kissed her, slow, sweet, sensual kisses.

They parted long enough to finish removing their

clothes. His vest and shirt, her bodice and jaconet. His boots and trousers, her skirt and flannel petticoats. They paused in their disrobing to touch and savor and fondle. But the cabin was chill, and soon they sought their bedrolls.

There beneath the blankets they came together skin to skin, opened mouth to opened mouth, a sweet damp heat mingling between them. She tangled her fingers in his hair and he stroked his palms down the length of her back.

There was such delectable comfort here, such tenderness and warmth and communion. Such joy and forgetfulness, such ease and sustenance. This was what he'd wanted—to be with her, to have her be with him. To lose themselves for a little while.

Kisses that had been filled with sweetness and succor became sleek and erotic. Touches flowed, bodies seethed with heat and provocation.

Cam lifted his hips against her mound. Shea moaned deep in her throat, soft and enticing. They began to move together in a slow erotic dance, their hands gliding and caressing, encompassing and exploring collarbones and bellies, breasts and thighs, shoulders and spines and hipbones. His sex and hers.

He had never made love to a woman he cared about the way he cared about Shea, and there was richness and delight in cherishing her. He gave of himself freely and for her sake, courting her pleasure. Shea gave of herself as well, communed with him with that same selfless generosity.

They played together until the worry and the weariness receded to the very periphery of their thoughts, and their senses were fogged with each other.

As she welcomed him into herself, Cam shivered with the heat and passion of that deep communion.

The sentient bonds drew taut between them, but they were linked by far more than the promise of pleasure. It was as if the boundaries between them had melted away, as if they were one flesh, one need, one soul.

They moved in a slow, sliding, sinuous measure, heads bowed to each other, their hips rolling in a rhythm men and women had shared forever. They were swept up in a deep mesmerizing voluptuousness, a communion without words, a search for sensation as much for each other as for themselves.

At length the tempo of their movements heightened. The friction of skin against skin, tongue against tongue, male into female became exquisite pleasure. That pleasure expanded, swelling from the places where their bodies joined, rising hot in their chests, leaping along their nerves, setting their hearts to thundering.

They cried out as completion rolled over them. He came, spilling himself into her, filling her, completing her. She came a moment after, drawing him deep into herself, binding him to her in ultimate and unconditional embrace.

They tangled together in the aftermath, petting, murmuring, drifting, replete. Cam had never known such fulfillment, such a sense of peace and satisfaction.

He wanted to tell Shea what that meant to him, what she meant to him, but he didn't know how. As he struggled to find the words, the haze of languorous perfection deepened, and together they drifted into dreamless sleep.

Shea awoke stiff and cold and alone amidst their tumbled bedding. She sat up with a start, the thick stew of worry bubbling inside her chest even before she'd opened her eyes. Was it light yet? Had the snow stopped? Were they going to be able to find Rand and Ty?

Shea scrambled from beneath the covers and wriggled into the clothes Cam had been thoughtful enough to gather up and set near the fire. As she fumbled with the buttons and hooks that had opened so easily the night before, she did her best not to think about Cam or about the marvelous and terrifying thing they'd done together.

Yet the merest thought of him brought a strange warmth to her chest and an anticipatory tightness to her belly. She did her best to dispel those feelings. She bundled and tied up their blankets, put water on to boil, and sliced up the last of the bread and cheese.

She was making their tea when Cam pushed open the door. A blast of fresh mountain air rolled into the cabin. Shea looked up and saw him standing in the doorway, tall and dark and magnificent against a world of shimmering white.

And in that instant she knew she loved him.

The realization rolled over her like ocean breakers roaring toward shore, stunning her, leaving her reeling and exhilarated. It shook her perceptions of him, of the world. Of herself. Her heart skipped hard beneath her breastbone, and she hastily averted her eyes, terrified that he would see what she was feeling. She busied herself setting out food and fumbled for something to say to him.

"Has—has it stopped snowing?"

Cam stomped the slush off his boots and came into the cabin. "Not only has it stopped snowing, but the temperature's risen forty degrees. Everything's melting."

She could smell the thaw, the warmth and earthiness that had swept into the cabin at Cam's heels.

"When are we leaving to look for the boys?"

"As soon as I get the horses saddled." He hesitated. "Is that all right?"

"Finding Rand and Ty is why we came," she answered and thrust the mug of tea at him.

Cam hunkered down beside her in front of the fire. He took a sip from his cup, then paused to tuck back the cluster of errant curls that straggled against her cheek. His touch was gentle, intensely intimate.

Though she shivered, the brush of his fingers against her skin sent heat blossoming at the pit of her stomach. Feverish agitation climbed up inside her ribs. Her throat went dry as tinder. It was a moment before she could raise her gaze to his.

When she did, he was close enough that she could see the crinkles at the corners of his eyes and the tenderness in the bowing of his mouth. For a moment she thought he meant to kiss her, but she managed to maneuver the plate of food between them.

Quirking one eyebrow, Cam retreated, helping himself to a slice of bread and a piece of cheese and settling down on one of the bedrolls to eat.

Shea set the plate on the floor between them and took a piece of bread for herself, but she was too overwhelmingly aware of Cam to swallow more than a mouthful.

She had fallen in love with him. One quick glance from beneath her lashes elicited the same clutch of elation she'd felt when he opened the door, the same fierce joy and warmth, the feverish awareness and possessiveness.

Only now that she recognized what this wondrous feeling was, she was forced to acknowledge everything that made loving him impossible—starting with the fact that he had adopted her child.

Cam must have sensed her uneasiness and edged closer again. "Shea?" he asked, his voice deep and tinged with concern. "Is everything all right?"

Shea started at the question. "Fine," she answered. "Everything's fine."

"Are you sure?" She could feel how closely he was watching her. "You're not sorry that we—"

"No!" Shea's head came up. She couldn't let him think that she regretted for a moment what might well be the most wonderful night of her life.

In truth they had come together because they were cold and tired and worried half to death about the boys. They'd needed the comfort of touching and bodies tangled close. They'd needed the solace of kisses and desires so deep they kept the world at bay. But in the end, what had passed between them had been something else, something extraordinary.

Shea had never known a man to offer up so much of himself in making love. Cam had courted her with the patience of his caresses. He had devoted himself to fulfilling her needs and desires. As they'd made love he had opened himself to her, showing her his innate loneliness and his longing for companionship, his joy in touching and being close, his willingness to reveal the most secret and fragile parts of himself to her.

Shea had never felt so revered and treasured as when she lay in Cam's arms. She'd never felt so connected to another human being—or so undeserving of his trust.

Her unworthiness stood out like a broadside, in the light of day. From the moment she'd realized Rand was her son, she'd been lying to Cam. She'd deliberately courted his confidences, then manipulated him to have more time with her boy. She'd even lied to him about her reasons for wanting to come up here with him. Even as she'd been taking shelter and comfort in his arms, she'd been nurturing the seeds of his betrayal in her heart.

Pure, gut-twisting guilt ate at her as she looked hard and long at what she'd done. She loved this man. She'd lain in his arms and shared the most tender intimacies a man and woman could have together. And all the while, she'd been keeping a secret that could destroy his world.

Then, all at once, Cam pushed to his feet and stood over her. "Well, then," he said, "if you're packed up and ready to head out, I'll go saddle the horses."

As he bent to grab up their saddles, the need to tell him the truth rose in Shea like a flood tide. The words she'd guarded so carefully sprang into her throat. The declarations burned like pepper on her tongue. She couldn't leave this place without telling him the truth about his boy, about her son. Without telling him the truth about herself.

When she'd revealed her secrets to him the last time, he had accepted them and comforted her. She couldn't imagine he would respond the same way now.

She turned to him while the resolution was burning hot in her belly. "Cam?"

He paused, silhouetted in the brightness of the open doorway. "Yes?"

For a moment the words were wedged tight in her throat, packed close by tears. Then she took a breath and revealed all of her secrets, all of herself. "I believe Rand is my son. I believe he's the child I gave away."

He stared at her, his eyes gone suddenly to flat blue planes, his expression stark and unreadable.

"He's exactly the same age as my son would be," she pushed ahead. "He came west on an orphan train to St. Joseph, Missouri, during the fall of 1866—just as my son did. Rand's eyes are almost the color of mine. He has that same special way with horses that both his father and my brother had. I believe he's mine."

"He's not your boy." Cam's voice was toneless, implacable.

She raised her chin. "I've never felt such an affinity for another child."

Cam didn't so much as question her. He just looked at her as if he didn't know who she was.

"He isn't yours," was all he said. Then he turned and went to saddle the horses.

Rand wasn't her son!

Shea was wrong. She'd made a mistake. What she claimed was impossible.

Cam was shaking inside, breathless and aching and coldly furious as he spurred his horse up the trail through the melting snow.

What could have possessed Shea to make such a claim? What was she thinking? How could those few coincidences and a handful of physical similarities convince her Rand was the child she'd given up?

It was ridiculous, preposterous.

It wasn't as if she'd tracked Rand down, arrived at the farm in search of the child she'd given up. She'd come to them by accident, by the purest chance.

Or the hand of fate.

Cam scowled and squinted into the snowy glare that lay ahead, and eased his horse along the slippery, twisting trail.

He didn't believe in fate. He didn't believe in miraculous reunions. He didn't believe Shea was right about who Rand was.

He sheared a glance back to where Shea was resolutely following him deeper and deeper into the mountains. He couldn't tell what she was thinking, but beneath the shadow of her hat he could see that her mouth was set in a thin determined line.

She really did believe that Rand was her child, god-damn her. She wouldn't lie about something as important as this, not something that could shatter so many lives. Shea might keep secrets, but she didn't lie.

Of course she didn't have proof of what she was claiming, either. Yet even if she'd come to him with sworn oaths and affidavits, he wouldn't have believed her, wouldn't have given up his son.

He couldn't give him up, even if he'd wanted to. Cam himself might love Rand as if he were his blood and bone, but that boy was Lily's life, the center of her world, the very bedrock of her existence. He couldn't let Shea—or anyone else—threaten his family.

He wouldn't *ever* let Shea take Rand away.

Not that she could. If Cam knew one thing, it was the law, and Shea had no rights at all before the bar. She had no way to prove she was Rand's mother. She'd forfeited her claims to him when she'd left him on the steps of that foundling home and walked away. It didn't matter that she'd gone back; it didn't matter that she'd been searching for him all this time.

What mattered was that Cam had taken Rand as his son that day in St. Joe. He had the papers the Children's Aid Society agent had given him, granting him custody. He had gone on to adopt Rand, all legal and proper. Rand was his, his and Lily's.

He stole another glance at Shea and his chest went tight. He thought that when they'd touched and kissed, they'd been sharing something fine and pure and extraordinary. He thought she'd offered herself to him because she had yearned for tenderness and communion as fiercely as he, because she sensed the bond that

had been growing between them. How could she have
made love to him with such sweetness and abandon just
last night, then told him what she believed about Rand
this morning?

For the brief, sweet whisper of time when they'd lain
together, he felt as if he'd wrapped his hands around
something solid, something worth having, something
just for him. Now everything he thought he'd found
had crumbled in his grasp leaving him with nothing.

Leaving him with less than nothing. Where once
there had been burgeoning hope that Shea was something special, there was now a cold hard knot of suspicion that she had lain with him for reasons of her own.

Whatever had made her do it, at least she hadn't
told either Lily or Rand what she suspected. Somehow
he'd have to find a way to convince her not to tell
them, find a way to make her promise—

"Cam, I see them!" Shea cried out.

He jerked around and looked toward where she was
pointing. Three riders were picking their way down a
snowy incline that breached the rim of the next rise.
Though they were still some distance away, Cam recognized Jasper's reddish hide and the size and shape of his
son astride him.

Feeling shaky and light-headed, Cam cupped his
hands around his mouth. "Hullo, Rand!" he shouted.

His voice echoed off the high rock walls, and Rand
waved back. The gesture was extravagant, filled with
confidence.

Damn fool boy! Cam found himself thinking, anger
chasing hot on the heels of relief. To his son all this had
been a grand adventure. Now he'd have to persuade
Rand otherwise, perhaps with the help of a hickory
switch.

"Oh, Cam!" Shea breathed from where she'd pulled up beside him. "They're safe!"

Cameron turned to her and was unsettled by the shimmer of tears on her cheeks and the gleam of possessiveness in her eyes as she watched his son picking his way toward them.

As they waited, he reached out and clasped her wrist. "Not a word to Rand of what you told me this morning," he warned. "I don't want him knowing about this until I've had a chance to look into your claims."

She stiffened, her eyes wide with reproach. "I would never do anything to hurt Rand," she averred. "Or Lily, either."

At least she understood what was at stake.

"Then see that you don't!" he hissed at her.

"Cam. Oh, Cam," she whispered so softly he wasn't sure she had meant for him to hear. "I didn't mean for any of this to happen the way it did."

Cam didn't have a chance to ask her what she meant, because Rand came loping toward them.

"You didn't need to come all the way up here, Pa!" he shouted. "We'd have been home tonight."

Cam rode out to meet his son, thinking how much older Rand suddenly seemed, how insufferably pleased he was with himself.

But as Cam closed the distance between them, Rand must have read the worry in his face. In the space of a heartbeat Rand's demeanor changed. He became a child again, one who'd suddenly realized just how much he'd displeased his father.

"Geez, Pa, I'm sorry," he began. "I'm sorry if I worried you. I didn't mean to. I'm really sorry. I didn't think—"

Cam drew rein beside his son, reached across, grabbed him, and hugged him hard. He needed the contact, the feel of his tall gangly boy against him, the reassurance that his son was safe. Rand's cheek came cold on his, and there was the smell about him of onions, tobacco smoke, and bacon grease. They were threatening smells, somehow, and Cam hugged him harder.

"Just what the devil were you thinking about, boy?" he demanded the moment he let Rand go. "Coming all the way up here, just you and Ty? Your aunt Lily's been beside herself since we found your note. How could you be so reckless?"

Rand bobbed his head. "I'm sorry, Pa. I didn't mean to make Aunt Lily worry. But when Ty said he was headed up into the mountains after his pa, I figured I couldn't let him go all by himself."

Cam scowled at the boy. "Ty's your friend; he isn't your responsibility. You deliberately left home without permission. You went somewhere you knew you shouldn't go and put yourself in a situation that might have been dangerous. It's only by the grace of God that you and Ty didn't get hurt or lost or frozen to death. Once we get back to the house, we're going to have a long talk and decide on your punishment."

"All right, Pa," Rand offered meekly. "I'm really sorry I worried you."

Shea nudged her pony closer just as Sam and Ty joined the group. Cam could tell by the expression in their faces that they were surprised to see her, but he didn't offer any explanations.

Instead he leveled his gaze on Sam Morran. "Are the boys all right?" Cam asked him. "Did you take good care of them?"

"They got up to where I was staying just before the storm blew in," Morran answered as if he didn't like being questioned. "We fed 'em, we watered 'em, and we gave 'em a place to sleep. I was bringing 'em back to Denver this morning."

Cam nodded, not quite satisfied. "Mrs. Waterston tells me you were at some sort of mining camp, is that right?"

Morran's eyes widened and his gaze flickered to Shea. "It's where she met the boy and me."

"And why did you go back there?" Cam asked.

When it looked like Morran didn't know how to answer, Ty spoke up. "Some of Pa's friends come and got him. You had business up there, didn't you, Pa? Something about the claims?"

Morran glanced at his son. "Yeah, something like that."

Cam wouldn't have minded questioning Sam Morran more closely, but gray clouds were beginning to crowd out the sun and the wind was picking up. Cam didn't want to take the chance of getting caught in another snowstorm.

"We'll talk, Morran, once we get back to Denver," he promised and turned toward home.

They all fell in behind him: Rand riding on his flank, Shea trailing after them, Ty and his father bringing up the rear. Cam should have been content to be bringing his son home safely. But his world had changed since he'd ridden out, and he didn't have any idea what to make of it.

It was just after dark when they turned up the lane to the farm. Shea was cold, saddle-sore, and tired all the way down to her bones. Yet for all her weariness, she was humming with tension, overwhelmed with remorse, afraid for the future in a way she hadn't been since Simon died. Fear sat like a weight on her chest, making it hard to breathe, hard to think beyond the terrible, life-altering mistake she'd made this morning.

Since the night she'd asked Cam about the man she'd shot, the two of them had shared a bond neither of them had expected to have with anyone. Shea saw things in him that no one else ever saw, and gradually he'd revealed the more closely held parts of himself to her.

In return for keeping his confidences, he'd opened his home to her, helped her establish her studio and start her business. He'd accepted her even when she'd told him about the child she'd given away, and held her close when everything she'd worked for had been reduced to chaos. The two of them had been good together as friends and confidantes.

She shivered, remembering just how good they'd been together as lovers in the smoky darkness of that mountain cabin. How each touch, each kiss had been imbued with overwhelming tenderness and deep communion. It was as if they'd joined on some level that was closer than skin to skin. As if their hearts had touched, as if their nerves had surged with the same impulses. As if they'd come together in some extraordinary way.

Then because she'd realized what being with Cam meant to her, she'd told him the last of her secrets.

Shea shivered again, this time with dread. How much had she lost by telling the truth? Certainly she'd lost Cam's trust, risked Lily's friendship, and maybe even forfeited contact with her child.

How could she make her way in the world if Cam refused to let her see her boy? How would she live without contact with her son, now that she'd finally found him?

As they rode up the drive toward the Gallimore

farmhouse, its windows glowed with their usual warmth and welcome. Yet somehow Shea had never felt more alone, more separate from the people she'd come to care for and depend on here in Denver.

As Shea pulled up behind Dr. Farley's buggy, Emmet led Lily carefully out of the house.

She took one look at the weary riders and gave a shout of joy. "Rand!" she cried, running down the steps and into the lane. "Oh, Rand! You're safe!"

Rand jumped off Jasper's back and threw himself into Lily's arms. They came together with enough force to rattle their bones, but neither of them seemed to mind.

"Oh, Aunt Lily, I'm sorry!" Rand exclaimed, hugging her. "I'm so glad to be home!"

Lily ran her hands across his shoulders and down his back, as if she needed to confirm that he was solid and real and here with her. "Are you all right, child?"

"I didn't mean for you to worry—"

"Did you get caught in the blizzard?"

"—but when Ty said he was going up into the mountains—"

"It got so cold!"

"—I thought I'd better go with him."

"You were you dressed warmly enough, weren't you, Rand? You didn't get frostbite, did you? Can you wiggle your toes?"

"My toes are fine," he assured her. "Oh, Aunt Lily, I wish I hadn't worried you so much!"

Lily hugged him almost off his feet and burst into tears.

Watching the two of them together, Shea's own eyes teared and her heart broke all over again.

Just then, Cam nudged his horse up close to hers.

"She's his mother now," he whispered. "There's

nothing to be gained by telling either of them what you told me this morning. It's here Rand belongs, here in the only home he's ever known."

The truth of his words tore into her, slicing so much deeper because what Cam said mattered to her. But neither the truth he'd spoken nor the pain he'd inflicted could keep Shea from longing for her son.

She wanted Rand and the life she'd missed and the family she'd never had. She yearned to be part of something as wondrous and enduring as what she saw between Rand and Lily, between Cam and her boy. She ached for that same closeness with her son. But what good would it do to claim her boy if he ended up hating her for depriving him of something so wonderful?

When Lily was finally done hugging her boy she tucked Rand tight beneath her arm and came to where Shea and the Morrans still sat their horses.

"I want to thank you for all you did to bring Rand home," she said. "I thank you Mr. Morran for seeing Rand was safe while he was with you. And Shea." Lily reached up and took Shea's hand. "What would I do without such a fine and faithful friend?"

Tears burned in Shea's throat and she dared not reply for fear she'd cry in front of Lily and Cam.

"Now," Lily began again, "won't all you folks come in and let me feed you supper? I've got good venison stew simmering, and it won't take me a minute to make some biscuits."

Morran spoke up first. "Much as we'd like to stay, Miss Gallimore, we need to get on back into Denver. Ty's got jobs he's been neglecting, and I got a few things of my own to take care of."

"I need to get back into town, as well," Shea murmured, knowing she couldn't help the Gallimores celebrate Rand's return. "I need to see how Owen's done without me."

As exhausted and as brittle as Shea felt, all she could think about was getting back to the studio, closing the door behind her, and crying until she'd spent the last of her tears. The life she'd always dreamed of was dissolving like sugar in tea, and there wasn't a thing in the world she could do to stop it.

THIRTEEN

For more than a fortnight, Cam carried Shea's belief that Rand was her son around with him like a bag of lead shot. Some nights he found himself squinting across the supper table, wondering if he saw a hint of Shea in Rand's smile, and if the similarity in their coloring was heredity or happenstance. He'd even gone so far as to look up the laws on adoption and parents' rights, just to be sure Rand was his, all legal and proper.

Still, Shea's claim that the boy was her son chafed at him, spoiling his appetite, disrupting his sleep, and fouling his mood. He'd been unduly stern with Rand when he'd done poorly on a spelling test. He'd snapped at Lily when she'd asked if Owen's cough was better—and he hadn't been able to tell her, either.

He wasn't aware of anyone but Shea when he stopped at the studio to get Rand at the end of the day. He kept watching her, wondering if she'd spoken to his boy about being his mother. He wanted to make her promise she wouldn't do that, but Cam couldn't bring himself to ask her.

He considered forbidding his son to go visit at all, but that would require an explanation. And what could he say?

"I swear, Cammie!" Some of the exasperation in Lily's tone finally reached him, and he looked up from the dinner plate he'd been drying for what could have been either two or ten minutes. "I don't think you've heard a word I said."

Cam put the plate aside and picked up another. "I'm sorry, Lil. What did you want?"

"I was asking if you could take me into town tomorrow. Rand brought a note from Shea. It seems they've gotten behind with their hand-coloring again and need my help."

"She should be paying you," Cam murmured, faintly aggrieved on his sister's behalf.

"She is," Lily informed him with a raise of her eyebrows. "I'm thinking of using my earnings to buy a new hat. Mrs. Franklin has a lovely blue mohair bonnet in her window."

"Blue?" Cam echoed. Lily hadn't worn anything but black since their mother died.

"Of course we'll need to add a veil, but Mrs. Franklin said she thought she had one to match. She was going to tack it on this evening to see if I liked the effect."

"Blue," Cam repeated.

"I'm also having lunch with Emmet tomorrow. Is that all right?"

Cam blinked at her, feeling as if the world had shifted under his feet. "Why—why wouldn't it be all right? Where are you having lunch with him?"

"We're eating at Emmet's house between his morning office hours and afternoon calls. He stopped by and asked me when he heard I was going to be working at

Shea's. He said it won't be anything fancy, but Mr. Wingate paid him in venison, and he needs someone to help him eat it up."

"Are Shea and Owen joining you for lunch?"

Lily lowered her gaze. "I'm not sure who Emmet invited."

Cam nodded, wondering if it was wise to let Shea and his sister spend time together. Now that Shea had told him about Rand, would she voice her claims to Lily? Was that why she'd asked his sister to come to the studio?

More than once he'd started to tell Lily what Shea claimed, and then he'd remember the odd mix of satisfaction and anguish in Shea's eyes as she'd watched Lily and Rand together when they'd come home from the mountains. Somehow he couldn't believe that anyone who so obviously cared for both of them would deliberately cause them pain.

But if Shea didn't intend to claim her son, why had she told him who she was? Or who she thought she was. What had made her think—

"Oh, Cammie, you're hopeless!" Lily interrupted, with a laugh. "Where on earth is your mind tonight?"

Cam glanced at her. "What did I miss?"

"I wanted to make sure what time we'd be leaving tomorrow."

He reached for a bouquet of silverware. "Seven-thirty," he answered, "just like always."

Once he'd seen Rand safely deposited at school and left Lily at Shea's studio the following morning, Cameron headed for the sheriff's office. Though he'd been distracted by tracking Rand and Ty into the mountains and by what Shea had claimed about his son, the discovery he'd made the night the studio was vandalized chafed at him.

When they'd been sweeping up, he'd managed to set that one particular shard of glass aside and smuggle it out of the studio. It lay now in the bottom drawer of his desk like an unexploded canister of grapeshot. Though the image on the plate was far from complete, he knew to the dregs of his soul that Wes Seaver had posed for that photograph.

Even when he'd pressed her, all Shea could tell him about the negatives was that the majority of the ones she'd lost had been exposed since she'd been in Colorado. Which meant Seaver had been holed up near Denver this summer. Cam was willing to bet he still was.

As Cam pushed his way into to the sheriff's office, Dan Cook looked up from his breakfast. "Well, good morning, Judge," Cook greeted him. "What brings you here so early? You want some coffee?"

Cam shook his head. "I was wondering if you'd let me look through your wanted posters."

"Sure," Cook agreed and pulled a two-inch-deep pile of papers out of the bottom drawer of his desk. "You thinking about taking up bounty hunting when your term as judge expires next summer?"

Cam braced a hip on the corner of Cook's desk and began leafing through the posters. "I've been thinking about giving up the law altogether."

It was the first time he'd actually spoken the words out loud.

The sheriff whistled in surprise. "To do what? Before you accepted the judgeship, you were one of the best trial attorneys this territory has ever seen."

"The law can wear on a man," Cam admitted on a sigh, thinking about the cases he'd heard, the judgments he'd made. And the hangings.

Cook rubbed his chin. "I know how that is."

"I just made an offer on the land adjoining ours," Cam went on, "and thought maybe I'd try my hand at farming."

"You got some good bottomland there where you are, and I hear they're experimenting up north with irrigation."

"You sound like a farmer, Dan."

"My pa farmed," the sheriff offered. "I suppose I could still plow a straight furrow if I set my mind to it."

Cam nodded absently and found what he was looking for halfway down the pile of posters.

"I haven't decided anything yet," he said, "and I certainly haven't said so much as a word to Lily. So keep my ambitions under your hat, will you, Dan?"

Sheriff Cook gave him a smile. "You can count on me."

"Thanks," he said, gesturing with the wanted poster. "You mind if I keep this?"

The sheriff shrugged. "Someone you know?"

Cam forced himself to laugh. "Maybe."

He tucked the poster in his pocket and headed for the door. Once he was outside, he clambered into the carriage and sat waiting for his knees to stop quivering. He pulled the poster out of his jacket and unfolded it carefully.

Though the drawing was crude, Cam didn't have any trouble recognizing the man. He remembered that long, spade jaw; the thick, fair hair; his carefully curled mustache. He didn't look as whipcord thin as he'd been eleven years ago, and new lines seemed to bracket his thin mouth. Cam supposed there were some who might consider this fellow handsome, but he'd always found something vaguely reptilian about his cold, unblinking stare.

The poster had been issued in Nebraska not quite a year ago and offered a five-thousand-dollar reward "for the arrest and conviction of Wes Seaver and the members of his outlaw gang." The small print at the bottom of the page detailed what Seaver was wanted for: three murders, eight bank robberies, two train holdups, and several instances of cattle rustling.

It was an impressive list. But then, Seaver had been given the best apprenticeship an outlaw could have, the same training as the James brothers and the Youngers. The kind Cam knew a good deal more about than he cared to admit, because they'd all ridden roughshod across Missouri and Kansas during the war with William Quantrill and "Bloody" Bill Anderson.

Heaving a sigh, Cameron tucked the poster away. He needed proof before he could go to Sheriff Cook with his suspicion that Wes Seaver and his gang had come to Colorado. He needed proof that they were behind the rash of lawlessness that had been sweeping across the territory since early summer. And in the next few days, he hoped he'd get it.

While Lily was off having her noon meal with Emmet Farley, Shea decided to run a few errands of her own.

"I'll be back in about an hour," she called through the door to the darkroom, then pulled on her coat and clattered down the stairs.

Shea wasn't used to being out of the studio in the middle of the day, and she was surprised to see how many buggies and drays clogged the streets. As she walked she saw fashionably dressed women scurrying from store to store. Several businessmen smiled at her as they brushed past. Cowboys sauntered along, their collars turned up around their ears. A monte dealer had picked a sunny spot at the corner and was attracting a crowd.

Since Shea's first order of business was to secure a bank draft, she set off for the Bank of Denver at the corner of Sixteenth and Holladay. It was an impressive stone building with an ornate corner entrance and three tall tiers of windows down each side. She climbed the steps and crossed the lobby to the tellers' grilles.

"I'd like a sixty-three-dollar bank draft made out to Anthony and Company," she told the clerk. She was finally money enough ahead to pay the last installment on her new portrait camera and order what she needed to repair her other equipment.

As she waited for the draft, she noticed Sam Morran step up to the teller's window just to her left. He looked better than he had in a very long time. His clothes and hair were clean. He was freshly shaved and, as near as Shea could tell, he was sober.

"I'd like change for this," he said and snapped a shiny, new double eagle down on the marble counter.

Now where on earth would Sam get a twenty-dollar gold piece? Shea found herself wondering. Where did a man whose son paid the rent get so much money?

As the teller counted out his coin, she noticed how Morran's gaze roved the interior of the bank, from the tastefully papered walls to the high, coved ceiling, and the mahogany depositors' tables. He seemed to take a particular interest in the row of brass-grilled tellers' cages, the cluster of desks behind them, and the vault at the rear of the bank.

Shea waited for Morran to take note of her so she could ask him to explain himself, but instead he scooped up his change and tipped his hat to the guard on his way out the door. By the time Shea finished up and got outside he was nowhere in sight.

She did notice that the sky was lowering, and it had gotten colder and windier while she'd been in the bank. The sun seemed muffled in layers of putty-colored clouds, and she figured they'd have snow before the day was over.

She turned up her collar around her ears and was just setting off toward Larimer Street when someone shouted her name.

"Hullo, Shea!" Lily cried waving gaily from the seat of Emmet's buggy.

Shea grinned when she saw that Lily was all decked out in her new hat and veil.

"Good afternoon," Emmet greeted her as he pulled the buggy over to the curb. "I'm taking Lily back to the studio before I start my calls. Would you like a ride?"

Shea thanked him but shook her head. "I've a stop to make on my way. But you're welcome to come with me, Lily, if you fancy a walk."

"Do you think I dare go with her?" Lily asked Emmet with what sounded like a giggle in her voice.

Shea turned and stared at her. Had Emmet served Lily wine with luncheon?

Emmet seemed rather flushed and ebullient himself. "I think you should dare whatever you like."

Lily hesitated, then said in that same giddy voice, "Then I think I *will* go with you, Shea."

Once Lily had climbed out of the gig, she paused. "I thank you so very much for everything, Emmet. I—I enjoyed our time together tremendously."

Emmet smiled at her, his eyes gone warm. "It was my very distinct pleasure to be with you, Lily."

The two women watched as Emmet drove off. "So," Shea observed, "you had a nice time with Emmet, did you?"

"Well, the venison was stringy and the potatoes were

burned," Lily confided, and beneath the thick blue scrim Shea caught the flash of a smile. "But he *does* make a tasty gravy."

For the second time in as many minutes, Shea stared at Lily. "And luncheon was just the two of you?" she asked.

"His housekeeper was somewhere out back."

As Emmet's sop to propriety, Shea thought. "Well, tell me then, how did the good doctor like your hat?"

Lily laughed and tossed her head, the thick blue netting lifting in the wind. "He loved the hat. He said I looked wonderful in blue. He said it was his favorite color."

Shea suspected Emmet would have thought Lily looked wonderful in vermilion, verdigris—or puce.

"Well, then, I'm just going to stop at the mercantile, before we head back—"

Lily stopped in the middle of the walk. "The mercantile?"

"I told you I had a stop to make," Shea reminded her. "It *is* all right if we stop there, isn't it, Lily?"

Lily took a long wavery breath before she answered. "Oh, I suppose."

"Rand was telling me just yesterday," Shea hurried on, "that Thursday is Ty's birthday. I thought I'd get a bag of licorice twists. Do you think he'd like that?"

"Rand's very fond of those," Lily encouraged her.

Then, in spite of her best effort to hold back the question, Shea turned to Lily. "And when is Rand's birthday?"

Lily shook her head. "No one with the Children's Aid Society could tell us exactly," she said. "But since our mother was born on the thirtieth of March, we decided to mark Rand's birthday that day, too."

"In the spring," Shea said almost wistfully.

If Rand *had* been born in the spring, she might not have fallen ill. If she hadn't been turned out into the wintry streets, she might have her boy with her now. How different all of their lives might have been if her child had been born a few months later.

They had nearly reached the mercantile's tall front doors when a cold, howling wind roared out of the north. It slapped their skirts against their legs and swirled dust into their faces. Leaves and papers mounted skyward.

And so did Lily's veil.

She made a quick, desperate grab for the square of dense blue netting, but it lofted out of her reach. Shea chased it along, watching helplessly as it snagged for a moment on the hanging sign for "William Smedley— Dentist," then roiled and whirled past the second-floor windows of Charpiot's Hotel. Another gust took it higher, swooped it along the roof of the laundry, and swept it out of sight. As hard as the wind was blowing, Shea figured Lily's veil would be in Castle Rock by suppertime.

Shea was still breathing hard when she got back and found Lily huddled in the alley beside the store.

"I'm sorry," Shea offered clasping the other woman's shoulder. "I just couldn't catch your veil."

"Then what will I do?" Lily whispered, pressing her palms against her cheeks. "How will I get back to the studio?"

Shea drew a breath and pressed her lips together before she spoke. "I think we should walk."

"Walk?" Lily lifted her head with a jerk.

"Walk along just like everyone else," Shea confirmed, knowing exactly what she was asking. "Don't look to the right or left, and speak only if someone speaks to us."

"I can't do that!" Lily protested. "People will see."

"Yes." Shea couldn't bring herself to be less than honest. "They probably will see. But Ty has seen your scars, and so has Agnes Franklin. Neither of them has behaved with anything but acceptance, have they?"

Lily shook her head.

"I think you're ready to do this," Shea encouraged her.

"Oh, Shea, no."

"You bought a hat today, didn't you, Lily? A *blue* hat."

Lily lowered her hands as far as her chin. "Yes, I did."

"Did Emmet like your blue hat?"

Lily blushed all the way to the hat's curling brim. "He liked it very much."

"Do you suppose Emmet thought you needed to add a veil to your pretty new hat?" Shea pressed her.

"He said right out I didn't."

God bless you, Emmet, Shea thought.

"Well, then. Emmet thinks you're ready to do this, too. We won't be going far, Lily. Just down a block and over a bit. And I'll be with you every step."

Lily looked dubious. No, worse than dubious—she looked terrified.

"I saved your brother from a necktie party, now, didn't I?" Shea prodded her.

Lily gave a sniff of startled laughter. "Well, yes, you did."

Shea took her hand. "I won't let anyone bother you, Lily. I promise I won't."

Lily heaved a sigh of resignation. "Oh, all right."

Together they stepped from the alley into the street, walking steadily but taking care not to hurry.

They had gone less than a block when a cowboy tipped his hat at them.

Lily broke stride and ducked her head, but Shea tightened her grip and tugged her along.

Two ladies passed; both of them nodded. "Mrs. Waterston," they murmured. "Miss Gallimore."

Lily turned and stared. "They called me by name," she whispered. But neither of the women seemed to have taken undue note of her.

As they paused at the corner to wait for a wagon to rumble past, Mr. Kent, who owned a drugstore down the block, turned and spoke to them. "Beastly wind, eh?" he mumbled.

Lily stood as if she'd been turned to stone.

"I do believe it's going to snow," Kent tried again.

Shea felt Lily fidgeting beside her and hoped her innate good manners would force her to reply to him.

"Yes, it certainly feels like snow to me," Lily finally ventured.

The man smiled at her, saluted with the handle of his walking stick, and moved on up the street.

Shea knotted her fists in her skirts to keep from throwing her arms around Lily and congratulating her for her bravery.

They were nearly back to the studio when Cameron came striding down Sixteenth Street. He walked like a man with something on his mind, with his shoulders bowed and his hands jammed deep into the pockets of his duster.

"Cammie!" Lily called out to him.

His head came up sharply, and for a moment he quite obviously had no idea where he was or who had spoken to him. Then Lily waved, and he started toward them.

He was barely ten feet away when he stumbled to a stop and stood gaping like a netted carp.

"Don't you like Lily's new hat?" Shea prompted, nudging him in the direction she wanted him to go.

"Her—new—hat," Cam mumbled a little uncertainly. "Why, yes. Her new hat. It's the blue one you were telling me about, isn't it, Lil? It's very handsome. Very handsome indeed. I—I like it."

"It had a veil," Shea went on.

"Oh, yes, it did," Lily picked up the explanation. "But it blew away in this horrible wind."

"Blew away," Cam echoed still looking stunned.

Shea bit her lip to hide a smile.

"Shea and I are on the way back to the hat shop to get another," Lily told him.

Cam seemed to be slowly recovering his faculties and tugged thoughtfully at one corner of his mustache. "You know, Lil, I'm not sure I'd be in a rush to add a veil, if I were you. I like the hat quite well without one."

Shea slid him the slightest of smiles, then made a show of considering Lily's hat herself. "I must say," she said with a nod, "I quite agree with him."

Lily pursed her lips to respond, but just as she did the barber from up the street brushed past them. "Judge Gallimore, Miss Gallimore." He bobbed his head. "Mrs. Waterston."

"Good afternoon, Mr. Furst," Shea acknowledged him.

Lily let out her breath in a huff and turned to her brother. "Ever since I started coming to town, people who've never laid eyes on me before have been calling me by name as if they've known me all my life. Shea says it's because they appreciate the notes and gifts I've sent to them but I don't . . ."

Cam took Lily's hand. "I think Shea's right," he offered softly. "You've been doing kindnesses for folks ever since we came to Denver. How can they help considering you one of them?"

Shea saw warmth flood Lily's eyes. "Oh, Cammie, do you think that's how they feel?"

Cam clasped her hand even tighter. "I know it, Lil. Emmet and I both hear how much people think of you; you're the only one who's never known it."

The look that passed from Cam to his sister made Shea's throat burn. It was soft with reassurance, ardent with respect for Lily, who had come so far.

After a moment Lily took back her hand and swiped at her own eyes. "Well, then," she said with a sniffle. "I suppose that explains it."

She straightened slowly and cleared her throat. "Now, I suppose we should be getting back to the studio. You have a sitting this afternoon, don't you, Shea?"

Shea nodded, willing to let Lily set the limits in this new situation. "Indeed I do."

"Well, then, ma'am," Cam drawled, and with the most courtly of bows offered Lily his arm, "I'd be proud if you let me escort you."

With a flip of her skirts and a smile that was pure coquette, Lily slid her hand through her brother's elbow. "I'd be honored, sir."

It wasn't very far to the foot of the studio steps, but when they reached them, Cam gave his sister a final pat and watched her glide all the way to the top.

Shea followed Lily up the steps, and when she turned at the landing to glance back at him, Cam was standing just where they'd left him, an expression of pride on his face and the bright glaze of tears shining in his eyes.

• • •

Lily. Oh, dear God! Lily!

Cam stood and watched his sister all the way to the top of the stairs, stood with emotion wedged tight in his throat and the shimmer of heat in his eyes.

He couldn't remember when he'd ever been so proud of anyone as he was of his sister today. His chest ached with elation at the confidence he saw in her face, at the wonder of Lily's liberation after all this time. He didn't know how this miracle had come about, but he was grateful—to the wind for tearing her veil away, to the people who had treated her so kindly in the street. And especially to Shea, who'd stood by his sister all the way back from the mercantile.

He saw her pause at the top of the stairs and look down at him. Across the distance their gazes held, and he could see Shea understood every bit as well as he how brave Lily had been this afternoon, how far she'd come. Cam also knew just how much of a part Shea had taken in Lily's transformation, and how much he owed her for her kindness.

Not quite sure how to put that gratitude into words, Cam tipped his hat and bowed to her.

He saw a flush creep into her cheeks, saw a smile feather over her lips. He saw her eyes go liquid and soft. She dipped her head in acknowledgment and went inside.

Cam stood at the base of the steps staring after her. He couldn't fathom why this woman had shared so much of herself with him, or why she insisted Rand was her son. Though he didn't believe her claims, he'd been afraid of what she'd do, to whom she'd reveal her convictions next. But after seeing the care Shea had taken with Lily today, he knew she'd never hurt his sister, never hurt his boy.

With the realization, Cam let out his breath, resettled his hat, and turned west along Sixteenth Street. He'd been on his way to a rooming house down by the depot when he'd encountered his sister, and he still had pressing business there.

He needed to talk to the man who'd been conductor on the train from Cheyenne the night it was robbed some weeks ago. He wanted to show him the likeness on the wanted poster. He wanted to know if his suspicions about Wes Seaver being in Colorado were right.

And if they were—oh, God, if they were, Cam's world would start to crumble.

He found Jim Peters in the big front room of the boardinghouse's second floor, recuperating from the wounds he'd suffered in the attack on the train. He was sprawled on an unmade bed wearing his rumpled conductor's pants and a knitted undershirt when the landlady showed Cam into the room. A bandage still swaddled Peters's head, and his arm lay strapped across his chest. From what Cam had heard, it was a wonder Peters was breathing at all. Two passengers and the engineer hadn't been so lucky.

Cam slowly approached the trainman's bed. "Mr. Peters," he began, "I'm Judge Cameron Gallimore. I've come to talk to you about the robbery."

Peters looked off toward the window and sighed. "I told the sheriff and the territorial marshal everything I know. Then I told the Pinkertons and the men from the newspapers. I can't think what I can tell you, Judge, that I haven't told someone else already."

Cam knew all about the robbery, how the outlaws had flagged down the train and killed the engineer. He knew how they'd gone through the baggage car and the coaches, taking what they wanted and shooting anyone who resisted.

"I didn't come to hear your story, Mr. Peters," Cam said. "What I have is a hunch and a picture to show you."

Peters seemed relieved and pushed up against his pillows. "All right."

Cam took the poster out of his pocket. He'd folded back the edges so only the drawing showed. "Does this look like any of the men who were on that train?"

Peters took the picture and stared at it. "The men were masked," he allowed.

"This man would have been tall and slim," Cam prodded him.

"Would his hair have been blond, kind of a tow color?"

Cam's throat went dry. "It might have been."

"And it was long on his collar maybe," Peters said, squinting. "I remember seeing his eyes above that bandanna and knowing I was going to die. They were black and cold as witch's tears."

Cam remembered Seaver's eyes—black, black eyes with heavy lids, eyes fierce with bravado and utter ruthlessness.

He knew what Seaver's being involved in the holdup meant, and shivered in spite of himself. "And you're sure this man was with the outlaws who boarded the train."

"The more I think on it, the more certain I am," Peters reckoned. "He had some sort of fancy weapon, too, a pistol with a pearly grip. And from the way he talked, he might have been their leader."

Cam nodded, gone cold to his bones.

"Who is he, Judge Gallimore?"

"A man wanted for robbery and murder in Nebraska," Cam murmured, and it was a moment before he realized Peters was passing the picture back.

"So if you're right about who this bastard is," Peters went on, "are you going to arrest him? Ham Wilson, the engineer on the train, was a friend of mine, and I'd like to see his killers hang."

"I'm trying to see there's justice done," Cameron answered.

"Well, do your best," Peters said as Cam turned to go. "Ham's murder deserves to be avenged."

"I'll do what I can," Cam promised.

He found his own way down the stairs and out of the boardinghouse. He crossed the tracks and stood staring down at the river.

Wes Seaver was here in Colorado. This confirmed Cam's own worst fears. He figured he could go ahead and approach the victims of some of the other robberies. He could see if they recognized Seaver, too, but he didn't really need that confirmation. He should take what he'd discovered to Dan Cook, tell him all of it, and let the chips fall where they may.

The few blood-soaked months he'd spent riding with Anderson's hellions at the end of the war had always been a slow-burning fuse hissing toward detonation. If they caught Seaver here in his district, if Cam was forced to preside over the trial, or even if he recused himself, everything was bound to come out. His good, loyal Union neighbors would hear how he'd ridden with the rebel raiders, burning houses and barns, pistol-whipping grandfathers for defending their livestock, and carrying off the slaves if there were any left.

When they heard that, he'd be ruined. He'd lose his friends, his reputation, his respectability. He'd lose the very thing that was his reason for living—the love of his family. Especially Lily's.

His extraordinary Lily.

He jammed his hands into his pockets and hunched his shoulders against the wind. He couldn't hope to escape retribution if Seaver was here, but maybe if he held his peace, he could eke out a few more days or weeks of normalcy. He could insure a few more quiet mornings doing chores with Rand, a few more companionable evenings with his sister and his son, a few more nights of going to bed knowing that the people he loved were safe and happy.

He could buy that time—but at what cost? How many crimes would Seaver commit, how many more men would he kill before Cam did his duty? Each moment he waited would eat at him like maggots at a corpse.

Cam closed his eyes and prayed for the strength to do what he knew was right, go to Dan Cook and tell him the truth. He prayed for the courage to face his son—and especially his sister—with what he'd done.

He prayed for the fortitude to accept the loss of everything that mattered to him, because that's what exposing Seaver meant. Once he set all this in motion, there would be no going back.

After a good long while, he straightened, feeling as if the weight of his family's future could crush him to his knees. In spite of knowing the cost, he turned and crossed the tracks. Through a grim, sleety curtain of snow, Judge Cameron Gallimore went back to the sheriff's office to tell Dan Cook what he'd discovered—and turn the sweetness of his life to dross.

FOURTEEN

*S*hea hurried up Sixteenth Street clutching the tails of her flapping shawl in one hand and a bag of licorice candy in the other. She'd put off this errand for the best part of a week, but Ty would turn eleven tomorrow, and she wasn't about to let his birthday pass without some small notice.

She was just approaching Holladay Street when she heard a quick, sharp crack that sounded for all the world like someone firing a pistol. She hesitated and glanced toward the corner just in time to see the man leaning against the hitching post in front of the bank snap to attention. A second man who'd been lounging on the steps tossed away his cigar. A third, the one nearest Shea, whisked back his weather-stained duster to reveal the gun strapped low on his hip.

Shea realized in an instant what was happening. Someone was robbing the Bank of Denver!

Before she could think where to go for help, the staccato rattle of gunfire rent the midwinter afternoon and five armed men poured out of the bank. As people on sidewalks ran shrieking in all directions, the gunmen charged down the steps toward their horses.

Shea bolted into the narrow brick doorway between two shops. From where she pressed back against the wall, she could see how the noise and confusion had spooked the robbers' horses. Several men managed to swing into their saddles, but others were still struggling to rein in their animals.

As a few more managed to mount, the bank guard burst out of the building's double doors and started firing. One of the thieves toppled out of his saddle. A man who had been grappling with his horse spun backward and fell.

The outlaw leader turned in his saddle and shot down the guard. He reeled back against the doors of the bank and crumpled.

Shea mewled in horror as the man she'd spoken to and smiled at more times than she could count sprawled dead on the steps. She cringed further back into the doorway.

More of the robbers were clambering into their saddles when one of the sheriff's deputies pelted up the street yelling and shooting. The outlaws shot back.

When one of the townsmen wandered into the line of fire and fell dead, civilians joined the fusillade. They fired around the corners of the buildings on both sides of the intersection, and from behind the horse trough and a delivery dray. Two men peppered the robbers from a building across the street. Shea saw Mr. Johanson race past from the direction of the livery stable, a pitchfork in one hand and his shotgun in the other.

Under the rain of heightened fire, one of the outlaws grabbed his shoulder and went down hard. Another of the town's defenders tumbled from the roof of a building and into the street.

The shop window to Shea's left exploded in a thousand glittering shards of glass. She yelped and dropped to her belly in the doorway as the firing escalated around her.

She lay with her nose in the dirt and only raised her head when she heard more yelling and the approach of hoofbeats. As the outlaws thundered past, she caught a glimpse of the first man's flapping duster and high-crowned hat. The second man's chest-length chin whiskers and the bullwhip looped over his saddle horn seemed somehow familiar. The third man blurred past clutching a battered valise, his luxuriant blond hair flowing well past his collar.

Shea pushed up onto her elbows and stared after him. She knew that hair. She knew that face. She'd photographed him in the mining camp.

The town's defenders ran past shouting and firing. But the mounted outlaws quickly outdistanced them.

Then all at once, the city fell still. The townsmen stood as if frozen in the pockmarked street. The air hung thick with the acrid singe of gunpowder. The wind blew cold, scudding scraps of papers up the block.

The instant of silence seemed to echo forever. Then from somewhere up beyond the bank a woman set up keening.

As if her weeping had shattered the spell that held them all immobile, the townsmen holstered their guns. People ran toward the bank from all directions.

In the doorway, Shea pushed slowly to her knees. Her legs were quivering, and it took some time before she was able to get to her feet and wobble as far as the corner.

A crowd had gathered in front of the bank. They whispered among themselves and stared at where the bank guard sprawled in a pool of blood. Abe

Nicholson's new young clerk lay dead at the fringe of the intersection. Bile churned up Shea's throat when she realized who he was.

Two of the robbers lay limp as bundles of old clothes between their horses' hooves. Two more sat moaning in the street, one wounded in the shoot-out, and a second who'd hurt his leg when he'd been thrown from his horse. A third man knelt in the mud, his hands raised and his body swaying in entreaty.

Armed, grim-faced townsmen stood over each of the men, clearly looking for an excuse to shoot them.

Just then Sheriff Cook and two more deputies came dashing around the corner from the direction of the jail.

"Just what the hell happened here?" Dan Cook demanded and detailed one of the men into the bank.

Shea felt someone step up close behind her and turned to find Cam at her elbow. "Are you all right?" he asked softly.

The question seemed to take the last of the starch out of Shea's knees. She tottered against him, and he wrapped her close against his side, holding her up.

"It's over, Shea," he murmured. "You're going to be fine now."

Shea nodded and pressed her face to the warm, woolly folds of his jacket, breathing in his sharp, clean scent. She let his solidity and the feel of his hand against her back soothe and settle her. Only when Sheriff Cook's deputy came out of the bank did she raise her head.

"The outlaws got away with all the coin and bank notes," the man reported. "Seems Mr. Simonson locked the vault before they shot him, so the gold and treasury bills are safe."

"Bill Simonson's dead?" Cook's face went hard.

"And Frank Justice, too. He must have been in there making his afternoon deposit."

"Dear God!" the sheriff mumbled.

Another deputy came from up the street bringing news of three wounded and two dead among the town's defenders.

Hot dread crept up Shea's throat as she turned to Cam. "I know who did this," she whispered. "I recognized two of the robbers as men I've photographed."

Cam didn't move, but his muscles seemed to have turned to stone. "Who was it?" he asked, a raw, deep thread to his voice. "Who did this?"

"It was a man called Wes Seaver."

Cam bowed his head even closer to hers. "Are you sure it was Wes Seaver?"

"Why? Do you know him?"

Cam waited an instant too long before he denied it. Something about his evasion chilled Shea's blood. Something in the taut, bleached look of the skin across his cheekbones and the narrowing of his mouth made Shea suddenly and irrationally afraid for him.

Before she could say another word, Cam gestured to where the deputies were hauling the captured robbers to their feet. "Do you know any of those men?" he asked her.

The first man, who stood clutching a bloody handkerchief to his shoulder, was short, brown-haired, and nondescript. "I don't remember him specifically," Shea murmured, "but the second man is Seaver's younger brother, Jake."

As the deputies dragged the third outlaw to his feet, Shea recognized the man in the dome-crowned Stetson and mud-stained duster. A chill of shock ran through her. She pressed her hand to her mouth and choked back a gasp.

Mary, Mother of God! It was Ty's father.

She looked around wildly, wondering where Ty was. Did he know his father and his cronies had robbed the bank?

Seeing Sam with these men made sense now—made sense of a mining camp where no one worked the claims, of the rowdies who drifted in and out of the Morrans' cabin. Of the gold piece she'd seen Sam cash at the bank not a week before.

"The robbers are men from the mining camp," she whispered half to herself.

Cam's hold tightened at her waist. "The mining camp where the boys spent the blizzard?"

"Do you think that's where they've been hiding out?"

Cam cursed under his breath and maneuvered her through the crowd of gawkers. "Sheriff Cook will take his prisoners back to his office before he heads out with a posse, and I think you can tell him where to look."

As they moved down Holladay Street, Shea looked back toward the bank, back to where Sam Morran stood between two tall deputies with his head bowed and his hands manacled.

Shea turned to Cam. "Will Sam Morran come out of this all right?"

Cam compressed his lips for a moment before he spoke. "Things don't look very good for him."

Cam braced his hands against the windowsill at the sheriff's office and stared up Eleventh Street. They'd been waiting half an hour for Dan Cook and his deputies to bring in the robbers they'd taken at the bank, and Cam was about out of patience.

Less than a week before, he had warned the sheriff

that the Seaver gang was operating in the Denver area. Now the Seavers had killed people, stolen money, and endangered the citizenry. Would it have made any difference if Cam had begun to investigate his suspicions about Seaver sooner? Could Cook and his men have located the gang in time to prevent what had happened today?

"Cam, are you all right?" Shea asked from where she'd settled in the chair beside the sheriff's desk.

How could he be all right when his reticence to expose his past might have cost men's lives?

"I'm fine," he snapped and wished Shea wasn't so damned perceptive. He was furious at his cowardice and unnerved by how many connections he'd had to Seaver all along. Shea had met the man in the mountains and taken his photograph. Tyler Morran's father rode with Seaver. Rand had been in Seaver's camp.

The very idea chilled Cam's bones.

What would Seaver have done if he'd known Rand was his son? Would Seaver have played cruel games with the boy to settle old grievances? But then Seaver wouldn't have recognized the Gallimore name. Cam hadn't been reckless enough to use his real identity when he joined up with the guerrillas.

Just then Dan Cook and his deputies prodded the three bank robbers into the office. "Put them in the cells out back," Cook instructed. "Then go get a doctor to look them over. I don't much care if they're hurt, but the taxpayers will expect them to be healthy for the hanging."

Though he could hardly keep from noticing them, Sam Morran didn't acknowledge either Cam or Shea as the deputies hustled the three prisoners toward the cells. Nor did Shea attempt to speak to him.

Once Cook had locked the outlaws' guns and

belongings in a brass-bound trunk, he turned to Shea and him. "Now what the hell do you want? I'm supposed to be getting up a posse to track those bastards."

"I saw who robbed the bank!" Shea answered.

The sheriff nodded and scowled. "We already know it was the Seaver gang. That's Jake Seaver locked up in there. He's been outlawing since right after the war."

"Wes Seaver was with them, too," she confirmed.

"I got half a dozen witnesses who'll swear to that."

"But can your witnesses tell you where Seaver and his men might be headed?" Cam asked with some asperity.

Cook looked up from the shells he'd been loading into his rifle. "And how would you know that, Mrs. Waterston?"

"I photographed Seaver and a goodly number of his men in a mining camp about a day's ride west of here," Shea began. "I even had some of their likenesses on photographic plates until the night my studio was—"

Cam felt her look across at him. She'd just come to the same conclusion he'd been harboring, that Wes Seaver was behind the photograph that had been stolen at the opening, Shea's midnight visitor, and the destruction of her studio.

"You say Seaver's hangout is west of here, Mrs. Waterston?" Cook asked.

Shea nodded. "It's tucked way back in the mountains and will be hard to find unless you know what you're looking for. But I could show you—"

"Hell's bells!" Cook exclaimed, pulling a second rifle out of the gunrack. "I'm sure not having a woman on this posse. Can't you just tell me where Seaver's camp is?"

"Would you like me to draw you a map?" she offered.

Shea had never offered to draw a map for *him,* Cam realized.

Dan Cook nodded. "Fair enough."

Shea was just finishing up her map when the door to the office burst open.

"Is my father here?" Tyler Morran demanded. He was white-faced and breathing hard. Dread emanated from him like waves of heat.

Before either Cam or the sheriff could answer, Shea crossed the room and clasped Ty by the shoulder. She drew him into the office and hunkered down beside him.

"I'm sorry, Ty," she murmured, closing her hands around his arms. "They brought your pa in a little while ago."

The boy swallowed hard. "Was he one of the men who robbed the bank?"

"Yes, son, he was," Cook confirmed.

Ty stiffened and turned to the sheriff. "He—he didn't kill anybody, did he?"

No man alive wanted to tell a boy his father had done murder, and Dan Cook was no exception. He came around the corner of his desk and looked down at Ty. "We don't think so, son."

Relief softened the set of Ty's shoulders. He let out his breath. "I knew he couldn't hurt anybody."

"No, of course not," Shea said, easing him toward her.

"I—I could tell they were up to something," he told her so softly Cam was sure he hadn't meant anyone else to hear. "More of them came into town every day, and Pa was sneaking around meeting with them. I found a pistol under the mattress. He'd never kept a pistol there before, so I should have figured something bad was going to happen."

"Oh, Ty, no," Shea murmured and tried to draw him into her arms. "How could you have known?"

"I should have known. I—I should have *told*," he said and his eyes began to shine. "I should have told someone, so they could stop it. I just didn't know what it was they meant to do. I didn't know so many people would get k-k-killed . . ."

Shea slid her arms around his back and drew him against her. This time Ty let himself take the comfort she was offering. He pressed his face into her shoulder, and Cam saw Ty's ribs bellow as he fought to keep from crying.

Shea hugged him tighter. "This wasn't your fault," she whispered fiercely. "Bad men did this. Grown men, outlaws did it. You're just a boy, Ty. There's nothing in this world you could have done to stop it."

His breathing stuttered. Ty shook his head. He believed the robbery was his fault—and nothing anyone could say was going to convince him otherwise.

Cam knew how that was.

Instinctively he stepped toward where Shea was swaying with Ty in her arms. He laid his hand on Ty's shoulder and waited for the boy to raise his head.

"You know Wes Seaver would have killed both you and your pa before he let you interfere with this." He spoke softly, man to man. "None of this was your fault, Ty. I won't have you blaming yourself."

The boy gave a jerky nod as if he'd taken Cam's word, but it was a minute or two more before he got control of himself. Once he had, he rubbed at his eyes with the heels of his hands, then looked up at the sheriff.

"D'you think I could see my pa?"

"That'd be highly irregular . . ." Dan Cook looked

across at Cam, half in concern for the proprieties, half in concern for the boy.

Cam gave the sheriff a nod. God knows, no one was going to begrudge this child time with his father when the man—however lacking—was all he had.

"Well, it *is* highly irregular," the sheriff reiterated, "but I don't see any harm in making an exception just this once."

He unlocked the door that led back to the cells and motioned Ty through. "Don't be long, boy."

Ty snuffled, wiped his nose on the cuff of his shirt, and straightened his shoulders. "Thanks," he said and went back to the cells to see his father.

FIFTEEN

Cam stared at the paper spread across his desk and swallowed, doing his best to keep from losing his breakfast. It had been a scant two weeks since the bank had been robbed and five of Denver's citizens killed. Two weeks of Dan Cook and his posse fruitlessly combing the countryside for the rest of the Seaver gang. Two weeks of angry mutterings in anticipation of a hanging.

For all of Colorado's respectability and impending statehood, Denver was still essentially a vigilante town. Only seven years before, mobs had strung up members of the Musgrove gang. Now, whenever two men got together for a drink or a smoke, the question they pondered wasn't whether the robbers would hang, but whether the hanging would take place by sanction of the court, or by mob rule.

Cameron braced his head in his hands and stared at the headline. It wasn't as if he thought these men were innocent. They'd been caught coming out of the bank; they'd shot down prominent citizens in front of witnesses. What distressed him most was that Sam Morran was going to die for being part of this, and Cam was going to have to pass sentence on him. What clawed at the pit of his stomach was the fear that something in the trial would bring the whole of his past to light.

Cam groaned and pushed to his feet. He'd be calling his court to order at ten o'clock, and he needed to get over to the courthouse ahead of time.

As he walked the few short blocks, he was aware of groups of men loitering in the streets; more were smoking on the courthouse steps, waiting to be admitted to the courtroom. The halls were jammed with prospective jurors, and Cameron had to elbow his way to the doors.

At his knock Sim Cummings, the deputy marshal who was serving as bailiff for the trial, let him in. His boot heels rang on the wooden floors as he made his way up the central aisle. He swung past the defense and prosecution tables, and the jury box that stood behind a wooden baluster off to his right. Cam stepped up behind the bench. As he looked over the rest of the courtroom, his heart lay cold inside of him. Never had he felt such dread at the start of any proceeding as he did now.

In spite of it, he opened his satchel and began carpeting the judge's bench with piles of books and papers. He was almost done when someone rapped on the door to the courtroom. Cummings opened it a crack, and Cam caught sight of Shea and Ty just outside. He acknowledged them with a nod and motioned for them to be admitted.

Ty had gone to live with Shea after the robbery. At first he had resisted leaving the cabin, but Shea simply packed up his scant belongings and Ty had followed her to the studio.

In the end, he seemed to like sleeping somewhere warm and safe, eating regular meals, and knowing someone was looking after him. Cam himself had arranged for Ty to visit his father at the jail whenever he liked, and in these last days, Morran seemed to have become more of a parent to the boy than he'd been in a very long while.

Cam stepped down from the bench as Shea hurried Ty down the aisle. "I thank you for letting us in early," she told him, looking harried. "The mob in the street is quite unruly."

"I can't imagine what either of you is doing here," Cam admonished, scowling at her, scowling at Ty. "Murder trials are no place for women and children!"

"Well, I ain't leaving," Ty announced. "You can't make me."

Shea raised her eyebrows in dismay. "I did my best to dissuade him," she said, "but he wants to be here."

"It's not like I don't know what he done," the boy argued, his chin jutting mulishly.

"And if Ty is staying, so am I," Shea averred.

Cam sure as hell didn't want the two of them here. No boy should be exposed to the kind of testimony Ty would hear about his father. No child should be in the room when a jury found his father guilty of murder, or hear the death sentence pronounced on him.

Cam didn't want them here for his own sake, either. He couldn't allow himself to be compromised in his handling of this case. He didn't want to know that Ty was here. He didn't want Shea watching, either.

She saw too much, understood too much. He didn't want her to guess that his belly went hot at the thought of facing the Seaver gang, didn't want her to see how afraid he was that this trial would expose his secrets. He didn't want to see her disillusionment if his life unraveled before her eyes.

He could bar them from the courtroom if he chose, but neither was likely to forgive him that.

"All right, damn it," he finally conceded. "Take seats down in front where I can keep an eye on you. And don't expect that this is going to be easy for anyone."

Shea lay her palms on Ty's narrow shoulders and spoke with conviction. "We'll be just fine."

Cam doubted that, but he ushered them into seats behind the defense table and nodded for the bailiff to open the doors.

Once everyone was seated or had found a place to stand, the lawyers took their chairs. The prisoners arrived and jury selection went off without a hitch. Every man in town wanted to serve, to hear the sensational testimony and bask in the notoriety of being on the jury that voted to hang the Seaver gang.

Once all the jurors had taken their places, Cam began to instruct the panel. "In considering this case, you will be dealing with acts of murder committed in the course of a robbery. The defendants will be judged guilty or innocent of either or both charges.

"I want you to notice that there is one lawyer for each of the defendants. Mr. Edwards will be defending Mr. Seaver."

Edwards stood, and the men in the gallery craned their necks to catch a glimpse of the stone-face outlaw seated beside him.

"Mr. Wallace is representing Mr. Morran," Cam went on. "And Mr. Kingston is counsel to Mr. Faber."

Sam Morran sat with his head bowed. Faber was pale and still bandaged from the wound he'd received in the course of the robbery.

"The reason each man has a lawyer of his own," Cameron went on, "is that while the charges against these men are to be considered simultaneously, you will be deciding the guilt or innocence of each man separately. Is there any one of the jurors who would like me to explain that further?"

The jurors shook their heads, and before he continued, Cam spared a glance for the rest of the courtroom. His gaze swept over the rows of avid faces. Newspapermen with their pads and pencils had come from as far away as Julesburg and Cheyenne. Cowmen had ridden in from their ranches. He recognized everyone from blacksmiths to bank presidents in the rows of chairs. Several members of the city council and three county commissioners were in attendance.

Yet not one saloon owner or employee was in attendance. Barkeeps knew murder trials were thirsty work.

As his gaze tracked back toward the jury box, Cam spotted a tall, lean man leaning negligently against the doorjamb. He had a long face, with a sharp jaw and stiffly waxed mustache. His expression was hidden in the shade of his hat, but hair the color of corn silk flowed in waves against his collar.

It had been ten years and more since Cam had put that part of his life away, but he would have known his old enemy anywhere. *It was Wes Seaver.*

Cam felt the blood leach out of his face; his head went light. He tried to point and shout the order to have Wes Seaver arrested, but he couldn't seem to suck in air enough to speak the words.

Seaver made the most of his reaction. He smiled, nodded at Cameron, then turned to go.

Cam sat helpless as Seaver stepped past the man beside him and disappeared down the hall.

As he fought to regain his composure, Cam caught a

glimpse of Shea. She had seen his reaction to Seaver in his face—and though he didn't think she'd turned soon enough to see the man himself, that wouldn't stop her from asking more questions than he could answer.

He straightened and cleared his throat, doing his best to buy time enough to gather his wits.

"I—I know there's been a great—a great deal of public—public outcry over the matter at hand," he managed to start again. "In the interest of fairness, I—I want you as members of the jury to do your best to put the sentiment of the community out of your mind as you consider the guilt or innocence of the men being tried, and make your judgment of these individuals accordingly."

Relieved to have this initial duty out of the way, Cam's heartbeat slowed.

"Mr. McGreggor the prosecuting attorney for the Colorado Territory will now make his opening statement," he concluded and sat back in his chair. What he vowed to do for the rest of today was keep his mind on the trial ahead of him.

From the moment she and Ty took the seats Cam had provided for them in the first row of the gallery, Shea found herself wishing she were anyplace but where she was. She didn't want to be in this close, crowded courtroom where Sam Morran was about to be tried for robbery and murder. She didn't want to watch Cam take his place on the bench and preside over the case, when his concern for the boy was eating him from the inside out. Heartache lay ahead for both of them, and Shea hated knowing she was helpless to save them from what was to come.

Once the deputies arrived with the prisoners, the din

of voices in the courtroom rose. Shea's gaze moved over
each of the three men—men she'd photographed not
all that long before. Jake Seaver's sandy hair was slicked
back with pomade, and in spite of a limp and the manacles on his wrists, he managed to affect a demeanor of
cocky disdain. Matt Faber, the outlaw who'd been
wounded in the robbery, stared straight ahead, his face
impassive.

It was Sam Morran who seemed to reflect the gravity
of the proceedings. He hunched like a man beaten
down by life, a man who expected this trial to be the
final blow. He raised his head long enough to seek out
his boy, and for an instant his eyes warmed and a smile
touched the corners of his mouth.

Ty inched forward in his chair as if he meant to go
to his father. Only when Shea laid a restraining hand
on the boy's arm did Morran's gaze move past his son
to her. He frowned for an instant as if he had expected
her to prevent Ty from coming here, then he lowered
his chin as if he knew no power on earth would have
kept his son away.

Once the prisoners had joined their lawyers at the
defense table, and Cam and the others had taken their
places, the bailiff bellowed: "This First District Court
for the Territory of Colorado is now in session, Judge
Cameron Gallimore presiding."

Cameron clapped his gavel, looking powerful and
judicial and so grave Shea's heart went out to him. He
had his duty to perform today, and he'd live up to it,
no matter what the cost.

She eased Ty back in his chair and settled herself
more comfortably to watch what went on. Yet as the
jurors were questioned and picked, she found her gaze
drawn to Ty and his father again and again.

Cam had arranged for the two of them to spend

time together at the jail, and once the alcohol had boiled out of Morran's system, he had reverted to the man he must have been before Ty's mother died. He'd become a father who had time for his child, time for a few soft words and a smile, time for a game of checkers and a moment or two of foolery.

As she waited for the jury selection to be completed, Shea saw the concern in Morran's dark eyes and the terrible longing in Ty's. They had found each other, now when it was very nearly too late for them.

As she watched, Shea couldn't help wondering what Ty wanted from this man who was his father, what he'd yearned for in the years since Sam had sacrificed responsibility for his boy to his own grief. Had Ty wanted love, guidance, a real home? Did he yearn for someone to take care of him so he could be a child again?

Shea trembled, knowing she meant to offer all that to Ty if he gave her the chance. She wanted to give him all the love, all the mothering she might have lavished on her own child if he didn't already belong to someone else.

She'd come to understand since he'd been staying at the studio, that she needed a son just as badly as Ty needed a mother. She didn't know if such a proud, independent boy would be able to accept from her the things his father had never been able to provide. She wasn't sure if she had the courage to ask him to stay. What would she do if she offered him a home and he refused? How could she bear to lose a child she loved a second time?

When Shea turned her attention from Ty and his father to the trial once more, she saw that the jurymen had taken their places, and Cam was instructing them about how the trial would be conducted. Halfway through the explanation, he paused and glanced around the courtroom. Shea could see contempt for the people who'd come to watch the trial in the line of his mouth and the way he narrowed his eyes. It was the same contempt she'd seen in him when he'd looked at her that day in Breckenridge.

Then all at once, his attention snagged on something at the back of the courtroom. His eyes widened; his voice faltered. His face paled to gray.

Shea craned around to see what had affected him so, but at first all she could see were the avid faces in the rows behind her and a line of men standing in rapt attention against the back wall of the courtroom. Then her attention shifted to a scuffling in the doorway.

She caught the slope of a man's shoulder, the line of his back, and a glimpse of pale hair. She hadn't seen nearly enough of him to be sure, but the man put her powerfully in mind of Wes Seaver.

But that had to be impossible. The sheriff and his posse had investigated every hill and hollow, every barn and home and outhouse between the mining camp and the Kansas border these last two weeks. Seaver and the rest of his gang had vanished like frost in the sunshine. They must be long gone from here, and not haunting the halls of Denver's courthouse.

After a minute's hesitation, Cam seemed to overcome whatever it was that had upset him. When she turned her full attention to him again, he was continuing with his address to the jury as if he'd done no more than taken a breath.

The trial went on all day, and for all of his usual exuberance Ty never moved. He paid attention when the prosecutor explained the details of the robbery and the roles each of the men had played in it. He sat and

listened when each prisoner's attorney spoke, declaring
his client's innocence.

He seemed to watch from someplace deep inside
himself as the witnesses were questioned and questioned again. Some were men who'd been in the bank
during the holdup; others had been close enough to see
the robbers' faces as they came out. A few were men
who'd shot it out with the Seaver gang. Shea wondered
what Ty thought, what this bright but illiterate boy,
this child whose future would be decided by what was
said and done here, made of the proceedings.

It was late afternoon when Cam set a time to recon-
vene and banged his gavel to dismiss court for the day.
The prosecution had rested its case, and the defense
lawyers would begin presenting their witnesses in the
morning.

The moment the prisoners were removed, the crowd
gushed out of the courtroom like rain down a gutter.
Doubtless they were headed for the saloons that
bloomed like summer daisies in the streets surrounding
the courthouse. There, over innumerable glasses of
whiskey, the men would discuss and ponder and argue
over the trial in anticipation of its inevitable outcome.

Shea wasn't sure if Cameron had plans to join them
for a drink, but she went to the head of the aisle and
waited while he gathered up his things, anyway.

"Where's Ty?" he asked, buckling his satchel closed
as he turned to her.

"He wanted to go over to the jail to spend time with
his father. I told him he could have supper there, and
I'd come by for him later."

Cam frowned, not quite meeting her eyes. "I can't
tell you how many times today I looked over and saw
him there, watching and listening. Probably understanding a whole lot more of this than is good for

him." Cam sighed and shifted the satchel in his hand. "He knows what's going to happen, doesn't he?"

"I think he knows," Shea answered slowly. "But I think he wants to believe there's hope."

He shook his head. "Ty hasn't dared hope for anything since his mother died."

Then, Shea thought, hope was one more thing she'd be able to give to Ty when this was over.

They walked out of the courtroom together and pushed their way along the crowded corridors. The din of voices was all but deafening, and Shea was glad when they reached the relative quiet of the sunny street.

As they stepped outside, she laid a hand against Cam's arm and looked up at him. "There's something I'd like to discuss with you," she began, "if you have time."

Before he could reply, a boy of twelve or thirteen rushed up to them. "Judge Gallimore?" he asked breathlessly.

"I'm Judge Gallimore."

"A man said for me to give you this," the boy told him and thrust a folded paper into Cam's hand.

"What man?" Cam asked, as he tried to catch hold of the lad's coat. The boy was a step too quick for him.

"What was that about?" Shea asked, staring after the child.

Cam shrugged and flicked open the sheet of foolscap with his thumb. Before her eyes, the strong, vital man beside her turned wizened and gray. His shoulders slumped; his hands began to tremble. Shea clasped his arm, half expecting she'd have to hold him up.

"Cam?" she whispered urgently. "My God, Cam! What is it?"

It seemed to take a very long time for him to hear

her, longer still for him to raise his gaze to hers. When he did, there was utter desolation in his eyes.

"It's nothing," he mumbled, and straightened as if he bore a yoke of iron across his shoulders. "It's nothing at all."

Then without so much as another word to her, he turned and strode down the street.

Charlie Gilbert.

That's all the note said. Charlie Gilbert—and with that hastily scribbled name Cam's past caught up to him.

He stood in the front of the courthouse feeling as if the world had dropped out from under his feet, as if his life were hurtling past him like landscape past the windows of a speeding train. Memories of his parents and sister and home remained as perfect and fragile as a bouquet preserved under glass. The years of the war blurred to a single harrowing recollection. He remembered how he'd felt buried alive by what he'd found when he returned to Centralia, and how the breadth and grandeur of Colorado had resurrected him. He'd rediscovered the finer parts of himself in Rand's love and Emmet's friendship and—

"Cam? My God, Cam!" Shea's voice sliced through the web of memories like a blade of Toledo steel. Her hand tightened on his arm. "What is it?"

He looked down at the note, down at her. He saw the concern in her eyes—and all but drowned in a swell of unworthiness.

"It's nothing," he said. "Nothing at all." Then, stuffing the paper in his pocket, he jerked away and bolted up the street.

Charlie Gilbert was running away.

The note confirmed that Wes Seaver had recognized him in the courtroom today, just as Cam had known Seaver from the broken pieces of the photographic plate he'd found in Shea's studio. And now that Seaver knew who he was, the truth about those days at the end of the war was bound to come out.

God damn me for a fool, Cam thought as he shoved his way through the crowd on the sidewalks. God damn me for thinking I could keep my secrets.

He'd done such despicable things in the name of patriotism, in the name of war. Those two scrawled words brought all of it back. He could almost smell the smoke from the barns and fields they'd torched and see the crows circling low above the carnage. He could almost hear the sobbing of the women they'd terrorized and the pleas of the men they'd killed. He'd forfeited his soul in those dark days, abandoned his honor, and sold out the people he loved. And what was worse, he'd never had the courage to own up to what he'd done.

Cam knew very well what Seaver would demand in return for his silence. He'd want his brother's life, his brother's freedom, and Cam couldn't give him that even if he'd wanted to.

Yet if he refused, everyone he cared about would learn what he'd been and what he'd done. Learn how little he deserved their respect or their trust—or their love.

Especially Lily.

Without once considering where he was going, Cam found himself barreling up the stairs to his office. He charged through the anteroom and slammed the door to the inner office behind him going to ground as if the hounds of hell were at his heels.

With blood pounding in head, he kicked his way

through the familiar comfort of that cluttered room. He'd always been safe here, safe to be just what he was—but not any more.

The weight of disaster sat hard on him, and panic sang along his nerves. He flung his satchel across the office then struck out blindly, sending the stack of lawbooks on the corner of his desk thundering onto the floor.

Breathing hard, he looked down at them, then with a sweep of his arm cleared the desktop. Pens and pencils and papers flew in all directions. Inkpots fell and overturned, bleeding thick, black stains into the rug. His humidor bounced across along the carpet, spewing cigars.

Bellowing with rage, he swiped the shelves of his bookcase clean. He trampled the pages of the tumbled law books beneath his boots and attacked the filing cabinet in the corner. He grabbed metal-bound corners and hauled the oaken case toward him, straining against its bulk. One by one the drawers tipped opened drunkenly and cascaded folders onto the floor. The weight of the cabinet shifted unexpectedly, and he stepped back, letting it fall. The crash resounded through the room, through the building like a bomb blast.

Panting with perverted pleasure, Cam grabbed up one of the leather wing chairs by its arms.

"Cam!" Shea gasped from the doorway.

He hadn't heard her coming, hadn't heard her open the door. He hadn't heard anything but the fury roaring in his head and the rasp of his own breathing.

"Get out!" he boomed at her.

Then with a grunt of effort hoisted the chair above his head and heaved it across the room.

"My God, Cam!" she cried.

He could see the shock in her face, the condemnation. "I told you to get out of here!"

She came toward him instead.

He snatched up one of the law books and shied it in her direction. When she didn't stop, he threw another.

He didn't want her here, God damn it. He couldn't bear anyone seeing him like this, mad and frightened, and falling apart.

He took a step backward. "Leave me alone."

His voice shook as he spoke. His hands shook. A thick tarry ooze of dread and self-loathing bubbled hot in his chest.

"I mean it. Go away!"

Her footsteps never wavered.

He came up hard against his desk and turned his back on her. He closed his eyes and stood there with his heart surging inside him and his muscles quivering. Sweat slid down his throat, soaked into his clothes. He stunk of desperation and despair.

Why wouldn't she go?

Shea insinuated herself on him, pressed up close against his back instead. His nerves rippled with the contact. Her energy crept along the surface of his skin.

She wrapped her arms around his chest.

Just this semblance of restraint when he was so raw and desperate made him thrash, made him moan. He grabbed her wrists and did his best to disentangle her.

"Shea." He meant the word to be a warning, an admonition. It sounded like a plea.

She clung to him more tightly.

"God damn it, Shea!"

"Tell me what's wrong," she whispered.

He couldn't tell her anything.

"It's all right, Cam," she whispered, splaying her hands against his chest. "Let me help with this."

He closed his eyes. He shook his head. "You can't."

"Please."

She pressed her face into his spine. Her breath condensed against his skin.

His heart beat harder. He could feel the sweet, damp suppleness of her body through their clothes.

"Let me take care of you," she urged him.

Cam didn't want her to take care of him. He didn't want her seducing him, either with her body or with her promises of help. He wanted her to destroy him. He wanted her to help him destroy himself.

He started to tremble.

"Oh, Cam," she whispered and her hands began to move on him. She stroked across his chest, along his ribs. She meant the touch to be gentle, soothing, but with his every nerve drawn taut, the stroke of her hands was like flint on steel—provocative, inflaming.

His nipples constricted. Heat flooded into his groin with a force and suddenness that made his head swim. His manhood engorged, straining against the front of his trousers. With all of his black soul he longed to turn to her, use her to obliterate his pain for a little while. But even he couldn't be that much of a bastard.

She seemed to sense his weakness. Her hands moved lower, down along his belly, past his navel, easing toward his . . .

Raw and trembling, he turned to her and dragged her against him. He lowered his head, kissing her aggressively, invasively, losing himself in the sheer raw pleasure of her mouth.

Shea kissed him back. Clasping his face in her hands, she drew him closer and thrust her tongue into his mouth.

"Take me," she whispered, and he tasted as much as heard the words. "I need to be with you!"

Sheer carnality tore through him. A flush of hot, heady lust seared the surface of his skin. Shaking like a man in the throes of fever, he seized her, bent her back across his desktop, and followed her down. He ground his hips into the V of her legs, caught in a frenzy so strong he burned with the joy and pain and insanity of it.

Shea lifted her hips against him, her tempo rhythmic, erotic. Incontrovertible provocation.

He moaned and retreated from her only far enough to ruck up her skirts and pull open the slit between the legs of her underdrawers. He tore at the buttons along his fly.

She spread her legs and offered herself, inviting him to take her. He groaned and thrust into her. She took all of him, encompassing him, holding him close and tightly sheathed. His every cell quivered in response. Every fiber of who he was wallowed in the sensation of being one with her.

Then slowly he bowed his back, all but withdrawing. She gasped and shivered with the loss, before he returned, plunging deeper.

The two of them mated there on his desk like pagans on the altar of some heathen god. Mated with her bodice still buttoned to her chin and her hat still pinned in place. Mated with his boot heels grinding into the rug and his watch chain rattling against her belly.

His breathing roared in his chest; his heartbeat thundered. He thrust and thrust and thrust, the pleasure outstripping the pain he'd sought, the joy of being one with her overwhelming his desolation.

She cried out his name as her climax took her. He felt her body tighten around him as the paroxysms began, and gloried in the madness of her release. Just when he would have pulled away to deny himself, she tangled her hands in his clothes and dragged him closer, willing him to follow her over the edge. He fought the tide, the throbbing, twisting ache at the base of his shaft, the tight pulse of anticipation.

"Please," she whispered. "Please."

And he was lost.

The world went white around him. Silence like the hush after a thunderclap resounded in his head. Then every nerve flickered back to life, caught fire, exploded in a flare of sensation so intense that when the peak upon peak of pleasure flickered out, there was nothing left but darkness, oblivion.

When Cam came to himself again, he had absolutely no idea how long they'd been sprawled across his desktop. Shea was flattened beneath him, but somehow she didn't seem to mind. She had one foot still notched behind his knee and was stroking his hair with a tenderness that made his throat burn.

He pushed up and off her, separating them with a roughness that denied all they'd just done and been to each other. He hated himself all the more for finding solace in her.

As he attempted to restore some order to his clothes, Shea braced up on her elbows and looked at him. "Cam?"

Her skirts lay crushed against her thighs in a most provocative manner. Feeling himself beginning to stir again, Cam hastily turned away from her.

"Cam," she insisted.

He jammed his shirttail into his trousers. "What?"

She drew a breath and let it out in a flickering sigh. "Will you hold me?"

It was the single thing he couldn't deny her.

He helped her down off the desk and smoothed her rumpled skirts. Then, settling into the remaining armchair, he pulled her down onto his lap. She nestled like a child, tucking her head beneath his chin and drawing her knees up close to her body.

The feather on her hat tickled the turning of his jaw. The soft lavender scent of her, mixed subtly with the musk of their lovemaking, was both scandalous and intoxicating.

It forced him to own up to the way he'd just used her—one more thing to be ashamed of in the tally he was keeping. He sucked in his breath and began to apologize.

"Oh, God, Shea. I'm so sorry. I should never have—"

"Have what, Cam?" she asked quietly. "Are you apologizing for giving me pleasure?"

Heat crept up Cameron's throat. "I'm apologizing for—for ravishing you. For taking you like—"

"Like a man in need?" He felt her turn and look at him. "I meant what I said. I came to help."

He sighed and shook his head. "You can't help with this," he insisted. "This is long past helping."

Shea sat up and fixed him with her most probing stare. "Tell me what was in that note. Let me be the judge this once."

Cam fished the scrap of paper from the pocket of his jacket.

Shea turned it toward the window where the last golden light of the day had begun to dim. She squinted at the words and then looked up at him. "Who is Charlie Gilbert?"

He was well beyond being able to lie to her, but he needed to put some space between them before he told her the truth. He eased her to her feet and relinquished the chair to her.

He made his way through the carnage to the far side

of the desk, then turned to face her. "Charlie Gilbert
rode with 'Bloody' Bill Anderson during the war,"
Cam told her, sickened by the memory. "He was a
guerrilla, a marauder. He trampled fields and set fire to
barns and ran off animals. He stood idle while men
were rousted from their beds and hanged in their night-
clothes. He watched women being terrorized and did
nothing to save them." He paused for breath, his self-
loathing like a miasma exhaled into the air around him.

"That was you, wasn't it, Cam," she said quietly.
"*You're* Charlie Gilbert."

Bile rose in his throat. He inclined his head. "That's
how Wes Seaver knew me—as Charlie Gilbert. At least
until today."

"Seaver was in the courtroom today, wasn't he?"

He couldn't answer outright; he was too ashamed to
even nod. He should have been able to do something,
to call to the bailiff, to have Seaver arrested. Instead he
had cowered in fear.

"Did Seaver ride with the guerrillas, too?" she
asked him.

"Lots of the men who rode with the Confederate
bushwhackers in Missouri and Kansas became outlaws
after the war—the Jameses and the Daltons and the
Seavers. Anderson and Quantrill schooled us all in lawlessness."

His own mastery of the guerrillas' lessons gave proof
to the paucity of his conscience, the bleakness of
his soul—no matter what reasons he'd had for joining them.

"Seaver sent that note to let me know he recognized
me," he went on. "To put me on notice that he means
to expose me."

"But what is there to expose?" Shea asked. "The

war's been over for a decade. Considering your reputation here in Denver, how could this hurt you?"

"Do you have any idea who the guerrillas were? Do you know what they did during the war? They were beasts, monsters, anathema to people of conscience on both sides of the conflict who had so much as a shred of decency."

"You couldn't have been part of that."

He was touched by her conviction, "Oh, but I was. I raided and burned with Anderson, who was mad with viciousness, and men like Wes Seaver, who developed an appetite for pillaging and killing. And after the attacks on Lawrence, Kansas, and Centralia—"

"*Centralia?*" Shea's head came up. "Lily was burned the day the guerrillas attacked Centralia, wasn't she?"

He nodded, determined not to spare himself. "So now you know the worst."

He saw accusation replace the shock in Shea's eyes, and knew her censure was nothing compared to what his sister's would be when she learned the truth.

"Lily doesn't know I rode with Anderson. She doesn't know how I came to be in Centralia the day she was burned."

While most of Anderson's troops were down at the station executing the unarmed Yankee soldiers they'd found on the train, Cameron had done his best to reach his mother and sister.

"And what will Seaver expect to ensure his silence?" she wanted to know.

Trust Shea to understand what was at stake. "He hasn't asked for anything," he hedged.

"I think you know very well what he wants."

She was going to force him to admit what Seaver was after. "He wants his brother's freedom."

"Will you give it to him?"

Cam stared past her and shrugged. "Jake Seaver's freedom isn't up to me."

"Who is it up to, then?"

"It's up to the jury and to the law."

"But you're the law," she insisted.

"Yes."

Shea looked into his face, daring him to tell her he would stand against Seaver and chance whatever came.

He shifted beneath the intensity of her gaze. After the intimacies they'd shared, he thought she deserved an answer. He thought she deserved the truth. "I don't know what I'll do."

Cam saw her eyes darken. He'd been bound to disappoint her in any case, just as he was bound to break Lily's heart. What he'd done all those years ago ensured that.

Shea rose and came toward him. "I know the man you are, Cam," she said softly standing before him in the dying daylight. "You won't give in to him."

"You don't know anything."

She took his hand in both of hers, into those small, dexterous hands, into those hands that had wreaked sweet havoc on his body not half an hour before. "I don't know what happened in the war, or why you rode with men like Seaver. What I know is that you've never spared yourself when it comes to doing what's right, what's honorable."

"I'm not the only one who'll suffer if this comes out. There's Lily and Rand." A sound of distress vibrated deep in his throat. "Especially Lily."

Shea's voice came softer; her hands tightened on his. "What would she have you do if you gave her the choice?"

Cam didn't know the answer.

"I've spent my life protecting her." He could hear

the defeat in his voice, feel it caught like a burr at the back of his throat. "I can't betray her. I can't let her know I rode with the men who nearly destroyed her."

"Lily's stronger than you think."

"I can't risk hurting her any more than she's been hurt already."

She touched his face, traced her fingertips down his cheekbone, along the edge of his mustache to the turning of his jaw. "You're a stronger and wiser and better man than you know, Cameron Gallimore," she told him.

He stepped away from her, not willing to let her lie to him. All he wanted was for her to go.

"Aren't you supposed to be meeting Ty at the jailhouse?" he asked pointedly.

Shea sighed as if she saw what he was doing. "I thought I might see Rand today. He hasn't been around much since Ty's father was arrested."

Cam heard the wistfulness in her voice, the yearning of a mother for her son. But that was something else he couldn't bear to think about tonight.

"Rand's been riding back to the farm with Emmet while I've been preparing for this trial." He looked around him at the inch-deep carpet of scattered files, the tumbled lawbooks, the broken and up-ended furniture. "Which I suppose is a very good thing, since it's going to take me half the night to put this back together."

She cupped his cheek for an instant, then turned and wended her way through the chaos to the door.

He stopped her as she reached for the knob. "Shea, I—" He hesitated, not sure what he wanted to say to her.

She gave him a slow nod and a tender smile. "I know," she murmured, and closed the door behind her.

• • •

Cam was halfway down the alley between his office and the livery stable when someone grabbed him from behind and jabbed a pistol into his back. A silky soft voice purred in the darkness.

"Well, if it ain't my old friend Charlie Gilbert. Or maybe I should call you Judge Cameron Gallimore, like everyone else?"

"What is it you want, Seaver?" Cam asked, though he knew very well what it was.

"You get my note, Charlie?" Seaver taunted him.

"Your note?"

"The one I had delivered to you after court let out," Seaver prompted.

"Yes, I got it."

"And what'd you think?"

Cam gave a snort of disgust. "I think your handwriting is illegible."

Seaver chuckled under his breath and rammed the pistol even harder against Cam's spine. "You ain't changed a lick, Charlie, since I knew you in the war. You still think you're smarter than me—and maybe you are. But being smarter don't necessarily give you the upper hand."

"Why don't you just tell me what you want?" Cam was tired down to his bones. He just wanted Seaver to either say the words outright or kill him and get it over with.

"You know what I want. I want you to see this trial goes my brother's way."

Cam gave his head a quick, little shake. "That's not up to me, Seaver. Juries decide which men are guilty."

Seaver cocked his gun. "You're a lawyer, God damn it, Charlie. You know how to bulldog a jury. Or if those bastards find Jake guilty, you sentence him light. You sentence him to the time he's served. I hear judges can do that."

"I can't let him off, Seaver. The law prescribes the punishment—"

"I don't give a damn what the law prescribes. You find a way to get Jake off or I'll have an an-nony-mous word with the men who write for the newspapers here in Denver. I'll tell 'em how you rode with 'Bloody' Bill and old Quantrill. How you kept close company with the James brothers and the Daltons." Cam could almost hear Seaver grin. "And me. It won't take much checking for them to find out it's true."

"This town'll lynch your brother if I let him off." Cam spoke the truth before he thought.

Seaver snapped Cam's head back and pressed the pistol to the base of his skull. The barrel was startlingly cold against his skin; the chill of it jolted down his back.

"If Jake dies," Seaver hissed, "I'm holdin' you responsible."

Cam took a long, slow breath and let it out. "You do what you need to, Seaver. But even if I don't sentence Jake to hang, sooner or later someone will."

"To hell with you, Charlie!" Seaver shouted. He gave Cam a hard little shove and cracked him with his pistol.

Cam's vision flared white, then blue. The next thing he knew he was on his hands and knees in the slush and the mud. He could hear Seaver's footsteps retreating down the alley, hear him mount his horse over somewhere toward Lawrence Street.

Cam eased back on his haunches, holding his head

in both his hands. Something sticky and hot was seeping through his hair and down his jaw. He crouched there, sick and shivering.

"Jesus," he whispered into the dark. "What am I going to do? *What in the name of hell am I going to do?*"

SIXTEEN

Dear God! Cam looks terrible, Shea thought as the bailiff led Ty and her to the seats they'd occupied in the courtroom the day before. Seeing the dark hollows scoured beneath Cam's eyes and the lines of weariness bracketing his mouth, she wondered if he'd slept last night at all.

She'd tossed and turned herself until almost dawn, grappling with the memory of following Cam to his office and what she'd found when she got there. Never had she imagined that the strong, calm, capable man she thought she knew could be so fragile and vulnerable. She had taken him into her arms instinctively, needing to comfort, needing to absorb as much of his confusion and pain as she could. She'd wanted so much to be with him, to offer him the balm of lovers' intimacy, the succor of her tenderness.

Close as they'd been last night, he'd finally given up the last of his secrets, trusted her with what he believed was the worst of himself. Even after he'd told her what he'd been and done, Shea's faith in him was unshaken.

God knows Cam had made his mistakes, but he wasn't brutal or cruel. He wasn't the kind of man Wes Seaver was, and she couldn't help believing Cam had had reasons of his own for joining up with the guerrillas so late in the war.

She only feared—especially when she saw how brittle and drained Cam looked this morning—that he would bend beneath the weight of Wes Seaver's threats, sacrifice his honor to protect his sister.

She couldn't bear the thought of that, of what it would do to him, of what it would do to Rand and Lily. Cam was the foundation the two of them had built their lives on, and while Seaver's revelations might rock their world, Cam's family would survive unless he crumbled.

Shea looked up at where Cam was giving a few last instructions to his bailiff and wished she'd had that insight to give him last night. Shea longed to go to him now, look into his eyes, and reassure him. She wanted to tell him he must stand against Seaver's threats for everyone's sake.

But the courtroom was quickly filling with lawyers and jurors and spectators. The trial was about to resume, and she'd have no chance to talk to him.

Beside her, Ty leaned in close. "Is Cam mad at us?" he wanted to know.

Shea smiled and gently smoothed down Ty's hair. He hadn't slept well, either. She'd heard him cry out more than once in the night, but when she'd gone to him, he'd turned to the wall to hide his tears.

"Of course Cam's not mad at us," she offered gently. "He doesn't want to be here today any more than we do."

Ty nodded as if he understood, but before she could say more the deputies brought in the defendants.

As he settled into his chair at the defense table, Sam Morran glanced back at his boy. A smile touched his lips, a smile warm enough to drive the fear and sadness from his eyes.

Ty reached out and closed his short, blunt fingers around the tails of his father's battered sack coat. He gripped it tight, crimping new wrinkles into the already rumpled cloth.

The brevity and the intensity of that contact wrung Shea's heart. What would this child do when the jury brought back their verdict? How would she console Ty when his father was sentenced to hang?

"First District Court is now in session," the bailiff intoned.

Cam clapped his gavel and the trial picked up with the presentation of the defense attorneys' cases. Cal Edwards, Jake Seaver's attorney, called his first witness.

Hyram Plumber was the barkeep at the Citation Saloon, one of Denver's seediest drinking establishments. After establishing that the man had been pouring drinks the day of the robbery, the lawyer went on to question him. "Were any of the men in this room drinking at your establishment that afternoon?"

"Why, yes, sir, they were," Plumber answered crisply. "Mr. Seaver and Mr. Morran were there, and Mr. Faber came in a few minutes later. The three of them ordered a bottle."

"Can you identify those men for the jury, Mr. Plumber?"

"Sure," Plumber said with a nod of his bald head. "They're the ones sitting over there, done up in manacles."

Mr. Edwards frowned as if he wished Plumber had used some other way of identifying his client and the others, but proceeded anyway. "Mr. Plumber, just how do you know these gentlemen were in your establishment at the precise moment the Bank of Denver was being robbed?"

"Well, sir, when we heard gunfire from the shootout at the bank, Mr. Seaver turned to me and said, 'What the hell is that?'"

A murmur rose in response to Plumber's answer.

Seaver's attorney waited for the din to die away. "And how did you answer Mr. Seaver?"

"I said, 'Damned if I know.' But then, for some reason, I took out my pocket watch."

"And what time was it?"

"It was ten minutes after one." Plumber paused for effect. "Which is amazing, you know, because that is exactly the time the *Rocky Mountain News* said the robbers came out of the bank."

"You're sure of the time?" Edwards asked.

"I said so, didn't I?" The saloon keeper took out a rumpled handkerchief and blotted perspiration from his upper lip.

"What did the defendants do when they heard the shooting?"

"Do? Well, sir, the three of them tossed back their drinks, and went out to see what the ruckus was about. I saw them head up the street in the direction of the shooting," Plumber testified, "so maybe that's how folks got the idea it was them that robbed the bank."

"And you're swearing these men were in the Citation Saloon at the day and time in question?"

The barkeep bobbed his head. "I specifically remember, because they left half a bottle on the table when they went out."

"Which you watered and sold to some other unsuspecting sod, you cheating bastard!" someone shouted from the back of the courtroom.

The place erupted with catcalls and laughter.

Cam straightened like a shot and banged his gavel. "There will be order in this court, or I'll have the bailiff toss the lot of you out into the street!"

Even at that, it took a minute or two for the crowd to settle. When they had, Cam turned to Mr. Edwards. "Have you any more you want to ask this witness, sir?"

"No, Your Honor."

Cam turned to Faber's and Morran's attorneys.

Morran's lawyer, Josiah Wallace, got up and asked one question. "And you're sure Sam Morran was in your establishment during the bank robbery?"

"Like I said. I know Mr. Morran real good. He's one of my best customers."

It was a dubious achievement, to Shea's way of thinking, but it established Sam Morran's identity.

Matt Faber's attorney asked specifically about his client, and received much the same assurances.

John McGreggor, the prosecutor, rose. "You testified, Mr. Plumber, that while the defendants were in your saloon, you took out your watch." Plumber inclined his head. "And that it was at exactly ten minutes after one o'clock in the afternoon on January the twenty-sixth, is that right?"

"Yes."

"You're sure it was the twenty-sixth?"

Plumber laid his hand across his heart. "It would have been my dear mama's sixty-first birthday. God rest her soul."

"Do you happen to have the timepiece in question with you?" McGreggor asked.

Cam frowned down from the bench. "Mr. McGreggor, is there a purpose to this?"

Shea's heart leaped and she couldn't help wondering why Cam was questioning the prosecutor's methods.

Was this what judges did, or was he preparing to undermine the prosecution?

"I think you'll see the purpose, Your Honor," McGreggor answered, "if you allow me another question or two."

Cam scowled and nodded.

"Would you mind if I took a look at your watch, Mr. Plumber?"

Plumber shot a quizzical glance at Seaver's attorney, then dug the watch out of his pocket.

McGreggor turned the shiny silver pocket watch in his hand and popped open the case. "This keep good time, Mr. Plumber?"

"Un-huh," Plumber answered, pressing his handkerchief to his upper lip again.

"And why do you find it necessary to carry this timepiece, sir?" McGreggor asked, shutting the case over the face of the watch.

"Well," the witness began with a grin, "for one thing, it ain't good business to have a clock in a barroom."

The crowd rumbled again, probably in agreement.

"I see," McGreggor murmured, flicking open the side of the watch case that protected the works. "So, Mr. Plumber, can you explain to me how you consulted this watch, the very one you claim to have been carrying on January twenty-six of this year, when it's engraved with your name and the date 'February eight, 1876'?"

Plumber paled, and Shea heard Cal Edwards curse under his breath. "Goddamned idiot!" he mumbled.

Cam banged and banged his gavel, but it was a full five minutes before the turmoil in the room sank to manageable levels.

When it did McGreggor continued, "I have a bill of

sale from Hense Jewelers, which details the sale of this watch and is dated the eighth of February."

Cam scowled over the edge of his bench at the witness. "Well, Mr. Plumber, you care to tell the court what happened here?"

Plumber had sweated through his shirt and vest. "I got nothing to say, Your Honor."

"Well then, I'm going to ask my bailiff to escort you to the room next door so we can have a little chat when I'm done here about what happens to witnesses who perjure themselves."

Once Plumber was gone, Cam turned to the jury. "Now then, it's my duty to direct you to disregard this witness's testimony and not to consider it in your deliberations."

The trial proceeded, and in the course of the morning, the defense called three more witnesses who proved hardly more reliable than Hyram Plumber.

Just before twelve o'clock, Cam banged his gavel and adjourned the court for the noon meal. Shea waited in the corridor, needing to talk to Cam, needing to convince him not to bow to Seaver's threats. But Cam never showed his face beyond the tightly locked door of his chambers.

The afternoon session was louder and more unruly than the previous one, probably owing to the fact that most of the spectators had sought their lunch at the saloons surrounding the courthouse. Once Cam had called everyone to order, he asked the lawyers to make their final statements.

Shea listened raptly, and found Prosecutor McGreggor's strong and relentlessly logical. Five citizens of Denver had been ruthlessly shot during the robbery. Numerous unimpeachable witnesses had identified the outlaws. All three of the defendants had been arrested outside the bank with their weapons drawn.

The defense attorneys attempted to convince the jury that their clients had been mistakenly identified in the confusion of the robbers' escape.

After all the lawyers had spoken, Cam turned to instruct the jury. As Shea understood it, this would be his chance to explain how they should consider the evidence, limit the scope of their deliberations, and temper the outcome of the trial.

Shea's heart beat hard inside her. If Cam was going to submit to Wes Seaver's blackmail, he would begin to guide the jury's purpose now. As if he knew what she was thinking, he glanced across at her, and the desolation in his eyes made her belly churn with dread.

"Sometimes," Cam began his directive, his voice ringing low and resonant across the crowded courtroom, "sometimes mitigating circumstances alter the deliberations a jury undertakes and affect the outcome of a trial. I believe that there are things about this case, this robbery, that might influence the way you judge the men being tried today."

Oh, Cam, no!

Shea bit her lip to keep from crying out, knowing it was already too late to change what was about to happen. If she'd wanted to help him stand against Seaver's threats, she should have held his hands in hers last night, promised him that Lily would understand and forgive him his past, and pledged to help and support him whatever came. She hadn't done that. Instead she had let him run her off, let him believe he had to walk this treacherous road alone.

Up on the judge's bench Cam continued his instructions to the jury. "I think that the deaths of your friends and your neighbors might well color the deliberations you are about to undertake. I know you are bound to feel bitterness and grief at the deaths of these good men. You may even long for revenge against their killers. That's more than understandable, but those feelings have no place in a juror's mind."

Cam compressed his lips before he went on. "When you agreed to serve on this jury you took an oath. You promised to set aside your personal considerations in the name of the law. It is my duty to remind you of that pledge."

His gaze moved over the jury, the courtroom, and came to rest on the defendants.

"You must consider the charges against these three men solely on the evidence presented here—and nothing else. No wishes to avenge these senseless deaths, no feelings of bitterness and hatred. It is the law that raises us a step above the beasts, and we must uphold the rights and responsibilities it demands of us."

Shea's throat closed and her eyes burned with pride. Cam had not bowed to Seaver's threats. He might be forced to confront his past, but he would do it as a man who stood for right and honor. If he let her, she would stand proudly beside him through whatever came.

Cam drew a long breath and let it out again before he concluded. "As you go off together, you must consider each of these men's crimes separately. That means you might well decide on different verdicts for each of them—and ultimately provide for different punishments. The bailiff will escort you to a room where you can consider those decisions."

Deputy Sim Cummings led the jurors out a side door of the courtroom. Cam rapped his gavel sharply to adjourn the court. There was nothing for any of them to do now, but wait.

• • • •

"Jury's coming back, Judge," Deputy Cummings said, seeking Cam out in the small spartan chamber down the hall from the courtroom.

Cam put down the cup of coffee he'd been drinking and pushed to his feet. "Be right there."

"We gonna have a necktie party, Judge?" Someone in the hallway waved a flask in his face as if the man were proposing a toast. Cam batted the flask aside.

"We'll have to see," he answered and promised himself that once this was over he was going to take a bottle of whiskey off somewhere and drink himself insensible.

The jury had come to their verdict even faster than Cam had anticipated. Nor did he think their efficiency boded well for the men on trial. Not that he was surprised; these three were unquestionably guilty of the charges brought against them.

Except maybe for Sam Morran. Cam couldn't imagine for a moment that Morran could have shot someone. Certainly none of the witnesses had said he did, but Cam supposed that didn't matter. Denver was in a hanging mood. The populace—goaded by the shrill headlines in the newspapers—had decided the men who'd died in the course of the robbery had to be avenged, and today that bill came due.

It was time for Cam to play his part in this—despite Wes Seaver's threats. Once the jury had published its verdict, he'd pass the sentence, set the date, and attend the execution.

The very thought of facing another hanging—especially this hanging—made his belly burn. Dear God, he hated being part of this!

He hated even more that he was going to have to condemn Sam Morran in front of his boy. He'd wished

he could count on Shea to keep Ty out of the courtroom, but he knew short of chloroform or hog-tieing
she wouldn't be able to prevent the boy from being
there. In a way Cam couldn't blame him. He'd needed
to be at his father's bedside when he died, and he
hadn't been a whole lot older than Ty was now.

As Cam took his place on the bench, he glanced
across and saw that Shea and Ty were seated in their
usual place. Though Ty's mouth was set, Cam could
see a glimmer of hope in him, some stubborn childish
belief that everything would be all right. Shea sat with
Ty's hand wrapped tight in hers, and Cam thought she
might be hoping for a miracle, too.

In any case, he figured he owed her some sort of
warning. He caught her eye, then nodded almost
imperceptibly. Still holding his gaze, she inclined
her head.

What surprised him even more than her perceptiveness was the compassion he saw in her eyes. She understood what having to pass this sentence was doing to
him, how speaking the words was going to flay his soul.
And he could see that no matter what he'd told her, no
matter what he'd done, she was willing to stand by him
when this was over.

The din in the courtroom rose as the prisoners were
escorted to their places, and Cam noticed the way Sam
Morran greeted his son. The communication that
flowed between them, the need to touch, the yearning
to speak of things that only boys and fathers knew
sliced to the quick of him.

He saw the fear beneath Jake Seaver's bravado, and
the acceptance in Matt Faber's eyes.

Cam straightened as the bailiff called the court into
session. "And have you come to a verdict?" Cam asked
the foreman of the jury a few moments later.

"We have, Your Honor."

Cam asked the defendants to rise, then turned to the foreman again. "How find you in the case of Matt Faber?"

"Guilty on all counts, Your Honor."

The courtroom buzzed like a hive of bees. Cam rapped his gavel for silence.

"And Jake Seaver?"

"Guilty on all counts."

Cam hesitated and let his gaze stray to the last man at the defense table. "And Sam Morran?"

"Guilty, sir."

To his credit, Morran's face gave nothing away. Cam suspected he had accepted what was going to happen long before. From what Shea told him, Morran had been trying to kill himself with drink ever since Ty's mother died.

Cam slid a glance at where Shea had her arm around Ty and his heart twisted hard. Still, he banged his gavel for silence, then turned to the row of defendants.

"Do any of you have something to say before I pass sentence?"

Faber's head was bowed. Jake Seaver looked scared down to the soles of his boots. Morran looked back at his son. None of the prisoners spoke.

Cam took a breath that burned all the way down. It didn't matter how hard men were or what they'd done, at the moment he condemned them they were more like children than monsters, more like terrified boys than heinous outlaws. Because Cam always saw that other self in men like these, he hated this part of being a judge. He hated it more today than he ever had.

"Very well, then," he began. "It is my determination that in accordance with the laws of the Colorado Territory you will each be hanged by the neck until dead."

He took another long breath. Knowing the mood of anticipation rife in the city, he continued. "I'll convene court to hear any appeals your lawyers care to make first thing in the morning. Otherwise, the sentences will be carried out tomorrow at two o'clock."

Ty gave a cry of protest and bolted out of the courtroom. Shea jumped to her feet and ran after him.

Cam watched them go, hating himself for doing what he'd sworn before the law to do. But now, by the grace of God and the new constitution of Colorado, Cam would never have to condemn a man to die again. He was done with the law. He meant to tender his resignation right after the execution.

He rapped his gavel one last time.

Cam elbowed his way through the crowds in the halls of the courthouse ignoring the score of men who tried to stop him, slap him on the back, and congratulate him on how well the case had turned out. What he'd never been able to understand was why they treated him as if he'd done something worthy of their praise, as if condemning three men was something he'd want to celebrate.

The jury had found Seaver, Faber, and Morran guilty of robbery and murder. All Cam had done was his job.

He drew a long shaky breath when he finally reached the street, then turned resolutely toward his office. If he hadn't spilled or broken it last night, he had a bottle tucked away somewhere. What he wanted more than salvation right now was to get to his office, unearth that whiskey, and drink until he couldn't see.

He hadn't gone more than a dozen yards when someone snagged his arm and pulled him around. He

hunched his shoulders and balled his fist, ready to
punch whoever had been imprudent enough to interfere with him.

Albert Root, one of the city councilmen, waved a
newspaper in Cam's face. "What's the meaning of
this?" he demanded.

"Of what?" Cam snatched the paper from Root's
grasp and scanned the headline.

PROBE INTO JUDGE GALLIMORE'S PAST
PROMINENT COLORADO JUDGE
BELIEVED TO HAVE RIDDEN WITH QUANTRILL

Cam felt the color drain out of his face.

"What the hell are they talking about?" Root demanded. "You didn't ride with those reb outlaws, did
you, Cam?"

Cam shoved the newspaper back in Root's face. "I
can't explain this to you now," he murmured tersely
and started up the street.

"I don't want an explanation," the councilman
shouted after him. "I want a denial!"

Cam kept walking, bile rising up his throat.

A short, wiry man in a rumpled coat stepped into
his path. "Men like you reb bastards killed my grand-
daddy defending his farm," he shouted, shoving at
Cam's chest with the heels of his hands.

Cam didn't say a word, just stepped around him
and pressed on. A thousand glaring eyes seemed to
pierce him as he made his way up Larimer Street. The
crowd parted as he passed, shrinking away as if he were
a snake.

"I wouldn't have believed that of him," he heard
someone say.

"Quantrill's men were brigands, sure as hell!"

"Goddamn Sesch outlaw," someone else hissed, and spat at him.

Cam finally reached Mr. Johanson's livery stable and saddled his horse. After what he'd just seen here in town, all he could think about was getting out to the farm. All he wanted was to explain to Lily about the war and the raiders and what had happened that day in Centralia, before she heard it from someone else.

He'd known this was coming from the moment he'd recognized Seaver's photograph at Shea's studio, known it from the moment he'd decided to fly in the face of Seaver's threats.

He'd run this trial exactly the way he had every other one he'd presided over these last four years. Once the jury had published their verdict, he'd passed the only sentence he could. It was the sentence the law provided for murders, the only sentence that would keep the citizens of Denver from storming the jail and lynching the prisoners outright.

But he *had* expected time before the truth about his past came out. He'd figured the editors would send a reporter to talk to him, give him a chance to explain himself before they printed Seaver's allegations.

He'd meant to use that time to take his courage in his hands and face his sister. He'd wanted to explain things he should have told her years before, wanted the chance to ask for forgiveness.

Now he had to reach her before the newspaper did.

The countryside he rode through seemed cowed and bleak beneath its tattered sheet of graying snow. The sky hung thick and low. The wind pierced through him like talons.

Everything he'd wanted, everything he'd tried to build in Colorado, every bit of the future he longed for depended now on Lily and how she accepted what he was going to tell her. He was terrified by the prospect of seeing hurt and betrayal rise in her eyes, frightened of what she might do. He'd accept whatever recriminations she heaped on him, knowing full well how richly he deserved her censure. But he hoped with all his heart that once he'd told her all of it, she'd find a way to forgive him for the things he'd done and the secrets he'd kept from her.

Cam reined in at the foot of the drive, turning his horse in circles while he tried to gather his courage. Once he rode up the lane his course would be set, his destiny decided. His mouth tasted like years-old rust and his chest was tight. Somehow he managed to nudge his gelding forward.

Cam's mouth went dryer still when he saw that Emmet's buggy was parked by the gate—though judging by the horse's lathered hide Emmet hadn't been there long.

Cam had been so intent on facing Lily that he hadn't even considered what he'd tell Emmet about all this. Or what he might say to his son. Confronting Lily wasn't the end; she was only the beginning of a round of explaining and begging forgiveness.

Still, he had to start by making this right with her. For these next few hours only Lily mattered—Lily's anger, Lily's grief. Lily's feelings of betrayal and loss.

He dismounted and opened the gate. He was halfway up the walk when Emmet stalked out onto the narrow porch. He braced his feet and curled his fingers into fists.

"Go away," he spat. "She doesn't want to see you."

Each one of those careful, quiet words bit into Cam like the tail of a lash. "Did she see the story in the newspaper?"

Emmet raised his chin, his color high and accusation

clear in his voice. "*I* brought her the newspaper. I thought she needed to hear the truth about her brother from someone she could trust."

Emmet's words made it hurt to breathe, hurt to speak. It made him ache to see Emmet acting as Lily's protector when Cam had dedicated his life to watching over her. It was agony to know Emmet was protecting Lily from *him*.

"Please, Emmet," Cam offered softly. "I need to talk to Lil, need to explain. I need to tell her why I took up with the guerrillas so late in the war. I need to make her understand why I wasn't there to protect Mother and her when Anderson and his raiders came through Centralia."

"So you admit it, then?" Emmet asked, his voice deep with loathing. "You admit you rode with that vermin? You consorted with that madman Anderson and the James brothers and the Daltons and the Seavers. Even though I fought for the South, I consider those men a scourge, a blight on a grand and glorious Cause."

In spite of Emmet's outrage, Cam stood his ground. "I want to talk to my sister."

"Do you think she's likely to forgive you for joining up with the men responsible for her being burned? Do you think she'll simply excuse you for lying to her all this time?"

"I have to ask her," Cameron offered again. "Emmet, please. Give me a chance to talk to her."

Emmet stood like a spire of granite between Cam and the door, between Cam and his sister.

Then, just as Cam was about to turn away, Lily stepped into the doorway. Though he couldn't see her all that clearly through the screen, he could tell her face was set, and she looked like she'd been crying.

"Lil—" Cam called out to her in entreaty. "Lily, please."

Emmet turned and glanced at her. "Go back inside," he bid her, softly, insistently. "Let me take care of this."

She hesitated as if she might change her mind, then swiped at her tears and stepped back into the kitchen.

"Lily, please . . ." Cam begged, but his sister was gone.

Emmet glared at him. "I'd as soon kill you where you stand," he offered softly, "as give you the chance to hurt her again. Go away, Cam. Get out of here."

Cameron had no doubt of Emmet's sincerity. He took one step backward, and then another. If Lily had seen the article in the *Rocky Mountain News,* she knew the worst. Perhaps if he gave her time to absorb what she'd read, gave her time for her hurt to subside, he could make her listen.

"I'll be back," Cam said, shifting toward the gate.

"You're not wanted here."

"But I will be back. I'll keep coming back until Lily agrees to see me."

"She'll never agree to that," Emmet assured him.

Cam was terrified that was true. "You will take care of her while I'm not here, won't you, Emmet?"

"You can depend on it."

"Emmet." Cam's voice dropped almost to a whisper. "Will you tell her I'm sorry?"

For a moment Cam thought Emmet meant to refuse, then he nodded his head.

Cam dragged himself out the gate and looked back at the house. Emmet stood at the edge of the porch, his feet braced wide and his arms crossed against his chest. He was the very picture of disapproval and obstinacy, and Cam was suddenly glad that if Lily and Rand didn't have him to protect them, they had Emmet.

He swung up onto his horse and rode away.

Shea cracked open the studio door and stared out at Cam, leaning against the brickwork at the top of the steps. "Shea?" he whispered. "May I come in?"

She glanced past him to where lacy swirls of snow spun through the dark and tried to judge the hour. Well past midnight, she thought. Well past the time when respectable women entertained gentleman callers.

She reached out and grabbed his wrist anyway. "For the love of God, Cam," she murmured as she pulled him into the entry, "where have you been?"

He braced back against the wall to steady himself, and she realized he'd been drinking. And by the bite of whiskey on his breath, drinking heavily.

"Is—is Ty here?" he asked her.

She shook her head. "He's spending the night at the jail with his father. The sheriff said it was all right, since they haven't much time . . ."

Cam sighed and, even in the filmy half-light, she could see how he sagged under the weight of the sentence he'd had to pass today. It was a weight distinct and separate from his usual mantle of guilt and responsibility. Shea couldn't help worrying that condemning Ty's father coupled with Seaver's revelations about Cam's past might be what finally broke him.

Because he was here—and in this condition—Shea suspected he'd gone to see Lily and that things had gone badly between them. She supposed she should ask about his sister, but it was late and she knew he'd tell her when he was ready.

"What can I do to help?" was all she said.

He shifted and curled his arms around her. "I need to hold you and breathe you in and taste your throat. I want to sleep with you in my arms and wake in the morning with you beside me."

His words surprised her, sending a shiver of pleasure down her back. Cam never spoke about his needs, never asked for help from anyone. That he'd come to her tonight gave proof of his yearning for warmth and solace, soft words and reassurances. His yearning for her.

She reached up and cupped his cheek. "Then take off your coat and come to bed."

He draped his duster on the coatrack with scrupulous care, then did the same with his gunbelt and hat. He wavered just a little as she led him into her tiny bedroom.

Rufus, who'd been snuggled deep in the covers at the foot of the bed, hissed as Cam plopped down on it.

"Even the cat wants me to go away," he murmured, loosening his necktie and working the buttons down the front of his vest.

"I'm glad you came," she murmured and reached out to trace the contours of his cheek and jaw.

"Why?" he asked.

Because I love you. Because I like knowing you need to be with me. But Shea knew she couldn't say those things to him now, couldn't expect him to respond to her when he had nothing left to give to anyone.

She shifted her shoulders and stepped a little away. "You know I hate being here by myself at night."

He accepted her at her word and continued removing his clothes. He was not nearly so incapacitated as she'd thought, but he seemed weary down to his bones.

Knowing he was going to pass judgment on Sam Morran had been wearing on him for weeks. Having to condemn Jake Seaver in the face of his brother's threats had taken a terrible toll. But it must have been facing Lily with the truth about his past—and hers—that left him so depleted, so terribly spent and hollow-eyed.

He'd tried to refill that void with whiskey, and ended up on Shea's doorstep instead.

When he was down to his knitted underdrawers, Shea lifted the covers on the bed and guided him beneath them. The springs creaked in protest as he eased down onto the mattress; they grumbled even more as she climbed in beside him.

Without so much as a word, she took him into her arms. It seemed right for him to be there, his head resting against her shoulder, his breath washing warm against her throat. He curled his hand at her waist, drawing her closer. She felt his mustache graze her collarbone.

Shea smiled to herself, weaving her fingers through the heavy raw silk of his hair. She liked having him here with her. She liked the way his scent surrounded her, liked the faint tang of vetiver, the crispness of the cold and snow, the malty sweetness of whiskey. She liked his breadth, his maleness, and the sense of safety he gave her by just being Cam. Even now, when he was so vulnerable, he was able to make her feel safe. He always made her feel safe. She closed her eyes and reveled in that safety.

They drifted for a time, half awake and half dreaming, communing in a way that transcended words. The time seemed imbued with priceless tenderness as each of them was wrapped in caring and warmth and acceptance.

As the night advanced they stretched and turned and twisted, always touching, always moving together, always nestling close. As Cam curled onto his side, he pulled her back against his chest, notching his knees to the bend of her legs, wrapping himself around her. Shea arched and snuggled deeper, drawn by his rich internal heat.

But now as they lay spooned together, a torpid voluptuousness began to flow between them. Gradually the whisper of sexual awareness came louder, more insistent. Slowly the need for rest was replaced by other more compelling needs.

Shea's skin tingled at the places where their bodies touched. An ever-sweetening intensity seeped through her. The hair along her forearms stirred; gooseflesh rippled over her buttocks and down her thighs. A warm, soft throbbing beat at the core of her.

She had not meant to bring desire to their bed. She had wanted to offer Cam a night of peace and consolation. She had wanted him to leave her renewed and armored for the trials he must face tomorrow. But the desire was here in spite of her.

Cam must have felt it, too, for the tempo of his breathing changed. His muscles flexed. He skimmed his palm upward from where it had lain at her waist and cupped her breast, splaying his fingers over her. The gesture was primitive, instinctive, blatantly and erotically male.

His erection rose against her. Deep inside, her body throbbed in answer. The wanting grew in both of them.

He nuzzled her gently, grazing the skin of her neck with his lips. He paused to breathe moisture into the hollow of her collarbone, paused to stain the pulse point midway up her throat with his heat, paused to savor the hollow beneath her ear.

He drew her earlobe into his mouth. She shivered with pleasure.

Though he murmured as if he meant to soothe her, he began to sketch slow lazy strokes around her nipple with the pad of his thumb. Strokes that made her want, made her yearn.

Sensation soaked into her, collecting low in her belly, hot between her legs. Sensual restlessness grew in her. She turned and sought his mouth.

They kissed in soft, exploratory couplings of lips and tongues. In slow, soul-melting scrutiny of every crease and every hollow of each other's mouths. In longer, deeper tastes where they could relish the pleasure they found in each other. They kissed until they were both trembling with the need for greater contact, closer communion.

Shifting beneath the covers, Shea caught the hem of her nightdress and pulled it over her head. Cam struggled out of his knitted underdrawers.

They came together skin to skin. The contact was delicious, provocative, warm, and intimate.

"I like this," he whispered, tracing her soft silhouette with the brush of his hand. "I like being with you like this."

"I like it, too," she murmured in answer.

She saw his features soften, saw the glow in his eyes intensify. Here in bed tonight, there was only him and only her. Only warmth, only pleasure and the kind of peace that came with closing out the world. It was the kind of calm and renewal Cam needed so desperately.

She rolled onto her back and drew him over her. He came nestling against her, draping one leg over hers, pulling her close. He lowered his head to her breast and drew the ripe knot of her nipple into his mouth.

"Oh, Cam," she breathed, arching against him.

As he drew on her in a rhythm as familiar as her own heartbeat, his hands skimmed over every inch of her exposed flesh. He charted the curve of her waist and the slope of her hip. He skimmed one palm the length of her legs. He traced a slow, lazy line along the vale of her chest and belly. He cupped his palm to the swell of her mound.

Everything inside her liquefied.

She reached for him, all but weeping with the joy of exploring the sleek, sweeping planes of his body. She liked his textures, the bristly vitality of his mustache, the whorly roughness of the hair along his thighs. She liked his taste, the rich dark flavor of his skin and the whiskey sweetness of his mouth.

She reveled in him, savoring him no less intimately than he was savoring her, no less provocatively, and with no less tenderness.

They stared into each other's eyes as they came together, joining flesh to flesh and soul to soul. They lay united, wholly one, cherishing an intimacy neither of them had ever known, letting the depth of that communion shape and nourish them.

In that moment of deep connection Shea might have told Cam how much she loved him, might have heard him respond in kind, but they were far beyond words. She was far beyond anything but her awareness of Cam, far beyond anything but anticipating the pleasure beckoning them.

With a few murmured endearments they began to move slowly and sinuously together. Cam breathed her name as he took her with a sweet, lazy carnality. Shea drew him deeper, engendering the pure, liquid spill of desire between them.

They held each other, whispering and kissing, giving and receiving shivery delight, keeping the world at bay for as long as they could. But in the end, those tender ministrations gave way to a wondrous tumble of

sensation that swept them up in a maelstrom of ultimate rapture.

They curled together in the aftermath, shifting,
breathing deep, finding bliss in each other's arms. Finding peace and renewal in the slow, sweet slide into
dreamless sleep.

SEVENTEEN

"*S*omeone must have slipped this under your door during the night."

Shea looked up at Cam, who was standing just inside the bedroom doorway, a crumpled envelope in his hand.

"Who could have done that?" she asked him.

Cam shook his head. "You recognize the handwriting?"

Her name ran downhill across the front of the envelope. Something about those scrawled, uneven letters chased a chill down her back.

"Do you want me to open it?" he asked her.

Shea finished buttoning up her bodice, then took the envelope from him, impatient with herself for letting the letter spook her. The tattered sheet inside bore a few wavery lines of script.

Dear Mrs. Waterston,
    Would you please do me the honor of stopping by

*the jail some time before they hang me. I need to talk
to you about my boy.*

Much obliged,
Sam Morran

"It's from Ty's father," she breathed on a huff of
relief. "I thought Wes Seaver had traced you here. I was
afraid . . ."

Though Cam made a dismissing sound, she could
feel his hand wasn't quite steady as he stroked her hair.
"Would you like me to go with you when you see
Morran?"

Shea glanced at him. "Would you mind doing that?"

He cupped her cheek, the graze of his thumb along
her cheekbone a dulcet reminder of the tenderness
they'd shared the night before. "Let me go get a bath
and a shave. I'll be back in half an hour."

She heard him go, softly closing the door behind
him, stepping lightly on the stairs, leaving before the
town was astir to spare her reputation. The thought of
him doing that for her made her smile, and she crossed
to the window to watch him up the street.

He walked with his head up and his shoulders
squared, walked like a man with purpose and assurance.
It warmed her to know that in the quiet passions of the
night she'd given that back to him, given back the sense
of who he was.

He'd come to her last night an all but broken man.
He'd come because he hadn't known where else to go,
and because he'd needed to be with her. This fine,
strong, intensely insular man had finally opened himself to her, laid his trials and fears and the treasures of
his heart before her. That he'd trusted her and made
her a part of his life filled Shea's chest with incalculable
pride.

As he reached the corner at Larimer Street she saw Cam pause and look back toward the studio—almost as if he was thinking of her.

She stepped hastily back from the window lest he see her watching, but the idea that she might be as much on his mind as he was on hers brought the heat of pleasure to her cheeks.

By the time she'd made coffee, Cam had returned bathed and barbered and wearing a fresh shirt. Together they set off for the jail on Eleventh Street.

Sheriff Cook looked up from his desk when they arrived. "The two of you are out early today."

Shea took the rumpled paper from her pocket. "I found this note under my door this morning. It says Sam Morran wants to see me."

The sheriff nodded. "Morran had one of the deputies drop it off while he was patrolling last night. Why don't you make yourselves comfortable, and I'll have Morran brought out here."

"That's good of you, Dan," Cam said with a nod, "to give us a little privacy."

The sheriff inclined his head. "It's the least I can do. You want the boy, too?"

"That's up to Mr. Morran," she answered.

A few minutes later Shea found herself facing Sam Morran across the sheriff's desk. Though Morran was manacled and an armed deputy was posted just outside, Sam didn't look like a desperado. He looked old and weary down to his bones.

Ty stood at his father's elbow, doggedly loyal to the man who was about to give him away.

"What I wanted, Mrs. Waterston," Morran began, "is to talk to you about Ty. Since neither his ma or me have kin I can send him to, I was hoping you'd agree to look after my boy once I'm gone."

Shea looked across at Ty, at his dirt-smudged face and rumpled clothes, and her throat went tight.

"I wouldn't expect you to adopt him outright," Morran went on. "Ty's headstrong, and he don't always mind the way he should, but he was raised up right. My wife saw to that, and for as long as I can remember, he's earned his keep."

The man hesitated, and Shea couldn't help thinking how hard this must be for Ty—to hear himself described in such a depreciating way, to have his future parceled out while he was standing there. To be helpless to change any of what was going to happen.

"You and I ain't always seen eye to eye on things, Mrs. Waterston," Sam Morran apologized. "But it'd ease my mind considerably to know my boy's going to live with someone who'll be good to him."

Shea pursed her lips, taking a moment to consider what she should do. She'd been drawn to this child from the moment she'd met him at the mining camp. She liked being able to offer him work and help and affection. She'd wanted to offer him more than that, and now she had the chance. But what she needed to know was if *he* wanted *her*.

"Ty," she said, looking deep into those solemn brown eyes, "I need to be sure you understand what your pa is asking me. He wants you to come and live with me permanently, and I need to know if that's what you want, too."

Ty's face screwed up as if he was trying not to cry. "I don't want to be no trouble."

No trouble. Just breathing made Tyler Morran trouble. He was eager and quick-witted, impulsive and full of mischief. He was the kind of child that would keep her busy extricating him from one scrape after another for the rest of her days. Yet he had such a good heart, and he tried so hard. She'd never known anyone who tried as hard as Ty.

"You won't be causing trouble by answering me honestly," she persisted. "But I do want you to know that if you come to live with me, I'll expect things of you. Minding what I say is one of them, and the other is going to school."

Ty straightened a little, as if he'd realized he really was going to be given a choice.

"You also need to know we might not be staying on here in Denver." She heard Cam shift on his feet behind her, but forged ahead. This wasn't about her or Cam; it was about this boy. "And I'd expect you to go with me wherever we went. I'd also want you to promise to live with me until you're of legal age."

"How old is that?" Ty wanted to know.

"Eighteen," Cameron answered.

Shea leaned forward in her chair, wanting to reach out to Ty and knowing she had to have his promise before she could.

"I'd like to have you as my boy, Ty," she went on, "but I can't tell your father I'll look after you until you agree to live with me and abide by my rules."

His eyes suddenly went desolate, the color of old bronze. Giving this promise would make his father's execution real to Ty in a way neither the trial nor the sentencing had.

"I don't want to promise anything," the boy answered mulishly. "Pa ain't dead yet."

Shea supposed Ty felt disloyal talking about a future his father would not see. Still, getting this settled was important. Someday Ty would understand that his father had only asked this because he loved his son.

"No, boy, I'm not dead yet," Sam Morran allowed, "but I'll go to my rest a whole lot easier in my mind if I know that you're provided for. I know I ain't been the best of fathers these last few years. I know I drank too much, and didn't look after you nearly enough. I know that after your mama died, I fell in with bad companions. I ain't proud of what I've done, but it's over now. I just want you to know I always loved you, Ty, right from that first day."

Ty swallowed hard and looked at his father. His eyes shimmered with tears, with anguish and love. "Is this what you want me to do, Pa?" he asked softly "Go live with Shea?"

The manacles rattled as Sam Morran covered his son's hand with his own. "She's been taking good care of you, hasn't she, boy?"

Ty nodded his head.

"Then promise her, Ty."

Shea could see color come into Ty's face, along with anger and hopelessness. He glared across at her, his eyes welling. He hated that she was making him do this, hated that giving his word meant acknowledging that his father was going to hang.

When he spoke his voice came out in a croak. "I promise."

Shea let out her breath. Sam Morran stared down at where his hands were linked with his son's. Ty stood like a rock beside his father.

Cam broke the heavy silence. "Would you like to make your wishes legal, Mr. Morran," he asked softly, "just in case?"

"Is there someone who'd object to Mrs. Waterston taking my boy?" Sam asked almost fearfully.

"A will would clarify things," Cameron assured him. "I'll help you write it if you like."

"All right," Morran conceded, swallowing hard. "Let's write that will—for Ty's sake."

• • •

The din of the crowd rose in intensity as the paneled police wagon rumbled across the broad, frozen field at the top of the river bluffs. Well over a hundred people had been waiting in the wind and the cold, and they were impatient for things to get underway.

As the wagon jolted to a stop at the foot of the gallows steps, Shea tightened her hands on Ty's narrow shoulders.

Once the driver had unlocked the doors, Cam stepped down from the rear of the wagon, looking as gray and grim as any man could. Sheriff Cook climbed out after him, followed by two young deputies.

The clamor of the crowd rose to a howl as the lawmen began handing the three bound prisoners to the ground. Jake Seaver immediately shook off the lawmen's hold and sneered at the people who had come to watch him die. Matt Faber glanced once at the gallows then lowered his head.

Sam Morran stood in the doorway of the van, seeming more composed than Shea had ever seen him. Perhaps he'd made peace with hanging, she thought. Or maybe he'd just grown so tired of grief and responsibility and failure that he was ready to give it all up and join his wife.

Shea felt Ty tense as the deputies helped Sam down. For an instant Shea thought the boy was going to pull out of her grasp and cross the field for one last word with his father. Instead he stayed where he was, though she could feel his breathing go labored and uneven as he tried not to cry.

It made Shea want to gather him up and take him far away from here. But none of them—not her nor Cam nor Sam himself—had been able to convince Ty he didn't have to come to the hanging. Still, Shea had deliberately picked a place for them to stand that was a good way back and on the opposite side of the field from the scaffold's steps. She knew from her own initiation in Breckenridge just what grim business hangings were, and she'd vowed that when the moment came, she'd stop Ty's ears and wrap him so close against her that he wouldn't hear the trap fall or see his father swing from the gallows beam.

As the little party of lawmen, prisoners, and newspapermen clustered at the foot of the scaffold's steps, Shea scanned the field. The crowd was better dressed and perhaps not quite so unruly as the one that had been in Breckenridge. Still, she'd heard them ranging through the streets all morning, visiting shops and patronizing the local eateries and saloons. Business at the studio had been brisk. Folks seemed prone to having themselves immortalized on days when other men were going to die.

She'd closed at noon, collected Ty at the jail, and made the walk out Sixteenth Street. She could barely believe her eyes when she saw that Owen had come to the hanging, too. When she'd decided to take that photograph last fall, he'd refused to go near the gallows, refused to help set up the camera. Now he was here, keeping his distance, but peering at them around a cluster of drunken cowboys. He'd come to look after Ty and her, she realized, and was warmed both by the gesture and his courage.

Then, just as the hangman, the deputies, and the prisoners seemed ready to mount the gallows steps, a tall, black-coated minister rode up to join them. Something about his whiplash build and the way he sat his horse caught Shea's attention. But it was the thick, yellow hair tucked down into the collar of his jacket that gave him away.

"That man's Wes Seaver," she shouted, trying to make herself heard above the yelling of the crowd. "It's Wes Seaver!"

As if *he'd* heard, Seaver pulled his pistol and killed the hangman and one of the deputies where they stood.

The newspapermen dove for cover. Cam and the sheriff fell back behind the police wagon and returned Seaver's fire.

At the sound of the shooting, the crowd erupted into a pushing, screaming mass of humanity. As people flooded past them, Ty twisted away from Shea and set off across the field, shouting for his father. Shea grabbed up her skirts and raced after him.

In the midst of the chaos, a second outlaw burst over the lip of the river bluff and ran to cut the prisoners' bonds. Four more gunmen galloped out of the trees at the north end of the field, firing into the crowd and leading a string of horses for the prisoners to use in their escape.

Over near the gallows, Cam and the lawmen fought it out with Seaver. A few of the citizens who'd come to watch the hanging drew their weapons and started shooting.

In the midst of the gunfight, the prisoners struggled to catch and mount their saddled ponies. Matt Faber went down still clutching his roan's bridle. Someone shot one of the other men out of the saddle. Another of the outlaws cut loose the spare mounts and spurred his own horse toward the center of town.

Against the fleeing tide of humanity, Ty fought his way diagonally across the field. Shea ran after him, pushing one woman aside in her haste and all but stumbling over a child who was curled up and crying. Ty was agile and far too fast for her.

Then, through a cloud of billowing gunsmoke, Shea saw Sam Morran pull himself up onto one of the extra mounts. He hesitated before he spurred away as if he were looking for Ty, and in that instant a bullet caught him.

Sam's features widened in surprise. Blood blossomed across the front of his shirt. He went boneless and crumpled out of the saddle. Shea knew he was dead before he hit the ground.

A dozen strides ahead of her, Ty cried out and leaped desperately forward.

Without so much as a flicker of recognition in his eyes, Seaver sighted on the child bolting across his path.

Shea screamed Ty's name, but she wasn't close enough to reach him.

In the split second before Seaver fired, Owen Brandt came pelting from somewhere off to Shea's left and bowled Ty out of Seaver's way.

Wes and Jake Seaver spurred past them, and galloped away.

Sobbing, Shea raced to where Owen and Ty lay on the hard, snow-speckled earth. Blood was already beginning to pool beneath them. Neither of them was moving, neither of them seemed to be breathing.

Shivering and moaning their names, Shea grabbed at Owen's shoulder and pulled the old man over onto his back. Bright blood pulsed from the wound in his chest.

"Oh, Owen!" she whispered, dragging off her shawl and pressing the folds into the wound to stanch the flow.

Cam suddenly loomed over her on horseback, pausing in pursuit of the Seavers. "You all right?"

Shea looked from Owen to where Wes and Jake

Seaver were galloping away. "You go get them," she sobbed. "You make those bastards pay for this!"

Only when Cam had thundered away did Shea dare to reach a hand toward Ty. He'd been tucked up tight in the arc of Owen's body and was covered with the old man's blood.

"Ty," she whispered. "Ty, are you hurt?"

He rolled up onto his knees, then rose shakily to his feet. "I need to get to Pa," he whispered and was gone before she could stop him.

She turned back to Owen, to where his lifeblood was soaking through her shawl, welling around her fingertips. Though she could see recognition in Owen's eyes, Shea knew she was losing him.

The last of the gunfire was fading away. As it did, Rand materialized beside her.

"Geez!" he whispered, his mouth hanging slack. "Geez!"

"What are you doing here?" she demanded, pressing even more frantically against Owen's chest. Then, without giving Rand a chance to answer, she gestured with her chin. "Go find a doctor! Bring him here as fast—"

"No," Owen whispered.

Shea looked down at him and their gazes held. Owen was dying and no one could save him. Sam Morran was dead, and Ty—

She turned to Rand. "Ty's with his father over by the scaffold steps. Can you stay with Sam and him until I get there?"

Rand went to do as he'd been bidden, leaving Shea at Owen's side. "You foolish old man," she admonished him, her vision blurring. "What the devil did you think you were doing?"

"Taking care—of Ty," he murmured.

In spite of herself, a sob worked its way up her throat. "Well, you did a very fine job of it."

"Worth it, then."

She could hear Owen's breathing going reedy and thin, and took one black-smudged hand in hers. "What you did was very brave," she told him, tears spilling down her face.

"Brave," he whispered and smiled. The word seemed to please him.

Shea tightened her grip as if she could hold him there by the strength of her will.

"Love you, Sparrow," he murmured.

Shea sobbed and bent over him, pressing her smooth, cold cheek to his whiskery one. "I love you, too, old dear."

And then he was gone.

She bowed her body over him, silently keening for this frightened little man who had died so gallantly. She wanted to gather him in her arms and ease his way on. She wanted to hold him for a time and remember the things he'd taught her and the places they'd seen together. But her other responsibilities dragged at her, and she knew Owen would understand her leaving him.

"I'll be back," she promised, touching his face in farewell. She forced herself to her feet, then draped her bloodied shawl over him.

Drying her tears, she straightened and turned and saw her two boys—*her two sons*—kneeling together beside Ty's father. Love for both of them welled up thick and potent inside, giving her strength to cross the field to where Sam Morran lay.

She crouched down beside them and drew Ty into her arms. He came to her ashen and dry-eyed.

"Pa's dead, isn't he?" he asked her.

She pressed her cheek into his tumbled hair. "I'm sorry, Ty. I'm so terribly sorry."

She felt his shoulders shudder and heard the sobs break free, raking up his throat, making him shiver in her arms. She hugged him to her as he wept, rocking him just as she'd once rocked her own child. As she'd rocked Rand in the weeks before she'd given him away.

With fresh tears in her eyes, she looked across at her boy hunkered down beside them, seeing him with both a mother's pride and a stranger's distance. Though she reached across and took his hand, she could see how separate he was from her now—lost over time and distance. Lost to fate and desperation and the choices she'd had to make.

He would always be her son, but she knew she could never tell him who she was. Or who he was. She could never take him back—and somehow, making the decision at last brought a kind of resolution, a kind of peace.

When at length Ty raised his tear-streaked face from her shoulder, he seemed younger and more vulnerable than Shea had ever seen him.

"What—what will we do now?" he asked her.

Shea cupped his face in her hands and dried his eyes with a swipe of her thumbs. "We'll pay our respects to your father and Owen," Shea told him gently. "Then we'll make ourselves into a family, the two of us together. Is that all right?"

Ty took a moment to consider then dipped his head. "Sure," he said.

Cam could see the Seaver brothers half a mile ahead of him pushing their horses every bit as hard as he was pushing his. The three of them were half an hour out of Denver and headed west.

Headed for the mining camp in the mountains, Cam figured.

As they rode farther and farther from town, Cam kept looking back, hoping to see the dust of a posse rising behind him. When Wes and Jake had escaped from the hanging, Cam had grabbed one of the outlaws' extra mounts and chased the Seavers up along the river and across the Fifteenth Street bridge.

He'd fallen back some as the ground turned progressively more rolling and gravelly underfoot, but he'd kept up. Now, ten miles beyond the outskirts of Denver jagged little coxcombs of rocks serrated the landscape, making the going even more treacherous. Still, the Seavers were kicking their horses, trying to outdistance him so they'd have a chance of losing him when they reached the foothills.

Then, as if their luck had suddenly run out, Jake Seaver's horse stumbled on the uneven ground. It staggered a wavery step or two, dropped to its knees, and rolled, its rider still in the saddle.

Cam pulled a Winchester from the saddle holster and kicked his pony hard. As he closed the distance between Seaver and himself, he could see the fallen horse scrabbling in the dirt as it tried to rise, hear it scream in pain as it fell back.

A good way ahead, Cam saw Jake Seaver kick loose of the stirrups and drag himself to his feet. He hobbled a step or two, pulled his pistol, and put his pony out of his misery.

The gunshot boomed across the empty landscape, rippling like a raindrop spreading rings across a pond. Two hundred yards beyond where his brother had fallen, Wes Seaver pulled in his pony, jerked him around, and galloped back.

Cam did his best to reach Jake first, but he was just too far away. As soon as Cam closed to pistol range, Jake started shooting. The first bullet whined past Cam's leg. The second blew his hat off.

Still clutching the Winchester, Cam dismounted on the fly, and dove for cover in a waist-deep ripple of upright rocks. He squirmed forward on his belly and sighted on where Jake Seaver was balanced precariously, hunched and obviously in pain.

"Surrender, Seaver," Cam shouted, and he fired, pecking up dirt a foot away from Jake.

The outlaw fired back, sheering off the rock just to Cam's right, sending up a spray of dust. Cam ducked and covered his eyes. When he looked back a few seconds later, Wes Seaver was turning his horse in small tight circles around his brother.

"Don't make me kill either of you, Seaver," Cam yelled to them. "You can come in peaceably."

"And what, Gallimore?" Wes Seaver reached down and caught Jake's arm. "Let you hang me?" He was doing his best to heave his brother into the saddle.

Jake foundered and fell backward.

While Jake fought his way to his feet again, Seaver shot at Cam, forcing him down behind the rocks.

Cam rolled to his left, popped up a yard away, and squeezed off another shot. He caught Jake Seaver square, knocking him backward, sending him sprawling in the dirt. He lay on the frozen gravelly earth, limp and utterly still. Cam couldn't see any sign that he was breathing.

Wes Seaver bent sideways in the saddle and looked down at him. For an instant his shoulders bowed. Then he turned and, bawling a bone-chilling howl of rage and grief, he charged Cam's position.

Cam got off one quick shot before Seaver rode over him. As the pony cleared the little rill, one of his hooves slammed into Cam's shoulder. Numbness chased down his arm. Another hoof thudded between his legs as Seaver swept past.

Seaver turned his horse and came at Cam again, yelling and firing.

Cam pumped off two shots, then scrambled away. As he did, something caught him hard and low in the ribs. Hard enough to make him flinch, hard enough to send that tight, achy weakness spilling through him. He knew he was hit.

Cam kept moving anyway, kept scrambling, kept seeking purchase along that shallow ridge of rocks. He'd lost the Winchester in the scuffling, but up this close his pistol was going to be more effective.

Grimacing, he jerked the pearl-handled Colt from his holster and checked the load. Was Seaver carrying this gun's mate? Who'd have the pair of them when this was over?

Wedged sideways in a notch in that low, rock wall, Cam swiped the sweat from his face with the back of his sleeve. He was protected on the left by a crumble of boulders. A rim of rocky coxcomb rose against his back. Beyond him, the low, striated wall curved toward the mountains like a dragon's tail.

In spite of the thick, hot panic pushing up his spine, Cam knew he was as safe here as anywhere. He wasn't in any condition to go looking for someplace better, anyway.

Taking a shivery breath, he finally looked down at his side. The bullet he'd taken was a good deal more than a graze, but it hadn't hit anything that would kill him outright. Still, blood had ruined his best waistcoat, and the left leg of his trousers was damp halfway to the knee. With a grunt of effort he fumbled for his hand-kerchief and pressed the completely inadequate square of cloth against his side.

Shifting even as much as that made his head reel and his hands shake. He was sweating like it was summer, not twenty degrees. He looked off toward Denver and wondered where that posse was.

Then, swallowing a sudden wave of sickness, he tried to concentrate, tried to figure out what Seaver was do-ing. He'd seen him dismount and take cover behind his own cluster of rocks. He was probably over there re-loading his pistol, assessing their positions, and making his plans.

Cam couldn't seem to do anything but pant and sweat and wait for Seaver to make his move. If he waited very much longer, Cam knew it wouldn't mat-ter what he did.

Finally Cam saw Seaver creep out from behind the rocks. Using his horse for cover, he circled around to Cam's left. It was the side where Cam was most pro-tected, where the rocks were highest. But the outcrop-ping also obscured his view.

Seaver was coming at him from the one place in all this open landscape Cam couldn't see. But then, Seaver wouldn't have stayed alive as long as this if he didn't play for the advantage.

Cam waited, his throat dry and his heart churning inside him. Even as sharply tuned as he tried to be to Seaver's movements, his mind kept wandering.

Who would look after Lily and Rand if he died out here? he wondered. Would they have money to live on if they sold the farm? He hated that he hadn't been able to explain to Lily about the guerrillas, that he wasn't going to have the chance to apologize.

He rubbed at his eyes and tried to figure out where Seaver was. When he came, Cam had to be ready. He'd get a single chance to defend himself. He cocked the Colt, but his thoughts kept drifting.

He hadn't told Shea he loved her, either. Because of Lily and Rand he hadn't so much as hinted at how he felt—how he loved Shea's softness and her courage, the sweetness of her body and the solace in her eyes. He hadn't dared to tell her, but now he wished—

Some instinct deeper than conscious thought prodded Cam hard. He shifted silently, not knowing what he'd heard or seen or sensed. His mouth went dry and his heart thumped so hard in his throat he couldn't breathe.

Then Cam caught the faint scrape of movement directly behind and above him. He jerked around and stared straight up at the muzzle of Seaver's Colt. The man loomed over him and there was no time to aim.

They fired simultaneously.

Seaver's bullet seared past Cam's hip, spattering gravel.

Cam shot straight up at Seaver. The bullet caught the outlaw full in the chest. Seaver blinked once, teetered on the edge of the rocks, and tumbled headlong. He landed on his back on the opposite side of the little ridge, his eyes wide and staring.

He was dead. Cam didn't have to check to know. The chaos spawned in the cruelty of the war had ended today—at least for Wes Seaver. Cam should have felt some satisfaction, some kind of vindication. But all he felt was spent and overwhelmed.

Yet there was one last thing he had to do. Groaning with the effort, he reached for the gun Seaver had dropped as he fell. It was the Colt Seaver had taken from Cam so many years before. He cradled that pistol against his chest, feeling as if he'd recovered some lost part of himself. Finally he slumped against the rocks and closed his eyes, shutting out the face of what he might have been and hoping he'd last until the posse came.

EIGHTEEN

In the cold winter twilight, Shea Waterston and
Tyler Morran stood over the two fresh graves. They'd
come together to bury their dead, Ty's father and
Shea's longtime companion. They'd done it just the
two of them, and the man who dug the graves.

He stood a little way off with his hat in one hand
and his shovel in the other while Shea read the simple,
comforting words of the Twenty-third Psalm. Then Ty
stepped up to the lip of his father's grave.

"I—I just want you to know, Pa," he offered quietly,
"I'm going to miss you, and that I hope dying didn't
hurt too much. I want you to know I really tried to be
a good son to you. I did my best to take care of you,
especially after Mama died. Shea says you're in heaven
with Mama now, and that she's looking after you instead of me. I know you been pining for her for a good
long while, so I hope that's where you are and that
you're happy again. I'm going to say good-bye now, Pa.
You know I love you. I promise I won't forget you—
nor Mama, neither."

Ty looked up at Shea when he was done. She saw that soft, earnest face through a film of tears and smiled at him. "You did well speaking to your father," she told him softly. "Would you mind if I said a few words to him, too?"

When he shook his head, Shea wrapped her arm around Ty's shoulders and pulled him close. She cleared her throat. "I just want you to know, Sam, that I'll do everything I promised this morning. I'll take care of your boy. I'll love him as if he was my own." Shea squeezed Ty extra tight. "I'll see that he grows into a man we can both be proud of. And, Sam, I want to thank you for trusting me with him. I'll do my very best to live up to what you expect of me."

Shea stood there listening to the wind humming through the grass, feeling the cold seep through her clothes. Feeling the warmth of the child she was hugging against her.

She'd done a good deal of thinking since this morning at the jailhouse. She'd thought about Sam and Ty, about Cam and Lily. She'd thought about Rand and his future and how she'd given him up a second time. It was different from the first. Though she still ached with love and regret, there was no sorrow or resentment or devastating sense of loss in it.

Maybe that was because she wasn't alone anymore, because she'd been given another child to mother and care for. Not that Ty was second best—he'd touched her heart from the first time she'd seen him. She understood Ty with a clarity and insight she'd never had for Rand. Ty was like her. She knew what drove him. She recognized her pride in him, her common sense, and her concern for people weaker than she. She was proud of the way Ty had looked after his father and the stubbornness with which he'd stood by him.

He was also a child with a dislike for school, a penchant for trouble, and an affinity for strays. Which probably meant they'd have a houseful of ill-tempered, scraggly things just like Rufus. The thought made her smile.

She hugged Ty hard, then stepped to the foot of Owen's grave.

She had some last things to say to him, a few final words to send him to his rest.

"Owen, my old dear," she began and drew a shaky breath, "you and I have traveled a long, twisting road together. I want to thank you for being my friend and companion for every mile. I ask your forgiveness for the times I was impatient with you, but I think you understood I just didn't know what it was you needed.

"I want you to know that my life is richer for knowing you and for everything you taught me. Every time I make a photograph I'll think of you and miss your company and your skill. You were a fine, brave man, old dear, and you were the very last person in the world to realize it."

When she finished it seemed wrong to walk away from the open graves, so she and Ty stood there together and watched the grave digger do his work. The sound of clods of dirt on a wooden casket was one of the most mournful sounds in the world, and one Shea had heard far too often in her life.

They stood there into full dark, and when he was done she pressed two silver dollars into the grave digger's loamy hands. Shea and Ty stood over the people they'd loved and lost a few moments longer.

"Sleep well," she finally whispered, "both of you." Then, with Ty tucked beneath her arm, she turned toward home.

· · ·

Shea had just gotten into bed when someone came pounding on the studio door. She snatched up a shawl and her Winchester and went to answer it. Sheriff Cook stood outside on the landing. With the help of one of his deputies, he was holding Cam up.

Panic swooped down on her and her belly went cold. "Mary, Mother of God!" she whispered, swinging the door wide to let them in. "What's happened to Cam? How badly is he hurt?"

"Not as bad as all that," Cam mumbled, though his head lolled to the side when he tried to raise it.

As Shea lit a lamp and led them into the cramped little bedroom, Sheriff Cook gave her a more precise answer. "He caught a bullet down low in the ribs. It doesn't look like it did too much damage, but he's lost some blood."

As the two men lowered Cam to the bed, his jacket and vest fell open. A big dark stain blossomed halfway up the front of his shirt, and his trousers were stiff with blood, too.

"Lost *some* blood?" she echoed as she fumbled open the buttons on his shirt. Someone had wrapped a makeshift bandage around Cam's waist, but red had soaked through the thick pad of cloth.

"Has anyone gone for Dr. Farley?" she asked, taking up a pair of scissors and snipping carefully through his clothes.

"Not Emmet," Cam protested, opening his eyes for emphasis. *"Not Emmet!"*

"We sent for old Doc Burns," Dan Cook told her. "He's dug out more bullets than any man I know. I figured if Cam didn't want Emmet Farley, Dr. Burns was the next best thing."

Shea didn't ask why Cam didn't want Emmet to
treat him. But he needed care—and quickly. There was
more color in her bleached muslin pillowcases than
there was in Cam's face.

The chill of seeing him like this began in the pit of
Shea's belly and spread outward, crystallizing the air in
her lungs, making her fingers clumsy as she worked
over him.

"Then hurry Dr. Burns along, will you?" she said
through gritted teeth, trying not to shout her frustration at the two tall men hovering at the end of the bed.

"I'll go get him," Ty offered from the doorway.

Shea glanced up and saw him standing there, shoving the tail of his nightshirt into the waistband of his
trousers. He was nearly as pale as Cam was, but she
nodded for the boy to go.

He didn't get far. Before he got his boots on and
made it out the door, there was the trudge of footsteps
on the stairs. Dr. Burns filled the doorway as he shouldered past Ty and the deputy to get to the bed.

"What happened?" he asked, setting his doctor's
satchel aside and bending over Cam.

"Cam got shot going after Wes Seaver and his
brother Jake," Sheriff Cook reported from where he
was easing off Cam's boots.

"And did he get them?" the doctor asked, peeling
back the bandages and prodding Cam's wound.

Cam flinched away from the doctor's touch and stifled a moan. For an instant Shea's knees went weak and
she had to fight down the burn of bile that backed up
in her throat.

"He got both Wes Seaver and his brother before they
shot him," Sheriff Cook answered with a hint of admi-
ration in his voice. "Looked like quite a fight to me."

"Good for you, Cam," the doctor said giving Cam's

wound another poke. "Didn't think for a minute that rubbish in the papers about him riding with the bushwackers could be true."

"Is—is he going to be all right?" Shea asked, in spite of herself.

"Oh, Cam's as tough as they come," the doctor answered gruffly, "but we need to cut that bullet out. You going to be able to help me with that, little lady, or are you going to up and faint on me?"

Shea had tended Simon all through his illness, but she'd never had experience with bullet wounds. Nothing with blood and the kind of pain that was hovering just beneath the surface of Cam's tense features. But she didn't want to be shunted off into a corner somewhere to wait for word, either.

She stiffened her spine. "I can help."

"Good," the doctor murmured. "Go get some water boiling. I'm going to need a pan to soak my instruments, and something to use for bandages."

The doctor tugged off his coat, then opened his bag and pulled out his case of instruments and several glass-stoppered bottles.

"Just get the damned thing out," Cam muttered when he saw that Burns was opening a bottle of chloroform. "I don't need that."

"The hell you don't," the doctor muttered and lowered a gauze mask over Cam's nose and mouth.

Shea was asleep in the chair in the corner of the bedroom when someone came scratching on the door of the studio. She roused with a blink and looked across at where Cam was lying on the bed, pallid and still as a corpse. Alarm crushed down on her at the pale waxen look of him. Though she could see the regular rise and fall of his chest and hear the rhythm of his breathing, it didn't help what she was feeling.

When the scratching came again, she rose stiffly and gathered up the blanket she'd wrapped around herself for warmth. She took up her Winchester, too, and went to see who was disturbing them now.

Emmet Farley stood hunched and shivering on the landing.

"What time is it?" she asked around a yawn.

"About three o'clock in the morning," he told her. "I was out delivering a baby and heard about Cam when I got back. How is he?"

"Doctor Burns says he's doing well enough, but he's scaring me half to death," she told him honestly.

Emmet pressed his lips together before he spoke. "Would you mind if I had a look?"

Her instinct was to let him in, let him examine Cam, let him reassure her. Instead she hesitated. "Why didn't Cam want you taking care of him?"

Emmet let out a heavy sigh. "It's as cold as the back-side of the moon out here. Can't I come in before I explain it?"

She could see the droop of his shoulders and dark smudges of fatigue beneath his eyes. His concern warred with her need to stand by Cam and what he'd wanted. Still, Emmet had come here instead of heading home to bed . . .

Shea capitulated and opened the door.

Emmet stepped past her and hooked his coat over the coatrack. Then, taking his bag in hand, he went directly into the bedroom. Without so much as a word, he took Cam's pulse, listened to his chest, and checked his bandage.

Cameron never moved.

Shea hung tight to the rail at the foot of the bed until Emmet finished his examination. "So how is he?"

"He's doing as well as can be expected. Dr. Burns did a fine job getting the bullet out, and there's no sign of infection. Cam's a little feverish, but that isn't uncommon as the body starts to heal itself. He lose a lot of blood?"

Shea inclined her head.

"That will slow him down some."

"But he's going to be all right?"

"He's going to be fine." Emmet did his best to smile at her. "But he's a damned lucky man. An inch or two in any direction and . . ."

Shea had figured by the cautious way Dr. Burns probed for the bullet that the wound could have been a whole lot more serious than it was. She couldn't bear thinking about how close Cam had come to getting himself killed.

She shuddered in spite of herself and pulled the blanket tighter. "If I make you a cup of tea," she proposed, "will you tell me why Cam didn't want you here?"

Emmet rubbed at his long, stubbly jaw and heaved a tired sigh. "I suppose I've done a whole lot more to earn a cup of tea. But, Shea . . ."

"Yes?"

"You wouldn't have a 'wee dram' of whiskey to put in that tea, would you?"

She saw all at once how shaken Emmet was that Cam had been shot, how much he regretted whatever it was that had come between them.

She flashed him a smile. "I've got a key to downstairs, and I know where Agnes Franklin hides her nip bottle."

A few minutes later they were seated on either side

of the desk in the entry, drinking tea laced with Agnes Franklin's excellent brandy. As the liquor started to warm her from the inside out, Shea glanced across at Emmet.

"So what was it that happened between you and Cam? Why didn't he want you here last night?"

Emmet braced his forearms against the table and looked at her. "Did you know Cam rode with the guerrillas during the war?"

Shea nodded.

"Did you know before you saw it on the front page of the *Rocky Mountain News?*" he demanded. When she nodded again, he went on. "Well, I didn't. I was stunned when I saw the newsboys hawking the paper on the street. At first I thought it must be some kind of mistake, but once I'd read the story and realized it was true, all I could think about was Lily. All I could think about was what that news was going to do to her. I thought I should be the one to tell her since Cam hadn't had the courage to do it in all these years.

"So I hightailed it out to the farm. I'd barely arrived, barely had time to show Lily the newspaper, when Cam came riding up the drive."

Emmet ran his hand through his already ruffled hair. "After I saw how devastated she was reading that news story, I would have done anything in the world to protect her, to spare her the pain of confronting him. So I met him on the porch and told him to go away."

"And she let you do that?" Shea asked, surprised that Lily had been so meek. "Didn't she want to know what Cam had to say? Didn't she want to give him a chance to explain? Didn't you?"

"She came to the door while I was talking to Cam. It was seeing how upset she was, seeing that she was crying that made him leave."

Having Lily refuse to see him, refuse to hear what he had to say must have all but torn out Cam's heart. Small wonder he'd showed up at the studio the way he had, so much the worse for drink, so in need of solace. In need of her.

"Is Lily all right?" Shea asked him. She knew what it was like to have your whole word crumble beneath your feet, to have everything altered from one moment to the next.

Emmet stared past her for a moment, then his angular face softened with the wisp of a smile. "Lily is a remarkable woman," was all he said.

"Should I send word to her about Cam?" Shea wondered. "If she hasn't heard about what happened already, she'll want to know. She'll want to know he's here with me, and that as bad as he looks right now, he's going to get better."

"I'm headed out there now. I'll explain everything that's happened," Emmet assured her and set his cup aside. "And now that you've let me examine Cam, I'll be able to reassure her."

"Do you think Lily will be in to see him soon?" she asked hopefully.

Emmet rose and reached for his bag. "I expect she'll come by in a day or so when his head is clearer so they can talk. But I doubt Rand will be able to wait that long."

"All this has upset him, hasn't it?" Shea asked softly, concern for the child as strong as it was for his father.

"He doesn't know what to think, and I hardly blame him," Emmet admitted on a sigh and pulled a small, corked bottle of amber-brown liquid out of his bag. "Did Dr. Burns leave you any laudanum?"

"For Cam, you mean?"

Emmet laughed and shook his head. "Not for Cam; for you."

"But surely I shouldn't be taking—"

"For your peace of mind," he clarified. "Cam's the worst patient I've ever treated. When he broke his ankle a couple years back, Lily was ready to throttle him before a week was out." Emmet pressed the square little bottle into her hand. "Cam's as strong as an ox, and he'll mend fast if he stays in bed. This is how you keep him there—for a couple of days, at least."

Shea looked down at the laudanum. "He won't like this."

Emmet raised his eyebrows. "Well, no, he won't. But it's what's best for him."

He reiterated Dr. Burns's instructions about Cam's food and medicine, and what she could do to make him more comfortable.

The night was turning to hazy gray when they stepped outside. "Thank you for coming, Emmet," Shea said quietly. "I appreciate it, even if Cam probably won't."

"Then just don't tell him I was here," he offered with a shrug. "And, Shea, I truly am sorry about Owen. He was a good man, and just beginning to find himself again."

"I think he found himself yesterday afternoon."

She reached for him, hugged him, and let him go. She watched him down the steps, then turned and went back into the studio. She glided through those dim, quiet rooms, checking on Ty, downing the last of her tea, and returning to the bedroom.

In spite of Emmet's reassurances, Cam hadn't moved and his stillness frightened her. She settled gingerly on the edge of the bed and took his hand. For a moment it lay cold and lax in hers, then slowly Cam's fingers curled, clasping hers even in sleep.

She let out her breath and stared down at him. How had this man come to mean so much to her? When had she begun to feel so much a part of him, so interwoven in his life and family? What would she have done if he'd died out there on the prairie today?

Stark, breathless dread quivered at the core of her, a feeling that was resonant and ominous, and far too familiar. She'd lost so much over the years, so many of the people she loved that Shea didn't think she could bear losing anyone else. Especially Cam.

Seeking closeness and reassurance and surcease, Shea eased down on the bed along Cam's uninjured side. She pressed her face against the smooth, firm flesh of his upper arm, and sought his warmth. Yet close as she was to him, as solid and safe as he seemed, the fear lingered in her as slow, silent tears crept down her cheeks.

NINETEEN

"*H*ow is he?"

Shea had opened the studio door to find Lily Gallimore hovering on the landing. It was four days since the hanging, four days since Cam had been shot. Rand had come to the studio every day to see his father and be with Ty. Now Lily was here, looking grim and a little pale, but armed with a crock of what smelled like chicken soup.

Shea stepped back and invited her in. "You know how Cam is. You've taken care of him. He's disgruntled, impatient, cantankerous . . ."

Lily handed the crock to Shea and hung up her coat. "Emmet says Cammie has remarkable recuperative powers."

"That may well be," Shea conceded, with a wry twist to her mouth, "but that doesn't make him any the less peevish."

The subject under discussion chose that moment to make his displeasure known. "Damn it, Shea!" he roared from the bedroom. "I can hear you whispering. Who's out there?"

Shea raised her eyebrows.

Lily raised hers in answer.

But when Shea turned toward the bedroom, Lily hung back. Still balancing the crock of chicken soup, Shea gestured Lily forward. "He needs to talk to you."

Shea thought what Cam had to say to his sister was at least half the reason he was so restless and out-of-sorts.

"I know he has things he wants to tell me," Lily whispered. "I'm not sure I'll know how to answer him."

"Just hear him out, Lily, please. Keeping this from you is killing him."

Lily reached over and touched Shea's hand, though Shea wasn't sure if it was Lily's way of reassuring her or gathering the strength she needed to face her brother.

In the bedroom, Cam lay propped up on pillows in the middle of Shea's bed, a bandage winding halfway up his broad, bare chest. Shea's stomach took that odd little dip every time she saw it there, every time she realized that in spite of his strength and vitality, Cam was fragile, vulnerable. He could be hurt, wounded in ways he might never recover from.

Right now his sister was wielding the weapon that could slay him.

As Shea set the crock of soup at the back of the stove, Lily crossed to the foot of the iron bedstead. "Hello, Cam," she greeted him.

"I wasn't sure after that day at the farm—" Cam's muscles constricted as he spoke, as if he were bracing himself for his sister's censure. "—that you'd ever consent to see me again."

Lily's soft chin rose. "Lord knows, I didn't want to

see you—at least not then. Not when Emmet had just come storming into the house waving that newspaper. Not when I'd barely had time to read the headline, much less absorb what it meant. Emmet knew how confused and upset I was, and he took it upon himself to protect me."

"Protect you from me, Lil?" The anguish in Cam's voice rippled from the core of who he was.

Lily leaped to the doctor's defense. "Emmet did what he thought was right. You understand what that's like, don't you?"

Cam aged ten years in an instant. The lines furrowed deep around his mouth and the set of his chin eroded.

Until that moment, Shea hadn't known how brittle he was, how barren and depleted. She was suddenly afraid for him.

"Was I wrong," he asked in a voice that was like the scuffling of dry leaves, "to shield you from what I'd been and what I'd done?"

Lily spoke on a long-drawn sigh. "Oh, Cammie . . ."

"Lil, please!" he begged her. "Let me explain about being with the guerrillas that day at Centralia."

Lily tightened her hold on the foot rail of the iron bedstead and faced him head on. "That attack was eleven years ago. What's kept you from explaining before today?"

A faint flare of color seeped into Cam's face. "I wanted to tell you; I swear I did. But every time I looked at you, I was so ashamed. Every time I saw how badly you'd been burned—"

Lily recoiled, her eyes widening with outrage. "You were ashamed of me?"

"No!" Cam pushed up from the pillows. "Oh, God, no! I could never be ashamed of you, Lily; I was

ashamed of myself!" He slumped back wearily. "I was
ashamed that I'd ridden with men who could do the
things the guerrillas did in Centralia, do the things
they'd done to you."

"How could any *decent* man have ridden with
them?" his sister hissed at him.

Shea bit her lip to hold back her instinctive defense
of Cam. He would never have consorted with outlaws,
would never have switched sides in the war unless he'd
had reason.

"While I was home recuperating after Spotsylvania,"
he went on, "an officer came to see me from the De-
partment of the West. They'd had intelligence that
General Price meant to join forces with the guerrillas in
southern Missouri and march on St. Louis. The army
needed someone to infiltrate the raiders and discover
their plans."

"And they asked you," Shea murmured half to
herself.

Cam started at the sound of her voice as if he'd
forgotten she was even there with them. For a long
feverish moment his gaze held hers, as if he wanted to
draw strength and sustenance from her faith in him.

"I'd heard about the guerrillas atrocities in Missouri
and Kansas," he went on, turning back to his sister. "I
did my best to refuse him, but he convinced me.

"In the end, I was able to send back valuable information about both Anderson's activities and Price's
plans." His eyes went dark, the specters of those days
astir in them. "But I hated what I had to do to stay
alive. I hated being party to their burning and their
looting."

I hated myself.

Shea heard the words as if Cameron had spoken
them aloud and she knew he would go on punishing

himself until Lily forgave him. Until he found a way to forgive himself.

He shifted against the pillows again. "I'd been detailed to another officer's bivouac to copy reports the day Anderson took his troops to Centralia. The morning was half gone when I heard where they went.

"I tried to get to you, Lil, before they did." His voice disintegrated more with every word. "I swear I did. I tried to protect you and Mother, but I was too late."

He raised his hand, beckoning Lily closer, needing the contact, the acknowledgment. Yearning for forgiveness. Shea prayed Lily would take it in her own. Instead she stood straight as a spire at the foot of the bed.

The hope faded out of Cameron's eyes like the wick of a lamp turned lower and lower. His hand fell lax on the coverlet.

When Lily spoke her voice was low and thick with years' old hurt. "Mother told me all of that before she died."

With those few words, the world seemed to stumble to a stop. The only sound was the faint hissing of the coals in the wood stove, the only movement the few flakes of snow drifting past the window. Not one of the three of them seemed to be breathing.

"Oh, Lil." Cam's words came delicate and friable, like motes of dust from a shattered soul. "I'm so terribly sorry."

Tears pooled in Lily's eyes. "Don't you realize," she shouted at him, "that I've been waiting all these years for you to own up to this? You gave me a home and security and Rand. I love you for doing that—and I *am* grateful." Lily's tears spilled over. "But you refused to tell me the truth or trust me to understand it.

"That day at the farm—you didn't come to tell me of your own accord. You came because what you'd been and done was in the newspapers. You came to me because you had no choice!"

Lily relinquished her hold on the foot rail and swiped at her eyes. "I've been waiting all this time, Cam, for you to talk to me about Centralia. It's what I needed to put what happened to rest. Because you've refused to speak, you've denied me the chance to do that. Maybe now I can."

She turned in a flurry of skirts and ran for the door.

"Lily, wait!" Cam called after her. "Lily, please."

Shea reached the entry just as Lily was stabbing her arms into the sleeves of her coat.

"You just can't leave him like that," Shea implored her. "You can't go without forgiving him!"

"What he's done isn't easy to forgive," Lily raged, her voice shaking. "He made me live with those memories every day because he wouldn't tell me the truth!"

Shea caught Lily's arm. "Think how it's been for Cam," she cried. "Your brother has been carrying those same memories around with him—and his guilt besides.

"He's kept his silence because he wanted to protect you. Every breath he's taken, every decision he's made has been made because he cares for you." Shea's grip tightened. "Lily, for the love of God, can't you forgive him?"

Lily jerked out of Shea's grasp and tore open the studio door. "All I ever wanted was to put the memories away, but he wouldn't let me!"

Shea watched Lily run down the steps and leap into the carriage, watched her whip the horses up the street as if demons were snapping at her heels.

She didn't have any idea what she was going to say to Cam once she went inside, but by the time she did, he was out of bed and dressing himself.

"I'm going after Lily," he told her as he pulled on one of the shirts Rand had brought from the farm. "She's my sister. We need to settle this."

Shea reached out to steady him as he pulled on his trousers. "Why don't you give Lily a bit of time? Perhaps once she's thought this through—"

"Lily can have until I catch up with her!"

Shea gently maneuvered him in the direction of the bed. "I'm not sure you're well enough to ride as far as the farm."

"Don't worry. I'll get there," he assured her.

"If you're so determined to go after her, at least let me go with you."

"I don't need you hovering over me."

"We can rent a carriage. I can drive—"

Cam plopped down at the edge of the mattress and reached for his boots. "This really doesn't concern you."

Of course this concerned her. *He* concerned her—and Lily was her closest friend. "Please, Cam, let me go with you."

Grunting with the effort, he tugged on his second boot. "This is between my sister and me. It's something we have to settle ourselves."

"I think I can help."

He dragged himself to his feet and stood over her, weaving ever so slightly. "Damn it, Shea!" he roared. "This is a family matter. You don't have any part in this!"

He might as well have laid hands on her and shoved her away. She stumbled back a step of her own accord. The air in her chest went cold and thin.

"I do so have a part in this!" she insisted, her voice starting to tremble. "You made me part of it by coming here when you needed me. You made me part of it by showing me things about yourself you never show anyone. You made me part of it by letting me fall in love with you."

Cam simply stared at her.

Tears breached the rim of her lashes. "People who love each other share more than what they do in bed. We've shared our secrets and our fears. We've had our moments of joy and wondrous pleasure. You've made me part of this, Cam. If you love me, you'll let me go with you."

He stepped in close and cupped her face in his two hands. "Please, Shea," he whispered, "try to understand. What happened with Lily is my doing, my mistake to rectify. No one can help. I have to make peace with my sister by myself."

She pulled out of his hold, angry at how determined he was, how completely he was shutting her out. She stood with tears on her face, shaken and disheartened that just when she thought she'd found her place in his life, he'd turned away.

Cam stepped past her into the entry hall and fought his way into his coat. She followed after him, helpless against his pull.

He jerked open the studio door and hesitated. "I want you to understand I'm not doing this to hurt you."

She shook her head. "I don't understand anything."

"Shea, please—"

"If you're going to the farm alone," she whispered, her voice wavering in spite of her efforts to hold it steady, "just go."

With a dip of his head, he turned and pulled the door closed behind him.

Once the unsteady tread of his footsteps had died away, Shea crumpled into the chair behind the appointment desk. She bowed her shoulders and raised her knees, curling tight into herself. Tears scoured her cheeks, and she pressed her hands to her mouth to hold back the hollow ringing of her sobs.

All her life she'd managed to make peace with the things she'd lost—her home and family in Ireland, her child, and her husband in New York. Even when grief lay heavy on her heart, she'd managed to draw on the will inside herself and move on. But here in Denver her losses had sundered the very fabric of who she was. She'd lost her son to the kind of family she could never provide, lost Owen to an act of senseless violence. Now she'd lost Cam—

Fresh tears stung her eyes, and she curled even more tightly into herself. She bowed her head to her knees and sat there huddled and holding herself together.

Ty found her there when he came home from school a good while later. "Shea?" he asked her, stumbling to a stop just inside the door. "You all right?"

She swiped the tears from her cheeks and smiled at Ty. Here amidst all of her losses she realized she'd been given a wondrous gift—this bright, scruffy, curly-headed youngster. She'd been given the chance to make a family, the two of them together. And she recognized that no matter what she'd lost she still had the strength for this. The strength for him.

She drew Ty closer.

He came hesitantly at first, not sure how to deal with a woman who'd been crying. He reached out gingerly and patted her. He didn't get the rhythm quite right, but something about his gentleness and his concern eased the ache inside her.

Shea sniffled one last time, then wrapped him against her. The notions that had been circling in her brain settled, solidified. Formed into the decision she'd been toying with since Cam left.

"I've been thinking that maybe we should pack our things," she offered softly, "and move on from here."

Ty pulled back, his eyes widening. "You have?"

"We'd be leaving in a month anyway," Shea went on, convincing both Ty and herself. "We could head up north and scout out opportunities for a lady photographer and her young assistant. We can come back for the wagon and the camera equipment when the roads are better."

After all the frequent and unexpected moves Ty must have made with his father, he didn't even question her. "So where do you think we should go?" he asked.

Shea said the first thing that came into her head. "To Cheyenne." The words came on the breath of a sigh. "We'll start looking for our new opportunities in Cheyenne."

The ride to the farm seemed to take Cam forever. The pain in his side and the cold, shaky light-headedness that swelled over him was only part of what made it so difficult. That he had no earthly idea how he was going to make peace with Lily preyed on his mind. But the thing that tormented him most was the way he'd parted from Shea.

He hated that he left her with tears on her cheeks. He hated that he'd left her believing he didn't care for her, that she had no part in his life. But as much as he'd longed to tell Shea how much she meant to him, he couldn't speak the words or court the consequences.

He was bound by the vows he'd made to his mother on her deathbed, bound by the commitment he'd made to his son when he and Lily had taken Rand as their child. They were sacrifices he'd made gladly, choices and restrictions he'd never minded living up to until today. Not until he'd looked into Shea's face and admitted to himself how important she'd become to him—and how little he had to offer her.

But before he could think beyond the depth of his regrets, the farmhouse appeared on the snowy rise ahead of him, and he turned his thoughts to Lily. When he'd come here not quite a week ago, she'd let Emmet turn him away. This morning at the studio, Lily had run from him, but he wasn't going to let her elude him again. They needed to settle things between them, and put their lives to rights for everyone's sake.

He cursed volubly when he rode up the drive and saw Emmet Farley's buggy parked at the gate. Still, he hadn't come all this way to be run off.

He pulled his horse up behind the buggy and clambered down. He was still clinging to the skirt of the saddle waiting for the dizziness to pass and his knees to stop wobbling when Lily burst out the kitchen door.

"Cammie! For goodness' sakes! What are you doing here?"

He raised his head and the yard swooped into focus around him. "I—I couldn't just let you walk away," he said, determined to get the words out. "Please, Lil, we have to talk, to work this out. I need to tell you—"

"What he needs," Emmet interrupted, bounding down the porch steps in Lily's wake, "is to have his head examined for getting out of a sickbed and riding all this way!"

"I'll be fine in a minute," Cam insisted.

Emmet didn't call him on the lie. He just eased an arm around Cam's shoulders and led him into the house. Cam wove toward the first chair he came to and sat down at the kitchen table breathing hard.

"Did you break open that wound with all your foolishness?" Emmet asked, kneeling and tugging at Cameron's clothes.

While Emmet poked and prodded, Lily brought Cam a cup of tea thick with sugar and cream. His ears had stopped buzzing by the time he'd drunk it.

"Well, I can't see that you've done any real damage," Emmet finally said. "Still, this was a damn fool thing for you to do. Didn't Shea try to talk you out of it?"

"Shea didn't have much say," Cam muttered. "What I came here to do was talk to my sister. *Privately.*"

Emmet raised his eyebrows. "Well, you're going to have to say what you've got to say in front of me," he said, leaning back against the sink, "because I'm not going anywhere."

Cam bristled at Emmet's tone, but he needed to talk to Lily far too much to argue.

"What I came to do, Lil," he began on a long, slow sigh, "is to apologize. I was wrong not to tell you years ago that I'd ridden with the guerrillas. I only did what I thought was best."

Lily stepped nearer, bracing her hands on the top of the chair across from his. "All your life, Cam," she began softly, "you've done what you thought was right. It's what made you load me into that carriage and take me to meet the orphan train. It's why you brought us to Colorado and bought the farm. Most of the time what you've done has been wise and well-considered— *and in my best interest.* But just this once, you made a mistake."

"I know, Lil, and I'm sorry."

She stepped around the chair and settled herself before him. "You're such a good man, Cammie," she said taking his hand. "You try so hard and you care so much. But you have to accept you can be wrong some-times—and that it's all right."

"Does that mean you're able to forgive me for the things I did," Cam heard the waver in his own voice, "and for all the things I didn't tell you?"

Lily tightened her warm, rough fingers around his hand. "I think that as much as I needed you to tell me about the raiders, I think you needed to tell me about them more. Maybe that's why Mama explained all of it before she died—so I'd be able to make you own up to what you'd done."

Cam ducked his head, thinking maybe his mother had been wiser than he knew.

"Getting this out in the open," Lily went on, sound-ing as if she was able to breathe again, "makes me feel as if I can finally stop being beholden to you, as if everything I have is something you've given me out of guilt."

"If I gave you things—" Cam tightened his hold on his sister's hand and waited for her to look up at him "—it was because I wanted you to have them. I wanted you to have a child to raise, a comfortable home, and a settled life."

"I always believed you gave me those things, Cam-mie, because you thought what you did had taken them from me." Lily lowered her gaze again, and the next admission came hard for her. "For awhile, right after mother told me where you were when I was burned, I—I thought you owed them to me, too."

Cam watched her face, hope pressing hard and hot behind his sternum. "But you changed your mind?"

"I grew up." Lily shrugged and gave him her one-sided smile. "I became a woman, a mother. And when I did, I came to understand that what happened that day wasn't your fault. That you'd have sold your soul to prevent it. That it's made me who I am. All I've wanted since I realized that was for you to tell me the truth, so both of us could put this behind us."

"But I wouldn't let you do that."

"You wouldn't let *you* do that, either," Lily amended softly. "You wouldn't own up to riding with the guerrillas because you didn't think you deserved to be forgiven. Or to forgive yourself." Lily clasped his fingers one last time, then took back her hand. "I know this isn't how either of us wanted things to work out, but it's over now and time for us to make a new start. Or at least I intend to."

Emmet set another cup of tea down in front of Cam, then went to stand over Lily's chair.

"You see," Lily went on, "I mean to marry Emmet."

Cam stared at her, stared at the two of them as if he'd never seen them before. "Marry Emmet?" he echoed. "Just when did you decide to marry Emmet?"

Lily tilted her chin defiantly "While you and Shea were off in the mountains looking for the boys, Emmet came to the house to be sure I was all right here by myself. He stayed to supper and we talked. Talking lead to other things, and well—" Color suffused her cheeks. "Emmet stayed the night."

Cam blinked, not entirely sure what his shy, virtuous sister was admitting. "He stayed because it snowed."

"I stayed because I love her," Emmet clarified, curling his hand possessively around Lily's shoulder.

"He's loved me for years." There was pride in Lily's eyes. "He's been waiting for me to spread my wings, to find myself. He's been waiting for me to be ready to be his wife."

Cam took a long swallow of tea and wished it was

something stronger. "And you're sure this is what you want?"

Lily looked up at Emmet, a sweet, soft glow coming into her face. "Oh, I'm sure," she murmured. "I've never been more sure of anything."

Emmet squeezed Lily's shoulder and smiled at her. Together they radiated a warmth the sun might envy, created a bond to keep the world at bay. Even Cam.

Cam watched them as he sipped his tea, thinking that for years he'd taken belonging for granted. He'd been one of the faces around this table, two of the hands that clasped as they spoke the blessing, a third of this family. Now the equation had changed. Emmet had taken a place in the circle. Cam couldn't have been more pleased for his sister's sake, but he was deeply aware of that shift, that alteration.

Here in his own house he suddenly felt like a stranger. Here where he'd always belonged he seemed oddly separate from the people he loved.

This must be why Shea had been so determined to come with him this morning, he found himself thinking. She believed she'd become part of this home and family, part of their lives. And he'd denied her her connection, shut her out. He'd seen confusion and hurt in her eyes, but he hadn't understood it.

Now he did.

Or maybe he'd been afraid to acknowledge how much a part of his world Shea had become. He'd been in love with her for a good long while. He'd loved her kindness and her integrity since that night in the kitchen when she came to him for Rand's sake. He'd loved her generosity and compassion for what she'd done for Lily. He loved her for what she was and what she'd been to him—a friend and confidante, a bulwark at his back. He loved her because she was a woman of character and strength, a lover whose passion and tenderness knew no bounds.

He hadn't been able to tell her any of that. He hadn't been able to offer her more than he'd given her already.

But now he could.

Seeing how Emmet and Lily looked at each other, thinking about the lies and guilt he'd cast aside made him realize all at once that he was free. Free to tell her how much he loved her. Free to show her what she meant to him.

Free to offer her . . .

"I have to get back to Denver!" Setting aside his cup, Cam shoved to his feet.

Both Emmet and Lily hurried over to stay him.

"Goodness, Cammie, you only just got here!" his sister protested, wrapping her arm around his waist.

"It would do you a world of good to rest a spell," Emmet agreed.

"I need to see Shea. We—we had words before I left, and I need to tell her she was right." Cam turned to his sister, his voice gone soft. "I need to tell her that I love her."

"I should think you do," Lily answered, smiling.

"I need to ask her—" A wave of sudden dizziness washed over him. "I need to ask Shea to be with me. To marry me. I only just realized how much I need—"

The dizziness came again, stronger this time. Cam wavered on his feet, and Emmet slung his arm around him, too. Together he and Lily eased Cam down into the chair as his head spun and his knees gave.

He stared up at them through a thickening haze of lethargy. Then all at once Cam recognized what this woozy, head-stuffed-with-cotton feeling was. He did his best to glare up at the man who was soon to be his brother-in-law.

"Goddamn you, Emmet! Did you put laudanum in my tea?"

Emmet didn't even bother to deny it. "You'd have fallen off that horse before you got halfway back to Denver. This saves us the trouble of having to search for you in the ditches."

"But I need to talk to Shea," Cam insisted.

"We'll drive you into town in the morning. You can ask Shea to marry you then."

"That isn't good enough," Cam slurred as the room faded around him and his eyes closed. With the protest still on his lips, he slumped across the table, dead asleep.

TWENTY

*W*ill you marry me, Shea?

Too straightforward, too simple. Women liked romance.

I love you, Shea. I want you to be my wife.

Better, but it didn't address the problem at hand.

Shea, I've been a fool! Will you marry me?

Now wasn't that a sterling recommendation for a husband?

"Cammie?" his sister interrupted from the front seat of the carriage. "What are you mumbling about back there?"

Cam looked up and realized where he was. Emmet had stopped at the foot of the steps to Shea's studio. A jolt of pure, raw panic rippled through him. God knows, he wasn't anywhere near ready to face Shea yet. Not when he knew their future hinged on what he said to her in the next few minutes.

Maybe he could convince Emmet to take another turn around the block. Maybe he should take Shea something—some gift to show her how he felt. He remembered a shop on Fifteenth Street that had had lovely fans in the—

"You need help getting out of the carriage, Pa?" Rand asked, from beside him, all concern and solicitation.

"No, son, I'm fine," Cam mumbled and blotted his upper lip with the back of his hand. "Just give me a minute."

Knowing he had no choice, Cam eased himself out of the carriage. He paused at the foot of the stairs and waited for Emmet to drive away.

The three of them sat watching him expectantly instead.

"You can go now," Cam urged them. He figured he'd pace a little before he went up to see Shea, and he didn't particularly want an audience.

"I thought we'd stay long enough be sure Shea doesn't throw you out," Emmet offered, grinning. Lily nudged him with her elbow, and Rand made it worse by snickering.

"I'll be fine," Cam snapped and started up the steps.

There seemed to be an inordinately large number of steps this morning. By the time he reached the top he was wobbly and running with sweat—and so nervous his hands were shaking.

This shouldn't be so difficult. What Shea wanted was what he longed to give her—a part of his life, a place in his family. The whole of his heart. He'd been drawn to her ever since he'd carted her off to jail that day in Breckenridge, and had been falling a little more in love with her every day since.

He nodded, swallowed, took a breath. He lifted his hat and smoothed down his hair. He reached for the doorknob and pushed, but for some reason the door didn't open. He turned the knob and nudged the panel with his shoulder. It refused to budge.

"Shea?" he called out softly and rattled the latch. "Shea?"

It was ten thirty on Saturday morning, Shea's busiest day. So why was the place locked up tight?

"Please, Shea, open the door." Dread crept in to displace his nervousness. "I need to talk to you. I need to talk to you *now*."

He pressed his ear to the door. There wasn't so much as a whisper of movement on the other side. She wasn't being stubborn; she wasn't there.

He half-stepped down the stairs.

"What's the matter?" Lily wanted to know.

Cam answered with a shake of his head before he pushed his way into Mrs. Franklin's millinery shop. "Where is she?"

"Who?" Agnes Franklin glanced up from the bow she was stitching onto a bright green hat.

"You know who I'm asking about."

Her eyebrows lifted. "You mean she didn't *tell* you?"

"Tell me what?"

"That she was leaving."

Cam had to grab the edge of the counter to steady himself. "Leaving?"

"She came downstairs yesterday, all red-nosed and tear-spotty, and said she and Ty were moving on." The disapproving look she sent him said she knew this was all his fault.

"Where—where did they go, Mrs. Franklin?"

Agnes Franklin stabbed her needle into the hat as if she wished it were his hide. "I don't rightly know," she sniffed. "Though I'd have thought a *respectable* man like you would have done the *proper* thing and married her. Staying up there nights without benefit of clergy, expecting her to tend you when you were hurt . . ."

Heat seeped up Cam's jaw. "I'm trying to find her so I can remedy that."

Mrs. Franklin paused with her needle in midair. "Oh?"

Cam hadn't meant to discuss his plans with anyone outside his family, but there didn't seem to be much help for it. "I mean to ask Shea to marry me. So if you could see your way clear to telling me where she went . . ."

"Well, then," Mrs. Franklin said with the air of a benevolent matchmaker. "They left for the depot an hour ago."

Cameron barely took time to mutter his thanks. As he clambered into the back of the carriage, he told Emmet where they were headed.

"The railroad station?" Lily gasped, as Emmet slapped the reins on the horse's backs. "Good grief, Cammie, what did you say to her?"

"It's the hundred things I didn't say."

He hadn't told her how she settled him and soothed him and made him feel as if he'd found something for himself in all of this. He hadn't told her how important it was for her to be part of his life, part of his family. He hadn't told her how he wanted to take care of her and give her children to make up for the son she'd given away. But then he hadn't been in a position to court a wife until yesterday.

Cam clung to the back of the front seat as Emmet did his best to maneuver through the crowded streets. But it was Saturday morning. The farmers and the ranchers had come to town and traffic was slow. The hoot of a train from over near the river made all of them jump.

After ten agonizing minutes, Emmet let him out right in front of the depot. With his heart hammering in his ears, Cam rushed into the station's waiting room.

The benches were full. There were miners in their flashy new duds and drummers with samples cases and several young matrons tending flocks of children. The gamblers had congregated in one corner to smoke and a few cowboys sat with their saddles at their feet, probably headed north to look for work.

There was no sign of a lady photographer.

What if he'd missed her? he wondered, concern crowding up his throat. What if she was already gone?

Desperation prodded Cam through the wide double doors and out onto the open platform. More passengers clustered out here, some pacing, some gathering up their children or their luggage, some pointing to the train steaming toward the station from the south.

Fresh panic clutched him, then he spotted Shea and Ty down at the end of the platform.

Relief dropped through Cam like cool rain. He went breathless and giddy. As long as Shea was still here, as long as he could talk to her, he thought he could find a way to make this right between them.

Just then the train from Pueblo came chugging and clanging into the station. Steam hissed and brakes squealed.

As the conductor swung down to the platform, Shea snapped to attention and took two tickets from her reticule.

"Den-ver. Den-n-n-ver station," the trainman bawled. "Five minute layover in Den-ver."

That didn't give Cam much time. He hadn't taken more than two steps toward Shea and Ty when the doors to the waiting room flapped open and he was engulfed in a gush of jostling passengers. Caught like a bug in sap, Cam watched helplessly as Shea hefted her valise, bent to say something to Ty, then turned toward where the conductor was beginning to hand people onto the train.

Ty lifted a big, square box that must have had Rufus inside and dragged along behind her. He was complaining, Cam thought by the set of his chin, or maybe arguing.

Whatever he was saying, Shea stopped, turned to him again, then cupped her palm to his cheek. She listened to him for a moment. A crease came between her eyebrows. She glanced toward the center of town, then sighed and nodded slowly.

At that moment, Cam managed to break free of the clot of passengers and called to her. "Shea, wait!"

She turned toward him in a rustle of skirts. When she saw who it was, she straightened from her heels to her hat.

Beside her, Ty gave Cam a grin so wide he wasn't sure how all of it fit on his face.

"What are *you* doing here?" she asked as he approached, tipping her chin like a queen addressing rabble.

As he drew closer he saw she had that soft, smudged look about her that women got when they'd been crying, and, selfish as he knew it was, Cam let it encourage him.

"I thought we ought to talk before you hightail it out of—"

The conductor cut him off. " 'Board! All aboard for Cheyenne!"

Shea glanced down the platform.

Cam stepped in close. "I don't think you should leave Denver."

She turned back to him, her eyes widening. "You don't?"

"You have people here who care about you." That wasn't what he'd intended to say. It wasn't very personal—or romantic. "I don't want you to go," he amended.

"Tell me, Cam, why is that? Just yesterday you wouldn't let me go with you when you went to talk to Lily. You told me what was between you wasn't my business. That I had no part in your life. Now you're here telling me not to go, that you care about me. If you care, why did you push me away?"

He took her hand, needing to hold her here until he'd found the words that would convince her to stay. "Shea, please, I—"

Just then Lily and Emmet and Rand burst out the doors of the station and bustled toward them.

The moment Shea caught sight of them, her gaze widened, softened. It lingered on Rand the way it always did, the way it probably always would. It brushed over him with affection and longing and more than a modicum of pride.

Then all at once Cam realized that by packing up and deciding to leave, Shea had made her intentions about claiming Rand clear. She was giving him up, giving him up all over again. Her sacrifice shook him.

"So have you convinced her to stay in Denver?" Lily asked breathlessly as they reached where Shea and Cam and Ty were standing.

"They're going to be here for the wedding, aren't they?" Rand asked.

"Wedding?" Shea echoed, flashing a startled look in Cam's direction. "What wedding is that?"

"Aunt Lily and Emmet are getting married," Rand

announced, more than delighted by the prospect of gaining Emmet as his second father.

With a little shout of joy, Shea threw her arms around Lily, and Cam heard the soft waver in Shea's voice as she hugged his sister. "Oh, Lily! I'm so glad you and Emmet finally realized how much you love each other!"

"This would never have happened if it weren't for you," Lily whispered, hugging Shea back.

Before Shea could so much as acknowledge the comment or offer Emmet congratulations, the conductor shouted again. "All aboard for Cheyenne. All aboard for Cheyenne, Wyoming."

Lily looked up at Cam with some alarm. "Has she agreed to stay?"

"Not yet—"

Lily all but shoved Shea in Cam's direction. "Then for god sakes, Cammie! Do something!"

Cam clamped his hand around Shea's wrist. "I fully intend to!"

He hauled her off down the platform away from where passengers were boarding, away from where Lily, Emmet, and the boys stood watching.

Cam stared down at her, the heat of longing budding in his chest. "As I was saying when the whole of the damn world burst in on us," he began again. "I'm sorry about what happened yesterday. When things overwhelm me, sometimes I crawl inside myself. I didn't shut you out because I didn't trust you. I didn't push you away to hurt you. I don't want you leaving Denver because you think I don't care about you."

"That was a very lovely apology, Cam," she said, and her chin came up. "And I'm glad you don't mind me living here, because I'd already made up my mind to stay."

"You what?" Cam dropped his hold on her wrist. "Then what the devil are we doing at the train station?"

He saw the color come up in her cheeks. "Staying was a fairly recent decision."

"How recent?" he demanded.

"I made it five minutes ago."

"What was it that changed your mind?"

"Ty convinced me," she answered. "He's barely given me a moment's peace since last night when *he* decided he wanted to stay. He got me thinking about how well the studio is doing and the friends I've made, and the people who are here that care about me. And I'm just plain tired of wandering, of running away."

Shea wasn't staying because of him. Cam couldn't help the dark seep of disappointment. She'd stayed for her friends and her business and her boy.

Cam saw quite suddenly that even if she stayed, he could lose her. She could have her work and a life separate from his right here in Denver, if that's what she wanted.

And he simply couldn't bear that. He wouldn't be able to bear having her so close without being able to see her and talk to her and touch her. Without her being his.

Cam caught her face between his hands and looked into her eyes. He could see all the way down to the core of who she was. He could see past her pride and her determination, to all her yearning and vulnerability, all her tenderness and humanity. And he knew he had to hang onto her forever.

"Oh, Shea," he breathed. "I want you to stay in Denver, because of me. I want you to stay because I please you, because I can make you happy. I want you to stay because I love you and I need you. I want you to stay because you love me, too."

He saw tears simmer in her eyes. "Oh, Cam," she breathed.

"For the first time in my life I've found someone who feels like part of me. Someone I can laugh with and trust, someone who trusts and wants me, too. That person is you, Shea, and now that I've found you, I'd be so happy and proud if you'd agree to be my wife.

"I want to be with you for the rest of my days. I want you to be part of my life. I want to make a home and a family for us together. Please, Shea, say you'll marry me."

A dozen yards away the train huffed and grumbled, stoking up its head of steam. The conductor bawled his last call for Cheyenne.

Ty came pelting toward them down the platform. "We going to cash in those tickets or what?" he yelled at Shea.

Shea looked down at Ty and up at Cam. He read the question in her eyes: would he take Ty as his son if she married him?

"Of course," he said and drew Ty closer.

She beamed down at her boy for a moment before she gave him her answer. "Not only are we cashing in the tickets, but Cam's also asked me to marry him. What do you think?"

Ty chewed his lip. "I suppose it depends on how you're gonna answer him."

"I think I'm going to tell him yes, is that all right?"

Ty threw his arms around both of them. "Well it's about damn time!"

Cam bent his head and kissed Shea right there on the platform. Right there on the platform while the train pulled out for Cheyenne, while Lily and Emmet and the boys clapped and hooted their approval. He kissed her with a good deal more enthusiasm than a sane man should five days after he'd been shot. Cam was woozy and gone at the knees by the time they were done—but he was grinning.

"Cammie," Lily said, stepping up close beside him. "You know it's only right and proper to seal Shea's promise with a betrothal ring."

Cam stared at his sister shaking his head. "But I don't have—You know there wasn't time—"

"I thought you might like to give her this." Lily opened her palm and in the hollow lay a small gold circlet of garnets, his mother's betrothal ring.

"Oh, Lily, are you sure?" he breathed. "You've worn that ring on a ribbon around your neck ever since Mother died."

Lily smiled softly and there was the shimmer of tears in her eyes. "I want Shea to have it. I think Mother would want her to have it, too," she insisted softly, "so that Shea will never doubt she's one of us."

Cam accepted Lily's offering and clasped the circlet tight in his palm. He felt the warmth, felt the connection to his mother and his sister through the gold and gems. He could see in Shea's eyes how much that connection meant to her.

Bending over her, he eased the ring onto Shea's finger and wasn't the least surprised that the circlet fit. "This is even more than a symbol of my love for you," he whispered. "It makes you one of us in every way."

Shea looked up at him, her face alight. "I love you, Cam," she whispered, then turned slowly to the others. "And all of you."

EPILOGUE

$\mathcal{C}$ameron Gallimore smiled to himself as he watched Shea and his new son—and his old son—preparing to take what would be their wedding photograph.

"Can you see everyone in the focusing glass?" Shea asked Ty from where she was hovering just outside of the dark-cloth. This was the first photograph Ty had taken completely on his own, and Shea was nervous.

"I can see everyone but you."

"And are they all in focus?"

"Everyone but you."

"Shall I take just one quick look?"

"No, Ma. It's fine."

Cam saw Shea's features soften. He knew her heart melted every time her boy called her that. So did Ty.

"It's the knob on the side of the lens you need to turn to bring everything into focus," she persisted.

"I know."

Rand stood off to one side carefully balancing the loaded plate holder in both hands. "Don't you think you should take your place, Shea?" he suggested,

beaming at her. "If it takes much longer to get everyone settled, won't this plate be too dry for us to use?"

Shea nodded reluctantly. "I'll just go take my place
then."

"Finally," Cam heard Ty mutter.

Shea came up the steps of the farmhouse and eased
between Lily and him. Cam slid his hand around her
waist and snugged her against him. He liked the way
she felt, soft and solid and so inviting. It was an invitation he was very much looking forward to accepting
once their guests went home.

He and Shea and Lily and Emmet had been married
right here on the veranda not two hours before. The
sky had been bright, cobalt blue, and the spring sun
had shone warm on them to bless the ceremony. Their
guests were still off eating and drinking and dancing in
the yard, but Shea had been determined to take their
wedding photographs before they lost the light.

"You ready?" Rand called out.

"That's good right there," Ty said, emerging from
beneath the dark-cloth.

Rand fitted the plate holder into the camera and
pulled the slide. "Stay really still, now," Ty told them.

"With this light that exposure should be to a count
of fifteen," Shea reminded him.

"You told me twice already." With a flourish Ty
removed the lens cap and began to count.

From the corner of his eye Cam noticed that in
posing for the photograph Lily had turned full-face to
the camera, and he couldn't help how proud he was of
her for being able to do that.

She'd be living in town after today, Emmet and
Rand and her. She'd be taking on the duties of a doctor's wife, overseeing his appointments and helping

with patients. She'd finally stopped hiding herself away. She'd emerged into the world secure in Emmet's love and Shea's fierce protectiveness and the friendships Lily herself had forged.

Ty finished his count and recapped the camera lens.

"We're going to make a second exposure to be sure we got the photograph," Rand informed them, as Ty closed the slide on the first plate and withdrew the holder.

Who would have thought, Cam found himself wondering, as Ty posed them for another photograph, that the stranger he'd brought to the farm last fall would change all their lives? Especially his.

Especially his.

Without his even realizing, his secrets and the law had been draining away his strength and optimism. Since resigning his judgeship in March, he'd bought some cattle, ordered seed, and plowed up the bottomland in preparation for planting. He was looking forward to running his beeves, tending his crops, and watching them grow. He was rebuilding his soul. Facing his past had been the start of it, and with Lily's concern and Emmet's friendship and Shea's love he was changing a little every day.

Once Ty had exposed that second plate, Shea and the boys disappeared into the house to develop it. While they were gone, Lily and Emmet and he rejoined the party.

It was well past dark when the last of the guests drove down the lane, and not long after the family gathered at the gate for their final good-byes. Cam stood with Ty tucked under one arm and Shea snuggled tight in the other as they waved Emmet's carriage out of sight.

"Oh, goodness!" Shea said on the breath of a happy sigh. "Hasn't it been a lovely day!"

"It's going to be an even better night," he whispered against her hair.

She stifled a laugh and wriggled out of his grasp. Still, something in the curve of her lips and the spark in her eyes made him want to swoop her off her feet and carry her directly to the bedroom.

"I had fun, too," Ty put in, reminding Cam that he and his new wife weren't quite alone out here.

Shea went to Ty and planted a kiss on the top of his head. The boy squirmed a little, but Cam could tell he liked it.

"I was very proud of you today," she told him. "You behaved like a perfect gentleman and were able to take two excellent photographs all by yourself."

"Geez, Ma!" Ty shrugged and took care to put a little space between them. "You taught me all about taking photographs, and Rand poked me in the ribs every time I started to do something he didn't think I should."

"Nevertheless, I was proud of you," she told him. "But it's late and you need to get to bed."

"I don't have to go to school tomorrow," he pointed out.

"Yes, but I'm afraid the stock doesn't know it's Sunday," Cam reminded him.

Cam thought he saw a flicker of uneasiness cross Ty's face, as he turned to him. "Can you come up and talk to me before I go to sleep?"

Cam was surprised by the request. Shea usually took care of tucking Ty in. Cam nodded anyway. "Sure."

"Now what do you suppose that's all about?" Shea murmured as they watched Ty scuffle and bang his way into the house.

"I'm not sure," he answered and drew her into his arms. "But I've got something I'd like to do while I'm waiting."

Her smile was saucy and wry. "And whatever could that be?"

"I'd like to kiss my wife," he said, lowering his mouth to hers, "right here in the yard."

Things might have gone a good deal further than kissing if Ty hadn't been waiting. As it was, Cam arrived in what had been Rand's room until yesterday, and found Ty seated and fidgeting at the edge of one of the narrow beds.

The lamp on the nightstand cast a soft, yellowish glow around the slope-ceilinged room. As far as Cam could see, the only change Ty had made in the place was setting the tintype Shea had taken of Ty and his father at the mining camp beside the lamp.

"Mind if I have a look?" Cam asked and gestured to the photograph.

"Sure, go ahead."

Cam lowered himself to the opposite bed and picked up the small, cardboard-framed photograph. In it Shea had managed to catch a precious moment in time, a moment when Ty had been happy and Sam had been sober. A time when both of them had come together to be painted by the sun.

Cam settled the tintype back on the nightstand and turned to the boy seated knees-to-knees across from him. "Well, then, what was it you wanted to talk to me about?"

Ty lowered his head and looked at Cam from beneath the froth of his curly forelock. "Well, I figured since you married Shea, that sort of makes you my father now."

"I suppose it sort of does," Cam offered. "But I don't expect you to call me Pa, and I'll never try to take your father's place."

"Well, no," Ty agreed as if he hadn't needed the reassurance. "Pa's Pa, and always will be. And you're Cam."

"Then that wasn't what you were worried about?"

"This is something else," Ty admitted and chewed his lip. "Something I need to tell you man to man."

Ty sounded so serious that Cam shifted to Ty's bed and put his arm around him. "All right, son. Go on," he encouraged him. "It's usually easier to just say things straight out."

"Well—" Ty swallowed hard. "—I thought— thought you should know my folks didn't get me the usual way."

"The usual way?" Cam echoed, taken aback. What would Ty know about "the usual way"? But then, he figured any child who'd learned to cheat at poker had probably learned a whole lot of other inappropriate things sweeping up in Denver's saloons. "What exactly do you mean by 'the usual way'?"

"They got me"—Ty ducked his head again—"from one of those orphan trains."

Cam felt like he'd been sucker-punched.

"Just like you got Rand," the boy hurried on. "That's why I'm telling you instead of Shea, because I figured you'd understand it better than her."

Cam very much doubted that, but he tightened his arm around Ty's shoulders anyway. "Of course I understand."

"I was really little when they got me," Ty said, still staring down at where his hands were knotted together in his lap. "I don't remember the train at all. I don't remember much of anything before the farm we had in Missouri."

"Missouri?"

"Yes, sir," Ty said with a nod. "We had a farm outside St. Joe until I was seven. When Ma died, Pa didn't care no more about farming."

Sam hadn't cared about much of anything. He hadn't even cared much about Ty until the weeks before he died, so Cam figured in some ways what had happened was a blessing.

"So since you and Shea are my folks now," Ty went on, "I figured I ought to tell you."

Cam took a moment to catch his breath. "I'm glad you were brave enough to tell me the truth," Cam said looking down at him. "It's never good to lie to people who love you."

Ty was still worrying his lower lip. "You don't think Shea will be mad about me being from an orphan train, do you?"

Of all the people in the world, Ty couldn't have found anyone to mother him who understood about children from orphan trains better than Shea.

Cam pulled Ty closer. "It won't matter to Shea one bit. I think she'll love you even more because of it."

"You think she will?" The magnitude of the relief in Ty's voice stirred a sweet hot current in Cam's chest.

"I've never been more sure of anything in my life," Cam said softly.

"Well, good," the boy said, and let out his breath as if he'd been holding it a week. "I got the papers the orphan train people gave Pa, and I want you to keep them someplace safe."

As he spoke, Ty drew two wrinkled, dog-eared pages from inside his pillowcase. He extended them to Cam, his small, blunt-fingered hands shaking just a little.

Cam could guess how much telling him this had cost him, how afraid he'd been that this would make a difference in how Shea felt about him, that it would make her send him away.

As he reached to take the rumpled papers from Ty, he looked down at their hands. Ty's were small for a child his age, yet blunt and capable. His fingers were short, spatulate, stained a little at the tips from the chemicals he and Shea had used to make the photographs this afternoon. They were oddly familiar hands.

Down in the pit of his belly something stirred.

He found himself staring at Ty's hands, noticing the scuffed knuckles, the almost circular nails, and the odd way his little fingers crooked.

Just like Shea's did.

A frisson of recognition chased up his back. A jolt of certainty thudded against his diaphragm. Cam lost his breath.

He looked at Ty as if he were seeing him for the very first time, took in his short stature and wiry build, at his tousled curls and the shape of his face, at the flecks of green in those wide brown eyes. He looked at Ty's hands again, and he knew.

He knew with a conviction he would never in a million years be able to prove that this was Shea's son. Ty was the child she'd given up. Ty was the child she had been searching for all this time. And somehow Ty had come to her now—after years of grief and longing—through some incredible twist of fate.

Cam's own hands shook a little as he tucked the papers inside his jacket and drew Ty closer.

"I know it wasn't easy for you to tell me this, and I thank you for being honest. But, Ty—" He stroked back the boy's curly hair, hair that had the same texture and vitality as Shea's. "I want you to know that whether you'd told us or not, you're our son. You'll always be our son. We'll always love you."

He hugged Ty hard, holding him against his chest, pressing his cheek for a moment to the froth of his curls. Holding Shea's son, and loving him every bit as much as he loved Shea.

"Now don't you worry about any of this," Cameron said, sitting back. "Everything is going to be fine from now on. But now it's time for you to get some rest. It's been a big day for all of us. Today we truly became a family—all of us together."

Rising to stand over him, Cam helped Ty slide beneath the covers. He drew the clean, fresh sheets up across his narrow chest.

"Are you going to tell her?" Ty asked in a very small voice.

"Don't you think I should?"

"I guess."

"This won't make any difference to her, you know," he reassured him, "except that she'll be so proud of you for being honest."

Ty nodded and Cam bent and squeezed his shoulder again as he blew out the lamp. "Good night, son," he said from the doorway.

"Good night, Cam. I'm glad you're going to be my new father."

Cam was still reeling a little from the shock of what Ty had told him, as he made his way downstairs. He still felt shaken by his own discovery. He took a moment to look over the papers in the kitchen, then shook his head.

Cam had no proof that Ty was Shea's son, he just knew. He knew Ty was her son as surely as he knew his own name, his own heart. He knew it as surely as he knew he loved this boy the way he'd always loved Rand.

He wandered through the house and finally found Shea out on the veranda, nestled into one corner of the swing. She was rocking softly, looking more at ease and contented than he had ever seen her.

He sat down beside her and took her hand. The contact of flesh to flesh carried a depth of connection that warmed him all the way to his bones.

"So what did Ty want?" she asked him, still swinging gently.

He hesitated, wondering if he should prepare her somehow, then decided just to tell her outright.

"He wanted to give me these," he told her, and withdrew the indenture papers from his pocket.

She took the pages and turned them to the light. She'd read no more than a few lines at the top of the page before she looked at him. "Ty was sent west on one of the orphan trains?" He could hear the waver of surprise in her voice and knew exactly what she was feeling.

He reached across and took her hand again. "He must have been adopted in St. Joe the same time we got Rand. They were probably on the train together. The dates are right—and their ages."

"But—but how is that possible? Why wouldn't Ty tell us?" Shea asked, incredulous.

"He just has."

"Why wouldn't Sam Morran have told me when he asked me to take care of Ty for him?"

He raised his fingers to her lips, the gesture more of reassurance than seduction. "He probably thought you'd change your mind if you found out Ty wasn't really his, if you found out where he'd come from."

"Sam must have known how I cared for Ty," she said, her voice full of reproach. She looked down at the papers again and rubbed them tenderly between her fingertips, almost as if she were caressing the child himself.

"Shea," Cam went on, softly, urgently. "Ty's your son. *Your son.*"

She raised her gaze to his. He saw a sequence of intense emotions cross her face. And then she laughed.

"Of course he's my son," she said. "Just as Rand is my son. Just as any children you and I may have will be our sons and daughters. Our family."

Cam opened his mouth to argue, to ask her to look at Ty's hair and eyes. And at his hands—smaller, but identical to the hand he was holding in his right now. Then he closed his mouth again. He had married a woman with a true and generous heart—a heart big enough to love a world of children. Big enough to give him a place of his own inside it.

It's why he'd wanted to make her his wife, why he wanted to live with her for the rest of his days. Why he wanted to lie with her tonight and experience again that sense of warmth and security and home.

"I love you, Shea." He rose to stand over her and drew her to her feet.

"I love you, Cam," she whispered back.

"I want to show you just how much I love you," he said and kissed her with all the tenderness and passion in his soul. "Will you come with me and let me do that?"

"Oh, yes," she breathed against his mouth.

He swept her into his arms and carried her across the threshold. It wasn't the first time he'd done it. It wasn't the first time he'd placed her in the center of his big bed. It was the first time he'd followed her down, and lain beside her.

He pulled her against him and nuzzled her throat. "I'm so glad this is our wedding night," he whispered.

Shea laughed and kissed him.

ABOUT THE AUTHOR

ELIZABETH GRAYSON was published for the first time in the fourth grade and had completed an historical novel by the time she was fifteen. *Painted by the Sun* is her tenth published work, several of which were written under the pseudonym Elizabeth Kary. She holds degrees in education and has taught art in elementary schools and at the St. Louis Art Museum. She lives on the outskirts of the city with her advertising executive husband and tabby cat. Contact her at P.O.Box 260052, St. Louis, Missouri 63126 or by e-mail at egrayson@MVP.net